FILTHY
RICH
VAMPIRE

FILTHY RICH VAMPIRE

GENEVA LEE

NEW YORK TIMES & INTERNATIONALLY BESTSELLING AUTHOR

Entangled Publishing, LLC
644 Shrewsbury Commons Ave., STE 181
Shrewsbury, PA 17361
rights@entangledpublishing.com

Amara is an imprint of Entangled Publishing, LLC.

Visit our website at www.entangledpublishing.com.

Cover art and design by Geneva Lee
Stock art byGluiki/Adobestock,Alena/Adobestock,
Murilo/Adobestock, Pixel-Shot/Adobestock, r_tee/Adobestock
Interior design by Toni Kerr

ISBN 978-1-64937-587-2
Ebook ISBN 978-1-64937-659-6

Manufactured in the United States of America

First Edition October 2023

10 9 8 7 6 5 4 3 2

AMARA
an imprint of Entangled Publishing LLC

ALSO BY GENEVA LEE

To Louise
Who waited forever for me
to write the damn vampire book.

At Entangled, we want our readers to be well-informed. If you would like to know if this book contains any elements that might be of concern for you, please check the back of the book for details.

CHAPTER ONE

Julian

"What year is it?"

I blinked as I raised my hand to shield my eyes. Daylight assaulted me through the windows, making it impossible to see. Still, a few things were apparent:

The world had not ended.

Despite this, I was awake.

And someone had opened the blinds.

There was only one soul who knew where I kept the remote control for the window shades—the only person I could trust. Someone who knew that waking me was not only stupid, but dangerous. Someone who'd seen me take off someone's head before for doing just that.

And she'd opened the blinds, anyway.

If Celia, my assistant, had disturbed me, there had to be an excellent reason. At least, there'd better be.

Celia moved noiselessly around the room as the blinds finished rising to reveal floor-to-ceiling windows. Light sparkled on the ceiling, dancing to the rhythm of the ocean waves outside. Quiet. Peaceful. The only sound came from the crashing surf.

I was utterly alone. That was the way I preferred it. People didn't bother me here—except for Celia, apparently. She had not only woken me up, but now she carefully skirted around my bed. She knew better than to be within reach of a vampire who hadn't had a warm meal in several decades.

"Celia, I'm not going to bite," I assured her.

Celia snorted and maintained her distance. "I've heard that one before, so I think I'll wait until I'm sure your gentlemanly side has kicked in."

"That could take a while." I grimaced, rubbing the back of my neck with my palm. I wasn't feeling very benevolent at the moment, not after my rude awakening.

"I have no doubt that's true." She busied herself arranging items on a silver tray.

A growl vibrated in my chest, and I gritted my teeth to contain my burgeoning annoyance. "Why am I awake?" I demanded. "And what fucking year is it?"

"I'm not talking to you until you're less grouchy." She didn't bother to look up from her task. Her silvery-white hair fell over one shoulder, blocking her face from view. But I heard the grin she kept hidden. I was glad *someone* was having fun.

I tried a more polite approach. "What year is it, *please*?"

"It's 2023, sir." She turned toward me with a sweet smile. I knew better than to trust it. Celia could rip a man's heart from his chest without breaking a nail. I'd watched her do it—more than once.

"Christ, I was hoping to get a few more decades in."

Her lips pinched together, erasing the smile, but she didn't respond. She simply shrugged her slight shoulders as though nothing was out of the ordinary. I studied her for a moment, trying to get some clues on what I'd missed while I'd been out. But she looked exactly as she had a couple dozen years ago. The scar that extended down one side of her face, a gift from a former lover a lifetime ago, remained uncovered. She'd hidden it as a mortal but now wore it proudly as a vampire. She called it proof she had survived and a warning to anyone who might wish to hurt her in the future. It was one of the reasons I trusted her. She didn't bother to hide her past or who she was now. She owned it.

But she was keeping something from me now. I could feel it.

That didn't bode well.

I moved to sit up and nearly ripped an IV from my forearm. I glanced at the crimson stream filtering through the tubing and sighed heavily. It was a thoughtful gesture on her part, but further proof my nap was over. I untangled myself from the blood drip as best I could and rested against my bamboo headboard while I waited for the transfusion to finish. It should take the edge off any lingering hunger, which might help my irritability over the current situation.

Somehow, I doubted it.

Now fully awake, I turned my attention to the turquoise waters lapping against the house. Not that it was a house, exactly. My private residence took up an entire island near Key West but was technically in international waters. So, unlike the Keys, the island was outside the reach of any government. It was an intentional choice, as well as my way of sending a message to everyone I knew.

Leave me the fuck alone.

I'd made the island my sanctuary. I had built my bedroom to jut out over the water, three walls surrounded by nothing but the ocean's vast, unending blue. The rest of the island was as large as a fully functioning resort, and a dedicated group of vampires and humans—all subject to my approval—lived on the three hundred acres for most of the year, vacating only for hurricane season. It was relaxing here, a luxury I suspected I should enjoy while I could. Celia had to have a damn good reason for waking me up.

"Anything happen while I was out?" I tried to sound casual, hoping she would finally reveal something.

Celia cleared her throat. "A fair amount. I have a dossier for you of major events, the last four presidents and various heads of state, and this morning's paper." She must have decided I was no longer a bite risk, because she placed the silver tray heaped with papers next to me in bed. She turned to inspect the blood bag feeding into my arm. "This is almost empty. Should I get another one?"

I shook my head. The older I got, the less blood I needed after waking. Picking up the *Wall Street Journal*, I skimmed the headlines. My lips turned down with each bit of news. I quickly moved on to the dossier, which proved to be even more depressing. "How did that moron get elected?" I flipped the page. "Or that one?"

I dropped the papers on the bed. The eighties had been a shit circus: too much hair, too many shoulder pads, and way too much cocaine. It had suited my siblings just fine, along with plenty of other vampires. But I'd needed a break. From the parties. From my family. From everything. I'd meant it when I'd told Celia to let me desiccate in my master suite until the apocalypse was at hand.

I'm not sure why she thought I was joking about that.

I stretched my now IV-less arms over my head, then pushed free of the sheets. I preferred to sleep in the nude, which now gave me a chance to see the blood drip had already done its job. I ran my palm over my stomach. The hard slab was as stacked and defined as it had been when I'd retired. Flexing my toes, I found my quads and calves had already regained their considerable muscle mass. There was no hint that I'd been sleeping for the better part of four decades, except maybe for the lingering erection inspired by my dreams. I'd been chasing a woman. It was the only dream I remembered having. I never caught her. The result was blue balls that had lasted decades and a hard-on that was as annoying as it was painful.

If Celia noticed, she didn't comment. She was good that way. It was another mark in her favor.

"So, about my undesirable awakening…" I dredged up my most charming smile. It hung crookedly on my lips from lack of use.

"Your mother has summoned you home," she said, averting her gaze and pointedly ignoring the sour change to my expression. "I've arranged the jet, but I should—"

Before she could finish the statement—or explain what my mother needed with her eldest son—the door to my room swung open on its hinges. A familiar figure stood in the doorway, grinning wickedly and giving no sign decades had passed since we last saw each other.

Sebastian Rousseaux was my brother. Not by birth, but by blood. While I had been conceived, our parents had turned him together, each using their blood in the process. It left us as far apart physically as we were in temperament. My muscular build took after our father, a byproduct of the line of ancient warriors he descended from, but Sebastian was lean and wiry. The last time I had seen him, he had bleached, spiky hair. He'd been leaning into the punk rock scene. Sebastian had adored every depraved moment of the eighties. Humans prone to excess were easy to manipulate, and vampires—who, as it so happened, liked cocaine as much as they loved opium—found it difficult to resist.

And no one loved drugs and humans more than Sebastian.

His hair had grown longer and faded to its natural blond in the intervening years. He'd given up the earring and dog collar that had been his signature look back then but kept the motorcycle jacket. He wore it now over a black T-shirt and loose, worn Levi's.

I observed all of this within a second of the door flying open. Sebastian might look different, but his cheekiness was fully intact, judging by the half-dressed woman leaning precariously against him.

"Good morning, brother," Sebastian called cheerfully. "I brought you a blonde."

The girl winked at me. Her gaze skimmed down my body appreciatively until it reached my groin and locked on like a heat-seeking missile. Her mouth rounded as she stared, eyes widening.

"I appreciate the thought," I said drily. I tossed the sheet back over my lap to block her view of my dick. "But I'm not hungry."

"I doubt that."

I ignored him. "Why are you here?"

Sebastian didn't answer.

It was never a good sign when I woke from a long sleep to find him in my house. Or any of my siblings, for that matter.

"I see you opted for a transfusion," he said, lips turning down as

Celia passed him with the spent blood bag. "But judging from that tent pole between your legs, you might need her for other matters."

"That won't be necessary." But I might as well have been talking to a brick wall, because Sebastian was already murmuring to the woman.

"Tell him how much you love to go for a ride."

"I love to ride," she said in a dreamy voice. "Can we go for one now?"

"See? The flesh is willing." Sebastian moved languidly into the room. He didn't rush like most vampires his age, who saw their speed as an advantage. No, my brother had perfected the art of taking his time. When he finally reached the bed, the blonde in tow, he nudged her toward it.

She dropped onto all fours, crawling toward me, but I held up a hand.

"As touching as your welcome gift is, Celia was in the middle of telling me why the fuck I'm awake."

"Allow me to share the good news," Sebastian told Celia, who tipped her head in agreement. But while Sebastian's grin remained, her lips formed a grim slash.

Anything that amused my brother and worried Celia was likely to piss me off.

"I'll check in with the airfield to make sure we're on track." She hurried out.

I'd never seen my assistant so avoidant. The jet would be ready to take me to whatever private residence my mother currently occupied as soon as I summoned it, and she knew as much. Unless there had been a financial catastrophe, the Rousseaux family name still meant open doors and swiftly snipped red tape. Our family had over fifty properties spread throughout the world, the results of a real estate portfolio that stretched back several centuries. We employed private pilots, owned multiple airplanes, and could buy whatever we wanted by simply snapping our fingers. So Celia didn't need to check with the airfield. She was putting a safe distance between us before my brother dropped a bomb.

This was going to be bad fucking news.

"What does Mother want?" I asked Sebastian as soon as Celia had left. The blond girl lay down at the foot of the bed and promptly fell asleep, looking a bit like a house cat. He must have fed her a fair bit of vampire venom before bringing her here. She was stoned out of her mind.

"Always straight to business." Sebastian dropped into a linen chair by the bank of windows. "Not even a little interested in what I've been up to?"

"Drugs and women, I assume." Probably a few men, too. Sebastian's appetite was always open to new experiences, as was his bed.

"I had another band for a bit." Sebastian tilted his head thoughtfully. "Mostly for the women and drugs. Then again, everyone had a band in the nineties. It was like the sixties all over again."

"I'm sorry I missed it," I bit out. I was not, in fact, sorry. Immortality hadn't gifted Sebastian with musical talent. Thanks to his obsession with the art, I'd sat through a couple of failed symphonies and one horrible opera. Punk had been okay for him, since it mostly involved screaming.

"Oh, and these are big now." He tossed a small, black, rectangular object toward me.

I caught it in my right hand and studied it for a second. When I turned it over, an image lit up along with a display of the time and neat rows of small icons. "What is it?"

"It's a phone," he explained.

"This is a phone?" I shook my head. "That's what humanity has been up to?"

"Nope. It's also a camera," Sebastian continued, sprawling in the chair. "Oh, and the internet. Wait, fuck, was that even a thing when you took your little nap?"

It must be show-and-tell hour. I dropped the phone on the

bed. It felt fragile, but I doubted it was too complicated to figure out. Later, I'd get a less narcissistic rundown of the major political, technological, and cultural events I'd missed from Celia, beyond what was in the dossier. For now, I needed to steer Sebastian's ego in the right direction.

"So why are you here?" I asked.

His mouth curved into a feline smirk. "Mother wants to…catch up."

"I better not be awake because Mommy had a bout of sentimentality." Those never ended well. The last time the entire Rousseaux clan was in the same city, we'd drawn local attention. By the time we'd realized it, it was too late.

"Oh no, it is an official summons." The smile grew wider, displaying a dazzling set of white teeth that could disarm and dismember within seconds. "I'll give you a hint. It's been about fifty years since the last one."

I picked up the phone again and peered at the screen. Under the time was a date. I groaned when I read October. Fifty years. October. It was all adding up. I didn't know why I thought I would get out of it. Nothing could stop it.

I'd gone to sleep expecting humanity to put the final nail in Earth's coffin while I was out. They'd been heading toward total devastation at a breakneck speed back then. I couldn't stand watching it any longer. But now that I was here, very much not dead, and facing the looming threat of the vampire social season instead, I wished they had. Armageddon would have been more fun.

"Fuck," I groaned. "Just stake me. I'll write you a note that says I asked you to."

"Cheer up, brother." His eyes glinted, which only made me further dread what he was about to say. "It's not just any season this year. The Rites are being revived. You know what that means."

Now I understood my brother's smugness. It wasn't just any social season. Not for the Rousseaux family. Not for me. The Rites changed everything. While vampires held a social season every fifty years to catch up and show off the wealth and numbers they'd accumulated since the last season, The Rites were more like an archaic mating ritual. Traditionally, they were held every couple of centuries. During The Rites, vampires dined with—and on—familiars, the descendants of once-powerful witches. Both groups came seeking matches that might produce new pureblood vampires, encourage alliances, and pad already swelling egos. It had fallen out of fashion by the twentieth century. Or so I had thought; it appeared something had changed while I was asleep. And as the eldest living Rousseaux, I was first up for offering.

"Don't look so pleased with yourself," I warned him. "Someday, it will be your turn."

"I figure I've got a couple hundred years unless you fuck this up."

I overlooked the barb, but ignoring the summons from our mother would be impossible. We both knew that.

"A Rousseaux answers when duty calls," I reminded him, even as I reached for the blonde, suddenly interested in a distraction.

"Still better you than me. I'll leave you two alone." Sebastian stood and walked toward the open door. He stopped just short of it. "Try not to drain her. I promised her I wouldn't kill her. See you at home."

He closed the door behind him as she climbed onto my lap, now fully awake. I didn't know if I was going to bite her or fuck her. Judging by the way the woman craned her head, she was ready for anything. She was pretty, in an artificial way. But there was altogether too much of, well, *everything*. Maybe Sebastian was still chasing the excess of the eighties, or perhaps he thought it might bridge the gap between when I had gone to sleep and the current year. Either way, I didn't care. She was willing, and her blood was warm.

I barely processed as she sank onto me and began to moan. I had other problems to worry about, and even a pretty blonde riding my cock wasn't enough to take my mind off them.

They had enacted The Rites. That meant the impending social

season would be far worse than tedious parties and pissing contests. There were strings attached. It had been at least two hundred years since the last time The Rites had been necessary. Our older sister had been alive then, and the duty had fallen on her to attend the balls and orgies and all the general mayhem the elite of vampire society could concoct in the name of matchmaking. Now it was my fucking turn.

I, Julian Rousseaux, had to take a wife.

CHAPTER TWO

Thea

Someday I would be on time.

Today was not that day.

The sun had already set by the time I raced through the back entrance of the Herbst Theatre. I was in such a hurry that I accidentally banged into a catering cart with my cello case. I squeaked, stopping to check that I had not destroyed any of the dishes. Thankfully, the chocolate tarts still looked sinfully perfect. A familiar pair of brown eyes peeked around the three-tiered dish of pastries, and I heard a sigh.

"Sorry, Ben!" I flashed an apologetic smile to the pastry chef.

"Cutting it close, huh?" he asked as he pushed the cart safely past me.

"I think we both are," I pointed out. Most of the Green Room should already be ready for the reception.

Ben shook his head, his wide mouth curving into a grin. "I know better than to leave chocolate unguarded for too long around you people."

"That's fair," I agreed. Nearly anyone who worked in the events business long enough had perfected the skill of pilfering off catering trays and artfully rearranging them to hide the evidence.

No chocolate tart was safe around this crew.

Most of the people here worked for the catering company connected to the San Francisco War Memorial and Performing Arts Center. The complex hosted the city's ballet, symphony, and opera, as well as a veteran's memorial. With some of the largest and most beautiful buildings in the Bay Area, the center was home to more social events than performances. Weddings and galas did more to shore up the center's expenses than productions of *Swan Lake* or symphony orchestras. That's why I was here: the string quartet needed a cellist for whatever high-profile event was next up on the docket.

I continued on to the kitchen instead of the dressing room. The only thing I needed more than an extra five minutes was a cup of coffee. It was the only way I was going to keep myself from nodding off midway through the gig. I propped my case outside the kitchen and sneaked inside, doing my best to stay out of the way. But I only got as far as the coffeemaker before I got caught.

"Don't even think about it." A kitchen towel smacked the counter near my hand. "I'm cutting you off."

I froze, my hand still poised to grab the pot, as Molly, the head chef—director of catering and keeper of coffee—stepped between me and my fix. I blinked innocently as if she hadn't caught me stealing coffee in a bustling kitchen.

"I didn't have any yet today," I lied.

"Try again." Molly crossed her arms and glared. Her corkscrew curls were pulled into tight pigtails with a handkerchief tied over them to keep her hair out of the food. She always wore it that way, along with her chef's jacket and checked pants. The handkerchief was the only thing that ever changed. Today's was crimson paisley. "You're practically vibrating. How much caffeine have you had?"

"Okay, I had a latte on the BART." I paused, hoping she would move away from the machine. She didn't budge. "And a cup before I left my apartment." I reasoned to myself that the cup I swigged after my shift at the diner didn't count. That had technically been last night.

"Two already, huh?" She swept one more suspicious look over me as if she was checking some invisible meter on my forehead. "You have more caffeine than water in your bloodstream. I'll brew some decaf."

"No! Death before decaf! Have mercy," I begged. "I got stuck with a double last night."

Molly sighed heavily before moving out of my way. She talked a good game, but she hadn't won on this topic yet. I didn't waste a second swiping the pot and pouring a mug. Breathing in its rich aroma, I felt my energy level instantly boost.

"You need to quit that waitressing job," Molly said, turning to nitpick a platter. She rearranged the garnish and nodded her approval at the waiting server, who grabbed the tray and disappeared in the direction of the event space.

"And retire with my trust fund on my yacht?" I asked with a laugh. "Maybe tomorrow."

Molly's mouth compressed into a line the way it did when she was about to deliver a real truth bomb, the kind that usually consisted of practical advice backed by facts and logic. We both knew making a living as a musician was a long shot. I didn't know how to get her to see that I loved music like she loved food. It wasn't my fault that cellists weren't nearly as in demand as award-winning chefs. "You can't keep going at this pace, Thea."

"I just have to keep paying my dues," I reminded her. It was something I told her—and myself—a lot.

"Well, make sure you get a receipt for those dues." Molly rolled her eyes and began arranging oysters on a silver platter of ice.

Between last night's double, two hours of sleep, classes, and not enough coffee, I'd failed to even look at the text I'd gotten about this evening's event.

"Is this some corporate party?" I guessed, hoping it wouldn't be a quiet affair that ended in me falling asleep with my cello between my legs.

"Not exactly. Seems more exclusive, but Derek is being ridiculously vague. You should have seen the menu requests I got."

"Gluten-free?" I guessed. Molly hated having restrictions placed on her art—as she put it—and distrusted people with dietary restrictions. Derek, the Director of Special Events, usually had to work some magic to soothe Molly's ego.

She shook her head with a grimace.

I braced myself. "Vegans?"

"Worse," she said in a lowered voice, and I stilled. I couldn't imagine what diet would be more restrictive than vegans, unless they were some unfortunate mixture of gluten-free vegans with allergies. "They wanted to forego the catering *altogether*."

Given the high demand for events, the center charged a hefty rental fee and required a catering order minimum. But I knew this wasn't about money. Not for Molly. I gasped conspiratorially. She was the keeper of the coffee, after all. "Don't they know you are a genius?"

"Derek told them." She seemed relieved I felt the same, but then she shook her head. "In the end, they wanted caviar, oysters, foie gras, steak tartare, and a bunch of pastries even Ben had never heard of."

"What uncivilized animals," I teased as I sipped coffee. "So what's wrong with that?"

"There's hardly any cooking for me. Sure, Ben gets to bake, but what am I supposed to do with a practically raw food menu? I mean, if that's what they want, why not just open a bag of chips and throw it in a bowl?"

"Clearly, they have no taste."

"It was just weird." Molly shook her head mournfully, missing my sarcasm. "Who has a cocktail party without appetizers?" She huffed. "At least they have expensive taste. They went from no catering bill to, like, six figures in ten minutes. Anyway, I'd brace for a very high-maintenance crowd."

"They rarely demand much of the cellist," I reassured her. Molly nodded, distracted by a passing tray of toasted baguette slices topped with black caviar. Meanwhile, I seized the opportunity to top off my mug before checking my watch. "I better go get ready."

"You better hurry," she said, adding, "and switch to decaf. You're going to stunt your growth!"

I laughed as I picked up my cello case, watching her turn to fuss over another tray. Molly loved to warn me about the perils of too much caffeine consumption, but I doubted I had any more growth left in me at twenty-two. I was precisely a third of an inch past five feet, coffee or not. People often didn't look past my height. Most seemed shocked that I was an adult in her final semester at Lassiter University. Their concern was annoying but well-intentioned. Plus, my height meant I could wear any shoes I pleased and never be taller than my date. Not that I had any time to date between my job at the diner, gigs, and practice. The only action I got was in my dreams. At least, when I found time to sleep.

I walked carefully out of the kitchen, afraid to knock over any catering carts in Molly's presence. Stepping through the large oak doors that separated the workers from the party, I turned the corner and ducked into a cramped room. The support area served as a place for us hired event musicians to prep. The mismatched furniture had been shoved to one corner to give the four of us enough room to move. Usually this space was reserved for brides and filled with flowers and tulle and lace. Right now, it looked like someone had shoved a bunch of adults into a closet.

I took one last swallow and braced myself for a long night.

"I'm here!" I checked my watch to see that we weren't due to set up in the ballroom for another five minutes. I got blank nods from Sam and Jason, who were more focused on their violins than on my arrival. Sam had retired from the symphony years ago, playing for fun and because, I suspected, he liked the attention he got from the ladies wearing a tuxedo. Between his salt-and-pepper hair and his easy smile, he fit into any crowd naturally. Jason, on the other hand, was only self-assured on stage. A head taller than Sam, he hadn't caught up with his long limbs unless he was playing. He had graduated last year and was hoping a spot opened for a full-time seat with the orchestra soon. Since we didn't play the same instrument, we'd avoided becoming rivals. Mostly. I couldn't say the same for the fourth member of our ensemble. She saw every musician, regardless of their instrument, as competition.

Carmen D'Alba had staked a claim on the small dressing table and mirror, more focused on checking her appearance than her viola. She strained to inspect herself in the room's dim lighting. She always looked more like a guest than the entertainment. Today was no exception. She wore a strapless black gown that swept the floor, and her thick black hair was up in a graceful twist. There was a raw, unapologetic sensuality to her. Her figure, soft and curving, matched her full lips, which were painted a vivid red that contrasted with her olive skin. Carmen was the second chair for the city's symphony orchestra. I'd never had the guts to ask her why she moonlighted with our quartet for events, and she had never offered the information.

"It's unprofessional to show up already dressed," Carmen informed me. She stood and finally took out her instrument. Her eyes flickered over my worn, black dress with distaste as she checked its strings. "Also, didn't you wear that on Tuesday?"

"I had an afternoon session that ran late, so I changed before I came." I forced a bright smile, pointedly ignoring her—correct—accusation about my being a repeat outfit offender. Carmen was hard to like, but I was determined to kill her with kindness. So far, that only seemed to annoy her more. Of course, complete frustration was Carmen's default setting. When Carmen made snide comments about my clothes, I always wondered if she thought she was doing me a favor, knocking me down a peg, or attempting her own warped view of friendship.

"You should invest in something new, especially if you'll be auditioning for the Reeds Fellowship. I already bought my dress for my tryout," she continued, tipping her chin importantly.

The Reeds Fellowship had been a sore subject between the two of us since we'd heard about it through the center. Some rich, anonymous donor had funded a year-long grant that paid all living expenses for a young musician. The rest of the details were sketchy. No one knew who had established the program, but the winner would provide private recitals to the donor throughout the terms of the arrangement. Considering the center was widely publicizing the fellowship, they had to be confident it was legitimate. Most of us simply thought it was an eccentric billionaire getting his rocks off. San Francisco had no shortage of those.

"You shouldn't have," Jason interrupted, "because I'm going to win the Reeds."

"We'll see." But Carmen's smug smile suggested exactly how likely she thought his chances were. Neither of them seemed at all concerned about me auditioning, which I tried not to take personally.

Jason and Carmen were too busy bickering with each other to notice me slip away to the relinquished mirror. I'd been too rushed to worry much about how I looked. Facing my reflection now, I groaned. The drizzle blanketing the city this afternoon had wreaked havoc on my hair, despite the careful bun I'd pinned up this morning. Considering I'd walked nearly a mile from the station with my cello in tow, it could have been worse.

The biggest problem was my hair. It had a disobedient streak made worse by rain. No matter what gels and mousses I tried, and no matter what miracles they promised, within moments, wisps of hair would escape and curl at the nape of my neck. I blew a rebellious strand out of my eyes and tucked it behind my ear. Surveying what I had to work with, I thought about letting it down. But it was slightly damp, which meant there was no telling how it would dry. Then I remembered Carmen's polished chignon. I'd never be as put together as her, but I could try.

I only had a few minutes, and it took every one of them plus two dozen bobby pins to tame it. Pinning my hair up also made it look less coppery and more auburn. I swiped Carmen's bottle of hairspray from the counter and applied it liberally. I dared my hair to disobey now, but I knew it would.

There wasn't enough time to deal with anything else but a dash of lip gloss. I couldn't help thinking Carmen might be right about my clothes, though. The long black dress I wore for performances was clean and wrinkle-free, but the color had faded to dark gray. That wasn't a surprise, given that my mother had found it in her closet a couple of years ago. The tag was long gone, but she swore it was designer. I was pretty sure she bought it for a funeral. A fact I did my best not to think about. Death and parties, even parties I was working, weren't a good combo.

As far as a new audition dress? I was about as likely to spring for one of those as I was to join the circus. San Francisco was one of the most expensive cities in the world, and despite my scholarships and sharing an apartment with two roommates, it was still a stretch to make rent each month.

My questionable designer dress would have to do.

"Guests are arriving. They're ready for us," Sam announced as he checked his phone, finally ending the argument between Jason and Carmen.

I hurried to take my cello out of its case as the others left the room. I made my way quickly down the hall into the Green Room, named for its distinctive color. I thought it looked more palladium blue than green. Maybe the gilt detail and five giant chandeliers made it look green to others. Towering urns draped with ivy and lilies perfumed the room with their heavy scent. Elegant and understated like the menu they'd demanded from Molly.

As soon as I stepped inside, I nearly ran into the group. They'd all stopped a few feet inside to stare, instruments still in hand.

"What is it?" I asked, trying to peek around them. I was too short to see over any of their shoulders.

"I think it's a modeling convention," Jason mumbled.

I elbowed him, and he finally moved over enough for me to see what he was talking about.

The most stunning people I'd ever seen mingled under the room's soaring ceilings. Every person I saw far surpassed good-looking, instead bordering on gorgeous.

Every. Single. One.

There was a statuesque brunette draped in a shimmery fabric that flowed down her flawless figure like liquid gold. A handsome man with deep black skin that almost gleamed was speaking with a petite blonde in the corner. And on and on. It took considerable effort to tear my eyes away from the group. I looked up to find Jason with a dazed look on his face.

"Close your mouth. You're drooling," I muttered to him. Not that I could blame him. We were mortals in the presence of gods.

"It's probably just a plastic surgery convention," Sam said with an unimpressed shrug. "We better get to it."

We found our music stands and chairs in a discreet corner of the room. I took my spot, forcing myself to pay attention to my cello instead of gawking at our patrons for the evening. I adjusted my posture, angling my cello just so that I'd have the best angle for my bow. Then I checked my music sheets.

Sam led us into the first piece, and I relaxed into the notes. The dull throb of anticipation I always got at the start of a performance began to fade, replaced by the music. When I was playing, the rest of the world melted away. My student loans didn't matter. Mom's hospital bills didn't exist. I wasn't caught in a rivalry with my fellow musicians. Everything was simply right. Everything was in harmony.

One melody shifted to another. I lost track of time, completely immersed in the music. My eyes closed as I played the last notes in the *andante con moto* from Schubert's *Death and the Maiden*. I vaguely heard Sam announce we would take a twenty-minute break. I lingered in the final sad crescendo. A sense of longing always ran through me after we finished this particular selection.

When I finally emerged from my trance, the others had already left. I gradually noticed the murmur of voices around me. I took a deep breath and lowered my bow. Awareness crept over my body, skittering up the back of my neck like spider legs, and my gaze roved across the room, locking onto the most handsome face I'd ever seen.

I gasped, but it wasn't the man's beauty that surprised me. It was the murderous look in his piercing blue eyes.

CHAPTER THREE

Julian

Nearly forty years had passed, and I'd missed nothing. I should have expected my mother to blow past normal and go straight to the extreme. But she seemed keen on surpassing even my expectations. She'd been so busy planning that she refused to see me after my arrival in California. She claimed it was her duty as one of the Bay Area's patron families to host an event to start the season. But I knew what this party was really about: bombarding me with possible matches from every angle.

Sebastian hadn't shown his smug face since we'd parted at the island. I had no idea where he'd gone off to, but I knew he would wind up here eventually. The elite rarely missed social season, but no one skipped The Rites. Even me. I recognized most of the vampires in the room, which was in no way a winning situation. We might mingle every fifty years, but the rest of the time we stuck to our own family trees.

I swirled the bourbon in my hand and braced myself for the relentless matchmaking about to begin. There were always a few romances during an ordinary season. Some even ended without bloodshed. But enacting The Rites meant something far worse than romance or mating or violence. It was a fate I was determined to avoid, regardless of tradition or my mother's meddling.

But duty beckoned, so I found myself in the Herbst Theatre, the most intimate building in San Francisco's Performing Arts Center. The ballroom wasn't the largest event space in the complex, but it was lavish enough to suit vampire tastes. Gilt flourishes decorated the arched windows and ceilings, complementing antique crystal chandeliers. Still, with half the country's pureblood vampires packed inside, it was a tight fit. That's why I staked a claim at the bar. It was out of the way, tucked into the back of the room. The others were here to mingle and brag, flirt and saunter. Everyone was looking for someone to boost their ego.

I was far more interested in being left alone.

Outside the soaring windows, city lights punctuated the dark. Night called to me, beckoning me to join it, but I was stuck at a cocktail party.

"Your time is up, my friend!" A pair of blue velvet gloves landed on the wooden bar top next to me with a *thwack* that dramatically announced their owner's arrival. The words were spoken by a slight male with a hooked nose and cruel, black eyes. He was undead proof that not all vampires were beautiful, towering creatures like most of the others in the room.

I sometimes wondered who had turned him and why.

"Boucher," I said by way of greeting, not bothering to raise my voice above a whisper. "Join me for a drink."

"Perhaps one." Boucher's own voice lowered to match mine as he held up a finger. The gesture had the air of someone important who would never lower himself to appear rushed. That was to say, it was very French, and Boucher was every bit the Parisian, down to his neatly polished dress shoes and up to the wool scarf knotted elegantly at his throat.

"You came all the way from Paris for this?" I asked. I knew the vampire hated to leave his beloved city.

"I had a disagreement with the new manager at the opera." He shrugged his shoulders. The bartender placed a glass in front of him, and Boucher tucked a crisp hundred-dollar bill into his tip bucket.

"Who won?"

"I did." He smiled, displaying rows of sharp, white teeth. I didn't bother asking how. If he'd left Paris over it, there had been violence. He'd probably been banished until whatever crime he'd committed faded from the public's memory.

"I'm lending my expertise to the orchestra here, for the moment."

"I'm sure they could use it."

"You have no idea," he said with a heavy sigh. "When did you arrive?"

"A few days ago," I replied in a clipped tone. Things were cordial between the two of us, but I'd hardly count him as a friend. It was impossible to trust vampires from other bloodlines. But Boucher and I both loved music, so it was easier to get along with him than most.

"Any favorites?" He eyed the crowd around us, his gaze skipping to the mortal women in the room. "I don't envy you. I'd never be able to choose. They smell so intoxicating."

My lip curled at the insinuation. I'd been doing my best to ignore the scent of blood perfuming the air. The mortal men and women present were all from families that dated back nearly as far as the vampires here. Like their ancestors, they had been groomed to be the ideal companion in hopes of making a match with a vampiric bloodline.

For humans, they were remarkably attractive. The families of familiars, which was how we referred to these mortals, spent years cultivating their best-looking and most talented children to catch our attention. Most matches between vampires and familiars were temporary arrangements that might last years, perhaps decades. But The Rites made things a bit more interesting. These humans were vying for marriage and the chance to help produce an heir.

As if the world needed more vampires.

"Why on earth are we still participating in this cattle call?" I asked him.

Boucher's dark eyebrows bunched in surprise like two wiggling caterpillars. "Didn't your mother tell you?"

"She's been avoiding me," I told him. I hadn't seen her since my arrival. I'd been informed of tonight's event by an engraved invitation and tuxedo waiting in my apartment downtown.

"Sabine does love her games." He downed the rest of his drink. "A party isn't the place to speak of serious matters, but the Council has decided an influx of new blood is in order."

"Don't you mean babies?" I said sourly.

"Seriously?" he asked. "You sound like you don't like them."

"What's to like? Diapers? Crying?" Vampire babies only differed from mortal infants in their diet and life expectancy. The rest was grotesquely similar.

"Your mother has her work cut out for her. I don't think she's avoiding you," Boucher said with a laugh. "I think she's devising her battle strategy."

I rolled my eyes at Boucher, who merely laughed as we watched them in the bar's lighted mirror. A row of bottles lined up like an army of soldiers blocked me from seeing them all. Why did all pretentious bars need a mirror? But the humans didn't hold our attention. Boucher's dark eyes moved to follow the more interesting vampires and familiars scurrying behind and between the bottles like a macabre rearview mirror.

"Shouldn't he be compelled?" I asked him, watching the human bartender's obvious interest in his unusual clientele. It was customary to mentally prepare any human attendants before large events, compelling them so they didn't realize what we were. Most humans wouldn't notice a vampire or two, but a large group was far too supernatural to ignore. The last thing we needed was humanity discovering vampires were real.

"The Council is getting progressive," he told me. I could tell what Boucher thought of this by the distaste coating his words. "Compulsion should only be used in extreme cases."

I grimaced. "Next, they'll cut off our balls."

"No one will let it come to that," he said darkly. But before I could press him for more information about The Rites or Council's sudden humanitarianism, he picked up his gloves. "I'm afraid I need to make the rounds. You won't hide here all evening, will you?"

"I expect at some point I'll leave," I said as he drew the gloves back down his fingers. I pulled my own leather ones from the interior pocket of my jacket. It was a necessary precaution in mixed company, but I hated wearing them.

"It wouldn't kill you to have some fun," Boucher threw over his shoulder as he finished adjusting his cuffs. He left me to join the throngs chatting and fawning over one another.

It wouldn't kill me. That was the problem. It was merely torture with no end in sight. But Boucher was right. I could have fun in San Francisco—as soon as I left this boring party. I made up my mind to find my mother and get her lecture about family duties and obligations out of the way so I could leave.

I turned to deposit my glass on the bar, dropping the gloves to reach for my wallet. The bartender stared as another large bill made its way into his bucket. It was too easy to forget that small amounts of money to us were much bigger to mortals. In the past, compulsion had eliminated any curiosity on their part regarding this. But now there were new fucking rules that made no sense. It was just like vampires to change the wrong behaviors just to be on the right side of history.

But before I could turn around, a scent rose like a warning in the air.

Blood. But not just any blood.

I smelled her before I saw her.

Crushed rose petals drifting over Marie Antoinette's dinner party. The burned sugar and velvet of violets dabbed on a porcelain neck. The warmth of a fire blazing in a Venetian hearth. The sweet almond scent of a woman's thighs wrapped around my neck. It was as if my life had been marked by her absence as much as this moment was marked by her presence. It took effort—more than I had exerted in centuries—not to turn to trace the path she made through the room. Patience was not one of my defining characteristics. But following her would imply interest, and I couldn't allow that.

Her scent grew stronger, and I cursed myself for bothering with a drink. I should have left here before now and avoided all of this. Was this part of my mother's schemes? Had Sabine Rousseaux finally succeeded in securing a familiar I couldn't possibly resist?

My fingers sank into the polished bar top as if it was carved of butter, my gloves abandoned on the counter. The bartender's eyes widened even more than they had at my tip, and I groaned inwardly. Later, I needed to ask Celia what qualified as an extreme enough scenario to warrant compulsion. For now, I was pretty sure sticking my hands through solid wood counted.

"You're getting me another drink," I told him, and he went still as our eyes locked. "You found the counter with these marks, but you didn't worry about it. You were too distracted by the huge tips you're making this evening."

He nodded and turned to pour another Scotch in my glass. Behind me, music began playing, and I relaxed momentarily. Withdrawing my fingers from the wood, I studied the gouges I'd made in the antique surface. I made a mental note to ease my guilt by making a sizable donation to the arts center in the morning.

I pulled my gloves on quickly before I accidentally maimed something else and accepted my fresh drink, pushing back from the bar. Another round would take the edge off. Whoever's scent had caught my attention would be gone by the time I was done, along with the familiar herself, lost amongst the many scents mingling in the room.

But when I turned around, the scent hit me again. A dark urge swelled inside me, something primal taking over as my eyes searched the room for its owner. I dared to take a step toward the crowd, only to find my attention pulled away from the mass of partygoers. I turned instinctively, and my gaze landed on the string quartet playing in one corner of the room. My senses rocketed past the male violinists and voluptuous brunette playing the viola and zeroed in on the musician tucked into the back of the group.

She sat at an angle, cello between her legs. Her dress was worn and shabby, and she lacked the polish of the other woman in the quartet. Her head remained tilted in concentration, preventing me from getting a good look at her face. But a single strand had escaped the tight knot of hair perched on top of her head. It curled at the nape of her neck, unwilling to be held captive. She struck me as equally unmanageable. Historically, that was a dangerous sign in a woman.

Altogether there was only one word to describe her: *human*.

She was definitely not the intended result of my mother's matchmaking schemes. But her blood was potent. Certainly, others would smell it even in a room choked with the olibane and citrus scent of witches and the spicy notes of vampires. She'd be lucky to get out of here missing a few pints of blood and suffering from short-term memory loss. Customarily, vampires didn't kill people, but there was a tendency to cut loose during the social season.

I lost track of how long I stood and considered what to do with the fragile creature. The longer I watched her, the more I became aware of something else. Her talent. It seemed as though she and her music had become a single entity, as though she existed entirely in this space and time for the delicate notes wafting around her. Her small stature seemed in stark opposition to the size of her instrument, but she was in complete control. It was intoxicating to watch. Unlike the others, she played with her whole being, and all of that would be lost if the wrong vampire got his hands on her tonight.

In that moment, I hated my whole bloody species. I hated the posturing around me. I hated that I'd been dragged out of my self-imposed exile to join them.

And I hated her, most of all, for forcing me to stay at this party. Because there was no way I could ever let her out of my sight.

I was still watching her when the group announced they would take a break. No one in the room seemed to notice or care. No one else seemed aware of them or the cellist and her intoxicating scent. The other three musicians exited quickly, but she lingered, as if stuck in the sheets of her music. Weren't humans supposed to have some sense of self-preservation? How could she sit in a room of vampires, unguarded, like a snack? Couldn't she sense the danger?

Suddenly, her eyes snapped open and looked directly into mine. Her mouth formed an *O*, and I heard a gasp drowned by the crowd but perfectly audible to my supernatural ears. It wasn't the first time a human had reacted that way when encountering our kind unexpectedly.

I narrowed my eyes, determined to scare her away. She had no business being here. I glared until blood pooled in her cheeks, locking my legs to keep myself from moving toward her. She turned away to reach for something behind her and exposed her slender, bare neck in the process.

My body interpreted the movement as an invitation—an invitation I was already moving to accept.

Whoever she was, it was too late for her now.

CHAPTER FOUR

Julian

I hadn't killed a human in forty years. That record would end tonight. It wasn't that I wanted to kill her. It was that I knew one taste of her would never satisfy me. Her blood sang to me across the space, its intoxicating lullaby luring me closer. She was young. I didn't care. She was talented. I didn't care. One word with her, and I'd be able to easily compel her to leave with me. Losing control here could get messy.

The activities I planned for her were usually reserved for the after-parties. The ones that took place at private manors and villas where the gates were locked and the guest list was much more exclusive. I didn't think I could wait long enough to find a new location. But the theater was filled with shadowy nooks and hidden places where I could sink my teeth into that alabaster neck.

She shifted in her seat as I approached, and her cello temporarily blocked my view of her. It had the effect of a talisman, warding her from evil long enough to stop me in my tracks.

I tore my attention from her and stalked out of the ballroom. With each step away from her, my head grew clearer. But in its place was a new, disconcerting desire. I wanted to protect her.

Protect her? How?

I had no idea how the fuck I hoped to do that when I was what she needed protection from.

A safe distance needed to be maintained. I would stay close enough to keep her from falling victim to any of my kind but far enough that I didn't lose my mind with hunger. I'd had years to get control of my bloodlust. I could do this. So why did my resolve feel like sand slipping between my fingers?

The corridor outside the Green Room was mercifully empty. I wasn't sure what might happen if a human stumbled into my path right now. There was one guaranteed way to sate my thirst. I started to slip off a glove when her petite form moved into view. Her scent hit me next. So much for my strategy.

It was a little harder to maintain distance when only one party knew the plan. I quickened my pace, stepping into a shadowy corner to let her pass. She only made it a few steps before a striking figure stepped into her path.

"Fuck," I said under my breath when I caught sight of Giovanni Valente. The vampire was only a century younger than me, but he had a reputation as a ladies' man. The trouble was that he had a tendency to kill it with the ladies—literally.

It was no surprise. In any era, he had the looks to get women behind closed doors. His black hair dusted his shoulders. It had been short the last time we met. We'd been fighting together in some war. After we lost, I hadn't seen or heard from him. Time was a tricky thing. Minutes might last an eternity while years slipped away in the blink of an eye. Giovanni's tailored tuxedo did little to hide his warrior's physique.

The woman fell back a step, her head tipping to take him in, since he had to be a foot taller than her. I listened, waiting for some reaction, but she made no noise. I didn't know her, but she was already driving me nuts.

"Forgive me," Giovanni said, giving her a charming smile, "but I wanted to thank you for the lovely music."

A human might not have picked up on her fingers tightening

around the neck of her cello, especially in the dimly lit hall. But I spotted it instantly. There was the survival instinct she seemed to lack in the ballroom. Hopefully, that meant she'd be smart enough to move away from him.

But she didn't. Instead, she laughed nervously. "It's my job," she joked. "And there's more coming soon, but for now I need to use the little girl's room."

She shifted uncomfortably, and I knew it was an excuse. He was making her uncomfortable, and she didn't know how to get away from him. If she knew what he really was, she wouldn't be uncomfortable. She'd be terrified.

"Little girl?" he repeated, clucking his tongue softly. "You shouldn't underestimate yourself. You're a very beautiful woman."

"I am?" She sounded torn between more laughter and annoyance now.

"Come for a walk with me," he said casually.

"But my cello..."

"Bring it. You can play for me," he said.

I heard the musical rhythm of his voice as he spoke. So much for using compulsion only in extreme situations.

Giovanni led her away from the party toward the theater, establishing exactly what his intentions were. I just had to let him take her. Once she was out of my sight, this temporary fascination would lift. I would leave. And the woman? Maybe his restraint had improved in recent years. But I found myself moving swiftly to follow behind them. I still wasn't sure why this was my fucking problem.

They vanished into the shadows, and I felt something snap inside me. I sped toward them, stopping so quickly that the woman startled, catching her heel in her long skirt in the process and pitching forward into my arms. Her cello crashed to the floor beside us, and she screamed.

"There you are," I said smoothly. "You disappeared."

She spluttered with confusion and tried to twist free of my arms.

"Wh—"

"Giovanni," I cut her off. "Excuse us for a moment. My lady is slightly accident-prone."

I bent and freed her shoe from her dress, then held it out for her. She slipped her foot into it and instantly turned to where her cello had fallen.

"Julian. I didn't know you were back in San Francisco or that this mortal was spoken for." He took a step away from us. He'd lived long enough to know how attached vampires became to their pets.

"This wha—" the woman tried to interrupt again.

I turned and stared at her. "Stay quiet, pet."

The girl froze, and despite the compulsion overpowering her free will, she glared at me. It was the first glimpse I'd had of her face. The end of her nose tipped up at the end, a smattering of freckles dusting it. In the dark, only a ring of green remained around her dilated pupils. A human wouldn't be able to see it at all, but it was clear to my vampire eyes.

"Yes," I said as though she hadn't spoken. "It's new."

"Obviously," he said with a dangerous current running through his words as he glanced in her direction. "I didn't detect your scent on her. If I had…"

"An innocent mistake." I angled myself between them, making my message clear.

"Perhaps. She's pretty for a human," he commented.

"Do you think so?" I shrugged my broad shoulders. "I'm more interested in her as a cellist."

Giovanni laughed and smacked me on the back. "I forgot how romantic you are." He began to walk away, then paused. "Do let me know if you bore of her?"

I forced a tight smile, not moving from my protective position until he was entirely gone. The woman wasn't safe here. The sooner she left the theater, the better. I'd have to compel her again. This time, I'd force her to leave and return home. Then I needed to see if Giovanni had lost interest. If he had, she would be safe.

If not…

"My cello," she shrieked, and I whirled around in surprise.

She picked it up and stared at its cracked body before lowering it to the ground solemnly. Then she did the last thing I expected. She stood up and poked me in my rib cage.

"What was that for?" I arched away before another jab could land.

"You scared the shit out of me, and I dropped it, and now…"

"That's not really important right now," I said. She glowered back at me, and I realized Valente was wrong. She wasn't pretty. She was stunning, even when she was mad.

Especially when she was mad.

"How can you—"

"Listen very carefully to me," I stopped her. "That man is not what he seems to be. You need to run."

I waited, but she didn't move.

"Run," I repeated, dialing up my compulsion.

She just stared at me.

"Why aren't you running?"

"Why would I run?" she asked.

"Because I told you to." My compulsion had failed. I didn't know why. She'd stayed quiet when I used it before, but now it was like she was immune to me.

She planted a hand on her hip as if to prove my point. "So?"

"That's usually enough." I didn't have time to explain compulsion to her. Or vampires. Or why she needed to leave. The longer she remained, the less likely I could clean up this mess.

"If that's all…"

I only had one more trick I could try—a human trick. "Okay, will you please run?"

She laughed. "One more time since you appear to be hard of hearing. Why?"

"Fine." I threw my hands up. I had tried to be gentle. I'd tried to warn her. I'd even tried to compel her. "Because that man is going to kill you and drain you of your blood."

She hesitated, but before I could feel relieved, she hit me with another question. "Why would he do that?"

"Why the fuck would he do that?" I exploded. "Isn't it enough that he might? A sane person would run."

"Look, I don't know how to tell you this," she said slowly, "but I don't think it's *my* mental health you should be questioning."

"I'm not crazy," I said through gritted teeth. I should leave her to her fate. Clearly, she couldn't care less if she wound up as Giovanni's evening snack. Why should I?

"That's the spirit," she said flatly. "Now if you'll excuse me."

I didn't trust myself to touch her, but I had to stop her from returning to that room. If Giovanni saw her without me at her side, his interest would be renewed. So I blurted out the only thing I could think to say: "Because he's a vampire."

"Vampire?" She said the word like it was a different language. There was a pause as she stopped to study me again. "Up until now, I thought you were just an asshole, but you really are crazy sauce."

I should have seen that coming, but I found myself trying again. "You need to trust me."

"Um, yeah, no."

Charm. Compulsion. Even the truth. None of it was working. And I was getting more annoyed by the minute. So what if this tiny human wanted to endanger herself? Why was it my job to save her? I stared at her, realizing she wasn't going to budge.

"I need to get back. They can't start without me." She looked over at her cracked cello. Pain flitted over her face. "On second thought, I can't play at all with that. You can come with me and explain."

Now we were going to fight over a bloody cello. I'd had enough. "No, you need to come with me. You can't go back to that party."

"Because you're going to save me from a vampire?" she guessed, and I realized that not only was she ignoring my warning, she wasn't a bit afraid of me. What the hell was going on? "How do I know you aren't going to get me alone and murder me?"

"I'm starting to consider it," I growled, feeling the tips of my fangs lengthen. "Are you always this stubborn?"

She crossed her arms, shrugging a single shoulder. "Are you always this weird?"

"I'm trying to save your life," I reminded her. "Some people might call that chivalry."

"Chivalry is dead," she said without missing a beat.

Clearly, I wasn't going to win this argument. "Well, let's not join it in the afterlife. You're not going to run, are you?"

She didn't move. That only left me with one choice. I swept her off her feet, threw her over my shoulder, and carried her away before she could even blink.

CHAPTER FIVE

Thea

found myself over the man's strong shoulder before I could answer. It happened so quickly that I felt a bit dizzy. He started away from the party before my shock could wear off. The corridor's white walls flashed by as he moved so quickly I could barely catch my breath. My eyes snagged on my cello as he carried me away.

My cello.

I had a crack in my cello.

Get a grip, Thea! There were more important things to worry about than a freaking cello. Like the impossibly strong, unbelievably gorgeous brute who had thrown me over his shoulder and appeared to be walking straight for the exit.

Was I just kidnapped? By a guy who believed in vampires?

Oh hell no. I was not going to let Mr. Crazy Pants drag me into his delusions, even if he was the hottest man I'd ever seen. If he thought he was saving me, maybe he'd let me go. Then I remembered the look on his face in the Green Room—a look that suggested he wanted to tear me limb from limb.

I needed to get away from him. Now.

He slowed his pace enough for the world to stop spinning. I caught sight of the janitorial closet, the last door in the hall before the exit. I didn't know what waited for me out there, but I decided to seize my chance before I found myself in the back of some van.

"Put me down," I said as firmly as possible, annoyed that my voice shook a bit on the words.

He ignored me. Balling my hands into fists, I beat at his back. Unfortunately, it was as effective as pounding a brick wall and hurt about as much. I wiggled in his grasp, trying to swing one foot toward his groin.

"Stop," he growled.

I continued hammering at his back, but I thought better of kicking him in the balls. "Not...until...you...put...me...down."

"Not until you're safe."

Fighting him was getting me nowhere. Reasoning with him seemed like a stretch. That only left one option. I released all the fear and panic I'd been bottling up since the moment I'd seen him staring murderously at me and let it spill out of me. "Please," I begged. "Please let me go."

He stopped in a shaft of moonlight streaming through the exit's glass door. My heart sped up, adrenaline pumping through my veins. I craned my head around his broad shoulder to see that one more of his giant strides would carry me outside into the dark memorial garden. I couldn't let him take me out there. I only needed him to let his guard down for a minute. But he didn't lower me to my feet and his grip on me remained firm.

"I'm not going to hurt you," he said in a strangled voice.

I went still, surprised by his obvious pain. My ragged fear ebbed a little, and I found myself scrambling to hold on to it. Because for some ridiculous reason, I no longer wanted him to put me down.

"Do you believe me?" he pressed.

I didn't know how to answer. There was something dangerous about him. I could feel it: the edge of violence mixing darkly with the raw power he exuded. This couldn't be real. This couldn't be happening. I had to be dreaming or something.

But maybe...maybe I'd imagined that hateful look back in the ballroom. Maybe the vampire thing was a weird joke. Maybe it had been too long since a man had flirted with me, and I needed therapy.

"Well, you *are* kidnapping me." I did my best to sound casual, but emotions churned inside me. Maybe he was a good kind of nutty, more like eccentric, like tossing millions of dollars out of a plane eccentric.

Or maybe he was rubbing off on me.

Something was definitely messing with me, regardless. I should be screaming for help. I should feel completely terrified, but since he'd said he wouldn't hurt me, my fears had been soothed.

I believed him.

At least, I believed the part about him not hurting me. The vampire bit? Nope.

Seconds ticked by, and I waited for him to respond. Finally, he lowered me to my feet. My heels clicked sharply on the tiled floors, and I stared down the long, dark hallway to an open door. I knew I should run for that door and the people laughing and visiting inside. But could I make it?

I glanced down at the chipped tile at my feet, knowing I'd have to lose my shoes to stand a chance of reaching the Green Room. He must have been thinking the same thing, because his hands remained on my hips.

"Don't run." This time it sounded more like a request, not an order.

I raised an eyebrow, acutely aware that he was still touching me. I felt his strong hands digging into my hips, his massive frame hunched slightly to keep his hold on me.

"Please," he added stiffly. His mouth tugged at the corners like he was resisting the urge to smile. It was that small, normal reaction that made up my mind.

"Okay," I agreed slowly, "but I need to get back and tell the others. They're probably wondering where I'm at."

His shoulders squared, a silent battle waging across his handsome face. I studied him while he fought himself. Cast in the moon's glow, his face remained half shadowed, emphasizing his chiseled jawline and the slight hook of his nose. His eyes watched me with a wary intensity that stirred somewhere deep inside me. I couldn't look away from him. He utterly captivated me.

So, if he was a serial killer, I was in serious trouble.

He cleared his throat and tore his gaze from me. "I will accompany you."

"You don't have to," I said quickly, earning a sharp look that silenced me from making further protests. Maybe I shouldn't provoke him. "On second thought, you do you."

"I will do that," he said, sounding confused. "Speaking of you and me, I've failed to introduce myself. My name is Julian Rousseaux, and I apologize for the strange introduction."

Julian. That was the name the other man had used. It took me a second to realize he was waiting for me to introduce myself.

"Oh," I yelped and stuck out my hand. "Thea. Thea Melbourne, and it's okay about the weird introduction as long as you aren't going to kidnap me."

I really needed to cultivate a survival instinct. Usually, I knew how to handle myself. I lived in a major city. I knew how to recognize danger. But now I was acting like nothing had happened.

"It's lovely to meet you, Thea." My name was intoxicating on his lips. I could fall into its spell and let it take me over. Cool leather wrapped itself around my palm and broke the enchantment. Looking down, I found he was wearing gloves. But before I could ask about the strange choice, Julian lifted my hand and pressed a kiss to the back of it. He seemed to linger for a moment, and I found myself feeling dizzy again. He released me and the sensation faded.

It was him. He was pressing all my buttons, and it was like he'd found settings I didn't even know I had.

He stepped to the side and crooked his arm. "Thank you for allowing me to come with you."

My mouth fell open. He frowned, and I snapped my lips together. Slipping my arm through his, I fell into step beside him. I relaxed as we started away from the exit and back toward the party. This was turning into the weirdest night ever. Still, maybe chivalry wasn't dead, I thought as we passed a collection of framed portraits hanging on the wall. I was having a hard time wrapping my brain around the last fifteen minutes, though.

"I will see to your cello," he promised.

I glanced to its dark shape waiting a few dozen feet farther down the hall. "You don't have to—"

"Of course I do," he cut me off. "I was responsible for its damage."

"I'm sure it can be fixed," I lied. It was possible it could be fixed, but I'd seen the crack. I doubted that even the most skilled luthier could fix that. I had waited tables for the entire summer before I started college to purchase it. It was the most expensive thing I owned. I had no hope of getting a seat on the orchestra without a full-size, professional cello, or even securing the Reeds Fellowship. The realization splintered my heart. Everything I'd been working for was gone.

I looked up, nearly straining my neck in the process, to see his eyes narrowed and wary. At the same moment, we passed by a sconce, and I glimpsed their bright blueness for the second time. My heart stuttered like the first time I'd found myself in his sights.

"If that is the case, I will see to it. If not, I will ensure a replacement," he said, leaving no room for further argument.

This time I wasn't going to be polite. He was right. He had caught me off guard and made me drop the cello. The least he could do was help me repair it.

"Your friend," I said, still trying to hold his gaze, which was quite a feat considering he had to be well over six feet tall, "he was a little weird."

"Giovanni Valente is not my friend," he warned me, "and you should stay away from him."

"I was just being nice," I said defensively. Actually, I hadn't wanted to go with the man he claimed was a vampire. I felt like I had to.

"Being nice is an excellent way to get yourself killed," he said as if he'd read my mind.

"You sound like a true-crime podcast." I rolled my eyes. "It wasn't like I was going to climb into the back of his van or anything." Nope, I'd nearly let Julian carry me off, though. This Valente guy had exercised an uneasy charm over me. Julian had just acted like I was a lost piece of luggage that he'd happened upon. What was going on tonight?

"A true-crime what?" he asked, looking down at me with a curious expression.

"Really?" He couldn't be serious, but his face remained inquisitive. "A true-crime podcast where they investigate old murders."

He blinked before rearranging his face into disinterest. "I've missed a few things. I've been away...on business."

"To where? 1999?" Everything about him was strange. He was missing a few pieces, and he swung wildly from brusque caveman to perfect gentleman. But how had he never heard of podcasts?

"Is it on these things?" He pulled a phone from his pocket.

"Um..." How was I supposed to answer that? "Yes. You need an app."

"An app," he repeated. He grimaced at the phone like he didn't trust it. "Would you call these things life-changing?"

"Phones?" I barely restrained a giggle. "Try living without one for a day."

"I might." He responded with a stiff smile. "I believe you needed the ladies' room."

Looking around, I realized he'd led me to it. "I did," I said in confusion. I hadn't told him that. He had been following me.

"I'll wait out here and then return you to your peers." He took a rigid stance next to the door, looking like a really beautiful statue of an ancient warrior. Except he was wearing a tuxedo and alive.

I reached for the door, casting one more look over my shoulder at him. He was still doing his impression of a bodyguard. Stepping into the bathroom, I waited for the door to close behind me and pressed my back to it, taking a deep breath. My life was busy. Hectic, even. But exciting? No. I wasn't sure if that was the right word for what I felt pulsing inside me.

I hadn't actually needed to use the toilet. That had been an excuse to get away from Giovanni. But, right now, sitting down for a minute seemed like an excellent idea. I took a few steps toward the stalls. Pushing open the first door, I gasped as I interrupted a man and a woman pressed against the side of the stall.

"Sorry!" I blurted out, whirling away, as something hit me. I turned my head back instinctively as I realized I recognized the strapless black gown puddling at the woman's feet. "Carmen?"

Could tonight get any weirder? Maybe I needed to take a few days off. But she didn't respond. The man she was with didn't move, either.

I took a step toward the door, averting my eyes from the kiss. "I'm sorry. I'll leave you two to…"

I was not about to finish that sentence. But before I could back out of the room, the man lifted his head to reveal two completely black eyes. Not a sliver of white or iris was visible. A single red drop dripped from the side of his mouth. Carmen slumped into his arms like she was drunk.

I opened my mouth to scream, but he murmured, "Silence. Wait there until I'm finished with this one."

My scream lodged in my throat and my body locked in place as if gravity had been turned to its highest setting. I couldn't move my feet. I couldn't lift my arms. It was as if I'd been frozen. I couldn't call for help. I could only watch as he lowered his lips back to Carmen's neck.

The only part of me I had any control over was my brain, but I could only think one word.

Vampire.

CHAPTER SIX

Julian

'd lived centuries, and somehow, I found myself lounging against a yellowing plaster wall waiting for a woman I barely knew—a *human* woman. I felt its slight orange-peel-like texture through my tuxedo jacket and shirt. My sharpened senses were still in overdrive. I tapped a beat on the wall to dissipate my energy, surprised at how it absorbed the sound. Then again, theaters were known for good acoustics. No one wanted a flushing toilet to interrupt a performance.

I glanced at the door of the ladies' room, wondering how long she could possibly take, and began devising a three-step plan for dealing with my colossal fuck-up.

Step one: get Thea away from the vampires here.

Step two: compel her to forget everything that had happened tonight.

Step three: fuck if I knew.

The problem was that I'd already tried compelling her. She resisted me entirely. If I hadn't already used it on the bartender, I might have been worried that something was wrong with me. The last time my compulsion had failed was…never.

It had never happened to me, not once in all my centuries. And the fact that Thea could resist me made it even harder to get rid of her. I wanted to know why. What was so special about the petite human? Yes, she was breathtaking and played the cello with a passion I hadn't experienced in ages. But she was also approximately the size of a teacup and just as fragile.

I couldn't satisfy my curiosity without putting her at risk, and that was a danger I was unwilling to accept.

"You know exactly what step three is," I muttered to myself. "Forget about her." If I could successfully compel her, I needed to walk away. I would provide her a new cello and see that she was never hired to play at another vampire function.

I glanced at my Rolex, relieved to see the cocktail party would be over soon. Minutes ticked by, and Thea didn't appear. After being alive as long as I had, time rarely registered with me. But waiting out here for her was a different story. I moved closer to the door. I wouldn't usually invade her privacy, but tonight was far from ordinary. After all, I'd just revealed the existence of vampires to a mortal. That was a decent justification for crossing the line. I leaned my ear against the door. As I suspected, no sound came from inside. It was deadly quiet.

Maybe she was right. Maybe I hadn't recovered from my extended break from the world. Perhaps I was breaking too many rules, but I couldn't ignore the dread tugging my hand toward the door. I'd nearly given in to my weakness when I managed to get a hold of myself.

I was not going to interrupt a lady in the toilet.

But before I could step away, I heard a faint slurp. Instinct flared inside me, and I inhaled deeply, catching another scent drifting in the air. I'd missed it before, too intoxicated by Thea's presence to realize I'd led her to another vampire. There was no time for second-guessing myself. My fangs extended instantly as I burst through the door.

Thea stood in the middle of the room, her body angled between the door and the stalls. Relief washed over me when I saw she was alone, but it was short-lived. Her eyes widened as I came into view, but she didn't move or speak. Frantic energy poured from her, and instinct took over. I bounded toward her, needing to place her within reach. But as I came closer, a drawling voice called out from an open bathroom stall. "These ones are taken."

I swiveled toward the vampire, placing myself between him and her. "I don't think so."

"Look, they're not familiars, and the food is seriously lacking here. I thought I was going to die of boredom." He released the woman in his arms, the other female from the quartet, and she slumped, unconscious, to the floor. Her head hit the toilet with a crack. "If you don't mind, mate."

He prowled toward me, obviously intent on finishing Thea off as well. He wore no gloves, and I wondered that he'd been allowed in at all. Dress codes at these things were strict.

"I do, actually, and I'm not your mate," I growled.

He smirked at me. I resisted the urge to take his head off. Barely. Tension gripped every muscle of my body. A low rumble started in my chest as I prepared to attack.

"Whoa!" He stopped and held his bare hands up, revealing a red slash tattoo on his wrist. "I didn't know."

"Know what?" I spit the words at him but didn't wait for him to respond. "That it's bad manners to dine on a mortal at a party? Or that it's illegal to drain one in public?"

"This is hardly public—"

I cut off the pitiful excuse. "Or maybe you simply didn't realize who you're speaking to."

The vampire's throat slid as he studied me. It was clear from his immaturity that he was young. He hadn't been born a vampire, either. While plenty of purebloods flouted the rules, he wore no gloves at a party full of witches. That either meant he was turned or stupid. No pureblood would be caught without them at an event like this. None of us would take that risk. I considered asking him who his sire was. Technically, they should be the ones to deal with this mess.

But instead of falling into line, his eyes narrowed. "You're one of them," he said. "A filthy pureblood. You think you can just order me around?"

"I know I can," I roared.

"I don't give a shit who you are, Granddad." He charged toward me, another smirk twisting his lips.

He might have a hang-up about purebloods, but I was older and faster. Only his body shifted along with that cocky smile. He never made it a step closer to Thea. My gloves were off before he even blinked. One second I closed my fingers around his neck. The next his head was in my hands. His body swayed for a moment before crashing to the floor and leaking blood on the tile. I dropped his head next to the rest of him.

But I didn't care about him or the mess that killing another vampire—even a fledgling jackass like him—could cause. Whipping around, I reached for Thea.

"Are you okay?" I asked as she began to tremble. Soon tremors racked her whole body. Her face tipped up to answer me, but when she opened her mouth, an ear-splitting scream tore from it. I pulled away from the piercing noise. "Well, your lungs seem to be working."

The cry finally died on her lips. She stared at me, then looked at the bloody remnants of the man who tried to attack her. "You killed him."

"I did," I said smoothly. She'd seen me do it, so there was no point debating the matter. Plus, it wasn't like I could charm her into believing otherwise.

"Why?" She spoke so softly I wasn't sure she meant to say it out loud.

I answered anyway. She was clearly in shock, so I tried to be gentle. Unfortunately, I was out of practice. "Because he deserved it," I said in a gruff voice. "Do you have a problem with that?"

She considered for a moment before she slowly shook her head.

I blinked in surprise. The response caught me completely off guard after her scream.

"Do you tear heads off often?" Her head tilted as if she was really looking at me for the first time.

"Only when—"

"They deserve it," she finished for me.

She was taking this remarkably well, but I suspected when the adrenaline wore off, she wouldn't be so calm.

"Now, will you finally let me escort you home?" I struggled to make it sound like she had a choice. If I had to throw her back over my shoulder and lock her up at my place, I would.

"He's dead." She licked her lower lip. It glistened in invitation, and I looked away. "Why do I need to leave now?"

I raised my hand and pinched the bridge of my nose, wondering if she ever ran out of questions. "Because I'm a vampire."

"I kinda figured that out when you, uh, ripped off his head." She shifted on her feet, but despite seeing what I was capable of, there wasn't an ounce of fear on her face.

"And that doesn't bother you? Because—and I realize this might be counterproductive to my plans—it should."

She lifted her chin a little. The small act of defiance tugged at me. Thea was brave. "You said you wouldn't hurt me."

She obviously had zero survival instincts.

"The others might," I reminded her.

"Others?" she echoed the word.

"The party." I lifted my shoulder closest to the door as if pointing her toward the missing clue. "We're all vampires."

"Oh. That explains it!" It sounded like she wanted to giggle. Perhaps she was prone to hysterics. That was common in cases of shock. But she didn't dissolve into a fit. She bit her lip like she was restraining a smile.

I needed her to stop doing interesting things with her mouth. It was giving me ideas. Bad ideas. Very, very bad ideas. Ideas we would both thoroughly enjoy.

"It explains what?" I forced myself to ask.

"Nothing!"

I arched an eyebrow. "I told you my secret."

She considered for a moment, and then she answered me. Thea Melbourne might resist my efforts to compel her, but she obviously appreciated the concept of give and take.

"You're all so good-looking," she blurted out.

"That's what you noticed?" Humanity was doomed. Still, I felt an unfamiliar twinge in my chest. Who else had she been looking at?

Before I could press her on it, a small moan interrupted us. I swiveled in surprise, and Thea took an unsteady step toward me. But she didn't fall into my arms. She pushed by me and rushed straight to the woman in the toilet stall.

"Carmen?" she called in a panic. She turned to me with searching eyes. "Is she going to be okay?"

I paused to listen for a heartbeat. I'd been too distracted by Thea to worry about the young vampire's victim. I could hear the racing beat of Thea's heart, the organ pumping so loudly that it took me a moment to make out the much fainter one in the room.

"She's alive," I said grimly. But she was definitely not okay.

"I thought he killed her," Thea whispered. Guilt flitted over her pretty face but didn't settle. When she continued, I understood why. "I didn't even think to help her. I just stood here. I couldn't move."

There wasn't time to explain compulsion to her, or to figure out why his had worked and mine had failed. Her friend's heartbeat was growing fainter. She was near death. Any moment now, she would pass into the next life. The jealousy I'd felt earlier was nothing compared to the bitterness taking hold of me now. But one more look at Thea's stricken face erased it. She blamed herself. She shouldn't, but humans were rarely rational creatures.

"I can heal her," I said softly, ignoring the fact that I shouldn't. Because it was definitely not part of my plan to get any deeper into the pile of shit I'd found myself in. "But I can't let her remember any of this."

Thea's tongue darted over her lip, her shoulders setting with determination, as she nodded. She moved to the side, giving me enough room to reach the victim.

"How…" she began, but trailed away as I drew one manicured finger across a vein on my wrist. Bringing it to the other woman's lips, I held it there until she began to drink. I felt Thea's eyes watching me as I fed my blood to her friend.

After a few sips, her dark eyes fluttered sleepily. I drew my wrist away and took a handkerchief from my pocket. Carmen bolted up—or tried to. Thea knelt quickly to steady her.

"What happened?" Carmen asked. She blinked a few times. Confusion was normal. She had lost a lot of blood, but there were also the aftereffects of feeding on vampire blood. "Why am I here?"

Thea chewed on her lower lip, searching for what to say. I tried to ignore the attention she was drawing to her mouth and failed. So I returned to dealing with the mess the reckless vampire had left behind.

"You fell," I said. Carmen startled at the sound of my voice, but as soon as she looked at me, she relaxed.

"I did?"

"Yes." Unlike Thea, she showed no resistance to my manipulations. "You tripped on your gown and hit your head on the toilet. Thea found you."

Her eyes widened in horror, and she glared at Thea. "I fell on the toilet," she shrieked, her voice hitting a pitch I hadn't thought humanly possible until this moment, "and you brought a man to help me?"

"I can see you're fine now," Thea said with a sigh. She glanced over at me. "You can go. I'll take care of her."

"Not fucking likely," I snapped. By my count, I'd saved her life twice tonight. I wasn't letting her out of my sight.

Thea squared her petite shoulders and stared me down. "Then wait outside."

I didn't budge.

"Please," she added.

"I'll find someone to deal with this mess." I turned back to the other woman. "You feel fine. You'll walk out of here without noticing the body. You won't remember the attack. You only remember smashing your head on the toilet."

"Thank you. I've got it from here." Thea's voice shook a bit.

My eyes narrowed, but I stalked toward the door. Not only was this tiny mortal not afraid of me, but she was also giving me orders. I slammed the door behind me and melted into the shadows to wait. This time, she hurried. My blood had done its job. There was no sign that anything had happened to Carmen when they exited the restroom. I only hoped Thea hadn't told her what really happened. Were they close?

I should find my brother. Sebastian had to be here by now. He could erase Thea's memories of the night. She could continue her normal life. As for me, I would see to my obligations. I would settle on some perfectly adequate familiar and see to the family business of marrying. Somehow that plan felt even less appealing than before, and before, I would have rather been staked.

"Thank you for your assistance," Carmen said, still avoiding my eyes. She was embarrassed by her understanding of tonight's events. "I can see myself back from here."

She glanced over at Thea and smiled tightly.

"Of course," I said, letting her pass. She walked confidently but swiftly down the dark hall and back to the party. As soon as she disappeared into the shadows, I turned to offer Thea my arm.

She just glared at me, not moving an inch. "Wait a second. Why can *she* just wander off without a chaperone?"

"She's in no danger."

"A vampire was drinking her like a milkshake five minutes ago." She crossed her arms, still refusing to move.

"She drank my blood, and now she has my scent on her. No other vampire will lay a finger on her," I said, my temper starting to rise. Why wouldn't she just listen?

"It's not your fingers I'm worried about," she muttered. "Okay, then put your scent on me, so I can go find my cello and explain where I've been."

A smile tugged at my lips, but I wouldn't let it loose. "It's not that simple."

"Why not?" she challenged me.

"Would you like to ingest my blood?" I asked her.

Thea gulped and shook her head.

"Would you like me to drink your blood?" I imagined that was an even less appealing option.

"You can't just rub against me or something?" Her hand flew to her mouth as soon as she realized what she had said.

"There is another way, but it would take a little more than rubbing, pet," I purred, taking a step closer to her. Her remark was innocent, but my thoughts weren't. Maybe all I needed was to get this unusual human out of my system.

But I knew that was a lie.

"What would it take?" she asked breathlessly.

I leaned down, lowering my voice to a murmur only she could hear. With vampires everywhere, I needed to be cautious. Bedding humans was frowned on, but during the social season, it was against every rule of etiquette to form a new attachment to a mortal. "I could take you to bed. No one would doubt you were mine after that."

She gulped, a battle beginning in her eyes. "I've never—"

"There you are!" A sharp, imperious voice interrupted before she could finish. I straightened and shot Thea a warning look as a beautiful woman in a red silk gown sauntered toward us. Next to me, Thea gawked as she took her in. That was how people usually reacted when they saw Sabine. I'd been suffering through its effect on her ego for nearly a millennium.

"You didn't come to the house," she said, placing a possessive hand on my bicep. Thea stiffened next to me. I looked to discover her lips turned down in a sour expression.

"Because you're avoiding me," I reminded her.

"I've been busy." She shrugged a shoulder dismissively. "Engagements don't plan themselves."

"I hope by engagements you mean parties."

"Of course." She blinked twice, a sure sign that she was lying. I'd learned to recognize her tells. It was why she always lost to me in games of poker. "What else would I mean?"

Thea cleared her throat politely. "I should be going. Thank you for your help."

"Help?" Sabine repeated, curiosity tainting her voice.

"It's nothing," I said before Thea could repeat any of this evening's disasters. It was bad enough that I'd gotten involved. It was worse that I'd nearly given in to my thirst for Thea. Sabine didn't need to know any of that.

"Nonsense." But she wasn't the type of vampire to roll over and accept that answer. "How did my son help you?"

"Son?" Thea choked.

Had I actually thought things couldn't get more complicated? Obviously, I'd forgotten how the world worked while I was desiccating alone in the Keys. This was a rather unpleasant reminder of who I was and of my duty.

Sabine waited expectantly for me to respond, and I knew I had no choice but to turn to Thea. "Allow me to introduce my mother."

CHAPTER SEVEN

Thea

"She's your mother?" The words slipped out before I could stop myself.

"Julian." The woman glared at him with a look that only a mom could muster in such a moment. "May I have a word?"

"Excuse us for a moment," he said tightly.

I nodded, feeling a bit numb, as I watched the two of them walk a few steps down the hall to a shadowy alcove. His mother was incredibly beautiful, her hair the same glossy dark color and her features just as striking as his, but softer. Not that she was his actual mother, probably. I mean vampires were made, as far as I knew. That was how it worked in stories.

Usually, I liked to consider myself a fairly adaptable person. Why fight change when you can run with it? But watching them whisper in the dark, my brain was on overload. Too much was happening too fast. This had to be a dream. One of those trippy, swiftly changing ones that felt so real you almost believed it was happening.

I closed my eyes. "Wake up, Thea. You're dreaming."

Usually that did the trick, especially when I was stuck in a nightmare. And this was a nightmare—wasn't it? Opening my eyes again, I found myself still standing in the corridor. Julian and his mother huddled a short distance away. I pinched my arm, just to be certain.

"Ouch."

This was really happening. All of it.

Vampires were real.

The sexiest man ever was one of them, and he might be flirting with me?

And his mother looked both younger and hotter than me.

I needed a drink. The memory of blood dripping from Carmen's neck swam to mind, and my stomach did a nasty flip. Or maybe a drink was a bad idea. Tonight had taken a surreal turn, and between my lack of sleep, work, and classes, I was too tired to deal with it. So what if Julian was beautiful? He was grumpy and controlling. Probably a byproduct of being alive during the Dark Ages or something. God, could he be that old?

It didn't matter. All I wanted was to go home, change into some joggers, and bury myself under the covers in bed.

Bed.

I heard his voice say the word, and my stomach knotted, coiling every muscle around it. I'd kept men at arm's length the last few years. I didn't have the time to think about a relationship between Mom's treatments, school, and work. A few guys had asked me out, but it had been easy to turn them down. But Julian wasn't talking about a date. What would it be like to go to bed with a man like him?

I imagined his bed covered in silk sheets and rose petals. Vampires in movies were always a little theatrical. What I couldn't begin to imagine was what it would feel like. I didn't have much experience in that department. I had never dated anyone long enough to go to bed with him. I'd never really considered it.

But now I couldn't help wondering what hid beneath Julian's tuxedo. I'd seen how strong he was. What could he do with it? I had no idea how long he'd been alive, but something told me his experience in the bedroom fell on the opposite end of the spectrum from mine. I'd never felt ready to sleep with a normal guy. There was no way I was prepared to lose my virginity to a vampire.

So why was I obsessing over it?

Probably because I couldn't think while he was this close to me. Another good reason for me to hide in bed until work tomorrow. I made up my mind to get my things, check on Carmen, and leave.

"I have to apologize for my son," the woman said, gliding toward me gracefully before I could take off. Her voice was warm and musical like his. I could listen to it all day. But meeting her gaze, I felt a chill. Her eyes were cold and hard as though she was sizing me up. "He told me that he was responsible for ruining your cello, amongst other things."

I glanced over at him, wondering what he had admitted to her.

"She knows everything," Julian confirmed in a low, irritated tone.

"Someone has to clean up the family messes." She didn't look too pleased about being the one who had to do it. "I already excused the other members of your quartet. When they returned a member short, the sound felt a trifle light."

"I am so sorry," I gushed. Guilt swelled inside me. Not only had I let everyone else down, they had to bear the consequences without me.

"It hardly matters. No one was listening anyway." She waved her hand dismissively. "You can go, too, Mademoiselle…"

"Melbourne. Thea Melbourne," Julian added, stepping into my path before I could do as she suggested. "I should have introduced you. Thea, this is Sabine Rousseaux."

"It's nice to meet you, Mrs.—"

"Madame," she corrected me. "Mrs. is a term humans use."

I nodded, not trusting myself to maintain a polite attitude if I spoke.

"Julian insists on seeing you home," she continued through gritted, but perfectly white, teeth.

"That's not necessary," I started.

"He's quite insistent." She shot her son a look as sharp as I expected those teeth were. "I am sorry you were dragged into this. If you'll excuse me…"

I resisted the urge to curtsy. It seemed like she might expect some sign of fealty. She brushed past me and then stopped.

"And Julian, be sure to see that she's looked after," she said meaningfully before continuing to the party like the queen she obviously was.

"Let's go," Julian said. He didn't offer me his arm this time. He didn't even look at me. Instead, he started straight for the front entrance.

"My case and purse," I reminded him. He stopped and turned slowly, looking as if spending another second dealing with me was absolute torture.

A lump formed in my throat as we walked in utter silence to gather my belongings. I swallowed, fighting back tears I didn't quite understand. The only explanation was that I was tired, and I wanted to put tonight and all this weirdness behind me.

I picked up my cello case, its lightness a reminder of what I'd lost, and felt a tear fall. I brushed it away quickly, hoping he didn't see. Julian reached over and took it from me, but he remained quiet. I followed behind him, digging my BART card out of my bag.

He beat me outside, and by the time I reached him, he was already speaking with the valet. The attendant rushed off with the speed of someone who knew a big tip was on the line.

I held up my pass. "I can get home from here. If I could have my case, I—"

"Don't be ridiculous," he cut me off. "I will see you home."

"I can take care of myself. I've been doing it for twenty-two years." Saying the words was like an incantation. After all of tonight's craziness, I'd started to question myself. Why? I had nearly finished school with a sick mom and two jobs. So what if vampires existed? I'd survived more than one tonight. If anything, I was more prepared now if I stumbled onto another one.

"Thea," he said stiffly. "I apologize for the suggestive remark I made earlier. I promise I will never lay a finger on you."

A wave of disappointment rolled over me, but I lifted my head. "And I promise that I can see myself home."

"No," he growled, his mask of polite detachment slipping to show the beast underneath. I resisted the urge to shrink away.

"What are you going to do? Throw me over your shoulder again like some Neanderthal?"

The muscles in his jaw ticked as he met my glare head-on. "Don't tempt me."

"Don't test me," I shot back.

We both refused to concede ground, so we stayed locked in a staring contest until a car roared to the curb in front of us. Julian grabbed my elbow and dragged me toward it, my cello case in his other hand. The valet got out, leaving the engine running, and glanced nervously at us. I knew nothing about cars, except that this one was expensive. Probably the most expensive car I would ever ride in. Julian placed my cello case on the ground as the valet came around to open my door.

"Thank you." Julian stopped him and handed him a crisp one-hundred-dollar bill. "I've got it from here."

"Thanks." He stared at the money before shoving it in his pocket.

Julian reached for the door, finally releasing his grip on me. He opened it and moved to the side. I crossed my arms and stood there.

"Get in the car, Thea," he said with forced calm.

I shook my head.

"Now," he added.

I raised an eyebrow and didn't move. We were locked in a vampire-human standoff.

"Please," he said with gritted teeth.

I waited for a second before releasing a sigh and climbing into the passenger seat, which took a bit of effort between the low ride of the car and my long gown. He closed the door, muttering a frustrated string of curses but looking relieved that I had given in. He thought he had won the battle, but I had questions for Julian Rousseaux, and he was going to answer every one of them.

Julian circled the car, pausing to put my cello case in the trunk, before sliding in behind the wheel. He filled the entire seat, reminding me again of his muscular body. I ignored the tick of interest between my legs that the thought sparked. He reached into his pocket but didn't pull anything out. Instead, he frowned and studied the dash.

"Fucking electronic bullshit," he swore.

"Huh?" I craned to see what had him so frustrated.

"My brother told me I could get directions on this," he said as he pressed a bunch of buttons. The display screen in the car flashed between settings as he searched for something.

"Like GPS?"

He shrugged one of his broad shoulders. "Is that what it is?"

"You don't know what GPS is?"

"I took a little break from the world," he admitted.

"Like a vacation?"

"Like a nap," he said.

"For how long?" I asked slowly.

"About thirty-nine years."

Another couple dozen questions added themselves to my list. For now, though, the flashing screen was making my head hurt. I shooed him away. "Let me."

He watched as I input my address into the car's navigation system. It spoke the first direction, and he grimaced. "This explains a lot."

"Like what?" I asked curiously.

"Nothing," he said as he pulled onto the street with a cautiousness that did not match the ostentatious car. We fell silent as he made his way through the streets of San Francisco. Cars zipped past as we drove.

"Do you always drive like a grandmother?" I finally blurted out.

"Only when I have fragile cargo." He didn't bother to look at me.

"Fragile? What…" It dawned on me that he was referring to me.

I was fragile—pathetically human—and he was stuck babysitting me. I slouched in my seat, no longer wanting to ask him anything. But one question kept resurfacing, even as I tried my best to ignore it.

"What did your mother mean?" I asked. "When she said to look after me?"

"You don't want to know," he muttered, his eyes never leaving the moonlit street. It had begun to drizzle, and the city's customary fog was rolling in.

"I really do," I said. Too many things didn't make sense. For one, Sabine Rousseaux had not seemed at all keen on me spending time with her son, so why tell him to look after me?

"She wanted me to compel you," he finally said after a few moments of silence.

"Compel?" I repeated the word as a traffic light turned red. "Like what you did to Carmen?"

"Yes." Julian slowed to a stop before turning to face me. "I'm supposed to make you forget everything you saw and everything you know about vampires."

I should want that, too, so why didn't I? My head fell as I murmured, "Oh."

"I'm not going to do it."

I lifted my head to stare at him. He didn't want me to forget. Hope blossomed in my chest. Maybe Julian didn't hate me.

Before I could question why I cared how the rude, old-fashioned vampire felt about me, he continued. "Because I have a better idea."

CHAPTER EIGHT

Julian

The BMW was a terrible idea. Not the car itself. I liked the car, apart from the electronic bullshit. No, it was the close quarters I regretted. It was impossible to ignore her scent, especially with the heat on. I couldn't exactly allow her to freeze to death. Hunger burned my throat, but it wasn't Thea's delicate neck I was thinking about. It was something else—something forbidden.

At least, for me, it was.

I didn't want to taste Thea's blood. I wanted to taste every inch of her, starting with her smart-ass mouth and her full lips. I wanted to drag my fangs along her tongue until she couldn't scrounge up any more combative responses to my demands. I would reward her then and sate myself. I'd start with her breasts. Then I would move lower and show her what I'd learned after centuries of pleasuring females—vampires and mortals alike.

I shifted in my seat, hoping she couldn't see my erection in the car's dim interior. Glancing over, I caught her staring at me with downturned lips. Thankfully, she was looking at my face.

"What?" I asked when she didn't bother to turn away.

"You said you had a better idea," she said, fiddling with her seat belt.

"Don't do that," I snapped.

She froze, her eyes darting up in confusion. "Do what?"

"It's there to keep you safe."

"My seat belt?" she asked. She smoothed it down on her shoulder dutifully, but as I returned my attention to the road, I caught her rolling her eyes.

It was a wonder that humans lived long enough to learn how to walk. Even after a couple of decades on this planet, the fragility of her body seemed a surprise to her. And every moment I spent with Thea suggested she had the survival instincts of a gnat.

"So?" she pressed. "What's your idea?"

"I'm still working on it." I really did have an idea, but even I knew it was far-fetched at best, impossible at worst. Was I simply responding to her nearness? That had to be it. It would be rash to make a decision without getting to know her first.

Thea huffed, her breath fogging the window. She stared at the city lights for a few minutes in silence before she swiveled in her seat. "Are you going to compel me to forget?"

"I don't know," I admitted.

"Why?" she demanded.

"I'm not entirely certain." I flipped on my signal as the map on the screen told me to turn.

"Why did your mother ask you to do that?" she asked.

I glanced at her, getting the sense she was trying to help me decide what to do with her. She was a strange, tiny creature. "Vampires are very selective about who they share private matters with. Usually, we know a human for years before we consider telling them the truth."

"Private matters?" She giggled. "Are you seriously suggesting that you're all beholden to some sort of vampire honor code?"

"No, I'm suggesting that a human usually finds out about us when we make them our snack," I growled.

"Oh."

A low rumble caught my attention, and it took me a moment

to realize the sound was coming from the delicate woman in the seat next to me. A second later, her intoxicating floral scent shifted, growing slightly sweeter. I studied her for a moment before I realized what it was. "Are you...hungry?"

"No," she said too quickly.

"Your stomach is growling," I pointed out, "and your blood sugar is low."

"How on earth...?" She stared at me as if that was the strangest thing she'd heard this evening.

"I can smell it," I explained.

"My hunger?" She shifted closer to me. It seemed like an odd reaction until I realized that she looked absolutely fascinated.

"That's one way to put it." My head throbbed a little as I tried to block out her changing scent. "You're hungry, so your body released glucose. It made your blood smell sweeter."

"You can smell my blood?" Finally, something freaked her out.

"That's amazing," she said after a moment of thought.

Or not.

"The point," I said through gritted teeth, "is that you need to eat."

She shrugged as if it didn't matter to her. "I could use a coffee."

"You could use food."

"Are you sure *you* don't need to eat?" she asked pointedly. "Because you're a little hangry."

"Hangry?"

"Hungry and angry," she explained. "You really have a lot to catch up on."

"Yes, I can't wait to learn all the ways humanity has butchered the English language." I pulled to a stop in front of a diner and parked. It was shabby, its paint discolored from pollution, but well-lit. Inside, a waitress darted between blue vinyl booths, smiling warmly. It looked like the sort of place a human might like. "Is this okay?"

"They'll have coffee." She reached for her door.

I was faster. A second later, I opened it from the outside and offered her my hand. Her mouth fell open, but she quickly clamped it shut. "How do you do that?"

"I'm a predator." I helped her out of the car. "I'm built to hunt."

Her throat slid, drawing attention to her porcelain neck. Her skin was so pale that it was nearly translucent, making it far too easy to see the blue veins running through it. I hadn't bitten a woman on the neck in decades. Marking a human there only said two things among vampire circles. I didn't respect her or I'd laid permanent claim to her. Neither were messages I wanted to send.

"Are you going to bite me?" she whispered, and I realized I'd been staring at her long enough that she had noticed.

I grimaced, wishing her question hadn't been so on the nose, and shook my head. "No. I'm not going to bite you."

"So you aren't hangry?" she pressed.

Goddammit, did she want me to bite her? It was bad enough that my fangs had yet to fully retract. It made my mouth ache for attention.

"No, I am not hangry," I said harshly.

"Look, if you needed to...um..." She stared at the ground as her cheeks flushed.

"To what?" I asked.

"Eat," she blurted out. "I mean, I owe you, and I guess—"

"Never offer a vampire your blood again," I seethed. Just the thought of a vampire—any vampire—drinking Thea's blood was enough to make my fangs lengthen.

Her eyes widened as she got a glimpse of them. "But you're hungry..."

It took every ounce of self-control I possessed not to pin her to the car and take her up on her offer. She wouldn't resist, not once I was inside her. The only trouble was that I couldn't decide what I wanted more: to sink my teeth into her or bury my dick inside her.

"Never," I roared again and stalked toward the diner. "Let's eat."

A bell tinkled as I opened the door. I held it for her, then followed her inside. We paused at an abandoned hostess stand. A deeply lined face appeared in the pass-through window, summoned by the bell. He waved a spatula in the air. "Sit wherever you want."

The diner was fairly empty at the odd hour—too late for dinner and too early for the late-night crowd. The few patrons here now weren't the type to nose around in another's business—probably because they wouldn't want anyone to nose around in theirs. There wasn't a speck of dirt on the checkered-tile floor or a single crack in the slick vinyl seats despite their age. Thea didn't wait. She just walked toward a booth in the far corner away from the windows and the other diners.

Thea was quiet as she scooted into her seat, which squeaked under her petite body. Before I could apologize for losing my temper, a waitress delivered menus to us, dropping them onto the tabletop with a plastic *smack*.

"Can I get you two something to drink?" she asked with a sugary sweet smile.

"Coffee," Thea murmured.

"I'll take one, too," I said. As the waitress left, I nudged the menu toward Thea.

"I'm not really hungry," she said quietly.

I raised an eyebrow, and she groaned.

"That's not really fair." She picked up the menu and flipped it open. "Why do you get to worry about feeding me when—"

"I'll eat," I said and grabbed my own menu.

"Wait, you eat?" she asked, peering over the top of hers at me. "Like real food?"

"Of course." Not that there were a lot of tempting options here. Nearly everything was fried, smothered in gravy, or came with a side of pancakes. "Why do they put hash browns on every plate here?"

She ignored the question. Lowering her voice to a whisper, she said, "I thought vampires only drank blood."

"That wouldn't be a very balanced diet." I folded the menu and placed it in front of me. "You have a lot to learn about vampires."

"About that…" She trailed off as our coffees appeared.

"You two want food?" the waitress asked.

"Two eggs," I told her. "Basted."

The waitress blinked at me, her pencil hovering over her order pad. "Let me ask."

"Never mind," I said with a sigh. "Whatever's easiest."

"Scrambled?" she asked.

I glanced at the line cook working the griddle and decided it was the safest option. "Yes."

"Cheese?"

"No." I handed her the menu.

"And you?" She turned to Thea.

"Same."

I shot her a warning look. After the shock she'd experienced, she needed more than a couple of eggs. "She'll have pancakes as well. The tall stack, please."

Thea pursed her lips like she was annoyed, but she didn't argue. "With chocolate chips."

The waitress gathered the menus as Thea downed half of her coffee with one swig. She caught me staring and groaned. "Please don't lecture me about my caffeine intake."

I lifted a shoulder and let it fall. "I'm just impressed. It was a long day."

"You have no idea." She shook her head, angling her body to catch the waitress for a refill. "I had a shift at my other job this morning and classes. I should have gone straight home and passed out."

Two jobs and school? That explained her worn attire. But she hadn't gone home. She'd agreed to come out with me. Maybe it was simply her natural curiosity, or maybe...

"You have questions," I reminded her.

"And you'll answer them?" she asked.

"Some." I took a sip from my mug and refrained from gagging. It tasted more like the dirt they grew the beans in than coffee. Thea took a long swig from hers without complaint.

"Because you can compel me to forget?" she asked.

"I could, but I will leave that up to you."

"Up to me?" Her voice pitched up with surprise.

"You were not given any other choices this evening. It only seems fair to let you decide whether you'd rather forget tonight ever happened."

Thea fell silent, and I waited for her to speak. Finally, she raised her eyes to meet mine. "I'm not sure."

"Because you have questions?" I guessed, and she nodded. "Ask me anything."

She didn't need to know that I hadn't been able to compel her back at the theater. No one did. Not until I figured out why. There was only one way to get to the bottom of that mystery. I needed to know what made Thea tick, and there was only one way to learn that. Over the centuries, I'd learned a bit about humans. There was one thing in particular that always held true. You could learn more about a mortal from the questions they asked than any answer they might give to yours. Maybe it seemed safer to them to let their guard down when asking rather than answering.

"On one condition," she said.

I hadn't expected her to issue an ultimatum. Not when she could barely hide her curiosity.

"You answer any question I ask, truthfully," she said firmly, folding her hands triumphantly in front of her.

"There are rules—" I started to explain.

"You said you could make me forget it all, right?"

Was she calling my bluff? I nodded slowly, wondering where she was going with this.

"Then there's no reason you can't tell me everything." She smiled sweetly.

Thea Melbourne was even more cunning than I thought she was. But before I could decide what that meant for me, she leveled a no-nonsense glare at me and asked the last thing I expected from her. "First question. Why do you hate me?"

CHAPTER NINE

Thea

"Hate?" He chewed on the word for a moment, and I caught another glimpse of his fangs. They weren't as long as they'd been earlier when I pissed him off, but they were still there. I mentally added fangs to my growing list of topics to discuss.

Julian lifted his broad shoulders, his face a mask of detachment. "I don't hate you. Why would you think that?"

So he was going to deny it. I didn't know where to begin. "It's just seemed that way from the first moment I saw you, when I was playing with the quartet. I caught you watching me."

"Yes," he said calmly, his long, graceful fingers molding around his coffee mug in an oddly human way. "People often watch musicians—or has that changed as well?"

"Watching is the wrong way to put it," I said, bypassing his question.

"What is the correct way you wish to put it?" he asked.

I thought for a moment before landing on it. "You were...uh... murdering me with your eyes."

He stared at me, his face still carefully blank, but shadows clouded his eyes. They didn't go completely black like the vampire who'd bitten Carmen, but his pupils seemed to take over. Yeah, I needed to ask about that, too. But after a moment, he snorted, and the darkness evaporated. "I'd been talking to an old friend and discussing some private matters. I apologize if you thought I was— how did you put it? Murdering you with my eyes?"

"Oh, okay." I grabbed my coffee and took a long drink of it, embarrassment washing through me, cheeks burning. I'd imagined it. I mean, why would he want to kill me? Apart from the obvious reasons a vampire might want to kill a human.

"Next question."

"How old are you?" I opted for a more benign one to avoid humiliating myself again.

Before he could answer, the waitress reappeared and plopped our plates down in front of us. "Syrup is over there." She pointed to the condiments clustered at the end of the table. "Can I get you anything else? Ketchup? Hot sauce?"

After all the blood I'd seen tonight, I didn't think I could handle the sight of any red-hued liquids. I really hoped that a vampire hadn't ruined french fries for me forever.

"Thirty," he answered when she left. "Give or take."

"Thirty?" I blinked as I tried to make that math work. "You said you were asleep for, like, forty years."

"Thirty-nine," he corrected me. "Pureblood vampires don't age past thirty."

I narrowed my eyes, wondering if he was going to twist every question I asked. So Julian Rousseaux thought he would be cute? I would be cuter. "What year were you born, then?"

"I was born around the Battle of Hastings," he said.

"And that was when?"

He muttered something that sounded like a curse. "Around the year 1066."

I nearly choked on a bite of pancake. "Did you say 1066?"

"I'm relatively young," he said. He waited for a moment while my brain tried to process that the man I was sitting across from was nearly a thousand years old.

"You said 'born,'" I pointed out when I'd finally regained control of my brain. "I thought a vampire bit you, and then you died, and you became a vampire."

"That is one way—quite a vulgar way, might I add—that a vampire can be made, yes." He grimaced as if the thought of it was unappetizing. "But that's not how I came into being." He pushed a bit of egg around with his fork. He'd yet to take a single bite.

"I thought you said you ate food, but you haven't really touched yours," I said.

"I'm not a huge fan of scrambled eggs."

There was something so spoiled and human about the way he said it—as if he'd been offered a sandwich without the crusts cut off—that felt so at odds with everything he was telling me that I couldn't help myself. I burst out laughing. Julian tilted his head, looking perplexed at this reaction.

"I'm sorry," I said, still unable to get my laughter under control. "It's just that you're a thousand years old—"

"Almost," he cut in.

"—and you're a picky eater," I finished.

"Maybe later you can explain the joke," he said drily.

"Sorry." I forced myself to stop. I had no idea how long my coffee date with a vampire was going to last. I needed to focus on getting answers. How else would I be able to decide if I wanted him to compel me to forget everything? "So what's vulgar about being bitten and becoming a vampire? Wait!" A terrible thought occurred to me. "Is Carmen going to become a vampire?"

"No, there are a few more steps involved to be turned," he reassured me.

"Thank God," I said with a groan. "I can't imagine how full of herself she'd be if someone made her immortal."

"Not best friends, huh?"

I shook my head. Now wasn't the time to discuss Carmen or me or any other petty symphony drama. "What else is involved?"

Julian sighed as if he'd rather not talk about the particulars of how one became a vampire. "A human must be drained entirely of blood and then offered vampire blood at the point of death."

"Why does that work?"

"Most vampires believe it's magic."

"But you don't?" I guessed.

"Some vampire scientists have researched it. There's clear evidence that vampire blood overwrites human blood."

"I feel like I should have paid more attention in biology class," I confessed. "So basically, if you gave me your blood, it would turn me into a vampire."

"As I said, it's a bit more complicated. Vampires generally don't discuss the process."

"Because they don't want humans to know how to do it?" I asked.

"Because it's rather private," he said. "At least, it should be. Making a vampire out of a mortal is an intimate choice."

"Have you ever done it?" I wasn't sure if I wanted him to answer that question. Not with the way he said *intimate*.

"Not like that," he said. "There are other ways."

"Oh." So he had made other vampires. Envy crept through me, and I stabbed a piece of pancake with my fork. I wasn't sure what I had to be jealous about. It didn't sound particularly pleasant to become a vampire. It was more the idea that Julian's fangs might have been sunk into another neck. It was a ridiculous thing to be upset over. He was over nine hundred years old and a vampire. He'd probably bitten hundreds—maybe thousands—of other women. "What other ways?"

"A ritual exchanging of blood," he said.

"That's it?" I asked.

"Believe me, you don't want to hear the rest."

But I did. I got the impression that Julian did not, however. "So then what do you mean you were born a vampire?"

"Exactly that. I was born to a vampire mother and father," he said.

"Vampires can have babies?" I dropped my fork. This couldn't get any weirder.

"Yes, Thea," he said in an exasperated tone. "Vampires can have babies."

"Wait, do you have kids?" I tried to imagine Julian with children. An image of him sitting grouchily at a soccer game while tiny vampires ran around formed in my mind.

"I have no pureblood children," he said.

"So vampires that are born are purebloods," I clarified. It felt like I should be taking notes to keep all of this straight. I doubted Julian wanted a notebook full of the vampire rules floating around the world, though.

Julian nodded.

"And you're pureblood?"

"Yes."

"And you have other pureblood siblings?"

"I had one," he said. "My twin. She was born a few minutes before me."

"Had?" I echoed the word carefully.

"She died." He didn't offer more details.

I tamped down my curiosity about his sister's death. As much as I wanted to know more about his twin, I understood grief. I'd experienced it myself. I saw it now contorting his gorgeous face. Apparently, sorrow was a place that vampires and humans found common ground.

I needed to change the topic and fast. I still had a million questions about how vampires were made or born, but there were other things I wanted to know, too. For one, how had I wound up playing cello at a vampire party?

My plate was nearly empty now. I had no idea how much longer Julian was willing to sit here and allow me to interrogate him. "What were you all celebrating tonight?"

"Celebrating?"

"The party," I explained. "I was told it was a reception of some sort."

"A party? Yes. A celebration? Not exactly. Every fifty years or so, we gather for parties—a social season, if you will."

"A social season?" I couldn't help but think of Jane Austen novels. "So you have balls and stuff?"

"And stuff," he confirmed.

"Why? That sounds a bit...old-fashioned."

"I suppose vampires are a bit old-fashioned, as you put it," he said. "We cling to our traditions."

And with lifespans that lasted hundreds of years, they probably had some ancient traditions. "So why bother with a social season?"

"Why do you think?" he asked, tilting his head to study me.

"Well, I've seen, like, every Jane Austen movie ever made, so I'm guessing it's to show off."

Julian's head fell back, and then to my surprise, laughter bellowed from him. When his amusement finally died, he nodded. "I suppose you're right. There are other matters, of course."

"Like?" I pressed. There was something romantic about the idea of these beautiful creatures gathering in expensive clothes and discussing the lives they'd led. I couldn't imagine all of the history they'd witnessed, the art they'd seen, or—a jealous realization hit me—the musicians they'd heard perform throughout the centuries.

"Matchmaking." His voice took on a bitter tone.

I stared blankly at him.

"You said you watched Jane Austen movies," he said. "I presume they're concerned with the same subject matter of the books."

Why wasn't I surprised that a vampire would have that *the book is better* attitude? I ignored the subtle dig and nodded.

"What are the mothers always worrying about?"

I thought for a moment. "Marriage?"

"Exactly," he groaned.

A strange sadness overcame me as I put all of this information together. "So you're all getting together to find someone to marry?"

"It's a bit more—"

"Complicated," I finished for him. While he'd been vague on

some points regarding vampires, he'd made it clear that nothing about his world was simple. "And your mother wants you..."

I couldn't even bring myself to say it, but I wasn't sure why.

"To marry a witch and make little vampires." He looked like he'd rather go back to his nap.

"So you're looking for a wife." It sounded strange to say it. It was the twenty-first century. People did not go around attending balls and making matches.

But apparently, vampires did.

"I'd rather not." He flicked one long finger against the tines of his fork.

"So why do it?" I asked him.

His mouth quirked as he studied me, something unreadable in his eyes. "Straight to the point, I guess." He shrugged. "Because of The Rites. It's expected."

I swallowed a groan. Why did every answer require another question? "What are The Rites?"

"That's a bit easier to answer." He leaned across the table, lowering his voice. "Promise not to tell?"

To the outside world, it must look like we were two lovers about to kiss. If anyone actually knew...

"Several hundred years ago, vampire bloodlines started to die out. It was about the time that they were burning witches at the stake," he said matter-of-factly.

I blanched, thinking of history lessons from high school. "I guess that was real."

He nodded with a grim smile. "Although they burned as many innocent people as they did witches. After all, it was never about stopping magic. It was about control."

"I always thought that." That had definitely been part of the history lesson.

"And then, accidentally, they found a solution to both of our species' problems. Only the oldest and most powerful vampires could still conceive purebloods. But they pretty much all hate each other. I mean, who can blame them? I don't think any couple would want to fuck after thousands of years."

I flushed and glanced away from him, pretending to study the grimy dessert menu. If they all looked like him... "They sound like the Greek gods."

"Where do you think humans came up with that?" he asked. I started to laugh until I saw the seriousness on his face. "Humans want to control what the world believes. Vampires decided to stop fighting them on that a long time ago. Witches, too. It was safer for all of us. So now our histories have been rewritten into myths and legends."

"That sucks."

But he only shrugged. "It did, at first. But it was easier than choosing between massacring a mob of ignorant humans or being massacred by them. Contrary to what some vampires claim, most of us have a conscience."

"Most?" I couldn't help notice his careful choice of words. Which category did he fall into? He hadn't hesitated earlier tonight. He'd killed that vampire without hesitation.

"Not everyone is happy with changes in recent centuries," he said darkly.

"Okay, so what does that have to do with The Rites?" I felt like I was sitting in Vampire 101. There was so much to learn. Not just about how things functioned in their world, but why.

"Sorry. There's a lot of history to keep straight, and I've forgotten half my life." He tapped his forehead.

"So have I," I said before realizing how ridiculous that sounded. I'd forgotten snatches of twenty-two years. He must have lost what—centuries?

"The Rites starts with witches and vampires. There's a whole debate as to whether vampires or witches came first and who had magic first. There were all different kinds of magic back then, but only very powerful vampires had much of it. Witches like to say they were the only ones with true magic—and that they created vampires. And vampires like to say they're older than witches, and if witches were so powerful, they'd live longer. Nobody's really sure who's right, but you didn't hear that from me."

"Like the chicken or the egg debate?"

He nodded. "The point is that witches didn't trust us, and we didn't trust them. There were lots of curses and secret alliances. This was all happening when I was very young, so I didn't know much about it. And things got out of hand. I mean, for an entire century, witches cursed vampires to burn in sunlight."

"Oh! So that one is true!"

"In a way. Thankfully, we got that reversed." He paused, waiting as the waitress stopped to refill our untouched waters. Clearly, she wanted to know what we were whispering about. When she gave up, he continued, "Long story short, something backfired or a witch betrayed their people—because magic was put to sleep."

"Put to sleep?" I had no clue what that meant, but it didn't sound good.

"It's still there in the blood—true magic—but the witches can't use it. They can cast family magic. Make potions," he explained when he saw my face. "But nothing like what they used to do. But it wasn't only the witches who were affected. Our own magic diminished as well. We've always depended on the magic we gathered when we fed."

"On witches?"

"All mortals have some magic in them. Some cultures call it the life force or the soul or whatever," he clarified for me. "But yes, witches contained the most concentrated source of magic by far. So once magic went to sleep, we found our own powers diminishing. Suddenly, it was harder even for purebloods to conceive new vampires, so more vampires were made, turned from humans. But these *made* vampires rarely—if ever—conceived and birthed vampires in turn. To grow our families, we had to turn people, and the more people we turned, the fewer humans there were. Until, for a while, there was an oversupply of vampires and an undersupply of blood. And the new vampires didn't always understand the old traditions—or the rules. Witches were not happy about that."

"But something changed. Vampires and witches don't hate each other anymore," I pointed out. "Or you wouldn't be marrying a witch."

His lips pressed together, and I knew he was holding back a smile. "There's still plenty of hate. We marry each other as a matter of survival. Witches, we call them familiars, needed vampires to hide and protect them. Vampires discovered that witch blood made them more powerful. But more importantly, they discovered a female familiar can carry a vampire's baby. And a female vampire can carry a male familiar's child. So we were keeping each other alive. Literally. A deal was struck, and everyone agreed the two species would come together for a social season every couple of hundred years. Vampires already host these all the time. Every fifty years, it's just nonstop balls and dinners and orgies, but every few centuries the witches are invited to join."

I swallowed a laugh at his obvious annoyance, especially since fifty years seemed like more than enough time to keep the social events from getting stale.

"Eventually, familiars began to care more about matching their children with the most powerful vampire families for reasons other than protection," he continued. "The better the match was, the more power or money or status came with it."

"Why are witches called familiars?" That bit still eluded me.

"It was a subtle insult—part of the agreement. Before magic went to sleep, witches could cast spells, and a spirit would appear to them in some form—a familiar. Their familiar would serve them in some way. Witches used to claim that they'd created vampires to be familiars and lost control of them. Eventually, to receive vampire protection, the power balance flipped and witches became the vampires' familiars, rather than the other way around. We still call them familiars today to remind them they are indebted to vampires for their survival."

"Aren't vampires in their debt, too?"

"Of course," he said with a shrug, "but we are in the position of greater power. And back then, we had the money and resources to fade into the shadows while the humans hunted both our kinds. Witches needed us. It's worked out better than imagined, until recently."

"Recently?" I pressed.

"Vampires are conceiving less, and there are rumors that witches are becoming less powerful. Their old spells and potions aren't working as well—if they work at all. It's why the Council decided to enact The Rites. Normally, the season ends in a few marriages. The Rites are a call for all eldest, eligible pureblood to marry. They want to ensure that the oldest bloodlines—which still have some magic of their own—don't die out."

"They want babies," I said in a hollow voice.

"Yes, it's like being around a bunch of hopeful grandmothers all the time. *When are you going to settle down? When are you going to have a baby?*" He rolled his eyes.

I'd met his mother this evening, and I tried to imagine her badgering him about this. It was impossible to think of Sabine, who looked far too young to even have a child Julian's age, as a grandma.

"Wait," I said as something occurred to me. "If vampires can have babies, why do you all look like you're in your twenties or thirties?"

"We age, but differently than you. It differs a bit for any of us who are born vampires, but aging stops around thirty. Although, we're still considered adolescents until we're a couple of hundred years old. Don't be fooled most of us have lived lifetimes."

"I never thought much about lifetimes until my mom got sick, and then I realized how little time we have," I told him softly. He raised an eyebrow, and I sighed. "My mother had cancer."

"Had?" he echoed.

"Yes, she's in remission," I said brightly, but the smile fell off my face as I recalled what it had cost us—what it was still costing us. "That's how we wound up in San Francisco. There was an experimental treatment. I applied to Lassiter, so I'd be close by."

"Experimental? Sounds pricey."

I swallowed and forced a smile. "It was." I paused. "*Is*."

He leaned back in the booth, drumming his gloved fingers together. "That's why you have two jobs? Medical bills?" he guessed, and I bobbed my head. "And student loans?"

"Scholarships don't cover much these days," I said, looking for a change in subject. I didn't need a vampire feeling sorry for me. "Humans must seem very small to you. Breakable. Finite."

"At times. Most of us avoid humans altogether. When we become attached to one of you, it feels like we lose you in the blink of an eye."

"But you marry witches? They're mortal, right?" I pointed out. Was that why he wanted to avoid marriage? Because it was a speed bump in his perfect, immortal life? Or because he didn't want to get attached to something or someone so fleeting?

"Yes, but sometimes, that's part of the marriage arrangement. After an heir has been produced, the vampire agrees to turn the familiar. But not always. Some vampires only care about producing an heir. Some familiars refuse to become vampires."

I couldn't decide if that made me more or less sad.

"It's a lot to take in." I bit my lip, slightly amazed that he'd told me all of this. "I guess this means you need to compel me."

"It's your choice."

I stared at him. "But you told me all of this."

"I'm not..." He paused as the waitress appeared to deliver the bill.

I reached for it, but he was faster.

"Don't tell me that men no longer pay for a meal," he said as he withdrew an expensive leather wallet from the breast pocket of his jacket.

"On dates, they might," I said, rummaging around my purse.

"Thea, what are you doing?" he asked.

I drew out a couple crumpled bills I found at the bottom of the bag and tossed them on the table. "I can pay for my half."

"Don't be ridiculous." He pushed them toward me. "I'm paying."
I shook my head, refusing to pick them up.

"Why won't you let me pay?" he asked, sliding the ticket and a large bill toward the end of the table. My contribution remained balled up between us.

I swallowed, deciding I would not give in to the strange confusion I felt. Lifting my chin, I smiled at him. "Because this isn't a date, Julian."

A second ticked by, and he didn't respond. The waitress reappeared and picked up the bill, but our eyes remained locked on one another.

"Let me get your change," she said.

"That won't be necessary." Julian continued to stare at me, not bothering to look at her as he spoke. "Keep the change."

"And here's a little extra." I shoved the ones toward her. Across from me, a muscle ticked in Julian's jaw.

"Thank you," she said, sounding shocked as she gathered the additional tip. Considering the amount Julian had given her, the tip had to have amounted to more than the bill. She vanished toward the kitchen, probably wondering when we'd realize our mistake.

"Why did you do that?" he asked when she was gone.

"I told you," I said, hoping he missed the way my voice trembled. "I can pay my way. This isn't a date."

There was another pause, and for a moment, I was sure that Julian could see past all my pretenses right down to the confusion churning inside my chest. Why did he care so much that I wanted to pay? Why was I so hell-bent on fighting him on it?

"Thea." My name sounded tempting on his lips, but I wasn't prepared for the offer that followed it. "What if it was a date?"

CHAPTER TEN

Julian

Thea gawked at me like I'd asked her to marry me. She probably thought I'd lost it. Hell, maybe I had. But I knew something she didn't. Five minutes ago, a man had walked into the diner and began to watch us. Thea's back was to him, but I'd gotten a good enough look to know he wasn't an idle stranger with nothing better to do. If he'd been here when we arrived, I might have written it off as a coincidence. But he couldn't hide what he was or why he was here.

Someone had sent the young vampire to follow us. After everything that had happened this evening, I wasn't surprised. I'd taken another vampire's life, and while my social status afforded me that right, I might find myself facing a pissed-off sire if news got out about it. Or my mother was having me followed. I wasn't certain which possibility was worse.

The trouble was that now I'd dragged Thea into this mess.

"You want to date me?" she asked in a confused voice. "But you don't like me."

This again. Apparently, I hadn't done a very good job covering my bloodlust. It was interesting that she translated my lack of control as something negative. I wondered if she'd still be sitting across from me if she knew what it really was.

"Not exactly, and I like you perfectly well," I corrected her in a low voice. This was not the place to discuss my idea now that a curious vampire was nearby. "Perhaps we can discuss this at your apartment."

"Now you want to come to my apartment?" She shook her head. "I'm not sure that's a good idea."

"Then let me see you home." I stood and gestured toward the door.

For once, she didn't argue. I steered her toward the exit, keeping my body between her and the other vampire and making sure he saw me sneer in his direction. He met my gaze with mild annoyance that he'd been caught, then his dark eyes hooked on Thea and lingered. I moved closer to her, brushing my body against hers as we reached the door. She looked up, startled, and for a moment I lost myself in the green pools of her eyes, tiny gold flecks swimming in them like stars. Her breath caught, and heat blossomed on her cheeks, flooding the air around us with her delicate scent.

"We need to go," I snarled and shoved open the door.

Thea flinched and shrank away from me, but I herded her outside. By the time we reached the car, she had grabbed the handle and opened it before I could open it for her. Judging by how she slammed it shut, she found my actions rude.

I didn't care. She was alive. If I had to make her hate me to keep her safe, so be it.

That wasn't going to stop her from punishing me, though.

We rode in silence the rest of the way to her place, which I only found thanks to the bloody GPS. Thea refused to even look at me. As soon as I slowed the car, she unbuckled her seat belt. She was already climbing out of the vehicle by the time I'd parked and sped to the other side.

"I've got it from here," she said coldly. "And I've made up my mind."

"You have?" She wasn't going to give me a chance to pitch my idea.

She lifted her chin, her lower lip trembling a little. "Make me forget. Compel me."

I'd forgotten about that entirely. I hadn't expected Thea to want me to compel her. She seemed far too interested in the vampire world. I waited for relief to hit me. Despite my string of glorious fuckups, she had given me an out. There were only two problems: I couldn't compel her, and even if I could, I found I didn't want to.

"I told you I had a better plan," I reminded her as it began to drizzle, making the already cold night even more unwelcoming.

"Not interested." She shook her head and stuck out her hand as if to shake mine. I couldn't help noticing that she was shivering. "It was nice to meet you. Now make me forget it ever happened."

I ignored the hand and took off my jacket.

"What are you doing?" she asked suspiciously as I wrapped it around her shoulders.

"You're cold," I said. "We should get you inside."

"*We* shouldn't do anything," she corrected me, but she clutched the tuxedo jacket tighter. "I can see myself inside."

For the first time, I bothered to look around us. I'd been so focused on her that I hadn't realized where we were. Her building was a run-down old Victorian with bars on the windows. The streetlamp flickered above us, casting shadows on a group of men conducting business on the corner.

"My cello?" she prompted.

"This is where you live?" I asked, ignoring the request as I continued to catalog my concerns. The list was growing longer by the minute.

"It's an expensive city."

"You need to move. This isn't a safe place for a woman to live." I couldn't leave her here. Not in this part of town.

"I'm fine," she said, "and I don't live alone. I have roommates."

"Roommates?" I eyed her.

"Olivia and Tanner," she said, beginning to walk toward the dimly lit entrance.

I followed her, taking stock of the broken exterior light. "Is Tanner a man?"

"Yes," she said drily. "Does it matter?"

"Are you...two..."

"Mr. Rousseaux," she said, feigning shock, "are you jealous?"

"Curious," I said, knowing that was a fucking lie. She lived with a man. Never mind the fact that her apartment was one step above a crack den in terms of comfort and safety. A man lived with her. "You didn't answer my question."

"You didn't ask a question. You insinuated." She smiled up at me.

"You know what I meant." Thea was wrong. I didn't hate her. I didn't dislike her. But she could really get on my nerves.

"Tanner is just my roommate," she said. "I'm not... I don't... date."

"At all?" I couldn't hide my surprise. Thea was pretty by vampire standards, making her beautiful by human standards. Surely, men must have noticed her. She'd already caught the attention of two vampires.

"I don't have time to date." A yawn overtook her.

I checked my watch to find it was nearly midnight. I'd been in no rush to decide what to do with Thea. It hadn't occurred to me that she might be tired.

"My cello?" She yawned again.

"I need to repair it," I said. "I'll return it to you tomorrow."

"Tomorrow? There's no way."

I smiled at her doubt. "I can be very persuasive."

Just not when it came to her for some reason.

"Fine." Her shoulders slumped, and she dug a key out of her bag. "Well, you know where I live."

"Yes." I grimaced and looked up at the building again. Something needed to be done about that, too.

She unlocked the door and turned to me. "Good n—"

But I was already inside, my hand catching hers and dragging her into the darkened hall.

"I'll see you to the door," I told her.

She studied me for a moment, an internal war flashing in her tired eyes, but then she led me up the stairs to the second floor. It was a minor improvement to find she wasn't on the ground floor, but it hardly looked any safer. She paused in front of a door marked with an iron letter *C* and turned.

"You aren't going to make me forget, are you?" she asked, her keys still in her hand.

"I should bring you your cello first. Don't you think?" I said smoothly.

She raised an eyebrow, clearly not buying my flimsy excuse.

"And I think you should consider my offer." I stepped closer to her, backing her slightly against the door.

"To date you?" she repeated. "I'm not sure I could handle your mood swings."

"About that." I paused to consider if I was making a mistake by telling her the truth. "There was another vampire in the diner. He showed up right before we left."

Her eyes widened into saucers, but after a second, she gathered herself back together. "There are probably lots of vampires in San Francisco."

"A fair few," I admitted. The older the city, the more vampires there tended to be. And by American standards, San Francisco was very old. More than a few of my kind had come during the gold rush, eager to fill their already bursting bank accounts with new wealth. Plus, the incessant fog made for easy hunting.

"Then it was a coincidence."

"Maybe." But it didn't feel like that. Until I was sure if that vampire had been sent after her or me, I needed to keep an eye on Thea.

"So that's why you were being so weird?" she asked. "Is that why you asked about a date?"

"Being under my protection would only afford you—"

"I've been taking care of myself for a long time," she stopped me, but sadness colored her words.

Without thinking, I slipped my arm around her waist. "Maybe you shouldn't have to."

Her eyes locked on mine. The scent of candied violets filled the air around us, her body beckoning me to claim it. What was it about her that was so irresistible? I had to find out. And it wasn't as if I could leave her here. This building wasn't safe against petty criminals. It could never stand up to a vampire. The more I thought about leaving Thea, the less I felt I should. She needed my protection, and I needed to satisfy the craving I felt for her one way or the other.

"You should invite me in," I murmured, lowering my face toward hers.

"I don't know if that's—"

My lips closed over hers before she could find another excuse. There was only one way to make Thea see this my way. I had to show her.

Her mouth parted, welcoming me to deepen the kiss. I slid my tongue into her mouth, drawing hers to mine. She responded with a moan that sent a rallying cry directly to my dick. I pulled back, scratching a fang over her lower lip just enough to make her gasp.

"Invite me in."

Thea swallowed, her hand fumbling for the knob behind us. She'd begun to shake, her arousal overwhelming her and flooding the air around us with her scent. I was about three seconds away from ripping the door off its hinges and carrying her to bed when it finally swung open to a dark living room.

She glanced shyly at me. "Come in."

I didn't need a second invitation. Lifting her into my arms, I spun us inside and kicked the door closed behind us. Thea grabbed my shoulders, her whole being now trembling.

"Which way?" I asked.

She tilted her head toward the hall. "First one on the left."

There were a million reasons I shouldn't be doing this. I should walk out the door, find someone to compel her, maybe Sebastian, and forget this pretty little mortal existed. But somehow I knew I would never be satisfied if I left now. I found her lips as I carried her to bed, ignoring the fact and giving into the bloodlust roaring inside of me. I wouldn't feed on her, but I would have her. I needed to have her. I could only think of stripping her out of her poorly fitted dress and then sating the hunger growing inside me.

Her room was more like a closet, and the mattress shoved in the corner hardly counted as a bed, but it would do for now.

Dropping Thea on her feet, I reached for her zipper and moved to kiss her.

But she placed a hand on my chest. "Wait, Julian," she murmured, "there's something you should know."

CHAPTER ELEVEN

Thea

My heart pounded so hard I was sure he could hear it. Apparently, lust mixed with nerves was a potent combo. I'd never invited a man into my room. I'd never wanted to, and for the life of me, I couldn't figure out why I'd chosen Julian to be the first.

Sure, he was unnaturally hot, but that probably had a lot to do with the whole "being a vampire" thing. He was also bossy and rude, which should have counteracted his looks. But for some reason, I couldn't stop kissing him. It was like I'd unlocked some secret cache of hormones I hadn't known was inside me.

He placed me gently on my feet, his fingers finding my zipper.

Oh my God, was I actually doing this?

I needed a minute to think. My body was speeding forward before my brain could catch up. Julian leaned to kiss me, and I stopped him.

"Wait, Julian, there's something you should know."

His response was immediate. Julian stepped back and waited. He might have passed for nonplussed if it weren't for his eyes. The electric blue that had struck me from across the room earlier tonight had disappeared. Now his eyes were black. I trembled, reminded of how the other vampire had looked as he fed.

It was clear Julian wanted to sleep with me. But did he plan to take more than my body?

Julian straightened and squared his shoulders before I could sift through how I felt about it. His eyes began to return to their breathtaking shade of blue. "Perhaps this was a bad—"

"I'm a virgin," I blurted out before I lost my nerve. Instantly, I wished I could take it back. My stomach clenched, humiliation finally trumping horniness.

"You're a what?" He blinked rapidly as if I'd smacked him.

He was going to make me repeat the single most embarrassing moment of my life? No way. I would own this. I hadn't been alive for a million years. It didn't matter if I was a virgin or a hooker, I'd never catch up to his experience.

"A virgin," I said firmly. "Is that a problem?"

He stared at me.

"I thought you should know before...um...well, you know."

Yep, I was absolutely killing this moment.

"I don't understand," he said slowly.

"What do I have to do? Draw you a diagram?" I crossed my arms and hoped he thought my red face was due to anger, not mortification. "You do know what a virgin is?"

His eyes narrowed to slits. "I know what a virgin is," he said drily. "I didn't expect..."

I arched an eyebrow as he trailed away.

"You seemed..." He stopped and shook his head. "Actually, never mind."

I'd clearly freaked him out. "It's not a big deal. I just didn't want to surprise you if—"

"Thea," he interrupted me, placing his hands on my shoulders. "I've been alive for nearly a thousand years, and I can say, with absolute certainty, that it's always a big deal."

I found myself highly interested in my shoes. Julian had rough edges, but there was an unexpected softness to his words. "I still want to."

"Want to what?" he asked.

"You know."

"Thea," he said, sounding exasperated, "if you can't say it, you shouldn't do it."

Was he turning me down? I felt my lower lip quiver, and I bit down to stop it. None of this was going like I'd expected it to go. I had always assumed I would meet a nice guy and fall in love or, at least, just get drunk and get it over with. But with two jobs and school, I'd never found the time. I never expected to find myself arguing over whether I was ready. I was so annoyed that I found myself actually reconsidering. It wasn't like I'd pictured finally sleeping with a guy while my two roommates slept across the hall. But still, the rejection stung.

"I shouldn't have told you," I murmured, more to myself than to him.

"I'm glad you did. You saved us both from making a terrible mistake." His words raked across me like nails on a chalkboard. That's what he thought? Sleeping with me would have been a mistake?

Tears smarted my eyes, but now they were fueled by anger. "Maybe you should go."

"I've upset you." He studied me for a moment like a serpent contemplating a butterfly. I couldn't be more than a fragile, silly creature to this god.

"It doesn't matter. You're right," I said, swallowing back an ache in my throat. "It would have been a mistake."

His eyes narrowed, and I half expected him to strike. "You misunderstand me."

"Oh, I understand you." I planted my hands on my hips. It was hardly an intimidating move considering he had a good foot and a half on me.

"It's more complicated than you realize," he said, his mouth twitching as if he wanted to laugh.

Just what I needed, more half-truths and mysterious insinuations.

The longer we stood there, the more adrenaline drained from my body. In its absence, all I felt was bone-deep exhaustion. It had been a very long day. "Look, I have class tomorrow."

"Skip it."

"I'm about to graduate. I can't," I said. Why was I telling him this? He didn't care. Also, had I really almost had sex for the first time with a vampire who knew virtually nothing about me?

"Music?"

I nodded, a pang hitting me as I thought of my cello. It was unplayable, which meant not only would I miss my fellowship audition, I might not be able to give my final performance. I stumbled a few steps and dropped onto my bed. "Look, just leave. I worked all day, and I have to be up in a few hours. Thanks for getting me home and feeding me."

"It was the least I could do, considering," he said slowly. But he made no move to leave. "Is something wrong? You seem... I hope I didn't offend you."

"It's nothing." I waved off his concern, hoping he would leave soon. "I'm going to miss an audition. I'm sure I can reschedule."

That was a lie. This wasn't the type of audition I could simply rearrange. Julian didn't need to know. He already felt obligated to me, and look where that had gotten us.

"Thea, I—"

"Please," I cut him off. "I just want to go to sleep."

He tilted his head, but he made no move to leave. "Go to dinner with me tomorrow night."

I sighed. My life wasn't exciting, but it was busy. It wasn't as if I could just drop everything to go out with him, especially since I wasn't sure I wanted to anymore. "I work until late."

"Your other job," he recalled, displeasure rippling through his features.

"Yeah, not all of us have had centuries to invest. Look, you already said this was a mistake. Let's just leave it there."

"I fucked up," he said abruptly. "All night. I'm sorry for that.

Let me make it up to you. Take tomorrow off."

His apology knocked the arguments out of me. I wasn't sure who Julian Rousseaux really was. Was he the handsome stranger I'd caught staring at me? Or was he the vampire who'd ripped someone's head off in front of me? The guy who'd demanded I eat something before he delivered me safely home? All of the above? I couldn't keep up with him and his constantly shifting personas.

"I don't know," I said, at last. "Thanks to you, I don't have a cello. I can't afford to miss work."

"I'll take care of that," he said brusquely.

"By tomorrow?" That would take a miracle. Finding a luthier capable of repairing that damage would take at least that long.

"If those are your terms."

I gawked at him. "Even you aren't capable of—"

He smirked at me. "Never underestimate me. If I say I will do something, I will."

His words were much, much hotter than they should be.

I searched for another excuse. I couldn't face him again. Not after his humiliating rejection. "I don't get off work until after eight."

"Think about it." He drew his phone out of his pocket. "I assume you have one of these?"

I suppressed a giggle. He really had been asleep for the last few decades. "Yeah, I do."

"How do I call it?" He waved the phone like it was a wand, and its screen lit up.

"Here." I took his phone and opened his contact list to add my name. Of all the ways I'd imagined tonight would end, adding my number to a vampire's phone hadn't been on the list. Honestly, I wasn't sure which one of us was in more danger in this city. I might not have known vampires prowled the streets until today, but he seemed equally lost.

"I don't know why anyone would want a phone everywhere they went," he grumbled.

I snorted, unable to contain myself any longer. Julian might look like a gorgeous thirty-year-old, but he definitely acted like an ancient vampire.

"What?" he asked suspiciously.

"Nothing," I said with a shrug. "You just sound like an old man."

"And that amuses you?" he said in a flat tone. It was clear he didn't share my sense of humor regarding the matter.

"It's just funny to see a big, strong vampire overwhelmed by a phone." I smiled sweetly in response to his glare. "Still want to take me to dinner?"

"Yes," he said through gritted teeth.

I couldn't imagine why. "I'll let you know." I handed his phone back to him. "I texted you my number, so I have yours, too."

"Why?"

"So I can let you know what I decide."

"I was going to call you," he reminded me.

"Yes, but I leave my phone off at school and work. It's easier if I message you." But he continued to cast a shadowy look of disapproval at me. "Relax, it's the twenty-first century. Girls can text guys now. It can't have been that different back in the eighties."

He grunted. I couldn't tell if he was agreeing or disagreeing. At least, he'd stopped glowering.

"I should let you rest," he said after a few moments.

I showed him to the door, keenly aware of his presence. Partially because I still couldn't believe he was here, but mostly because he made the cramped space look even smaller. When I opened the door, I stepped to the side and pressed my back against the wall. Tonight had been a mistake. We'd both agreed on that. But what would happen now? Would he kiss me again? Did he really want to take me out?

Julian paused, his striking form filling the doorframe. Light from the hall spilled around him like a halo. He was beautiful, and I found myself unable to look away. But he was no angel. He was deadly. Why did that draw me to him even more?

"Thea." He leaned down, bringing his face closer to me, and I found my eyes closing in anticipation.

I held my breath, waiting for the electric touch of his lips, but it never came. Instead, he laughed under his breath. "Don't forget to lock your doors, pet. You never know what's lurking on the city streets."

My eyes snapped open, embarrassed that I'd mistaken his intentions and annoyed by his little nickname. Was that what he thought of me? I was just a helpless kitten? "Will do, old man."

A low growl rumbled through him, but I didn't wait for whatever clever comeback he'd fire off. I did exactly what he told me to do. I shut the door with him still standing there, turned the dead bolt, and hooked the chain. I doubted any of it would hold against him if he decided to take offense at the door being slammed in his stupid, gorgeous vampire face. Slumping against it, I half hoped he would knock it off its hinges and carry me back to the bedroom. But I gave up after a few minutes. Besides, if he had, someone would probably call the cops before anything happened.

The last thing I needed was my roommates *cop-blocking* me. I giggled at the thought. The fact that I found it funny meant I was edging from tired to delirious. I needed to go to bed and sleep until my head was clear. Pushing back onto my feet, I took two steps toward my room before a dark form rushed toward me.

CHAPTER TWELVE

Julian

My hands rose automatically to break down the door she'd just slammed in my face. But before they made contact with the wood, I caught myself. Tonight had been enough of a shit circus. I didn't need to add breaking and entering to my growing list of regrets.

Instead, I waited by her door for a moment, listening—for what I wasn't sure. Inside I heard the slow, even cadence of her breath. Her heartbeat, which was fainter, remained slightly elevated. She'd gotten a rush of adrenaline from kicking me out. After a minute, it returned to normal, and I stalked away, forcing myself to leave. She had made it clear I was unwelcome, and I wasn't sure what I would do if she let me back in now.

When I was younger I'd had a few doors slammed on me by humans fleeing their inevitable deaths. I'd never had a human do it after insulting me. Thea now held that dubious honor.

Old man.

By vampire standards, I was in my prime. I suspected Miss Melbourne had never met a real man before. Most human men didn't live long enough to outgrow their own stupidity. It wasn't my fault she was remarkably naive and unnervingly fragile.

And a virgin.

Virgins and vampires didn't mix for so many reasons. Not anymore. The risks were too great for each party. Even well-bred familiars aiming to marry up no longer saved themselves for their vampire spouses. The Council had issued several official warnings on the matter in the late nineteenth century before forbidding vampires from sexual relationships with virgins altogether. It was part of a plan to sever our world from theirs. At the time, it had been a natural evolution, and since humans were finally starting to catch up with reforming their own society, we needed to be one step ahead.

But I hadn't expected to meet a virgin in the twenty-first century. The thought hadn't crossed my mind when I'd given in to my desire to claim Thea.

Apparently, the beautiful cellist had an attitude that matched the coppery highlights in her hair. Part of me hoped she wouldn't call or...text, whatever that was.

As I stepped out onto the dark walk in front of her building, I made up my mind. The cool night brushed across my skin as I surveyed the street. She thought I couldn't repair her cello in time. She was right. I had a better idea.

Circling to the driver's side of the BMW, I pressed the handle and heard the doors unlock. I might hate some of the modern world's new conveniences, but I had to admit that was cool. Before I could open it, though, a dark figure ambled toward me. For a human, he was moving quickly. Something glinted in his hand. A knife.

"Give me your keys, man," he said, his face hidden by the hood of his jacket.

I glared at Thea's building. Part of me wished she was here to witness this, because it would prove I was right. This wasn't a safe place for her to live, even with her bloody male roommate. But if she had been here, I wouldn't have been able to handle the situation accordingly.

Turning, I studied him for a moment. He edged a little closer.

"Don't make me fucking hurt you. Give me your keys," he demanded.

"No." He paused for a second, surprised by my response, and I chuckled. "Do you even know how to use that?"

"You want to find out?" he shouted, lunging toward me.

Honestly, I was almost impressed. He was clearly prepared to back up his threats. But he had no idea who he was fucking with, and I was already low on patience. My hands closed over his wrist before the knife came anywhere near me. With one swift twist, his bones cracked and he screamed, dropping the knife.

"Quiet," I instructed, and his cry died in his throat. The hood covering his face fell back, revealing his face in the streetlamps, mouth open and features contorted with pain and fear. Of course I could compel him, too. Only Thea was immune to my charms. That only placed her in more danger from my kind, and she had enough to worry about with scum like this guy hanging around where she lived.

The least I could do was take care of this guy.

"You shouldn't steal cars," I told him, increasing my grip on his wrist. His knees buckled and he crashed to the street. "But if you do, you should do it right. Stay there."

He didn't have a choice. I'd taken his away. He couldn't call for help—not that anyone was likely to help in this neighborhood—or run away. Tonight, he'd chosen his prey poorly, and he would pay the price. I leaned down and picked up his knife. I held it, holding it close to his panic-stricken face. "With a knife, you have to be intentional," I explained. "You can't just jab and hope it's enough to hurt a man. You need to get it up under the ribs—if you want to kill him, at least."

I whipped the knife into the air and demonstrated for him. His eyes widened, telling me what I already knew. He was a petty criminal, at best. He had no intention of killing me. If I'd been human, and he'd managed to mortally wound me, it would have been due to luck, not skill or design. Desperation drove him. I pitied him, but that didn't mean I could give him a pass. He might be a thief, but he was dangerous. At least he would be useful.

Grabbing his jacket, I yanked him to his feet and tore into his throat in one fluid motion. His blood tasted bitter on my tongue, lacking the sweetness Thea's had promised, but it was hot and plentiful. That was enough. He struggled weakly against me before my venom overwhelmed him and he stilled. Blood coursed through me and the darkness shifted. Neon glowed on the edges of the dark night, stars twinkled through the fog hanging in the sky, and a chaotic symphony of city noises crashed into me.

After a few swallows, I dropped him to the ground. He crumpled into a bag of bones and stared up at me with dazed eyes. The edge of my hunger had dulled, but it still lingered. I suspected that even if I'd drained every drop from him, I would still want more. Because it wasn't his blood that I craved.

"Now, what do I do with you?" I asked him. He couldn't respond, since he was still under my compulsion, but he blinked rapidly, one hand pressed to his wounded throat. "I can't have you on these streets, but I'd really prefer not to kill you. I don't want to lose the bet I made with my brother."

The bastard had said I wouldn't make it a week without killing a human.

He cringed against the wet street. Now he was afraid. That I could work with.

"You're not going to remember what happened," I told him, taking out my wallet and drawing out a few bills and a business card. "You're going to find the nearest hotel, clean yourself up, and sleep. In the morning, you will check into the Fremont Free Clinic and give them the name Rousseaux. You'll stay there until you are clean. Then you will call this number and take the job the man offers you. No questions asked. As repayment for my mercy, you will never take another drug recreationally in your life."

Not that he had any choice. I tossed the money into his lap along with the card.

"Go," I commanded. "You can speak, but you may never raise

your voice to me."

He scrambled onto his feet with a frightened look. "Th-thanks," he stammered, even as blood seeped through the fingers pressed against the place where I'd punctured him.

But I was already climbing into the BMW, somewhat disgusted with myself. I was getting soft. There was a time when I would have been content to drain him and rid the world of another lost soul. Maybe Thea was right. Maybe I was old.

Inside the BMW, I smelled Thea everywhere. Venom pooled in my mouth, my fangs still lengthened from my quick feed, and I felt a magnetic pull tugging at me. Every inch of me wanted to get out of the car, run back inside her building, and knock down her door. So much for taking the edge off. Instead, I seemed to have made it worse. I hadn't felt bloodlust this strong since I was a teen.

I punched the ignition switch so hard the plastic cracked. A second later, I swerved onto the rain-slick street. The back end of the car kicked out behind me as I sped onto the streets of San Francisco. The city rushed past in a spectacular rainbow of color. I crested a hill, the BMW lifting off the pavement for a moment, and drove, wanting to put as much distance as I could between myself and the woman I'd left behind.

I was halfway across the city when a call came over the car's speakers. A name flashed on the navigation screen, and I groaned. There was no escape for me. Not tonight. Not with The Rites enacted. Not with Thea's scent lingering in the air around me.

"What?" I answered.

"I need to talk to you now."

"Not even a please?" I bit out, but she'd already hung up.

CHAPTER THIRTEEN

Thea

Going to bed wasn't in the cards. Not if my roommates had anything to say about it.

"Who was that?" Tanner asked, dragging me toward the living room. I knew better than to try to resist their curiosity.

Olivia had vanished the moment they'd ambushed me at the door. She returned and plopped down on one end of the couch with a pint of chocolate peanut butter ice cream. She patted the spot next to her and held out a spoon. As soon as I sat down, Tanner took the seat on my other side. I was the meat in an awkward sandwich.

"Is that from the emergency stash?" I asked. Ice cream was well established as a luxury in our apartment. Fortunately, we all shared a favorite flavor, so we split the cost of two pints every month to keep in the freezer just in case.

"I'd say this is an emergency." Olivia pried off the lid and took a spoonful before passing it. She must have been asleep when I came home with Julian, because her hair was up in a wildly messy bun, and she still had one foam earplug in.

"It's not. I just got a ride home." I passed the pint to Tanner, not bothering to take a bite. I didn't feel like ice cream. The taste of Julian's kiss lingered on my tongue, and for reasons I didn't care to consider, I wasn't ready to wash it away.

Tanner shot me a sideways glance and shook his head. He was fully dressed. He had probably been up playing games online and heard me come in. "A ride that delivered you all the way to your bedroom, shut your door, and stayed for twenty minutes?"

"You timed it?" I said casually. "That's pathetic. It's not like it's a big deal."

"Um, excuse me." Olivia turned her body, folding her legs gracefully under her as she shook an accusing finger in my direction. "When was the last time you had a man in your room?"

I shrugged, even as my cheeks began to burn.

"I think it was..." Tanner paused, so Olivia could join him.

"Never," they said simultaneously.

They had me there. The only way to get them to let up was to give them some juicy details to gnaw on. But that was a little complicated given the circumstances. All I could think of were the things I couldn't tell them. There was no way I was going to admit Julian was a vampire. They would think I'd lost my mind. And not telling them that meant I couldn't tell them about Carmen or the vampire who'd attacked her or the gig being cut short. But the biggest issue was that I was a terrible liar. Anyone who'd known me more than a few hours knew that.

"He brought me home because he felt bad." I'd stick to the truth, I decided, but be careful to only give away parts of it. "There was an accident."

"Oh my God." Tanner nearly dropped his spoon as he searched me for signs of trauma. "Are you okay?"

"I'm fine." I forced a smile. "My cello isn't."

"Oh, Thea." Olivia confiscated the ice cream from Tanner and forced it into my hands. "I knew this was an emergency."

Now that she put it that way, I had to agree. I dug into the pint until I hit a chunk of frozen peanut butter and then shoveled the spoonful into my mouth.

I'd met both of them my sophomore year at Lassiter. Tanner

had been a year ahead of Olivia and me, but we'd all wound up in the same history class from hell. The bonding experience had turned into a friendship, so when they suggested we rent a place together and avoid the cost of the on-campus dorms, I'd jumped at the chance. Tanner had stayed after he'd graduated. I didn't plan to do the same, and they both knew it. I saw my cello as a ticket to a better life—somewhere far away from San Francisco and its hospitals.

"That doesn't explain why he walked you all the way to your bed," Tanner said drily.

"Don't be a dick." Olivia threw a pillow at him. "She's in mourning."

"I'm fine." At least, I needed to believe that I was, and convincing them was a step in the right direction. "I ran into him and dropped my cello. He wants to pay to have it fixed."

"Good." Olivia sounded relieved at the news.

"And you thanked him for his assistance by..." Tanner waggled his thick, black eyebrows suggestively.

"Nothing happened." But my voice cracked, giving the fib away.

"What? Oh my God!" Olivia shrieked and grabbed my hand, almost knocking the ice cream out of the other in the process. I clutched the pint protectively to my chest.

"Seriously, nothing happened. Not really," I added, pleased that I sounded much more convincing that time.

"That sounds like code for something did happen, but you wish more had happened," she said, speaking to Tanner like she was translating girl talk for him.

"Yeah, I got that. So what does 'not really' entail?" he asked. "Did you two get naked?"

"Tanner," Olivia groaned.

"We didn't get naked," I interrupted before a fight erupted between the two of them. "We just...kissed, and then he freaked out."

Olivia crooked her head, trying to make sense of my story's change in direction. "Freaked out how?"

"I told him," I said miserably, digging out another spoonful of ice cream. Now that I was talking about Julian, I found myself wanting to get him out of my system. Not because I regretted tonight, but because I knew it wasn't going to happen again. His reaction to my confession had made that clear.

"Told him what?" Tanner asked.

"You know, stupid," Olivia hissed through her teeth.

"I don't. What?"

"That's she's..." Olivia shot him a wide-eyed look of warning. "...you know."

"I don't see what could be so bad that—"

"I told him I'm a virgin," I blurted out.

Tanner's mouth formed an *O* shape, but he didn't speak.

"Yeah, the kiss of death, I know." I sighed and abandoned the ice cream to our beat-up coffee table. "I just thought he should know if..." I caught myself before I said it, but it wasn't soon enough.

"You were going to sleep with him?" Olivia clapped a hand over her mouth and did a little shimmy of happiness in her pajama pants.

"It's about time," Tanner said, but at least he wasn't dancing.

"You act like I'm some sort of freak of nature." I slumped back against the couch and glared at them both. "I haven't exactly had the time to meet anyone."

"But you did," Olivia said. She could find the bright side to any situation. Usually, I could, too, but tonight I was struggling to see the silver lining. "I can't believe it. Are you going to see this mystery man again?"

"His name is Julian, and no," I said firmly. Then I remembered his dinner invite and frowned. I wasn't going to take him up on that. I couldn't after I'd slammed the door in his face. Right? It wasn't like he could actually get my cello repaired, and I'd made it clear that was part of the deal. "It was a temporary lapse of good judgment."

"Are you sure about that?" Tanner had an annoying habit of knowing exactly what I was thinking.

I rolled my eyes and reached for the ice cream again. I might as well just commit to eating the whole thing now. It had been one of those nights. "I mean, I have to get my cello back."

"If you don't want to see him again, you could just ask him to have it delivered," Olivia said gently.

I groaned, knowing she was right but feeling all wrong about that idea. "I sort of dropped it. It was my fault as much as his. It feels wrong to expect him to pay for it and not even say thank you."

Olivia grinned triumphantly, and I realized I'd played into her trap. "You do want to see him again!"

"She let him inside her bedroom," Tanner said with a laugh. "That's the first suitor she's had since we moved in here. Of course she wants to see him again."

"Suitor?" I repeated.

"Yeah, you make it sound like he's from 1892," Olivia backed me up.

I nearly choked on a bite of ice cream. If she only knew the truth. Tanner slapped my back helpfully.

"Careful there," he cautioned. "Are you sure you're okay?" He was studying me now with his intense, dark eyes. It was just like Tanner to see through my carefully constructed truth to the missing pieces I'd hidden from them.

I had no idea how dangerous Julian's world really was, but I wasn't about to drag my friends into this mess. "I will be. I'm just embarrassed."

"So he left because you're a virgin?" Olivia pressed, bringing the subject back to his painful rejection.

"I guess." I gave the ice cream to Tanner. "He acted like it was a huge deal."

My roommates' eyes met over my head.

"What?" I demanded when they remained silent.

"Thea, it is a big deal," Olivia said. "You've waited all this time."

"You make me sound like an old maid."

"No one is saying that," she added quickly. "But why wait and just jump some random guy..."

Because there was nothing random about Julian. He wasn't just some guy. He was unlike any man I'd ever met. Precisely because he wasn't a man. He was so much more than that. Just the thought of him sent the memory of his burning kiss to my lips. My fingers drifted to my mouth as I remembered.

"You really like him," Olivia said quietly.

I snapped out of my trance. "What? No. He's annoying and pushy..."

"And?" Tanner pressed.

"Gorgeous and rich," I added with a sigh.

"Rich?" Olivia sat up straighter.

"Gorgeous?" Tanner said. "Maybe you should see him again."

"I have to, don't I? I need to get my cello back."

"Sure, your cello." Olivia winked at me.

"He did ask me to dinner." I instantly regretted mentioning it, because they both launched back into the topic.

"What are you going to wear?" Olivia asked.

"Who cares? We need deal with the virginity thing. That's the problem, right?" Tanner teased. "Look, if you need help with that, I know some guys—"

"Ew, Tanner!" Olivia cut him off. "Maybe Julian just wants to take her somewhere special before he relieves her of that 'problem' himself."

In my friends' book, the fate of my virginity was already sealed. At this rate, I was going to be up all night while they decided exactly how I should give it up.

"As much as I'm enjoying your insinuations, I'm exhausted." Yawning to prove it, I got to my feet.

"We're not through discussing this," she warned me as I carried the empty pint of ice cream to the kitchen, then tossed it in the garbage.

"Yes, we'll talk about this tomorrow, young lady," Tanner mimicked Olivia's lecturing tone.

She smacked him and then followed me down the hall. "Don't

listen to him," she whispered, so only I could hear. "And if you want to talk or ask questions, I'm here."

"Questions?" I repeated blankly.

"About what to expect when...you know."

If you can't say it, you shouldn't do it.

I frowned, remembering what Julian had said. Maybe he was the one who needed to loosen up. I mean, what could I expect from a nine-hundred-year-old vampire?

"Thanks," I said. "I will."

I said good night and gratefully closed the door. Olivia's offer was sweet. But I wouldn't need to accept it, because Julian had made it perfectly clear he wasn't interested in taking me to bed. Not anymore.

But then he'd gone and invited me to dinner. I wasn't sure what to make of him, except that everything about him seemed like bad news on paper. So why did it feel so right to be in his arms?

I slipped off my dress, then climbed into bed in my underwear. It felt small and cold. I burrowed into the covers, but it didn't help. It was hard to believe that an hour ago, he'd been here with me. Telling him was the right thing to do, but I still regretted it. If I hadn't, would he be here now? It was impossible to imagine him in my tiny, single bed, but I tried to anyway.

I slid my hand past the band of my panties, my fingers searching for relief. But before I could find it, my phone lit up on my nightstand. I reached for it, expecting to see a suggestive text from Tanner or Olivia, but the number was new to me. I had two messages from it.

My finger skimmed over the screen to check them. I recognized the text I'd sent to my phone from his. It was him. I held my breath as I scrolled to the second message.

Dear Thea, it began. I giggled at the formality of the message. It sounded like he was writing a letter. I supposed that I needed to teach him more about text messaging.

I'll pick you up at nine.

Sincerely,

Julian

So much for waiting for me to decide. It seemed he had chosen for me. Arrogant, grumpy vampire. I stared at the message for a moment, trying to determine how to respond.

CHAPTER FOURTEEN

Julian

There are mansions. There are palaces. And then there are homes so obscene they could only be called monstrosities. My mother had a taste for the third.

Sabine Rousseaux's Pacific Heights enclave took up nearly a city block. Its size was bettered only by that of a neighboring romance author's residence. My mother said she preferred the view from her balcony—a panorama of San Francisco Bay and the Golden Gate Bridge—to the square footage.

The BMW's engine kicked into third gear as I made my way up the steep hill my family home sat atop. The house itself was a glorious bastard of design my parents had concocted over the course of a century. There was a revival-style portico mixing with French flourishes around the front. Arched windows sat in its limestone walls. I noticed a bit of scaffolding on the north side. No doubt my mother was still trying to match the original stone with what needed to be replaced following the 1906 earthquake. A twenty-foot-tall wrought-iron fence surrounded the perimeter to keep curious tourists from straying into our home, more for their protection than ours.

I rolled down my window at the gate and smiled grimly at the security camera. A moment later, it creaked open, and I drove into the private underground garage. While my family liked cars a bit too much, it was clear she had guests.

Was this why she needed me so fucking urgently? Did she have a parade of potential familiars lined up and ready to present?

I picked my phone up from the passenger seat. I was not going to spend every second I had in this city making small talk with other rich vampires, their bastards, and a bunch of desperate witches. Navigating to the text messages, I found the last one sent.

This is Julian's number.

It had to be her. The rest of the messages were marked by name, except for one about my phone bill. There was no response. It must be the one she sent? I was still unclear on exactly how this worked. Was I supposed to wait until she sent a yes or no about dinner tomorrow and why? Was I supposed to ask again on this infernal device? Was it so hard to just answer me in person?

I decided to do it for her. It took me a second to punch in my message on the tiny digital keyboard. When I was finished, I had more questions than answers about why today's people liked these crappy devices. There had to be a better way to communicate. After a few seconds, three dots blinked back at me.

What the hell did that mean?

They disappeared.

I waited, dimly aware that the elevator had arrived in the garage. The three dots appeared again, and I ignored whoever had joined me. Another few seconds passed before I got a response.

Okay.

It was a start. Although to what, I wasn't sure. Stepping out of the car, I slid the phone in my pocket, then turned to find my assistant waiting for me across the garage.

Celia greeted me at the elevator. "Sebastian is hosting a party in the opium den, but your mother requests to speak with you in her sitting room before you're stoned out of your mind."

I raised an eyebrow, and she held up her hands in apology.

"Her choice of words, not mine."

I followed her inside the elevator and pressed the button for the second floor. I had no interest in attending Sebastian's so-called party. No doubt "orgy" would be a better term for it. But I did need to speak with my brother.

"Is there anything I can see to?" Celia asked me as the elevator carried us upstairs.

I was about to tell her no when I remembered that I owed Thea. "Yes, call Ferdinand and find out what cellos he can bring me by tomorrow, and then figure out where the Stradivarius is being kept."

"Are you taking up a new hobby?" Her forehead wrinkled like she was trying to decide if I was feeling unwell.

"I owe someone a cello," I said with a shrug. There was no point in telling Celia about Thea yet. Not since I suspected Thea would continue to slam doors in my face.

A smile played on my assistant's lips. "She must be very beautiful."

"She is very annoying," I corrected her, "and as I said, I owe her a cello. Something happened to hers."

"Were you that something?" she guessed.

"Yes and no," I said, bracing myself as the second-floor button lit up on the elevator panel.

"Julian," Celia said with a long-suffering sigh, "whoever she is, your mother isn't going to be happy if you give her a twenty-million-dollar cello."

"It's my cello." I adjusted my cufflinks as the doors slid open. Holding my arm across the elevator's threshold, I waited until Celia stepped onto the gallery's landing before joining her. "And I'm not giving it to her. I don't see why the hell anyone would care if I did, though. None of us play. What good is it doing collecting dust?"

"I believe it's what mortals call an investment piece," she said drily. "Is there a budget for the ones Ferdinand will bring?"

I shook my head. "But I prefer something Italian."

"You always have." Celia walked with me toward Sabine's rooms. Her eyes wandered over the paintings lining the walls, widening every now and then when she spotted a Cézanne or a Van Gogh. Sometimes I forgot how much younger she was than me. Mostly because she spent so much time mothering me.

"Care to join us?" I asked when we reached the oak double doors that led into my mother's private wing of the house.

She rolled her eyes. "I think I'll sit this one out."

She was too smart to get in the middle of a family disagreement, especially when it involved me and my mother.

"I'll let you know what I find." She paused. "Shall I have whatever Ferdinand finds delivered and save you the trouble? I'll just need the musician's name."

"I'll handle the delivery instructions. I want to include a note."

She inclined her head in deference to my wishes before moving to leave. As she turned, I caught a glimpse of unmistakable satisfaction on her face. I opened my mouth to clarify again that this was simply an issue of courtesy, but she sped down the hall before I could.

I watched as she disappeared into the servant's corridor, deciding to let her think what she wanted to about the matter. I knocked softly on the door and waited until I heard an imperious "come in" from the other side.

Striding into the sitting room, I found my mother lounging by a marble fireplace, dressed in a silk dressing gown embroidered with large fuchsia blooms. The fire danced over the goblet in her hand, the glass reflecting the flames. Another filled glass sat on the eighteenth-century coffee table in front of her. She twirled a finger lazily in her own drink before lifting a blood-soaked finger to her mouth and delicately sucking it clean.

It was an old habit of hers, to think over a warmed serving of O-negative. In my younger decades, I came home to find her in a similar state frequently, usually the result of worrying over some mischief caused by one of my brothers. It had been years since I'd seen her like this, not since...

"I'm sorry for this evening," I said stiffly. She'd called me here to tell me off for speaking so openly in front of a human. An apology would minimize her concerns.

She lifted her blue eyes to stare at me, studying me with silent judgment, before she pointed to a plush chaise lounge across from her.

I might be the heir to the Rousseaux name and fortune, but my mother held a firm grip over me and the rest of our family. That was natural, given that vampires were matriarchal in nature. A male vampire's job was to marry, produce heirs, and contribute to the betterment of society during times of peace. When war was called for, we were well-trained to protect our mothers, sisters, and wives. It was a skill we learned during friendly skirmishes at home and honed on real battlefields. A male vampire always stood ready to protect the females he served, even if most of them didn't require much protection.

At least, I'd been raised with those traditional values. Even the wildest of my siblings fell into line where our mother was concerned. For the most part, she respected her adult children, but every now and then one of us disappointed her.

I had never been the one to do that before tonight.

Taking the seat across from her, I waited for the lecture I knew was coming.

"You knew this was coming," she said softly. She didn't need to raise her voice. That was the power of a vampire queen. She knew just how strong she was and where she stood as leader of the family. "When Camila died..."

She trailed away for a moment, the slight flare of her nostrils betraying the grief she hid like an old scar.

"I understand," I said, wanting to spare her the pain she still felt over my twin's untimely death.

Sabine's eyes flashed to mine, and I realized too late that I'd said the wrong thing. "You cannot understand the death of a child," she stormed, "until you have one of your own, and by the way you're acting, I assume you never will."

"There's an entire year for—"

"Who was that mortal?" she interrupted. "The pretty little human in the cheap dress? What was her name again?"

She knew perfectly well what her name was. My mother never forgot a thing. "It doesn't matter. She was just a human."

"Oh?" She reached for the phone in her lap where it lay hidden amongst pools of embroidered silk. "But you felt the need to dine with her?" She held it up to showcase a photograph of me and Thea at the diner.

"That was your man?" I fought to suppress the rage boiling inside me at this revelation. I'd known it was a possibility, but it was another stark reminder that being back in San Francisco meant dealing with my family's boundary issues.

"That one was," she said sharply. "Who knows who else saw you?"

"And who cares?" I challenged her. "So I fed her. She'd had a rough evening."

"I don't expect you to understand," she hissed, slamming her glass so hard on the coffee table's marble top that its stem shattered. She groaned and caught the globe in her hand before a drop was spilled. A second later, her own blood trickled down her wrist from the broken glass. If it hurt, she showed no sign of it. "This is not just any season—"

"The Rites have been enacted," I cut her off. "I know."

"Being seen with a female during The Rites signals unavailability. You know this!"

"I do," I said coolly.

"I don't understand." She drained the rest of the blood in a single swig and tossed the broken glass into the hearth. "What did I do to deserve this? I gave some of the best years of my life to raising my children, and now? If your father were here…"

"It's good to see your theatrical side is intact," I said flatly, "and speaking of which, where is my father?"

"Vienna." She dismissed the details with a flick of her wrist. "Or Venice? It's not important. We needed a little space."

In my parents' case, they often needed to put an ocean or two between them after an argument. I decided not to press her for details. It would either distract her or make her more upset. It was hard to tell.

She pinched the bridge of her nose before calmly continuing, "You have to be more careful. What would happen if you were linked to someone right now? It could hurt your marriageability. I won't live forever."

"Promise?" I grumbled.

"That's a terrible thing to say to your mother!" She clutched her chest as if I'd physically wounded her, and I murmured a quiet apology. "The point is that someone has to be ready to take my place."

"When?" I cut her off. "A couple hundred years from now? A millennium? We're not in a rush, exactly."

"Julian, we must protect our way of life and the family name. I don't want people to get the wrong idea about you. Not now."

"And what idea would that be?" I slung an arm over the back of the chaise and lounged against it. "I've never hidden my disinterest in marriage and all of that other shit."

"All of that other shit," she repeated, fangs glinting as she spoke, "is tradition, and you can scoff at that all you like, but a girl like that could never be part of our world."

"Is that what you think?" I asked quietly. I thought of Thea's face after I'd put a stop to our reckless kiss. She hadn't been simply disappointed. She had looked rejected.

"There are lovely, accomplished familiars that were waiting to be introduced to you this evening, but you were too busy with..."

"Thea," I offered her.

"Whatever. The point is that you can't waste any more chances, and you can't risk being seen with her."

I got to my feet. I'd heard enough of this conversation. "I had no idea that you were so prejudiced, especially after all the lovers you've taken over the years."

"A lover is one thing. Take as many of those as you want after you're married and after you've produced an heir."

"How romantic," I muttered. "Is that why Dad is abroad? Did he catch you with your latest boy toy?"

"Your father and I are very happy with our arrangement, and if you'd just be open to meeting someone, you could be one day, too."

It was the vampire way. Find a match that stroked your ego or your alliances or your bank account, spit out a kid or two, and then go on with your lives. Make a few more vampires the easy way. Take a few more lovers. Get a little richer and a whole lot snobbier. I'd been stuck on this hamster wheel of privilege long enough.

Sabine mistook my silence for compliance. A smug smile settled on her face. "I knew you would see it my way. Now, you should go join Sebastian in the den. He's invited the Bennett sisters and the Fairfields. Lovely girls. Sarah just graduated from Yale. I'm positive one of them can make you forget about whatever her name was."

Thea. I wanted to shout the name at her, but I bit my tongue.

I'd stopped myself from propositioning her to play the part of my girlfriend earlier. She was too innocent, too naive, *too human.* But she was more than my mother saw. She was a talented musician. She was brave. She was curious. The familiars downstairs were only after one thing; even Sabine wouldn't deny that. And why would she? To her, it was perfectly natural to marry to strengthen relationships between the mortal witches and our kind.

But I wasn't interested in a life of duty. I didn't want to go downstairs and find some sycophantic familiar to fuck. Even if I did, I doubted it could erase Thea from my mind. I doubted anything could. Not until I tasted her, which, given the situation, was now impossible.

"Julian." My mother's voice coaxed me from my thoughts. "Just be more careful who you are seen with. We wouldn't want people to get the wrong idea."

I glared at her, realizing I had nothing to lose but a spot participating in this season's cattle call. "That could be a problem," I murmured, enjoying the way her shoulders tensed, "because Thea is my girlfriend."

CHAPTER FIFTEEN

Thea

Julian's hands skimmed across my shoulders and down my arms. I sank against him, trying to turn my face to see his, but he lowered his head to the curve of my neck. Warm lips brushed my skin, followed by the gentle scratch of a fang. I twisted into him. A thin sheen of sweat covered my body. This close to him, I felt trapped in my clothes. I wanted to rip them off. Or better yet, I wanted him to rip them off me.

His palm slid to my hip, gripping the fleshy curve so roughly it hurt a little. A moan spilled from my lips, and he laughed darkly. I squinted in the darkness, trying to see his face. He thought I was ridiculous and fragile, and I didn't care. Not as long as I was in his arms. But it was too dark to make out anything other than the sculpted lines of his lips. They parted, and I melted willingly into him. I waited for him to kiss me. My breath caught, hanging on the moment, but then he pulled away, retreating into the shadows.

"Don't!" I called after him. It was the same as before. Teasing. Provoking. Igniting. And then a door slammed between us.

But he lingered in the shadows. I felt him more than I saw him. I held my hand out, an olive branch in the darkness. He took one step closer, and my heart jumped in my chest. I didn't dare speak.

It wasn't that I was afraid I would scare him off. I got the distinct impression that his reticence was for my benefit. Julian took another step closer, bringing half his body into the moonlight, but he paused again.

Once, when I was a child, I was playing in the desert on a camping trip with my mom when I stumbled across a Mojave rattlesnake. The dry, rocky earth concealed it until it reared up, its rattle shaking in a blur. I froze, unable to move as it decided whether to strike. Julian reminded me of the snake. He wasn't afraid of me; he was deciding what to do with me.

He took a step closer.

"Thea!"

I turned away from the sound of my name. Not now. Julian held out a gloved hand. Why did he wear those gloves?

"Thea!"

"No!" I moaned, earning another low chuckle from Julian. The wicked sound of it sent heat pooling in my core.

A light snapped on, illuminating the night, and he vanished into the air like magic. I flipped over and buried my head in a pillow.

"That's it!" Olivia's voice was muffled by the pillow. "Don't blame me if you fail your final semester."

Fail.

Her choice of wording had the intended effect. I bolted up, tossing the covers off, and mumbled, "I'm awake."

"I can see that," she said drily. "Also, your mom is trying to reach you, sleepyhead. She called me. I've got to run. Call your mom!"

"Crap!" I fumbled for my phone, practically ripping it from its charging cable, and found I'd missed three calls from her. I hit the redial button as my thoughts began to race. It wasn't like her to bother me during the week. We'd arranged to video chat every Monday, since my schedule was so packed.

"Did Olivia wake you up?" she asked when she picked up the call.

"Are you okay?" I ignored her question. "Do you need me?"

Since my mother's diagnosis a couple years ago, I dreaded

unexpected calls from her. Every time I was certain she was about to deliver more bad news. I'd started to breathe a little easier since she finished her last round of radiation, but somewhere, deep down, I was always waiting for the other shoe to drop.

"Calm down, sweetie! I didn't mean to worry you. I just wanted to check in," she said quickly.

I slumped into the bed and breathed a sigh of relief. "I'm fine."

"You sound tired," she said with that uncanny knack mothers had for seeing anything you tried to hide.

"Late night," I croaked, wishing I had some water. I sandwiched my phone between my ear and shoulder as I got out of bed. "I had a gig."

"Oh, is that all?"

"And work." I yawned, stumbling into our narrow galley kitchen where I discovered a pot of coffee waiting for me with a note.

Figured you needed some go-go juice.
XO, Olivia

She knew me too well. I bypassed the water and poured myself a cup of coffee. Cupping my palms around the mug, I savored how its warmth spread through me.

"Okay, but nothing's up?" Mom pressed.

I was still shaking off my dream, but it sounded like she was worried.

"Not really." As soon as I said it, the particulars of the night before crashed into my conscious brain. My cello. Vampires. Julian. Was I okay? I mean, mostly. The stranger thing was that she was asking. "Are *you* okay?"

"It's nothing." There was a pause on the other end of the line. "A nightmare, I guess."

"Well, I'm in one piece." I didn't have the heart to tell her about the cello. It would only make her frantic, and we had enough hospital bills to worry about. I had to trust that Julian would stay true to his word and get it fixed. There was no sense worrying my mom. "What about you? It must have been some nightmare."

"I think it's the radiation," she admitted. "I swear it's made me have the strangest dreams. Look, Thea, I know this is silly, but—"

A knock at the door interrupted her.

"Hold on a sec." I cradled my coffee mug in one hand and unlocked the door to find a uniformed man holding a box.

"What is it?" Mom sounded almost panicked.

She really was on edge.

"Just a package," I told her, smiling at the delivery man.

"Thea Melbourne?" he asked, and I nodded. "Great, sign here."

I scratched my signature across his pad, and he handed me the box. It wasn't a typical package. Instead of a cardboard box covered in printing labels, it was a large gold gift box wrapped with a white satin ribbon. I scanned it for signs of who it was from, but there was no label. "Thanks," I said and began to close the door.

"Wait!" He stopped me. "There's one more. I wanted to make sure you were here before I brought it up."

"Okay," I said slowly.

"Be right back," he called as he dashed down the stairs.

"That's weird," I muttered, forgetting I was still on the phone with my mom.

"What?" she asked.

"Two packages," I said, yawning again.

"Were you expecting something?"

I loved my mother, but I couldn't help rolling my eyes at her question. Why would I think it was weird if I was expecting it? "Nope."

"Well, open the first one."

"Okay, hold on. Let me put my coffee down."

"I have no idea how you juggle all these things," she said. "Where are your roommates?"

I slid my coffee onto the kitchen counter, past a pile of dishes and an old pizza box. "Olivia has class. Tanner is probably asleep."

"Has he gotten a job yet?" She didn't wait for me to answer

before she rattled off her concerns that he was going to kill himself playing video games day and night.

I untied the satin bow and slipped the ribbon off the package, murmuring half-hearted ums and ohs in agreement with her. I lifted the lid and found an envelope resting on neatly folded pink tissue paper.

My hands shook a little as I drew out a card of thick ivory stock and read the words scrawled across it.

I couldn't text this. Sorry. I'll pick you up at nine.
-J

My mouth went dry. I'd already told him okay, but was I really doing this? Swallowing, I pushed open the sheets of tissue to reveal an emerald velvet dress. I picked it up gingerly, and its skirt rippled down to puddle on the floor.

"Thea, honey," my mom said on the other end of the line. "Are you there?"

"Yes, sorry, I think I'm half-asleep." I hated lying to my mom, but telling her I had a date with a vampire probably wasn't going to ease her mind.

"Maybe you should go back to bed," she suggested.

"Can't." I checked the clock on the microwave and felt a fresh wave of panic. "I need to get to class."

"You're stretching yourself too thin."

"Not much longer, I promise." I'd lost track of the number of times that I'd said that to her since I started at Lassiter. I told myself it was a lot as well. "Oh, hold on, the delivery guy is back."

"Another package?" she asked as I opened the door.

"It's for Olivia." Why was I lying so much? Because I didn't want to put any more stress on my mother, not with remission looking so promising.

But when I saw what the delivery guy had in his hands, I dropped my phone. Quickly, I picked it up and apologized to Mom.

Julian hadn't just sent me a dress for our date tonight. He'd also made good on his promise about the cello. It wasn't my cello case in the man's hands now. Mine had come with my cello, both purchased secondhand. And while they had been well cared for, they'd also been well-loved. The case he held was a Bam L'etoile in a striking violet purple. It must have cost a couple thousand dollars.

"Mom," I said softly, "I need to let you go." I was vaguely aware of her saying goodbye as I ended the call.

"Looks nice," the guy said as he passed the case to me.

As soon as it was in my hands, I knew my cello was not inside. Julian hadn't repaired my cracked instrument. He'd bought me a new one. "Thanks."

After shutting the door, I carried the case inside and placed it carefully on the kitchen counter. I closed my eyes as I unfastened the locking clips. When I finally looked, I nearly fainted.

• • •

Two hours later, I was not in class. I was sitting on a stool, velvet dress in my lap, staring at the cello Julian had sent me. Tanner ambled into the living room, rubbing sleep from his eyes, and stopped when he saw me.

"Shouldn't you be in class?"

I looked at him, blinking as I processed his question. "Oh, yeah. Probably."

"Earth to Thea." He snapped his fingers. "What's going on?" He moved closer and peered into the open case. "Is that a new cello?"

"Yes," I said numbly but quickly added, "or, no. Not really."

"You need some coffee?" he asked. "Because you aren't making much sense."

"It's a Grancino." I sighed when he gave me a blank look. "It's from the seventeenth century."

"An antique." He reached to touch it, and I batted his hand away with a shriek. "Whoa! Sorry. Is it worth a lot of money?"

I swallowed and repeated the value Google had placed on it

when I'd searched earlier. "Half a million—give or take."

Tanner took a step backward as if he'd found himself past a velvet rope in a museum. Then he sank onto the stool next to me and joined me in staring at it. After a minute, he finally spoke, "So when you said rich..."

"*Filthy* rich." Honestly, I hadn't known how well-off he was, but this was probably a good indication of the status of his bank account.

"And he's in love with you," Tanner added.

This snapped me out of my daze. "What? No! I just met him."

"I don't care how much money you have. You don't send someone a half-million-dollar present just because."

"Mine broke," I reminded him, but even I knew my reasoning was feeble.

Tanner poked at the dress in my lap, and I passed it to him. He held it up and whistled. "And this?"

"For our date tonight," I said weakly.

"So you're going." It wasn't a question. We both looked at the cello and then the dress. I was going.

Julian had given me no choice.

CHAPTER SIXTEEN

Julian

I arrived at Thea's apartment shortly before nine. Despite receiving confirmation from the delivery company, I'd had no word from her about the packages I'd sent. I assumed she was pleased. Then again, she had a tendency to surprise me.

I wasn't certain if she would be grateful or furious over the cello—or, for that matter, the dress. Given that I'd only known her for twenty-four hours, it shouldn't bother me as much as it did. Something about Thea demanded my attention. She was an itch I couldn't scratch. In my nine hundred years on this earth, I'd never met a woman like her.

"Wait here," I ordered the chauffeur as he pulled to the curb. "I'll only be a minute."

"Yes, sir."

I left the limousine idling in front of her building. When I had asked her to dinner, I'd failed to mention that dinner would be taking place amongst vampire society. There was hardly a day between now and this time next year where there weren't some bloody engagements penciled on my calendar.

I smoothed the jacket of my tuxedo as I walked inside, wondering why there was no buzzer or extra security for her apartment building.

It was yet another reason she wasn't safe here. The thief I'd nearly drained to death last night could have easily broken into where she was sleeping.

White-hot anger burned inside me at the thought, my brain already beginning to form a plan to deal with the unacceptable situation.

I knocked, and the door opened almost immediately. But it wasn't Thea standing on the other side. The woman gawked at me for a second, her head tilting up like she was getting a panoramic look.

She was attractive for a human, with rich, olive-toned skin and a mass of glossy black hair piled on top of her head. She moved infinitesimally, giving me a glimpse of dancer's tights beneath her robe.

"I'm here to pick up Thea," I told her when she failed to muster a greeting.

She blinked dreamily and then shook her head as if she was clearing out fuzz. "You must be Julian." She emphasized my name in a way that told me she had heard about me. "I'm Olivia, her roommate."

"It's a pleasure to meet you."

Olivia took one final look at me, sighed, and gestured for me to come inside. "Let me go get her."

I took a few steps into the cluttered living room while Olivia skipped off. It was amazing to think that three living beings resided here. Not because the proof of it wasn't scattered all over the room— books, clothes, dirty dishes—but because it was hard to see how they had enough space. Human domiciles always felt a bit like cages to me. But this was worse than normal. Did Thea feel trapped in this world, or was it all she'd ever known?

Turning to take it all in without the presence of Thea to distract me, I spotted a violet-colored cello case sitting on the kitchen counter. I crossed to look at it and found it open. The Grancino was the only acceptable option I could get so quickly in San Francisco. I hadn't even seen the instrument, only the bill, when I'd signed off on the banking transfer.

It was beautiful—not as lovely as my Stradivarius that I'd asked Celia to track down, but a true work of art. Standing in the tiny apartment in the poorly secured building, it occurred to me that if any of the drug addicts that roamed the street outside knew what was sitting here, Thea wouldn't be safe. Why hadn't that occurred to me?

It wasn't enough to get Thea the cello. I needed to get her a new place to live. Or at least some security cameras, a security system, and some bars for her windows.

A gentle cough interrupted my thoughts, and I turned to find Olivia had returned. "She'll be out in a minute."

I'd attended enough Royal balls and courts and galas in my time to know when a lady was being presented. This time was a little different, though. Usually, a courtier read out a formal name instead of someone in their pajamas.

But as soon as Thea appeared next to her, I realized that it didn't matter where I was standing or who had advised me of her arrival. She was more beautiful than any woman—human, familiar, or vampire—that had ever entered a room before.

Her auburn hair hung loosely, sweeping over her shoulders in loose coils. As she walked into the living room, the light caught its red highlights, which were complemented by the deep emerald green of her dress. Its fabric hugged her curves, showcasing her full, shapely hips and the tempting swell of her breasts. An ivory leg slipped past a slit that ended at the apex of her thigh. I'd made a call to a friend in Paris, who'd compelled an atelier to overnight a piece from his latest collection. It fit Thea like it had been made for her, and I couldn't look away.

Thea clasped her hands together, glancing between me and the cello. "I hope…" She paused as if struggling with what to say. She turned to Olivia, who shot her a pointed look. "I mean, thank you."

"You're welcome." I swallowed. What had I done? The lie I'd told my mother was getting out of hand. How was I supposed to pass Thea off as my girlfriend without giving in to temptation?

I couldn't touch her, but seeing her like this, how the fuck was I supposed to resist?

"Shall we?"

Her eyes swept over my tuxedo—an Armani I'd picked up at the same time as her dress. Thea's teeth sank into her lower lip, sending a spike of testosterone straight to my dick. I was in trouble. "I guess."

I sensed her hesitation, although I didn't quite understand it. She had consented to spend this evening with me. "Unless you're having second thoughts." I sounded as stiff as it felt in my trousers. "If you'd prefer I leave—"

"No," she said quickly. "I just... Where are we going?" She adjusted the strap of her dress, anxious energy rolling off of her.

I held out a hand, noticing the curious expression on Olivia's face when she saw the black silk glove I wore. "I'll tell you in the car."

Thea nodded, but she didn't take my hand. Instead, she turned and hugged her roommate, whispering something she thought I couldn't hear. Someday I would inform her that vampires had excellent hearing. Tonight, I found myself wondering what she meant by her words.

Turning, she accepted my hand, and we moved to the door.

"Have fun!" Olivia called after us. "Should I stay up...?"

I bit back a laugh at Thea's horror-stricken reaction.

"We'll be late," I answered for her. Let her roommate decide what that meant.

Thea continued to chew on her lip as I led her down the stairs, making my slight erection harder by the second. If she wasn't careful, I was going to do something we'd both regret.

But thoroughly enjoy.

When we stepped out of the building, she stopped and gasped. I turned to see what had caught her attention. A thick haze enveloped the street, making it difficult to see more than a few feet ahead of us. She couldn't stop staring at the limousine. I hadn't considered it would surprise her. It had been too long since something so mundane had wowed me. It was yet another reminder that she was not part of my world.

So why was I dragging her into it?

"Where are we going?" she repeated.

"A party," I said simply. "I forgot I had a prior engagement." That wasn't precisely true. I'd willfully ignored the social calendar Celia had tried to present to me. But avoiding The Rites wasn't going to make them go away. I needed Thea for that. By the time my family realized I wasn't going to marry her, the social season would be over, and I would be saved from dozens of hopeful familiars.

At first, I'd seen Thea's virginity as a problem. Then I realized it was an opportunity. She was the perfect ruse—a female I wouldn't get attached to, since sex was off the table, and a mortal without an overbearing magical family trying to ensure the match. Perhaps, though, I could make it easier on myself to resist temptation when picking out her dresses.

"What?" She whirled toward me, catching the skirt of her dress on a heel and careening into me.

I caught her easily. Steadying her, I let a hand linger on her waist. Even through the fabric of her dress and my gloves, electricity sparked in my fingertips. I should have released her, but I didn't.

"You don't have to take me." She turned wide doe eyes up to look at me. "We can reschedule."

"But I want to take you," I murmured. In more ways than one.

She blinked rapidly, sending her lashes fluttering. "But why?"

"Do you have any idea how beautiful you are?" I brushed a finger down her arm, searching her eyes for the answer to my question—and the dozens of other questions crowding my brain. She didn't speak, and before I could stop myself, I bent to search for the answer in her lips.

Her mouth parted, accepting the kiss eagerly. The floral scent that hung on her skin like a delicate cloak deepened into something earthy and intoxicating. I swept my tongue over her teeth, and she allowed her own to tentatively slide across mine. She gasped as it caught on the sharp end of a fang, and I drew back quickly. If she drew blood, I wasn't sure I'd be able to stop myself. I'd have her on the nearest flat surface, relieving her of her pesky virginity before I could think better of it.

"Careful, pet." I fought the darkness swelling inside me. "I might lose control."

She pressed her lips together and swallowed, the movement sending the tangy scent of iron to join the perfume surrounding her. I turned my head, trying to clear my nostrils before I lost control.

Why was I convinced this was the perfect plan?

"What if I want you to lose control?" Thea's breathless answer sent a fresh jolt of desire through me. Christ, she was acting like I'd fed her my venom. I needed to get a handle on this situation. Fast.

I spotted her lower lip tremble and hated myself. "Thea, I—"

"It's nothing," she cut me off. Shivering, she wrapped her arms around her shoulders. "Once we're in the car…"

I'd been cut off from humanity for far too long. She wasn't upset. She was cold. It hadn't even occurred to me that she must be freezing. Whipping off my jacket, I draped it around her shoulders, relishing how she clutched it tightly against her.

"Let's get in the car," I suggested. "I'll tell you about the party."

Thea nodded, but instead of starting toward the limo, she took a deep breath. "And we need to talk about the cello."

"What about the cello?" I asked slowly.

"I can't keep it," she blurted out before falling silent. Her answer stunned me.

"Is there a problem with it? I assumed it would be up to your standards."

"My standards?" She blinked, looking a bit dazed before she snapped back to her fiery self. "It's not about my standards or how much you spent. It's the blood, sweat, and tears I poured into earning an instrument of my own."

I hadn't considered that. Hopefully, my luthier could repair it.

We stayed locked in a silent battle of wills for a moment before I forced myself to speak. "We can discuss it in the car."

"Julian, I—" she started, but I'd already crossed to open her door. Thea's shoulders slumped as she made her way to me. She stopped with one hand still clutching my jacket and turned to me. "Maybe this isn't a good idea."

Before I could stop myself, I laughed so loudly it echoed in the night around us. "No, Thea," I said softly, gazing into her eyes, "it's a terrible idea."

CHAPTER SEVENTEEN

Thea

His words hit me like a slap in the face. Wasn't a man supposed to soothe your anxieties about things like that? I made a mental note never to ask him how my butt looked in jeans.

"Come," he urged me toward the limo.

The limo. Limos were reserved for weddings and funerals, not dates, where I came from. What had I gotten myself into? Julian thought this was a terrible idea, I was about to be surrounded by vampires, and I wasn't going to keep the cello. I couldn't. It just felt...wrong.

I snuggled into his jacket as he guided me toward the back passenger door. A hint of exotic, spicy cologne lingered on the jacket, combining with something that could only be described as Julian. It was the centuries of experiences he'd lived before me, the places he'd seen and I'd only read about, the people he had met, and then, strangely, the music. There was something that hung on him that I'd only ever known when I was playing my cello or listening to music.

I'd tasted it in his kiss, too. I wanted to taste more of it. I wanted to experience his lifetimes, one lingering kiss at a time. It was going to be hard to keep my head on straight around him. It didn't help that his hand rested on the small of my back. Between that subtle contact, the memory of his lips on mine, and the scent of his jacket, my head was swimming.

The chauffeur jumped out of the car as we reached it. He dashed over to open the door, but Julian angled himself between us. The driver paused, his eyes widening, as Julian drew to his full height, squared his shoulders, and...growled.

It was more of a low rumble—a warning—than anything else. But it had its intended effect on the man. I was stunned.

"Did you just growl?" I asked him slowly.

He ignored my question. I couldn't tell if he didn't want to answer me or if he felt he needed to keep his eyes on the driver. His jaw tightened, but he didn't take his eyes off the other man. Julian opened the door for me. "Get in the car, pet."

"Pet?" I raised an eyebrow.

"It's a term of endearment."

That seemed doubtful, but I didn't object.

"I'll get in the car as long as you stop acting like a Neanderthal," I grumbled.

It turned out that getting into a limousine while wearing a dress wasn't all that easy. Or maybe I, as a limo virgin, didn't know the trick. Regardless, I found myself a bit relieved that Julian was too busy with his pissing contest to watch my less-than-graceful crawl across the limo's backseat. I bumped my head against the felt roof liner, and static electricity prickled all over my skull. Given the slightly squat seat, it took me a second to arrange my skirt. I quickly tidied my hair, which was trying to fly away due to the static. Julian slid in just as I settled, and I did my best to look casual.

That was hard because this was worse than driving with him in the BMW. Those had been close quarters, but there had been a center console between us and his attention couldn't stray too far from the road. Now I was alone in a massive backseat with a man who kissed like a reincarnated sex god, bought half-million-dollar presents, and growled if another man got too close to me.

I wanted to mind the last one more.

Honestly, he'd been born in the Middle Ages, not a cave. Instead, arousal ticked in me like a time bomb, and I pressed my thighs together, trying to keep myself from exploding.

I had no idea what Julian saw in me. He had to have met far more interesting women in his life. I also felt more confused than ever because he'd made it clear that a relationship with me was out of the question. Then why had he acted like he owned me?

Better yet, why had I liked it so much?

Julian remained silent next to me as the limousine pulled away from the curb. Something was preoccupying him, too. He stared out the window. How could he be so close that my whole body felt on edge and so far away at the same time? At least the distance that hung between us made bringing up the cello a little easier.

I took a minute to gather my courage before I plunged into the speech I'd practiced with Olivia's help all afternoon. "I want to thank you for the cello."

His head swiveled toward me, studying me for a moment. "So it did please you?"

"Definitely," I said quickly. He was paying attention. That was the first step. "I can hardly believe I touched something as beautiful as that Grancino. I was almost too scared to pick it up."

A smile spread like warm honey across his face. "Pet, you have to touch it to play it. Were you satisfied with its sound?"

"Actually, I didn't play it." I felt like I was confessing to a murder, but he only lifted one dark brow.

"Why not?"

"It's too much," I blurted out. I was already off-script; so much for delivering my decision calmly and smoothly. "It feels indulgent. You shouldn't have."

"I want to indulge you," he murmured.

His words sounded like how I imagined sex felt. I found myself wanting to play for him. I saw a vision of me, completely nude, with the cello carefully placed between my legs. My mouth went dry as he joined the fantasy. His bare hands brushed my shoulders as I played.

A finger danced up my neck and unpinned my hair. Julian draped a long arm around my neck and began to play with my nipples. I gasped audibly, and the vision evaporated. Next to me, Julian straightened instinctively, his protective demeanor returning from its short hiatus.

"Are you feeling well?" he asked.

"Fine," I lied. Now it wasn't only my head spinning. "I was imagining playing it for you."

His head tilted, and he studied me for a second. "Interesting."

"What?" So much for taking control of the situation.

"Nothing." He waved it off, but wheels continued to turn in his eyes. It was definitely something. "I would like that."

"What?" I asked, now completely confused.

"For you to play it for me."

I swallowed before nodding. "I *can* do that, Julian, but I can't keep it."

"I broke yours." He folded his hands in his lap as if waiting for me to respond to his move.

"I didn't need such a luxurious replacement." Why couldn't he see that? Or maybe vampires always bought stuff at antique stores because they preferred to shop in them? It hardly mattered. "I'd be afraid to even touch it. What if I broke this one like I did the other?"

"Then you'll likely have to settle for something other than a Grancino. There aren't many of them left in the world."

It was a very practical answer to my hypothetical question. But it illustrated the ocean between us. "It belongs in a museum," I continued. "Or a private collection. It's not meant to be played."

Julian leaned closer and took my chin in two gloved fingers. "Don't be ridiculous, pet. It wasn't crafted to be in a display cabinet. Grancino would want you to have it, and he would want you to play it."

Grancino would... Of course he'd known him. Who else had Julian known over his many lifetimes? I wanted to kiss it out of him like the rest of his truths, taste them on my tongue.

He mistook my silence for anger, and he released my chin with a sigh. "I can get you another, of course. I'm sure there's something under one hundred."

"You mean a hundred dollars, right?" I asked weakly. "Not a hundred thousand?"

He narrowed his eyes. "Is this about the instrument or the money?"

"Can't it be about both?" The price tag alone was bad enough, but the thought of playing something so old and precious felt wrong. "I don't deserve that cello."

"I've heard you play, and I disagree," he said quietly. "There's another arrangement we could reach if you're concerned about its cost."

God, I hoped he wanted me to play it for him. Naked.

"Consider it compensation."

Patrons of the Arts used to be common. "Are you giving me a job?" I glanced down at the dress. My gaze snagged on the uncovered swell of my breasts. Was that why he'd sent me something so sexy to wear? Because he wanted me to be his escort—in the human, legally questionable sense of the word?

"In a way," he said, "and trust me, after tonight alone, you'll have earned it."

He dropped the statement with a casual air that made me nervous.

"Why is that?" Did I really want to know?

"Because my mother is going to be at this party," he said simply.

I collapsed into my seat and groaned.

Outside, the city shifted into rows of houses, each neatly contained in its own box, surrounded by carefully trimmed shrubs. As the limo traveled, the houses got larger, taking up lots the size of two or three of the neat little houses. Then they sprawled into mansions peeking out from security gates that separated the world inside them from the rest of us. I couldn't imagine where I would find myself this evening. Would it be one of these estates? If his mother was going to be there, it must be.

This date, as he called it, was not what I'd been expecting. His mother hadn't been very friendly, and I doubted she would be happy to see me again. Being asked to be an escort was starting to sound okay in comparison. "Why is she there?"

"Because the party is at her house this evening," he explained.

Could tonight get any worse?

"Is this a good idea?" I forced myself to ask. "Your mother didn't seem to like me too much. I doubt she'll want me"—*in her lair*—"at her party."

"She's been warned to be on her best behavior." The way he grimaced as he spoke told me that would hardly matter. "And she's expecting you."

"Why?"

He paused, choosing his words carefully. "Because I told her you're my girlfriend."

My jaw unhinged, and I stared at him, waiting for him to smile and tell me he was joking. Julian didn't move. He only studied me as if to determine how I felt about this revelation. "I'm sorry," he said finally, "I didn't mean to upset you."

His apology snapped me out of my daze. "Upset? That doesn't feel like a strong enough word for it. Why would you do that?"

"Because I need a girlfriend to keep me from staking myself to get out of these fucking parties," he started.

"How romantic," I grumbled. "I completely understand now."

He appeared lost in thought for a moment. "It wasn't my intention to hurt you. I'd hoped the cello might open your eyes to what I can offer you."

"And what is that?" I channeled all the anger inside me into glaring at him. If I didn't, I was worried that I might cry. Had I actually thought this was a real date? He'd made it clear last night that he wasn't interested. Today, when the cello and dress arrived, I'd thought he had changed his mind. But this had nothing to do with romance. He wasn't interested in me. He saw his gift as a sign-on bonus for hanging off his arm at parties.

But his answer wasn't what I expected. "The world," he said softly. "I can offer you the world."

"Gift-wrapped?" I asked in a flat voice. I had no clue what he meant by any of this or why he would choose me—a woman he didn't even want to sleep with—to be the one at his side.

"If you'd like." His lips twisted into a smirk.

My heart fluttered at the sight, but I refused to give in to its reckless ideas about Julian or his lips.

"You can't just buy yourself a girlfriend!" When had he taken his nap? The eighties of the eighteenth century?

"In my world, you can." He took one look at my face and swiftly added, "But that's not the point."

Before he could enlighten me on exactly what the point was, the limo paused in front of a wrought-iron gate.

Julian groaned as he looked out the window. "I will explain this to you later," he promised. "But we're here. I would like you to accompany me, but if you'd rather be taken home, that can be arranged."

"Maybe we should finish our conversation." I felt sick to my stomach. I wasn't prepared to face his mother or hordes of beautiful vampires.

"I would much rather sit in here with you and debate this, but I'm expected inside." His tone had taken on a sudden violent edge that shocked me. I cringed into my seat, and his expression softened. "Please, will you come with me?"

"In exchange for a cello?" I asked bitterly.

"The cello is yours." There was no questioning the finality of this as he spoke. "You can do what you want with it."

"I want to give it back."

"Except that," he said through a clenched jaw. "Play it, burn it, sell it. You're just graduating, right? Pay off your student loans, buy a cheap instrument, and travel."

I stared at him. Half a million dollars would do more than pay off my student loans. It would also pay off my mom's medical debts.

Julian smirked. "What do you say?"

CHAPTER EIGHTEEN

Thea

The question rang in my ears. He'd finally found my forbidden fruit—the one temptation I couldn't possibly resist. "You can't mean that."

"I do. The cello was a gift."

"I thought it was compensation," I reminded him.

"That was a cheap tactic. I'm not trying to buy you, Thea." Underneath the stormy exchange, I heard something new creeping into his voice: sincerity. "I can give you a fresh start, and you can give me an out."

"An out?"

"I'm not interested in marriage. I need you to go to these parties with me so everyone thinks I'm off the market. In exchange, I'll see to the debts. Both school and medical."

He couldn't be serious. The offer clearly fell into the "too good to be true" category, and worse, it didn't make any sense.

"Why would you want *me* to go to these parties with you?" He'd already pointed out that I didn't belong in his world, so why was he escorting me to its literal gates now?

"Because you are interesting."

I narrowed my eyes. "Interesting? That sounds like a

consolation award."

"Let me finish," he said sharply. "You never respond the way I expect you to respond."

"I'm not like all the other girls?" I guessed with a roll of my eyes.

"What human is like another?" he asked, misunderstanding my point entirely. In fairness, he'd missed out on the sexual politics of the last few decades. "You play the cello with a passion I haven't seen in centuries. I would like you to play for me again. You're young and innocent..."

Was he planning to corrupt me? I fought the thrill I felt at that idea. Should I be focused on his praise of my musical abilities? Probably. Okay, definitely. But I hadn't forgotten the sharp edge of his fang and what it promised.

"...and I can show you the world," he continued. His choice of words echoed what he'd said earlier, but this time I listened. "Next week, I need to travel to Paris. There will be events in Venice, Hong Kong, and a dozen other cities around the world."

"You mean, you need me to leave San Francisco?" My throat went dry as I considered this. "I can't leave. School. Auditions. And I can't be that far away from my mom."

"I'm offering you something most people only dream of, and your obligations here will be seen to."

"Wait, are you saying that you're going to pay my bills?" After the picture he'd painted, this felt like he'd thrown cold water on me. "I can't leave my mother. She just finished radiation last year and—"

"Thea," he stopped me. "We will be traveling on one of the family's jets. Anytime you need to return home to care for her, it can be arranged instantly."

"My roommates and the quartet." I was scrambling for reasons to stop myself from saying yes because each barrier he removed made it that much easier to picture what he was offering me.

"Rent will be paid, and I'm sure the quartet can find another broke cellist," he said drily. "You're looking for excuses. What do you want?"

I wanted the world at my fingertips, and I knew experiencing it with Julian would be beyond my wildest fantasies. He hadn't just been to those places before; he'd lived there. He didn't know history; he'd lived it. I would be taking the trip of a lifetime with access to parts of the world most humans didn't even know about. But there was just one problem.

"And all I have to do is *pretend* to be your girlfriend?"

His blue eyes sparkled in the dim light of the limo. It was clear he knew I was attracted to him.

"What about the right to get married or whatever?" I asked.

"The Rites?" His bemused smile faltered into a frown. "The Rites are why I need you with me. If I'm already off the market..."

"No one will try to catch you." I'd stumbled into a really screwed-up Jane Austen novel.

"Exactly."

"Wouldn't you rather ask someone you're attracted to?" I picked at a piece of lint on my velvet skirt.

"Why would you think I wasn't attracted to you?" he asked slowly. "Or did I misunderstand that kiss?"

I flushed so deeply that I wanted to crawl across the limo and hide on the other side. I was the one who had brought it up. Tactfully. Why did he have to be so direct? I screwed every ounce of courage I had and looked directly into his beautiful eyes. "You wouldn't sleep with me."

"That's complicated," he muttered. "You're a virgin."

"Not a leper." Despite everything, courage burst through me. He did find me attractive. He liked my playing. He wanted to kiss me. He wanted to put me on a private jet and fly me around the world. If this was a dream, I prayed Olivia didn't wake me up.

"You've waited"—he held up a finger to stop me from interrupting—"for your own private reasons. That is a gift you should save for a man who deserves it."

"Oh." I wasn't sure how to respond to that. Julian thought I deserved better than him. He needed to adjust his standards. "So I will accompany you to parties, and then we say good night?"

Julian shifted in his seat and pressed his lips together. "I never said I would keep my hands off of you."

"But you won't take my virginity?"

He studied me for a second, the brightness of his eyes fading with each second that passed. Was the monster overcoming the man? Or was I only hoping he would?

"How far have you gone with a man?"

"I don't know why you think…" I spluttered as I tried to come up with a response that covered up the truth.

"Or a woman?" he added apologetically, misreading my reaction.

"I've done things," I hedged.

Julian's tongue licked across his lips as if he could taste my lie. God, I hoped vampires didn't have that ability. He moved closer, angling his head so his mouth was near my ear. "This is very important, pet," he whispered. "I sense your embarrassment. That's unnecessary. I'm simply asking you to answer one question. Has anyone ever made you come?"

I gulped, suddenly thankful that the angle of his head kept him from seeing my face. Finally, I forced out a small "no."

"I see." He placed a gloved hand on my knee and stroked it with long, soothing sweeps. "Have you made yourself come?"

My body tensed, readying for battle. There was no way I was going to answer that question. Then again, not answering it was probably answer enough. Julian continued his gentle touches as I waged war against myself. I had—not that it was any of his business—hadn't I? I took a deep breath and tried to shrug it off.

"Of course," I said, laughing nervously.

He lingered without another word until I swallowed my pride.

"I don't know," I said quietly.

"If you don't know, then you haven't." He wasn't teasing me, although I couldn't guess why. The hand stroking my knee slid higher up my thigh, and I stopped breathing. "Tonight, I would like to rectify that."

Oh my…

"But first, we need to attend this party," he whispered. He moved slightly and brushed a kiss over my lips. "And appear madly in love. Can you do that?"

Could I cling to him like I was living for his touch? Something told me I could. "Can *you?*" I countered. "You're the one who doesn't want relationships and love and all that baggage."

"Yes," he agreed, and I ignored the pang in my chest, "but I will be thinking of all the ways I'm going to introduce you to pleasure. Not a vampire in there will question that you belong to me. You're covered in my scent, after all." He fingered the tuxedo jacket I still wore. "And I have a feeling I won't be able to keep my hands off of you."

I bit my lower lip, and Julian swore under his breath.

"I'm not sure I can wait until later," he growled.

I braced myself as he reached to push up my skirt, but a knock on the window interrupted.

"If it's the bloody driver, I'm going to tear his head off," Julian stormed. There was another knock. He punched a button on the door, and the tinted window slid open. A moment later, a grinning blond peeked inside.

"Mother wants to know why you've been parked in front of her house for an hour. She said that if you don't come into the party, I have to drag you inside—and that looks like a new suit," the vampire informed Julian cheerfully. The stranger's grin widened into a disarming smile when he spotted me. "Well, now I understand."

"Thea, this is my brother Sebastian," Julian said through gritted teeth. "He has a death wish."

"Unfair." He pursed his lips, attempting to look put out, but it didn't stick. "I didn't know you had a date in here."

"We're coming." Julian pressed the button, forcing Sebastian to step away from the closing window.

"That's your brother?" I asked. The two were as different as night and day.

"Half brother." Clearly, the distinction mattered to him. "May I?" He gestured to his jacket. "We'll only be outside for a moment.

Next time, I'll be certain you have a coat."

"Oh, yeah." I shimmied it off and passed it to him. His words had turned me into molten lava. I didn't need the jacket for warmth, but I already missed his scent.

Julian reached between his legs and adjusted something. I stared curiously, trying to figure out what he was doing. Was his zipper stuck? He looked up, catching me, and raised an eyebrow.

"What was that?"

He barked a laugh. "Fuck, you really are innocent, pet."

I frowned as I tried to figure out what was so funny. Then it hit me. "Wait, were you…?"

"Hard," he finished for me, and I tried to turn away, feeling stupid. "No, don't. I wasn't laughing at you. It was cute." He took my hand and moved it to the hard bulge in his pants. "Do you still think I'm not attracted to you?"

I cupped my hand over his erection and stroked.

"Christ, we'll never get out of this car if you keep doing that," he hissed through his teeth.

"What if I want to pleasure you?" I asked in a small voice.

Julian closed his eyes and groaned.

"I don't really know how…" I admitted.

He gripped my wrist and lifted my hand from his lap. "I will happily show you that, too. But we should go inside now."

Julian got out of the limo and paused to put on his tuxedo jacket before reaching to offer his hand. Thinking of what lay before me tonight made it easy to take. But when I straightened, I saw what he'd reacted to earlier. A plush carpet had been rolled from the gate up a set of stairs that circled around to a lavish portico draped with purple wisteria blossoms.

"This is…"

"Extravagant," he finished for me.

"I was going to say pretty."

He glanced down at me as he offered his arm. "Stick close to me, pet. You're too sweet. They'll eat you alive."

I swallowed at his words, knowing that he didn't mean them figuratively. Julian took the stairs carefully like he was afraid I might stumble and plummet to my death. When we reached the entrance, two attendants stood by the door, each with a large silver tray holding a selection of masks.

"Familiars will enter through the salon." The female held out a tray of masks made of plaster, lace, and painted with gilt accents. "And vampires will enter through the opium den."

Opium den? I mouthed to Julian. But he was busy glowering at the woman.

"She stays with me," Julian informed them. The woman with the masks shrank nervously. But the older male attendant shook his head. Judging from his age, he must have been with the family for years. Was he a vampire? It seemed unlikely given his wrinkles. Human? Did he have a choice about his job? Or had they compelled him to serve them?

"Lord Rousseaux," he said, and my mouth hung open to hear him address Julian like that, "The Rites have been enacted."

"Like I don't fucking know that. Isn't it a little early in the season for this shit?"

The man continued as if Julian hadn't spoken. Maybe he was compelled. How else could he be so calm, staring down the furious vampire by my side? "Madame Rousseaux insists parties be separated."

"I'm not a familiar," I interjected, hoping this might sway them to make an exception.

"The Rites must be observed—"

"Oh, shut up," Julian grumbled and swiped a mask from the tray. Spinning me toward him, he looked deeply into my eyes. "I will find you immediately. Try not to be...overwhelmed."

"Julian, what kind of party is this?" I tried to sound calm, but there was a hysterical edge to my voice.

He cast one more sharp look at the attendants as if any of this was their fault and then took a deep breath. "Welcome to your first *blood orgy*."

CHAPTER NINETEEN

Julian

I could kill my mother for failing to mention the type of party she was hosting. Introducing Thea to vampire society was dangerous—for both of us—but this was worse than throwing her into the deep end. It was tossing her into the open ocean. I shouldn't have told Sabine that Thea was my girlfriend. Clearly, she was going to force me to prove it.

"Julian?" Thea held up her mask. "Can you help me?"

I took it with a grim smile. "Of course."

Thea turned away from me, and I placed the mask over her eyes. She reached up and adjusted it carefully. I'd discounted the effect seeing her at a blood orgy might have on me. I'd expected it to be a test we faced weeks from now, at the earliest. After I'd introduced her to sexual pleasure and sated my desire for her. I could stop myself from claiming her virginity under normal circumstances, especially if I was allowed to have her in other ways. But blood orgies were designed to arouse, every element an aphrodisiac meant to encourage bloodlust.

Generally, the wilder parties were reserved for smaller groups or held much later in the season, after more matches had been made. Hosting an orgy this early meant the event would live up to its name.

Usually, couples paired off, preferring dark corners and privacy for their mating rituals. Tonight there would be no such courtesy.

I tied the mask around her head. The ends of its ribbons slipped through my fingers as easily as my chance to be the one to educate Thea about her body. Thea moved to face me, her green eyes catching the light reflected in her mask's gold flourishes. She didn't look human. She would easily pass as a familiar with her dazzling beauty and easy grace. But that was a different problem altogether. A human might find herself lured into becoming a snack. I was prepared to face that danger. But if others believed she was a familiar, they'd also assume she was eligible.

I brushed a gloved finger over her lips, trying to decide what to do. I couldn't let her walk in there alone, even for a few minutes. Hopefully the scent lingering on her from my jacket would be enough to keep any overly eager parties away. But there was only one way to mark a human or familiar as off-limits—and I'd sworn I wouldn't do it.

I'd have to improvise.

I ran my tongue over my teeth as my fangs lengthened. There wasn't time to explain the stakes to her, so I hoped she would forgive me. And if she didn't? Maybe it was for the best. If The Rites meant hosting orgies a few days into the season, I wasn't sure she could survive the next eleven months.

"I'm sorry," I said in a quiet voice, hoping the vampires at the door were discreet. I couldn't imagine they'd been employed in such a position if they weren't. Moving closer, I angled my face over hers. Venom pooled in my mouth the closer I got.

Thea gazed up at me, mistaking my intentions. "It's okay. I'll be fine. I'll just find a bunch of humans on my side, right?"

I paused and considered her point. Why hadn't I thought of that? Yes, it was imperative to reach her as soon as the party started and the groups began to intermingle. But she wasn't in danger of falling into another vampire's hands before then. Not that familiars couldn't be as vicious as my species.

"Still," I said tightly, "don't get too friendly."

The last thing I needed was Thea to spill any juicy details to someone else. If anyone found out that she was a virgin, heads would roll. Quite possibly my own. And there was no way my mother would buy that I was in a serious relationship with Thea. But explaining this to Thea was a whole different headache and a subject I'd rather avoid, if possible.

She grinned at me, her eyes dancing behind her mask.

"What?" I asked.

"You're very overprotective," she whispered. "It's kinda adorable."

Adorable? Adorable was one word that had never been used to describe me. Apparently, I needed to rip a few more people apart in front of her if she was joking at a time like this. The sooner she dispelled any romanticized notions about me, the better.

"Pet, I am a goddamn Neanderthal, remember?" I growled. "Stay out of trouble."

"Or you'll punish me?" Did I detect a hint of hopefulness in her words? My cock twitched in my pants as if expressing its opinion.

"You'd like that," I murmured, moving closer to her in the darkness. "Just remember that if you're in trouble, I'm likely to behead whoever's standing between us."

She gasped, her eyes widening. Thea didn't say anything as she processed how serious I was about this.

"I'll behave," she murmured dutifully before drawing an *X* over her chest. "Cross my heart, I won't flirt with any other vampires."

Something rumbled in my chest, and I barely contained the jealousy vibrating inside me at her playful suggestion.

"Julian, I—"

The arrival of another party interrupted her, and we stepped to the side. The newcomers chose their masks and hurried into the party.

"Sir," the elderly attendant said, "guests should be inside by now."

"I'm not a guest," I growled at him.

"I'm aware of that, which is why the festivities are on hold."

"Hold?" Thea repeated in confusion.

"They can't start without us," I told her, gritting my teeth so hard that a fang sank into my lower lip. My mother wasn't just having a party. She was putting me on display for every eligible familiar to lust after. The sooner I showed them all that I was spoken for, the better. "We should go inside."

Without thinking, I leaned down and kissed Thea. I'd meant it to be a gentle parting and one more opportunity to plant my scent on her. But she responded with an urgency that left me questioning if she was more scared than she let on. I took her mouth roughly, forcing my tongue past her lips and reminding her exactly what I'd promised her later tonight. She'd be rewarded as many times as I could manage for playing along with these silly vampire traditions.

When we broke apart, she smiled dreamily at me and then slipped away toward the entrance reserved for attending mortals.

The male vampire at the door cleared his throat and stepped to the side to allow me passage into the other wing of the house.

I stalked toward the entrance, getting more annoyed with him by the second.

"Enjoy yourself this even—"

He choked as I lifted him by the throat off his feet and slammed him into the stucco facade. "Try to manage me again, and I'll rip your heart from your chest and feed it to you." I released him to his feet.

He caught himself easily and pinned a blank look on his face. "Of course."

There was more he wanted to say. I sensed it. But whatever orders my mother had given wouldn't extend beyond her exact demands. He wouldn't dare speak freely with me about anything else. Whatever the old human had overheard me discussing with Thea had probably given him a few opinions. I wasn't interested in any of them. But even compelled servants talked, so I hoped my threat would keep him from sharing my private business with anyone else.

The opium den had been added to my parents' San Francisco home in the late nineteenth century before it became hip among the humans. Vampires and Sumerians had discovered the drug around the same time and were the most responsible for the dens that sprang up in cities around the world. A den was an easy way to find fresh blood. Humans flocked to them willingly, and vampires enjoyed the delicacy of dining on the rich, opioid-drenched blood.

Naturally, that had gone wrong quickly. It had been an ugly affair with humans using the drug and its highly addictive nature to vilify minorities and working classes. Who would believe the dens were the invention of vampires? The Council had intervened, outlawing the entrance of humans and familiars into opium dens. Only a handful of open dens remained, although all the richest families had at least one somewhere on their various properties.

Ours was inspired by Venice. My father had taken a trip there while the estate was being built. It was a far cry from the back-alley haunts used to lure humans. The den itself could better be described as an opium parlor, seeing as it took up nearly a quarter of the first floor. Tonight it was nearly full. Vampire families crowded the space, leaving hardly any room to move.

No one wanted to miss an orgy hosted by Sabine Rousseaux.

Delicate seven-foot glass chandeliers hung from the twenty-foot ceiling. Each was hand-blown by Milanese artisans to look like flames blazing above guests. Venetian silks covered the floor pillows scattered around antique tables someone had found in Paris. Opium pipes lay on most of them, an extravagant party favor. Judging from the glassy eyes of some of the vampires I passed, most had already indulged. My father had added Roman dining couches in a fit of nostalgia, and most of them were already being put to use.

The party had yet to officially begin, but the orgy had started. It was customary for eligible familiars and vampires to engage one another in feeding and fucking at these events. For those already spoken for, there was clearly no need to wait. And the ineligible were more than happy to entertain themselves with each other. I spotted several of my peers glaring at the frenzy beginning around them while they waited for the doors to open to the real event. A female I'd met in London a few centuries ago tipped her head in greeting in my direction and then bent to whisper something to her friend. They looked back at me with predatory eyes.

It wasn't unheard of for pureblood vampires to marry each other, but it was the rare pairing that produced a match that might survive The Rites. I ignored them, knowing their interest would fade when they got sight of the male familiars on offer.

I passed a trio of guests pressed against the wall, already half undressed. The female draped over one of the males, moaned loudly as they took turns thrusting inside her. Her head dropped, and she caught my eye, flashing me an encouraging smile. Apparently, two wasn't enough to satisfy her. Another time I would have gladly joined them and relieved the need that had been building up since the moment I'd first seen Thea. Now I couldn't muster the slightest interest.

"Rousseaux." A hand clapped me on the shoulder, and I turned to find Giovanni Valente. His smile didn't reach his eyes. They watched me with the wariness of a snake. "I wondered if you would be here."

I tipped my head in greeting. "I didn't have a choice."

"And your lady?" he inquired. "Is she with you tonight?"

"She's here, but she's waiting with the familiars," I said lightly.

"I was unaware that she possessed any magic." He was baiting me now. Searching for information about the relationship that I'd claimed to have with Thea last night.

"Only over me." I smiled. "Still, she couldn't be brought in here." I gestured to the opium den.

"Ah yes. I forgot the Rousseaux family still followed the old rules."

"I was unaware there were new ones." My relationship with him had always been one of mutual necessity. He wasn't what I would call a friend. He could be counted on when fighting on the same side, but the rest of the time his interests lay purely in himself. That wasn't unusual for a vampire, but unlike most, he held little regard for his own bloodline. Of course he would think it was off for me to be here. If he hadn't wanted to come, no one held enough sway over him to force the issue.

"What do they say? Rules are made to be broken." He shrugged. "Perhaps someday, she will be allowed in here. Your relationship must be serious if you're letting her anywhere near your family."

"You mean my mother?" I let my boredom seep into my voice. The less interested I was, the sooner he would leave to find more fascinating company.

"Sabine can't be happy that you're involved with a human."

"Mothers are rarely happy when status is on the line."

"True." Giovanni laughed. "Perhaps, though, your lady will enchant her like she did to you—and me."

I froze. I didn't have a choice. Inside me, darkness raged, urging me to attack him. The comment sounded innocent, but I understood the suggestion behind it. Humans were fair game until they were bound to another vampire through one of the many archaic methods at our disposal. His message was clear: he would respect my claim to her until there was reason to question it.

After that, he could and would do as he pleased.

After I regained enough control, I smiled wanly. "I'm certain she will."

"But The Rites," he continued. "You are a firstborn, correct?"

"My sister," I corrected him. "A few minutes before me." It was a gamble that he didn't remember her—or the fact that she had died.

His eyes narrowed for only a moment as if searching through some internal Rolodex. In the end, he grinned. "Naturally. It will be your turn during the next season."

"I doubt The Rites will be in play then."

He leaned closer and lowered his voice as if the vampires fucking and smoking all around us gave a shit about what we were saying. "Not if the rumors are true."

"Rumors?" I repeated.

"I think you need to catch up on the Council's activities," he advised. "Or decide what you're going to do with that pretty little piece of flesh soon."

"What are you talking about?" I'd lost patience with Giovanni and his exploratory conversations that only led to more questions.

"They want to host seasons more often. Stir the blood. And as for The Rites," he murmured, accepting an opium pipe from a passing attendant. He sucked a long drag from it, his eyes turning to glassy onyx. "They've enacted them permanently."

CHAPTER TWENTY

Thea

Nothing could have prepared me for what I found on the other side of the door. I stepped into a ballroom that looked like something out of a fairy tale. Ropes of white flowers hung like delicate rays from crystal chandeliers bigger than my entire apartment. A few tables dotted the perimeter, but otherwise there was no furniture. Instead, the gleaming oak floor had been reserved for dancing—or whatever other activities were planned for the evening. All around me, beautiful people in masks primped and gossiped as they waited for the orgy to begin.

Orgy. The word kept tumbling around in my head. It had to be some type of joke. It couldn't be a real orgy. People weren't just going to get naked and go at it, right?

I slipped into a corner, doing my best to keep to myself and not draw any attention. If they'd been waiting on Julian's arrival, as I suspected, it would only be a few minutes before they let us loose and I could find him. I couldn't help picturing a large gate being thrown open and all the pretty people in here stampeding into an arena like the running of the bulls.

"What's so funny?" A Black woman joined me in the corner. She waited, watching me with curious brown eyes framed by a mask lined with glittering peacock feathers. Although it obscured her face, it couldn't hide her stunning beauty. High cheekbones held the mask in place over a wide, shapely nose. Her closely cropped hair had been styled into old-fashioned waves. She smiled when I didn't speak. "Come on, I'm not going to bite."

"*You* might not," I said drily, earning a laugh from her.

"I suppose we are in mixed company." She held out a hand to introduce herself. "I'm Quinn Porter."

"Thea Melbourne." I reached to take her hand, but she stared at mine.

"No gloves?" she asked with an arched eyebrow.

"Oh." I withdrew my hand quickly, realizing her own hands were covered in elbow-length plum velvet gloves that matched her beaded dress. "I didn't know I needed them."

"I'm sorry." Quinn shook her head and grabbed my hand. "That was rude. I was just surprised. They aren't technically required for us, but it's tradition, and I'm told vampires hate when we go bare-handed. What did you say your family name was?"

"Melbourne," I said feebly. She grew thoughtful, and I knew she was trying to attach the name with a bloodline. "I'm not a familiar."

"Well, that explains it." She sounded relieved. "I thought I'd forgotten a whole family, and my grandmum would not approve! I swear I've been studying vampire and familiar bloodlines since I learned the alphabet."

"You didn't forget anyone," I reassured her. "I'm nobody."

Her head craned back. "That's funny because I'm looking at you right now. How many nobodies can you see?"

I grinned a little, relieved that I'd managed to find a kind soul. I'd been prepared for a den of vipers.

"So you're a human, then?" she asked conversationally.

"Yep, and I have no idea what I'm doing here," I confessed. The longer I stood in the room and waited, the dizzier I felt. It had to be my nerves getting to me. Thanks to hundreds of cello performances, I usually felt comfortable at parties. But I was also usually the entertainment, not a guest. Was that why everything felt so strange?

"That sounds like a story." She leaned a hip against the wall, showing off her impressive curves. "Let me guess, it starts with a boy? Or a vampire?"

"Yes. A vampire, I mean." I couldn't fathom thinking of Julian as a boy.

"It must be serious," she said. "It's unusual for vampires to bring human companions to The Rites."

"How unusual?" I asked before I thought better of it. There were more questions I wanted to ask. I had a lot of them, but Julian had warned me about being too casual with details. If we were going to trick his family into believing we were a couple, I couldn't admit that I'd just met him or that I had no idea what was going on or that with each passing second, I felt more and more like my brain was going to burst from trying to wrap my head around his crazy world. "Julian didn't mention it."

"Julian Rousseaux?" Her voice pitched up an octave. "That explains it. He's not a big fan of these things. At least, according to my grandmum's *extensive* notes."

"Yeah, I get that impression, too." I wished I had extensive notes to help me navigate this. I wanted to know what she'd learned about my fake boyfriend during her research, but I couldn't ask. Or could I? "I have to know what people say about him. The Julian I know is very different away from all of this." I gestured to the ornate space around us.

Her gaze followed, drinking in the velvet-flocked wallpaper that covered the walls. Every few feet, a floor-to-ceiling mirror framed in gold had been hung, making the already massive ballroom look even bigger. More than a few familiars were preening in front of them, practicing flirtatious glances or curtsies.

"I believe that," Quinn confirmed. "He tends to avoid vampire society when he can. Not that he has much of a choice since his sister died. That makes it his turn."

My mouth went dry, but I managed to keep my face composed.

Puzzle pieces began to fall into place. He'd mentioned his sister but no details. Julian might have been leaving me clues, but I was far from having a complete picture. I needed to change that if I was going to keep passing as his significant other.

"I'm surprised he brought you here, knowing that he's expected to marry a familiar." She sounded sympathetic. Try as I might to heed Julian's warning, I felt comfortable around Quinn.

"It's complicated," I agreed. "When we got here, he seemed really surprised that this was"—I lowered my voice—"a Blood Orgy."

"Oh wow!" Her dark eyes widened behind her mask. "You didn't know? You poor thing! Did he at least tell you what to expect?"

"He was a bit too pissed when we got to the door and found out," I admitted. I was doing a pretty good job at making this all sound normal without giving away any clues that I'd known Julian for all of five minutes.

"Shit. Okay, hold on." She looked around her in a frenzy. "We probably only have a few minutes."

As if to back her up on that, the familiars around us started to act strangely. Whispers rippled through the groups, and then people started taking off their clothes.

"This is a real orgy, isn't it?" I asked hopelessly as I took in a lot of naked flesh. Most still wore something. I'd mistaken the velvet and silk robes worn by many as party attire. Under them, though, were a dizzying array of lace and leather, velvet and chiffon.

A man across from us shucked off his robe, revealing a golden, muscled chest. His lean torso tapered into a hewn *V* that disappeared under the low-slung waistband of his silk pants. He turned, and I got a glimpse of…everything. Silk, it turned out, didn't leave much to the imagination.

Several women had opted for lace bustiers that lifted all their assets into prime viewing, but a few wore nothing more than chiffon slips that floated dreamily over their nude forms. My core clenched, winding tighter with each sensual glimpse I caught. Julian had worked me up in the limousine and then dropped me into a roomful of sexy people. I was going to have a word with him later about managing expectations.

"Yes and no," Quinn said quickly. "It is an orgy, but you're taken. I mean, Julian brought you, so he'll come to find you right away."

I nodded, swallowing hard as a woman passed her sequined robe to an attendant, leaving her clad in a fringe skirt with nothing under it. Several ropes of pearls were draped artfully over her pert breasts. She was breathtaking. I couldn't tear my eyes away from her. I wished I could be like that: fearless in the face of all these strangers.

I glanced up at Quinn. "Should I...get naked?"

Julian really should have mentioned more specifics around this bit.

"No! I mean, unless you want to. We're not all parading around like meat," she murmured, sounding a bit peeved at the whole ordeal. "I'm keeping my clothes on. I mean, orgy or not, I'm going to need some foreplay first. Or, at least, some venom."

"Venom?" I whispered absently.

"He hasn't fed you his venom yet?" she asked curiously. "He must be a gentleman, but word to the wise, don't let him hold out on you. You'll have the best sex of your life."

If only that was true. Standing here, watching as familiars readied themselves to seek pleasure with the waiting vampires, I wished I'd never told Julian I was a virgin. If I had just kept that little nugget to myself, I wouldn't be one now. How was I supposed to cope with the war drum beating down there all night?

"You asked why I was laughing before," I said. "I was imagining everyone in here stampeding out to find a vampire, like it was a bad game show or something."

"You're not far off," she said with a giggle. "Just hang back when they sound the gong, so you don't get trampled. Let the eager ones go first."

"Thanks." I took a deep breath, grateful Quinn was here to guide me through this. "You don't have to hang back on my account, though."

"Believe me, I'm not interested in running out there and jumping on the first vampire dick I see," she said in a flat tone that left no room for misunderstanding.

"Sorry, I didn't mean to—"

"Don't worry about it. All that studying and preparing, and I'm my family's worst nightmare come true." She leaned closer and whispered, "I want to fall in love. I know I'm not supposed to care about that. A good match is a good match, but..."

"What's good about a match without love?" I said softly.

"Exactly. I mean, I know the perks of making a good match. I mean, look at this place! Of course, most familiars who produce an heir are turned." She sighed. "But I don't want a match. I want a mate. I guess I want it all."

"Why settle?" I agreed with her. It would be easy for anyone to be taken in by the fabulous wealth and privilege on display. Add a chance at immortality to the mix, and that would be enough for most people. I liked Quinn for wanting more than that.

"If only my family agreed. But they're so obsessed with the damn treaty—"

The deep, vibrating crash of a gong. On the other side of the room, two double doors opened. Quinn's arm flew out, shoving me against the wall as familiars crowded toward the party. She hadn't been kidding about the eager ones.

Once the majority were past us, we stood and smoothed our dresses.

"Thanks," I said breathlessly.

"Are you ready for this?" she asked.

I took one look at the doors that led to the Blood Orgy, gulped down a surge of fear, and nodded.

"Stick close to me until you see Julian," she advised.

I did as she suggested, moving by her side as we made our way into a stunning multi-story atrium. Lush, exotic plants were clustered around velvet couches and benches. My mouth fell open as I watched one of the women in a black bustier approach a vampire lounging against the sloped back of a divan. She dropped into his lap and stretched her neck in invitation. He smiled at her, his hand drifting between her legs to her naked sex before his mouth clamped down, and he began to feed.

"Do you think they know each other?" I asked numbly as the woman began to moan. I wasn't sure if she was responding to the hand intimately exploring her or his feeding.

Quinn shrugged. "Who knows? I mean, there is another way to snag a vampire."

"Which is?" I murmured.

"Get knocked up. Oldest trick in the grimoire," she teased. Then the smile fell from her face. "I'm sorry, that was thoughtless."

"Why?" I couldn't look away from the vampire and the woman. She had shifted to straddle him now, grinding her bare bottom over his trousers until he reached to free himself for her. I looked away, embarrassed to be watching such an intimate act. That was silly, since they didn't care.

"Because you can't give Julian an heir." She patted my arm, chewing on her lip as if delivering bad news. "Only familiars can conceive with a vampire."

Something twisted in my chest, but I hid the sharp, unexpected pain behind a smile. "Oh, that," I said, forcing a laugh. "Sorry, I'm a little distracted."

"Why would that be?" she said with a snort.

We maneuvered our way through the crowd, managing not to get swept into any of the small groups forming in clusters throughout the atrium. Moans filled the air around us, and with each step I took, I found it harder to block the sights and sounds out. The strangest thing was that I *wasn't* embarrassed or shocked. I was turned on. It was beginning to take hold of me when Quinn elbowed me and pointed.

"Is that him?" she asked.

Julian stood halfway up the stairs as if he'd been surveying the crowd. My eyes met his, and I knew he'd been looking for me.

He nodded, one unspoken command, to stay put, and then started toward me. The crowd parted for him. Even people mid-ecstasy seemed to shift to allow him passage. The world shifted on its very axis as Julian crossed to me through the orgy.

"Doesn't look so complicated to me," Quinn whispered before he reached us. "I think he knows exactly who he wants."

That made two of us. But as Julian approached, his blue eyes never leaving me, I couldn't help but wonder.

Why?

Before he reached me, the gong rang out again, causing even Julian to pause. The crowd fell silent as Sabine Rousseaux made her entrance, sashaying to the top of the stairs with effortless grace.

"Welcome, my friends." She spread her arms out in an elegant gesture, reminding me of a conductor before his orchestra. Of course, that's what we were to her: instruments for her to direct, players meant to entertain. "Before you enjoy your evening, I'm afraid we have a pretender in our midst. Please give us a moment to remove our uninvited guest."

And then all eyes fell on me.

CHAPTER TWENTY-ONE

Julian

It took a lot to stop an orgy. My mother had managed it, though. I would have been impressed, if I hadn't been so pissed off by her power play.

A hush fell over the room after her shocking announcement. I started through the crowd again, ignoring her decree, taking care not to draw too much attention to myself. But all around me there was a soft whoosh as collectively every being in attendance turned in my direction—or more specifically, in the direction of Thea.

"Fuck," I muttered. I had expected my mother to be cold and condescending. I hadn't thought she'd go as far as throwing Thea out of our house in front of the entire party.

Everyone moved in, trying to catch a glimpse at what had stoked Sabine Rousseaux's ire. The swarming masses closed the distance between us, and I lost sight of Thea. Something pounded in my chest, propelling me forward to the spot I'd last seen her. I shoved through the crowd, earning a few harsh words and glares. But I was no longer concerned with being polite. I could only think of reaching her before anyone else did.

I spotted her just as the security team arrived. Thrusting aside a couple of curious onlookers, I stepped in front of Thea like a shield.

"Julian," she whispered, sounding relieved. Her delicate fingers closed around my bicep. She held on to me like I was an anchor as the guards stalked toward us.

"Gentlemen," I said in a tone rich with warning. I'd known most of these men my whole life. Three of them were vampires, and two were humans. We weren't exactly friends, but they felt like members of the family. None of that mattered now. I would do whatever I had to do to keep their hands off her.

"Sir." Cassius, the head guard, gave me a stiff nod. "Don't worry, we have this under control."

He continued past us and stopped a few feet away in front of a vampire clad in all black. Unlike the partial disguises the other partygoers wore, a mask the color of midnight with a single red slash painted across it covered his whole face. Where had I seen that mark before?

"Please come with us," Cassius said quietly but firmly.

The vampire remained in place as if he hadn't heard the request. People began to pivot from Thea and turn toward the unfolding scene as the other guards circled the masked vampire. A musty, sweet smell filled the air—the scent of fear. I'd smelled it on battlefields and back alleys, but never in a ballroom filled with vampires and witches.

"Don't make this hard," Cassius urged him as two guards flanked the uninvited guest.

He didn't resist them, but they only made it a few steps toward the door when the party crasher called into the hushed room. "*Carpe Noctem!*"

Instantly, the mood in the room shifted. Whispers filled the space along with a number of harsh rebukes. The murmurs quickly turned into a buzz of conversations that filled the space. A few shouted back, hurling vulgarities at him.

"What's going on?" Thea asked me.

I shook my head. I had no idea. But something felt off. I had never witnessed a public display of defiance during the social season, but I had no doubt that's what this was. As Cassius and his men escorted the stranger from the room, a few people around us applauded as he was led past.

"What did he yell?" Thea whispered.

"*Carpe Noctem*," I repeated with a sigh.

"Like *carpe diem*," Thea said softly, continuing to cling to me. "But *noctem*..."

"Means night," I said. "Seize the night." I had no idea what it meant, but I doubted it was anything good.

"Why would he...?" Thea trailed off as Sabine reappeared on the stairs.

"What's a party without a little excitement?" she called to the crowd. "May each of you find matches that strengthen the bonds and bloodlines of our families. Born of blood!"

"Born from magic!" the crowd responded.

"What...?"

I shushed Thea, reaching for her hand. I spun her around until we faced each other. "Let's find somewhere more private."

A red flush appeared where her mask rested on her cheeks. The air around us filled with the scent of her blood. Darkness crept along the edge of my vision, and venom pooled in my mouth. Over her shoulder, I spotted Valente watching us. Hooking an arm around Thea's waist, I yanked her to me and kissed her deeply. It was meant to remind him of my intentions. Regardless of what customs dictated, I'd staked my claim on Thea, and I would protect her from predators like Giovanni until I figured out how to extricate her from vampire society permanently.

But the kiss became something else. It was in the nature of kisses to do that. I'd found myself in bed with a woman more than once after an innocent kiss good night. And I'd felt the unspoken goodbye in a lover's final kiss.

Thea's lips parted for me, responding to my desire to lay claim to her, and I invaded. There was no part of her mouth that mine didn't explore. I would taste every inch of her, starting right here.

I kissed her until the powdery scent of flowers transformed into a garden at midnight. Jasmine washed in wood smoke. Rose blossoms laced with absinthe. Every vivid color met a million shades of black. She bloomed in my arms as I wrapped her in my darkness.

We broke apart as an impatient cough interrupted us. I turned to find my mother glowering at me. "Playing with your food?"

My lip curled, revealing a fang, and her eyes widened a fraction of an inch. Thea wouldn't notice her reaction, but I had caught it. My mother wasn't just concerned. She was afraid, and I knew not of me. It almost seemed like she feared my public display with Thea, but why? It couldn't be *that* important that I marry this season. Plenty of vampires took their time finding a familiar to become their consort. What was the fucking rush?

I recalled what Giovanni had said earlier. There had to be a reason for the Council to enact The Rites permanently. I just needed to keep my head clear long enough to find out, but as long as Thea was nearby, that seemed impossible.

"You remember my girlfriend," I said pointedly.

"I don't believe she was introduced as your girlfriend." Sabine swept closer, her smile full of ice. She'd chosen a silver evening gown that wrapped around her from one shoulder to her feet. "Welcome to our family home."

Thea shivered as if she felt the chill in Sabine's welcome, too. "Thank you for inviting me."

It was a perfectly polite thing to say, but vampires only ever took etiquette so far. "I didn't invite you, mortal. But all the same, you are welcome *for the evening.*"

I didn't miss the subtle deadline on Sabine's welcome. Neither did Thea, because her hand slipped down to squeeze mine. I took it protectively.

"Thea will always be welcome in a Rousseaux home," I said in a low voice.

"Careful, my son. Don't write invitations to others' parties," she warned me with the same cold smile on her face. "I'd like to speak with you alone."

Thea tugged the hand I held, trying to pull away, but I tightened my grip.

"She goes where I go."

Sabine rolled her eyes. "This is private family business. For the blood only. I'm sure she'll understand. Sebastian is already waiting, and your father is supposed to call."

For the blood was code for a family meeting.

"And the others?" I pressed. "Where are they? Or were my brothers left off the guest list?"

"They are busy and ineligible until you make a match. Besides, it's not necessary to involve the others," she said.

"Why?" I'd always been present, even when my mother called a family meeting to discuss a papercut. It was odd to leave my younger brothers out even if they were otherwise engaged.

"Because I'm not waiting for them to join us from the ends of the earth when you are the one in trouble," she seethed. "I'm sure she'll be fine left to her own devices for a little while."

"I'll take her to my quarters." I didn't care what my mother thought about the situation.

But she was one step ahead of me. "Your quarters are being used."

"For what?" I immediately regretted the question as I caught a glimpse of a familiar writhing on a vampire's lap in the corner. "Never mind. Then I will find her somewhere safe."

"Are you implying the party isn't safe?" Sabine asked with downturned lips.

"Not for a human," I muttered. Looking to Thea, I found her staring at the two of us with a dazed expression. Dealing with my mother would have been bad, and going to a vampire party would have been overwhelming. We had blown past all of that and straight to a fucking fever dream. "Pet, let's find somewhere for you to catch your breath while I speak to my family."

Thea blinked before nodding.

"I will see you in the study," my mother said, tossing one last disdainful look at Thea.

"Come on." I led Thea through the crowd, keeping her close to my side. Every now and then, I would steal a glance to find her watching the frenzied fornicating around us with curious, round eyes. This hadn't been what I'd meant when I'd told her I would teach her about pleasure.

We stole up to the second floor where Han, one of the family guards, was turning lost guests back toward the rooms open to them. I nodded to him as I slipped past with Thea in tow. Han cut off a few grumbling guests with a sharp word, and they fell silent, staring after us.

"Do you live here?" Thea asked.

I shook my head, catching Han pointing the wayward guests toward the wing my quarters were in. My mother had actually opened them up for an orgy. I supposed it was her not-so-subtle way of pushing me from the nest. "I have my own place, but I usually stay here after events."

"Will..." Thea swallowed and asked a different question as we started up another flight of stairs. "Where are we going?"

"Somewhere quiet," I said. I wouldn't leave her to fend off advances at the party, and after her blunt introduction to vampire society, she needed to catch her breath. She needed somewhere not choked with the fumes of blood and sex. By now, she had to be rethinking our arrangement.

When we reached the roof, even I breathed easier. The heated pool reflected the stars overhead and streaks of city lights from a distance. Up here, it was quiet, except for the sound of falling water from two fountains mounted near the end of the pool. Most of the summer furniture had been taken inside, but a few loungers had been left clustered around a gas fireplace. But it was the view that caught her attention. She took one step toward the railing that ran along the perimeter of the roof and gasped.

Low fog rolled like smoke across the bay, which stretched as far as even I could see. The bridge was illuminated against the night, its lights sparkling on the hazy water below like stars. Thea shivered, wrapping her arms around herself as she drank in the view.

"Here." I showed her to one of the loungers and found a blanket in a nearby basket. "This should help, but let me start this." I walked to the fireplace and turned it on. After a few seconds, the heat began to radiate around us.

"Thank you." Thea snuggled into the blanket around her shoulders. She might have looked cute, but she was biting her lip, which sent my mind to a decidedly different place.

"You're welcome," I purred, kneeling in front of her. Every ounce of my being wanted to stay here with her, slowly erasing all the things she'd seen downstairs with my hands and lips and tongue. My desire must have been obvious, because Thea lowered the blanket enough to slip an arm free. She wrapped it around my neck and brought her mouth to mine, her fingers tangling in my hair.

Or maybe she was having the same thoughts.

It took effort to break away from her, but the second I managed to, she lunged forward and stole another kiss. I surged forward, cradling her body as I maneuvered us onto the lounge. Her skirt pooled open, and Thea lifted her legs to frame my body.

"Pet." I nibbled her jawline as my palm slid to cup her ass. "I need to go."

"Don't," she moaned, reaching to draw me back to her siren lips.

"If I don't go, someone will be sent to find me, and then we'll be interrupted." I continued down, trailing kisses along her throat. I paused to linger over a bluish vein where her scent was so strong I could almost taste her blood on my tongue. "And I have a hard enough time keeping control of myself as it is."

"Screw self-control." Her eyes were wild, and I laughed softly.

"Believe me, I want to," I grunted, brushing my mouth lower until it swept over the velvet peak of her bust. Thea gasped, and the air filled with new, earthy scents that promised I would find her wet between her legs. Could she make this any fucking harder? Or make *me* any fucking harder, for that matter? But there was one thought that swept through the dark desires shadowing my mind.

"I won't have my first taste of you like this," I whispered against her skin. "I need to take my time. I need to be alone with you where I can worship your body as it deserves to be worshipped. You've been patient, Thea. Not much longer, and I will give you exactly what you deserve."

Her hips stopped rocking against me, and she stared up at me, panting heavily before she finally managed a nod. The arm around my neck slackened and fell to her side, and I bolted to my feet before I lost control again. I wrapped the blanket around her shoulders and dared a kiss on her forehead before I strode away.

I didn't dare look back until I'd reached the door leading to the stairs. When I did, I found her watching me with eyes that sparkled as brightly as the lights on the water.

"Julian?" There was no tremble or hesitation in her voice as she called into the night. "Don't make me wait."

I swallowed the urge to return to her now and screw self-control as she'd suggested. Instead, I opened the door and sprinted down the stairs.

CHAPTER TWENTY-TWO

Thea

Even without Julian here, heat lingered on my skin. I'd felt it since he'd kissed me in the atrium. I'd barely heard a word Sabine had said downstairs. Even now, I couldn't pin down a single thought. I threw off the blanket he'd given me and let the night's breeze cool me.

I could only think in sensations. How it felt when his lips grazed along my jaw, the shuddering pleasure as they brushed over my breasts, the warm glow of his palm resting on my ass.

I wanted more.

No, I *needed* more.

With each second that passed, I felt his absence more acutely until it became hard to even breathe. Every gasp of air I took flooded me with new sensations that rushed down until they rooted between my legs and began to grow. And grow.

And grow.

I stood on trembling legs and tried to shake myself free, but the swelling desire only intensified. My foot caught the leg of the lounge chair, and I nearly wound up in the pool. But I straightened and pressed forward. I needed to find Julian. Now. I didn't care if I had to pass a thousand hungry vampires. I couldn't wait for a second longer.

I'd only made it a few more steps toward the door that led back into the house when it swung open, and two figures stumbled onto the roof. I froze, waiting to be discovered. But the couple wasn't interested in me. My heart pounded in my chest as I watched the man lift the woman off the ground. His hands pushed her skirt to her hips as he slammed her against the door they'd just come through. I opened my mouth to call out, but my warning died at the sound of her first moan.

I had nowhere to go. I darted a bit closer to the pool, where a slab of stone was fashioned into a spectacular fountain. I couldn't hide behind it without winding up in the water, but from this angle it was harder to see them. That meant they might not see me. But there was another problem.

It started in my stomach. Hunger seized control of my body. I felt hollowed out. Empty. Every inch of me was desperate to find relief. Without thinking, I took a step away from the fountain toward the couple. Then another. Before I realized what I was doing, I was standing a few feet from them. There was nothing to hide behind now.

But they were too preoccupied to notice. Not that I could blame them. I'd gotten a few glimpses downstairs, but this was entirely different. I'd been too embarrassed to look then. Now, I couldn't tear myself away. It was like watching a play on my own private stage. The man's hands slid up the woman's bare thighs as she wrapped one long, perfect leg around his waist. He was buried inside her, blocking any view I might have of the action. It was too dark to tell if they were both vampires. Every familiar I had seen while waiting had been beautiful and polished to the point of being nearly indistinguishable from their hosts. These two were no exception.

The throb between my legs continued to grow, refusing to be ignored. In this dress, there was nothing I could do about it. I wasn't even certain where to start. Julian was right. There was no longer any question in my mind. I'd never experienced anything like the desire coursing through my veins now. All I cared about was finding a way to relieve the tension I felt. I closed my eyes, hoping that I could break whatever spell had taken hold of me. Something was wrong.

This wasn't normal. I hadn't spent my entire life barely interested in sex to suddenly become some type of pheromone-crazed animal.

There had been drugs downstairs, opium—maybe I'd accidentally breathed some in.

"Well, well," the woman called out, and my eyes snapped open to find her looking directly at me. "It appears we have an audience."

"I'm sorry," I squeaked as the man's head swiveled to look at me over his shoulder. Something dark dripped from the corner of his mouth, and there wasn't a hint of white left in his eyes. They'd gone completely black.

Yeah, he was definitely a vampire, and I'd interrupted his feeding.

That should scare me. The last time I'd interrupted a feeding, I'd almost become the second course. Somewhere deep down there was fear. I was certain of it. The trouble was I couldn't scrounge up enough of it to trip my survival instincts.

His nostrils flared as he breathed in the air. "A human. Interesting. Are you a guest or an appetizer?"

I swallowed. "A guest."

"What a shame," he said thoughtfully. "Do you need us to move from the door? Or would you rather join our party?"

Was he suggesting what it sounded like he was suggesting? I stared for a moment, trying to think of a polite way to say no. But my brain wouldn't cooperate. It wanted me to stay and accept his invitation.

"I think she wants to join us," the woman said with a breathy giggle. She beckoned me with a finger.

I tried to shake my head, but once again my body refused to comply.

"Come here," the vampire demanded. His words hit me like a magnet, pulling me toward him. I was powerless to resist, and somewhere in my hormone-soaked brain I wasn't certain I wanted to resist at all. But when I got a few steps from them, he held up a hand.

"Wait. It seems you're spoken for." He inhaled deeply, his chest expanding, and I realized he was smelling me. "Rousseaux should know better than to leave his belongings lying about, especially when he's been feeding them."

Feeding me? What did that mean? My brain was too fuzzy to make sense of any of it. But the pull toward him that I'd felt moments ago evaporated. The lust lingered, however.

"Rousseaux?" the woman repeated. "Surely, he wouldn't mind if..."

The vampire chuckled darkly. "She's drenched in his scent, sweetheart. He's made it clear to stay away."

"But like you said, he left," she argued.

"And you need to do your homework," he told her, dropping her onto her feet. He smoothly fastened his trousers and began to buckle his belt. "I thought they prepared familiars better these days."

"I've been preparing since I was seven, you condescending *switch*," she hissed.

For a moment, his shoulders went rigid before they relaxed again. "Find another vampire to get you off. It's not worth my life to piss off Julian Rousseaux."

"If I'd known you were—" she began.

"Careful what you say next," he cut her off. "You insulted me once, and I took it like a gentleman. Call it a courtesy, since I just fucked you six ways to Sunday. But my patience is wearing thin."

She looked as though she was about to say something else. Instead, she released a frustrated shriek and began adjusting her clothing. She threw one furious glance over her shoulder before she wrenched open the door and started back to the party.

The fight had been enough to distract me for a few minutes, but now the overwhelming sensations crowded inside me again. I took a step forward, swayed unsteadily, and started to topple. Strong arms caught me before I hit the ground, and an instant later, I was resting comfortably on the chaise lounge by the fire. My vampire savior watched me from the other side of the outdoor hearth.

"When Julian smells me on you, would you mind telling him I was being chivalrous?"

"What?" I asked. None of this made any sense, and now my head was swimming. I tried to push up and get to my feet. "I should go find him."

"If I let you leave like this, he will definitely kill me." There was a blur, and suddenly he was standing at the end of the lounger. I startled and fell back into the seat.

"He wouldn't." But wouldn't he? I'd seen him kill another vampire already. What would he do if he found me out here with one now?

"You're not in the best place to think rationally, so I'll let that go." He remained nearby, guarding me with watchful eyes. "Where did he go?"

"He was summoned to a family meeting." I pressed an index finger to my temple. My head had started to pound, and despite the coolness of the night, I was so overheated that I wanted to rip my clothes off. I wrapped my arms around myself, hoping I could cling to control until Julian returned.

"And he just left you up here?" He shook his head with disapproval. "He should have known better than to bring a human here tonight. I imagine he's being reminded of that as we speak."

I couldn't take it any longer. I bolted onto my feet, but my new vampire friend blocked me.

"Just wait here for him." His eyes, which had returned to normal, contracted as he spoke.

The compulsion to find Julian dissipated. Now I was just left with a piercing headache and the same gnawing hunger I'd felt since he'd left me here. I needed something to occupy me until he returned. "Who are you anyway?"

"Bellamy. Pleased to meet you…?"

"Thea," I said softly. "Are you a Rousseaux?"

"No." He laughed as if the idea was preposterous. "I'm unaffiliated. Just a poor wayward switch."

"Switch? That's what she called you," I said, remembering the way her lips had curled disdainfully around the word as it left her mouth. "What does it mean?"

"Just that I'm a poor vampire bastard. I have no idea who turned me. It's just a nasty way of pointing out that I was made by someone who didn't want me."

"Oh. I'm sorry. It's none of my business." I felt bad for prying, but Bellamy shrugged.

"Don't be. That's the lottery of life. I could have just as easily been born to the Rousseaux family and been treated like a prince."

"A prince?"

"You haven't noticed?" Bellamy grinned at me. "Julian is pretty much vampire royalty."

"What does that even mean?"

"You know how kings and queens have all sorts of money and land and crowns and shit?" he asked, and I nodded. "They're not half as wealthy as the Rousseaux family and not nearly as powerful."

I stared at him, wondering if he was pranking me. "You aren't serious."

But the cello. The limo. It was all adding up. But still, vampire freaking *royalty*?

"As a stake through the heart," he said, drawing an *X* over his chest for good measure. "I'm surprised you didn't know."

"What does that mean?" I narrowed my eyes.

"Things must be serious between you two," he said, bypassing my question and circling around to answer it in a roundabout way. "I can't imagine he would ask you to brave meeting Sabine otherwise."

I couldn't admit that Bellamy was right without admitting to my ruse with Julian.

"Have you known Julian a long time?" I needed to steer this conversation in a different direction.

"A couple of centuries."

Would I ever get used to answers like that? Would I ever fit into this world? A sudden surge of dizziness answered for me, and I nearly fell off my seat.

"Are you okay?" Bellamy was at my side, kneeling to check on me.

"I don't know what's wrong with me," I murmured.

"I do," he said grimly. "You should lie down."

I didn't have much of a choice since I could barely stay upright.

Bellamy stayed crouched next to the chaise. "Once Julian gets back, he'll make it better."

"How?" I moaned. My skin felt too tight. I wanted to rip it off like I'd nearly done to my clothes earlier.

"You really don't know, do you?"

"Are you a sphinx or a vampire?" I grumbled. "Just tell me what he did to me."

"Well, when a girl and a vampire meet," he began in a teasing tone.

"I think you covered the birds and the bees earlier when you were making love to...what was her name?" I couldn't remember.

Bellamy snorted. "Hell if I know. But I would hardly call that making love."

"I was being polite."

"Polite doesn't really belong at an orgy, princess."

"Do you call every woman you meet by some cutesy name?" I muttered.

"Only the ones who hate it," he assured me.

My body began to tremble. Shivers rolled through me like waves battering a shoreline. Bellamy stood and took off his jacket. He placed it over me, looking worried. "Maybe I should go find Julian."

I tried to agree, but my teeth began to chatter too hard for me to get a word out.

"I could kill him," Bellamy said with a sigh.

"You could tr—" An inhuman growl drowned out the rest of my response. I sat up, dropping Bellamy's jacket in the process. He didn't notice because he'd turned in the direction of the voice, too.

"Julian..." I trailed away as he prowled closer, and I got a good look at him—and his jet-black eyes.

CHAPTER TWENTY-THREE

Julian

Bloodlust wasn't what humans imagined it to be. They conflated the term with violence. Not that bloodlust and violence weren't bedfellows. They usually came hand in hand. But bloodlust always *preceded* violence. Violence never sparked the frenzy I now felt. That always started with desire—some craving left unfulfilled. I didn't just crave blood. I craved flesh on my lips, against my skin, under my bare fingertips. And if I didn't get it—if something or someone got in the way—that's when the violence occurred.

"Julian," Bellamy's deep voice ran like an electric undercurrent in the background. "Get control."

I snarled, sweeping one arm at him like a hook. Bellamy was not suffering from bloodlust, so he dodged me easily. A younger vampire might have frozen and wound up shorter by a head. A stranger might have attacked. I'd known Bellamy for centuries, and we'd been in enough bar fights and battles to know how to handle each other.

"Why does she smell like you?" I snarled, stalking toward him. Thea scrambled to get between us, but instead, Bellamy shielded her.

Anger bellowed out of me, tearing through the air like a crack of thunder.

Thea tried to push Bellamy aside as if she understood she was the key to defusing my rage.

Bellamy held his ground, looking unimpressed. I might rip him apart just for acting like a total bastard. "She was freezing."

"And you thought you could claim her?" I lunged toward him, but Bellamy sidestepped me. He twisted and caught me in a chokehold.

"I forgot how stubborn you could be," he grunted as I fought his grip on me.

"I forgot you wrestle." Every time I managed to get loose, he caught me again. That was the other thing about bloodlust. It was usually only dangerous when all parties were suffering from it. If a vampire kept a clear head, they could easily handle an opponent being controlled by a raging hard-on.

"She is stoned out of her mind," he hissed so that Thea couldn't hear. His arm remained locked around my neck.

"What did you do to her?" I asked in broken gasps.

"I didn't do a thing. Your scent is all over her. Another vampire wouldn't have come within ten feet of her. Are you trying to tell me you didn't feed her your venom?"

That was exactly what I was telling him, except that he made a damn good point. Some of the blind fury I felt seeped away. I'd made a point to mark Thea as mine. Only a suicidal vampire would go near her. Or Bellamy. "She smells like you now. Maybe *you* fed her venom."

"Now you're just being a dick." He didn't release me. "Think about it."

I'd kissed Thea, that was all. I'd thought about doing more to her. I'd even fantasized about someday watching her enjoy the true perk of being a vampire's lover. I hadn't intentionally fed her my venom. I wouldn't.

But I hadn't been thinking very clearly, either.

My fangs had been out since we'd arrived. Venom was a natural byproduct of that, so when I'd kissed her...

"Fuck," I muttered when I realized what I'd unintentionally done. "Let me go."

"You sure?" he asked. "I don't feel like getting my head ripped off. It's been a long night."

"Yeah," I said grimly.

Bellamy's hold loosened. By the time I was on my feet, dusting myself off, he was on the other side of the roof. So much for trusting my word. Not that I blamed him. Bloodlust was a fickle thing.

"She's going to need—"

"I know," I cut his shout off. This wasn't how I wanted this to happen. But I'd left myself no choice. I was going to have to revisit the question of whether I could maintain my self-control around her after this.

Bellamy lingered in the background as I made my way to Thea. He wouldn't get in the way, but he cared enough to make sure I did the right thing. I owed him. Big time.

Thea had curled into a ball, her knees tucked to her chin and her skirt fanned open around her. She looked up at me with round eyes. Her voice was so small that the night nearly carried it away as she asked, "What's wrong with me?"

I hated myself as I tried to find the easiest answer. I'd left her here to face this alone.

"When I kissed you, you got a taste of my venom," I explained, taking a seat beside her. I paused for a moment, wondering if I had any right to touch her before I leaned over her body. She could make that decision.

Thea reached up for me, and I didn't hesitate. Scooping her into my arms, I cradled her shivering body against me.

We stayed like that for a moment before she asked, "Did you poison me?"

"No," I said with a humorless laugh. "Venom doesn't work like that. I'll explain it later, but right now I need to help you get this out of your system."

Holding her close, I stood and moved toward the door. Bellamy raced ahead and opened it.

"When did you become a gentleman?" I asked as I passed him.

"Time changes people."

It was a lesson we both knew too well.

"I owe you a drink. Thank you," I said, nodding in acknowledgment.

"It was no—"

"No, really," I interrupted him. "But I better see to her."

He chuckled softly, shooting me a sympathetic look. "Enjoy."

I forced a grim smile.

I made my way to the bedroom my mother insisted on keeping for me and hoped I wouldn't have to scare off any guests. I carried Thea down the hall, past dozens of framed oil paintings by Picasso and Rembrandt and Vermeer. I took the paintings as a sign of welcome, a gesture meant to make me feel at home. She knew how I loved art. But by the time they'd built this house, I already had residences of my own. I had never lived here. I couldn't even recall spending a night save for a handful of times I was here for a party, and usually then, I was too caught in the haze of whatever recreational substance was on offer to remember much. I'd had my own place in the city since the earthquake.

"Where are we going?" Thea murmured as we stepped into the darkened room. I was relieved to find it empty.

"I'm taking care of you," I said in a strained voice. I shut the door with my foot. Thinking better of leaving it like that, I turned to lock it.

As the bolt clicked into place, she lifted her head and looked around. Her eyes widened when she realized I'd taken her into a bedroom. "Are we...I mean...?"

"Relax," I shushed her. I needed to explain, but I wouldn't allow her to suffer any longer. I carried her to one side of the bed and laid her on it softly.

Thea writhed, her arms reaching out for me. The venom left unspent in her system had reached fever levels. Curls of hair stuck to her forehead and neck. A slight sheen of sweat glistened on her neck and collarbone.

Every impulse I possessed wanted to hike her skirt to her waist and take her. But that was the bloodlust talking. I should have known in the limo to keep her away from this place. Now I'd put her in a dangerous situation—entirely of my own making.

Thea was laid out like dessert on a platter. I looked away, but it did nothing to distract me from my desire. I slipped off my jacket and tossed it onto a bench at the foot of the bed. My shirt followed, and when I turned to look at her, she watched me with hooded eyes.

"Earlier you wanted me to touch you, pet," I murmured, lowering my body over hers.

Her legs coiled instinctively around my waist as she bucked her hips, seeking satisfaction. Her hands reached for the buckle of my pants. I grabbed her wrists and brought them over her head, but she continued to grind against me. Pressing my hips firmly against her movements, I pinned her body to the mattress.

"Not so fast."

"Julian." My name was honey on her lips as she breathed an invitation. "I want you."

Fuck. How was I supposed to resist that? My lips traced along her jawline. "That's the venom. It makes you want me."

She needed to know the truth.

"I wanted you before," she whispered, twisting her face to bring her lips to mine. "Now, I *need* you."

Need? That was definitely the venom talking. But it didn't matter. Neither of us had a choice, and even if we did, it was clear we wouldn't choose differently. I wished we'd stayed in the limousine long enough for me to deliver her first tastes of pleasure.

"Please?" Her soft petition sealed our fate.

My mouth covered hers, and I let my lips answer. Thea relaxed into the kiss. Her body ceased to fight as her tongue licked across my teeth, gathering any lingering venom there. That wasn't going to help my fuck-up. I reared back, breaking the kiss while keeping control of her body.

"I'm going to undress you," I explained before I released her. "Do you trust me?"

Her lip tugged between her teeth as she stared up at me. Finally, she nodded.

My fingers found her zipper. Her eyes fluttered closed as I unzipped it, revealing inch after inch of perfect skin. Now that the gown was undone, I slid its single strap off her shoulder. I couldn't resist pressing a kiss to her bare shoulder. Thea moaned. The sound spurred me forward, and I drew the dress's bodice down to expose her breasts. Her nipples pebbled as air brushed over them.

"You are so fucking beautiful," I growled. Closing my mouth over the furl of one, I plumped the other with my hand.

Thea gasped and grabbed hold of my hair as I worshipped her breasts. Her heart began to beat faster, making it easier for me to see a bluish vein pulsing under her pale skin. My fangs tried to protract, but I fought the urge. I wouldn't feed on Thea. Not in this state. Not ever. But the effort it took to hold back made my mouth ache. I continued past her breast, away from the tempting pulse of her blood and toward the only other way to sate my craving.

I circled her navel with my tongue, earning a whimper that told me she wanted this as much as I did. Her fingers circled my wrist.

"Your gloves?" Her eyes questioned me.

That was too complicated to explain at the moment. All I managed was a grunted, "I can't."

I kissed her hip, intent on making her forget the leather gloves I wore. It was safer for both of us if they stayed on, given our mutual problem: fraying self-control.

"I want your hands on me," she pressed, attempting to wiggle her fingers past the cuff of my left glove.

"No!" I thundered, jerking it away. With one swift motion, I pressed my palms to her thighs and spread her open for me. I wouldn't give her time to argue.

Instead, I sank between her legs and offered a distraction. As I pressed a soft kiss to the inside of her thigh, one thought rose above the bloodlust roaring in my veins: Thea Melbourne was going to be the death of me.

CHAPTER TWENTY-FOUR

Thea

"If you won't—"

My objection fell away as his lips brushed the soft skin of my inner thigh. He paused, as though giving me a chance to finish my thought. Maybe he was waiting for me to reject him. Maybe I should have.

But I didn't.

I'd demand some explanations later. Venom. Gloves. My confusion muddled my brain almost as much as whatever he had done to me. Still, each time he touched or kissed me, my head felt a little clearer and the fire burning at my core flamed brighter.

"Yes, pet?" His breath whispered over my swollen, feverish flesh, and I gasped. He chuckled and resumed his descent, blazing a trail of desire in his wake. My eyes clenched shut, savoring each delicious touch. I didn't know what to expect. I didn't care. I only wanted to find out what he would do next.

He stopped, his mouth hovering over my skin until I dared a glance. For a split second, shyness overcame me. No one—man or vampire—had ever been this close to me, had ever touched me this intimately. I was so caught up in the haze of his venom that I'd failed to grasp how exposed I was. The top of my dress was bunched at my waist, and thanks to the slit in my skirt, my lower half was nearly bare, too. All that remained between us was the thin lace of my panties.

Julian kept his gaze locked on mine as his fingers grabbed the flimsy elastic band that held that final barrier in place. He lowered himself, his eyes never leaving me until he disappeared from sight. I pushed onto my elbows, wanting to see what was about to happen.

"Do you have any particular attachment to these?" he asked as he fiddled with my panties.

My mouth went dry at the implication in his words, but I managed to shake my head. He bent his head, blocking my view, and then I heard the sharp snap of rending fabric. Cool air rushed against the warm wetness between my legs, and I swallowed a gasp as I felt the ruined lace flutter against my thigh.

He'd ripped my panties off me—*with his teeth*.

Thank God I couldn't have his babies, because I was pretty sure my ovaries had just exploded.

"I'll buy you more," he said, not sounding the least apologetic.

"Okay," I squeaked, wondering if it was wasteful to hope all my current and future underwear purchases suffered the same fate.

Julian smirked as he bent the final fraction of an inch, and our eyes locked. The darkness had left his, but in its place burned the fire I felt inside me. I held my breath as his mouth closed over me and then his tongue dragged clean up my center.

"Ohhhhhh." It was nothing like I'd expected. Warm, promising waves broke over me as his tongue delved past my folds and found its target. He began to coax with languid circles, and my head fell back against the mattress. But each turn of his tongue brought me closer to some unknown edge. Each demanded a little more pleasure from me.

A new trembling overwhelmed my limbs, seizing control of me and slowly erasing the painful need I'd felt only moments ago. He devoured me until, at last, my hands clenched the sheets, and he carried me over. I shattered beneath him, ripped into a hundred pieces that knew nothing but this.

I couldn't move. My arms and legs didn't seem to be working properly. In fact, they now seemed to be made of jelly. Julian straightened to his full height and licked his lips. None of the heat had faded from his eyes. He might not be under the effects of venom, but something else plagued him.

"You taste even better than I imagined," he said in a low voice that sent desire coiling inside me again.

He had imagined tasting me? I bit my lip, trying to dredge up even a morsel of resistance to his flattery. Instead, I found myself twisting around and crawling to the edge of the bed. I could think of nothing but my need to give him the release he'd just granted me.

Julian made no move to stop me. He only watched as I knelt on the bed before him. My fingers shook slightly as I found his belt and unbuckled it. Then the button of his pants. I pushed them down, revealing his boxers. Taking a deep breath for courage I plunged on, and his cock sprang free.

I paused a moment to stare. I didn't have much to compare him to, other than a few accidental glimpses of Tanner coming out of the shower. That was enough for me to know Julian wasn't just bigger than average. He wasn't even on the same chart as average. I'd been too feverish to appreciate his body before. Now I couldn't look away from him. His torso was pure muscle that narrowed into sharply hewn hips at the center of which rose his cock. I couldn't imagine how it would fit...anywhere.

Maybe it was a good thing Julian refused to claim my virginity. Now that I'd seen him naked, I felt even more intimidated than when I'd found out he was a vampire. But I was determined to return his favor. Not simply because it seemed like good manners, but because I was dying to give him an ounce of the pleasure he'd given me.

The trouble was: I didn't know how to do it. I wrapped my fingers around his length and tried to figure out what to do next.

"You don't have to," he said softly.

I turned my eyes up to him. "It's not that," I admitted. "I don't really know…" My head fell, shame flushing my cheeks.

A hand slid under my chin and lifted my face to meet his. "You're embarrassed."

I nodded.

"Why?" He waited for my answer, curiosity sparking in his blue eyes.

"Because…" I sucked in a deep breath and plunged forward. "You're, like, a thousand years old, and you've probably been with thousands of women who knew what they were doing—and what if I mess up and hurt you?"

Julian's face contorted for a second, and I braced myself for a storm. Instead, he laughed. "I'm sorry," he said quickly. "I think I should be the one worried about hurting you. I'm the one with fangs, remember?"

"I've got teeth, too," I reminded him stubbornly.

"Noted." He tilted his head to the side and smiled. "And Thea, I haven't spent the last nine hundred years bedding every female I met."

"It's none of my business," I said, feeling stupid for vomiting my insecurities all over him.

"You're holding my cock. I think we're past worrying about keeping out of each other's business," he said drily.

I allowed a corner of my lip to curl up, but I couldn't quite muster a smile. "So you haven't been with thousands of women?"

"No, I have not." He didn't offer me further clarification, and I was left to wonder if that meant he'd been with hundreds or dozens.

"And I'm not going to hurt you?"

There was a pause followed by the ghost of a smirk. "I'd say it's doubtful."

"I still don't know what I'm doing," I whispered.

Julian's hand closed over mine and guided it up and down. "That's it," he encouraged me.

That couldn't be it. It was too easy. "What else?"

His eyebrow rose as he cast a glance down at me. "You can use your mouth."

A new throb started between my legs as I considered this advice. I had a lifetime of licking ice cream cones behind me. That had to count for something.

I ran my tongue over my lower lip, then wrapped my mouth over him. Julian sucked in a sharp breath, and his hand shot out, gripping my hair in a loose hold. I flattened my tongue and drew it up his hard shaft, circling it over his tip before looking up at him. "I don't know if I'm doing this right."

"It feels fine," he said in a strained voice, peeking down at me with one eye.

"Fine?" I repeated, doubt beginning to throb in time with my pleasure.

"Christ, it feels fucking amazing, okay?"

I took that as a sign I should keep going. It was easier than I thought to take his full length in my mouth, so long as I focused on what I wanted most at this moment: to please him. I wanted to make him feel as good as he had just made me. I wanted to cool the fire that blazed in our veins.

He groaned, the sound catching the attention of the space between my legs. I wished he hadn't refused to sleep with me. What would it feel like to have this powerful man inside me? I swallowed at the thought, my mouth closing hard over his dick, which earned me another strangled groan of pleasure.

"Oh my God, how are you doing that?" he asked. His fingers were massaging my head, encouraging me. "I'm going to come in your sweet mouth if you don't stop."

But I didn't want to stop.

Still, I knew very little about what to expect. When the first heat of his release hit my throat, I responded with a rough, choked swallow. I struggled to keep up as he emptied himself, his hips bucking slightly with his climax.

When I finally sat back on my heels, my eyes were wet with tears from the effort. Julian looked down, his rapture quickly shifting from bliss to worry.

"Are you all right, pet?"

I was taken aback by the concern. My mind couldn't understand it, but my body seemed to understand something I couldn't, sending the desire building in me bubbling over. I nodded, barely stopping myself from reaching out for him again. I didn't want his blood to cool. I didn't want to leave this bedroom or his body.

He dropped to his knees, mistaking my silence, and took my face in his hands.

"I'm fine," I whispered, worried that saying more might betray the turmoil I felt. Our arrangement was temporary. No matter how good it felt to be here with him, I knew there was a deadline for our relationship. "Just tired."

His eyebrows knitted as if considering my explanation before his face relaxed. "Let me help you sleep."

He drew my body up into the bed, tugging my gown off entirely and exposing the parts of me he'd yet to discover. I was worried he'd tuck me in and leave me to rest. Instead, he spent the night sucking and kissing, as though he couldn't sate the longing between us. He was always careful to keep our bodies separate, even as I offered myself to him over and over, until sleep finally claimed me.

CHAPTER TWENTY-FIVE

Julian

I watched her sleep from the shadows, waiting until her breathing slowed to languid waves. I stayed there for moments—or hours. Time ceased to interest me. Given how much I'd screwed up tonight, it was reassuring to see her at peace. But I didn't trust myself to let her sleep if I stayed in bed. A naked Thea was far too tempting a thing to resist. Instead, I lingered, not wanting her to wake up alone. Then again, finding a vampire hovering over the bed and watching you sleep was creepy. In the end, I opted to slip out and deal with my mother.

The lights in the corridor had been dimmed to mimic the flickering glow of candlelight. My mother, not fond of having to find matches, had never relinquished her preference for firelight. Even with the modern heating and cooling systems that had been installed decades earlier, hearths could be found blazing day or night, summer or winter. It wasn't a matter of warmth, since vampires required none. It was a matter of habit, a nod to our past lives. But despite the remnants of the past, I wouldn't consider my mother sentimental. She didn't have time for it.

Tradition was another story, as I'd been reminded earlier. I'd left that conversation enraged, which, in hindsight, might have made my bloodlust a bit worse than usual.

When Sabine found out Thea had stayed the night, she was going to be livid. It was better I told her, rather than a member of the household staff. There were still partygoers lingering about in various stages of undress as I made my way to the lower levels, unwilling or unable to waste even a minute before sunrise. By dawn everyone would leave. It would be safer to speak to my mother when the house was empty, but I couldn't risk waiting.

I found her sitting quietly in the morning room, watching the world through her window. Sunrise was still a ways off, so the sky felt heavier and darker than when I'd taken Thea to bed a few hours ago.

Sabine didn't look up. She had traded her party attire for a silk lounge set and had taken off her makeup. Even without the added glamour she was beautiful. When we were children, she used to tell my sister and me that at least three wars had been started over her—before my father won her heart. Now I knew better. She hadn't been at the center of those wars because of the choices of other men. She'd been there because *she'd* started them.

"Good morning," I said, staying near the door and out of Sabine's immediate reach. Keeping a room between us—or preferably a country or two—when disagreeing was a wise tactic. A servant misinterpreted my pause and hurried over to offer me a selection of breakfast items ranging from pastries to fresh blood. "No, thank you."

"You should eat," Sabine announced as the man disappeared from the room. "Or have you found other ways to satiate your thirst?"

"Thea is my girlfriend," I reminded her. "I attended with her."

"Girlfriend? *Cortigiana*? Gold digger? It's all the same thing."

While Thea and I remained in San Francisco, I would be civil, even if my mother wouldn't. I moved toward the fire, then stood near the hearth and drew off my gloves. After placing them on the mantel, I turned to her with bare hands.

"That was quite the show. Are you planning to fight me?" she asked.

At least she'd gotten my hint. It was a subtle warning among our kind. Even humans knew what it meant when the gloves came off. I shook my head. "Not now. But if you insist on insulting her..."

"Julian." She said my name with a sigh that carried nine hundred years of maternal disappointment behind it. "She is not like us."

"She's human. That's hardly revolutionary."

"For a switch, perhaps. They don't know any better."

"And what about all the human lovers that vampires have had over the years—that you've had over the years?"

"I didn't hang off their arms at social events," she hissed. "I didn't show them off, and I never called them my girlfriend!"

"What is it Sebastian is always saying?" I asked with a yawn. It had been a long night, and this wasn't how I wanted to start a new day. "Welcome to the twentieth century."

Her lips curled into a cruel smile. "It's the twenty-first century."

"Exactly. Things have changed."

"Things haven't changed that much!"

"I just waded through two dozen naked, writhing vampires and familiars—I know."

"How are you going to meet a nice familiar if *she's* here to distract you?" she pressed. "The Rites can't be ignored."

"I realize that."

"Do you? Because you're acting like a teenage vampire. Now is not the time to think with your fangs or your cock."

I bit my tongue to keep myself from reminding her that she'd just hosted a party where I was supposed to do precisely that.

"Humans have become—"

"Stop! Don't even say it," she cut me off. "You are a Rousseaux."

"You keep telling me that, but it doesn't change my relationship with Thea."

"She is *la belle dame sans merci*." Sabine spat out the term like an unsavory bit of gristle.

I groaned. Quoting poets? Now she was being dramatic. She was going to whip herself into a frenzy if I wasn't careful, and that was the last thing I needed while Thea was under the same roof. She'd survived my bloodlust. I wasn't about to introduce her to blood rage in the same twenty-four hours.

Still, it didn't hurt to be prepared. I stepped closer to the fireplace—and the collection of swords displayed above it.

Sabine's eyes narrowed on the weapons cache behind me. "Those are antiques and no way to win an argument."

I wasn't certain there was a way to win an argument with her. Centuries of wisdom kept that comment in my throat. "Dad says it's best to have a sword within arm's reach at all times."

I left out the rest of that bit of advice—*around your mother.* Sabine was known for her temper as well as her beauty.

"Your father clings to the past."

"And you?" My mother perceived herself as the progressive of the Rousseaux sires. To humans, her beliefs changed at a glacial rate, but for a vampire of her vintage, she was a fucking radical. That was the difference between most humans' reckonings and a vampire's. When you have a thousand years behind you and forever ahead, change was never urgent. Still, she came around. Usually.

"You've chosen a mortal consort with no ties to magical bloodlines. She's been on your arm at two social functions now! The Rites don't exist for our amusement, Julian. They are a matter of survival. She can never..." There was more she wished to say, judging from how her lips thinned into a line, somehow helping her contain her next thought. "She can never be your wife."

"Why?" I challenged her. It was ridiculous to keep pushing this. I barely knew Thea. I certainly had no intention of marrying her. But I hadn't expected such an aggressive reaction from my mother.

She pinched the bridge of her nose between her fingers, which remained gloved. "You can't be serious."

"You know better than most that we vilify what we do not understand—what is not like us. She's only human. There's no harm in it." I'd known it would take considerable effort to sway her feelings toward Thea, but I hadn't expected an almost violent prejudice. After nearly a thousand years, she still didn't trust my judgment. Maybe mothers never did.

"Spoken like a human," she said. "She's already infecting you."

"Human? Vampire?" I shrugged. "We share more similarities than differences. They outnumber us, so we hide. We persist in the idea that if they knew, they would hate and fear us. Humans believe we're monsters. All a mechanism of prejudice."

"It's a mechanism of survival—as old as the sun that gives us life and the moon that gives us rest. Dualities exist to complete us, my son. Humans fear us because they should. They prove there is something superior in our blood—that we top them on the food chain." The words spilled from her, even though she remained as motionless as an ivory statue. Nothing but Sabine's lips had moved in over a minute. So unlike the woman who had been in my arms a few hours ago. It was an eerie reminder that there were discernible differences between the two species.

"Then why the blood banks and the rules and the Council?" I countered her. "I thought we were over all this bullshit."

"Over the fact we are above them? That we feed off them?" Her dark hair swung around her shoulders as she shook her head. Finally, a movement. "Blood banks and etiquette do not erase the fundamental fact. We are the superior creature. It simply means we learned to coexist. We've risen above our baser instincts, but they are still there. Never forget that."

"Careful, Mother, you're beginning to sound like Freud." My eyes flicked to the clock—an astronomical prototype from fifteenth-century Prague. If it was broken, it could never be fixed. The clockmaker was long dead, but his work remained to remind me that soon the sun would rise.

"And you sound like a fool. A lovesick one at that."

"I think—"

"You *aren't* thinking. That is precisely the problem. You think I'm revealing my bigotry, but you're missing the bigger picture."

"This should be good," I grumbled. "What am I missing?"

"What is above us in the food chain?"

"Nothing."

She shook her head. Her voice teetered on the edge of a whisper, yet her words filled the room as she quoted, "*I saw pale kings and princes, too. Pale warriors, death-pale were they all… I saw their pale lips in the gloam with horrid warning gapèd wide.*"

"That was written by a human." It seemed important to point out.

"An unusually perceptive one." Sabine had been fond of the fragile Keats. She'd hated the girl he'd been meant to marry, too. But Sabine was not wrong about Keats or his poem. "Her blood sings you the *canticum ad infinitum*. You know what the trouble is? It's not that you're screwing a pretty little human. She's something more than human."

Sabine had always seemed closer to the gods than most vampires I'd met. Some said Hecate herself had given her otherworldly sight. I imagined she'd lived long enough to always have the measure of those around her. She saw through most creatures to their true motivations. At least, I chose to believe that. It was better than thinking she could read minds. Still, there was something about Thea. Something even I didn't understand. If Sabine thought she heard…

I had hoped the vampire who attacked Thea's friend in the bathroom was a coincidence. Now…

No, I stopped myself. It had been a game, meant to draw me away from a companion my mother found unsuitable. I'd almost fallen for it. I'd almost forgotten that my mother had won as many battles with her wits as her weapons.

Thea was human. I'd held her in my arms. I'd touched her. I'd watched pleasure overcome her fragile, *mortal* body.

"Every vampire thinks they hear the blood-song from time to time. You're probably hungry," I drawled, even as my fingers tapped a frantic beat on the mantelpiece.

I blinked and found an antique blade at my throat.

It seemed my mother was taking matters into her own hands.

CHAPTER TWENTY-SIX

Thea

A nightmare roused me, and I rolled over and found myself in an empty, luscious bed. Pink light dusted the San Francisco horizon as the sun began to rise, peeking through the heavy silk curtains. Inside, a fire crackled in a marble hearth. I felt the warmth of both like a living thing inside me. But it wasn't the sun or the fire; it was a spark that hadn't been there before. Julian had promised me the world. Last night was my first glimpse, and it would stay with me forever.

I looked around Julian's room, realizing I'd been too far gone to notice any of it last night. The room itself was larger than the entirety of my apartment and furnished with antiques that probably made collectors weep. Paintings with signatures that made my head spin. Books were piled next to the gilded chairs and crammed into shelves next to the fireplace. In the corner, a large desk sat covered in papers and notebooks.

Memories of yesterday burst through me, and I began to shiver as I recalled the number of times Julian had taken me apart—and put me back together again. The memories stoked that lingering spark into a hungry thrum inside me. I gathered the sheets and hugged them to my body, wondering how dangerous it was to walk around the Rousseaux mansion looking for Julian. The party had started late. Considering it was an orgy, I guessed it was still going.

I could either wait here for Julian to come back to me, or I could seek him out. My legs slipped out of bed, and I stood, dropping the covers behind me. It took a few minutes to gather my belongings and get my dress zipped up. I was almost to the door when it opened to reveal a complete stranger.

"I'm sorry." The elegant, silver-haired woman stared at me a moment, as though she might blink and find I'd vanished. "I didn't expect to find anyone in here." She looked me up and down, a smile forming on her face. "You must be Thea."

I swallowed and nodded. It was embarrassing enough to wake up in a huge bed alone. It was somehow worse to be caught doing the walk of shame, especially since it was the first time I'd ever done it.

"I'm Celia, Julian's assistant," she said, carrying a tray to the other side of the room and cradling it in one arm as she reached for the handle of a French door.

"Let me!" I rushed over to help rather than continue to watch.

Her nostrils flared slightly as I came close, but she only smiled to decline my offer.

"Julian likes to take his coffee outdoors in the morning. Although he never actually drinks it," she said. She opened the large French doors with one hand, revealing a small balcony, and placed the tray she carried in her other hand on a stone table. "I didn't realize you had stayed the night. Would you like something? Breakfast?"

"Coffee would be great," I said quietly.

"Use his cup. I'll get another."

"I couldn't—"

"Nonsense. Julian would want me to see to your wishes in his absence." She sniffed again.

I got the impression she was smelling me. Oh my God, did I smell like sex? Not that we'd had sex. But I *had* spent most of the night in a state of sheer, sweaty bliss while Julian introduced me to what I'd been missing.

"Okay." I bit my lip, somehow feeling even more out of place than when I showed up to the orgy last night. I moved to join her on the balcony and picked up the delicate china cup she'd brought him.

Her gaze swept over me. "And perhaps a change of clothes?"

"You really don't have to go to so much trouble."

She waved a hand dismissively. "It's no trouble. There will be something in Camila's room. It might be a bit dated, though."

"Camila?"

"Julian's sister," she told me.

"His twin." I felt a surge of curiosity about her. They still kept her things. When had she died? I couldn't ask Celia any one of these questions. "It won't upset him to see me in her things?"

Celia tilted her head and studied me for a moment. "Humans can be so thoughtful. Well, some of you can..." She forced a smile. "No, it won't. I'm certain I'll find a dozen items she never wore with the tags still on."

"If it's—"

"If I might give you a piece of advice," she interrupted me. "You'll never survive this family if they think you are weak. But don't worry about all of this." She gestured to the room around us. "They have more money than they could spend in an eternity. Objects mean little to them. If one of them offers you something you want, take it without apology."

I nodded, feeling my eyes widen at the thought of being expected to take what they offered. "It's just..."

Celia remained silent, but she radiated an encouraging kindness.

I took a deep breath. "I don't want to be in their debt. I could never pay them back."

"Who could?" she said with a snort. "You're Julian's guest, so you should be prepared for what that means."

My mouth went dry as I looked back at the room I'd spent the night in. All I could manage was a small nod.

Celia patted my hand. "Let me see about those clothes and get Julian his cup before he returns."

Almost instantly, she was at the bedroom door, and I barely caught her in time to ask, "Where *is* he?"

"He's speaking with his mother. I'm certain he'll be up here soon."

I wasn't. It seemed like his mom wanted to talk to him a lot. Even worse, I realized as Celia disappeared into the hall and closed the door behind herself, she probably wanted to talk about me.

After all, I was supposed to be his excuse for avoiding whatever courting ritual these insane Rites were all about. But last night? Last night had complicated things.

My body hummed from how many times we'd complicated things.

It was like I'd woken up and found myself in a surreal fairy tale. I was dating a vampire. An insanely rich vampire. But I also wasn't dating him. That part still confused me, especially after he'd spent last night giving me orgasm after toe-curling orgasm. Maybe he saw it as part of the payment package for being his decoy. Not that I'd needed the incentive after what he'd offered me, but it certainly made it easier to put up with him when he was being grumpy.

I shivered in the misty morning, last night's dress no match for the weather. Everywhere in San Francisco was near the water, and everywhere near the water was cold. I decided to take Celia's word for it and make myself a cup of coffee. I poured from the highly ornate, silver teapot into the delicate, bone china cup. Next to the pot there were a number of folded newspapers from all over the world. I glanced to find *Le Monde*, *Corriere della Sera*, *The Guardian*, *The New York Times*, and several others that appeared to be written in languages I didn't recognize.

How many languages could he freaking read? Clearly he hadn't wasted his lengthy time on Earth doing nothing. I dug out the crossword from the *Times* and padded back inside his bedroom with my precious coffee. A crossword would distract me from my ever-fraying nerves.

I put my coffee on the side table next to the bed and walked over to Julian's desk to look for something to write with. A collection of yellowing papers and letters were strewn across the desktop. They had to be decades old, but I resisted the urge to look through his things. I didn't need any more proof that he was out of my league. Reaching for a pen sticking out of a leather checkbook, I accidentally got a glimpse of what looked like a bank balance dated with the year 1982. Except that there was no way it could be because, as far as I knew, numbers didn't go that high. Before I could stop myself, I picked up the checkbook and looked, convinced I was seeing things.

I wasn't. I tossed it back down like it was a snake that might bite.

What was I doing here? I didn't fit into his life, and that had nothing to do with him being a vampire. And everything to do with the balance of our bank accounts. Mine probably had twenty bucks in it. His? I didn't even know what category that number fell into. Not millions. Not billions. I mean, why bother even keeping track?

I took the pen, which turned out to be a Montblanc, of course, and returned to the crossword puzzle. Sipping my much-needed coffee, I tried to concentrate, but I'd only filled in a few answers when Celia returned.

"These should fit you, and they're brand new, so there's no need to worry about Julian," she added as she laid a sweater and leggings across the bed.

I got up, ready to change. Being in an evening gown was only adding to the surreal feeling I was experiencing here. I picked up the creamy sweater and knew from its buttery softness it had to be expensive. The price on the still-attached tag proved it.

"Cashmere," I murmured. I'd never felt anything so decadent in my life. No wonder it cost a small fortune.

"Would you prefer something else?" Celia asked, misunderstanding me.

"No," I said quickly. I shot her a sheepish grin. "I've never worn cashmere before. Maybe I shouldn't. What if I spill something on it?"

"It's been sitting in a closet for over forty years," she told me. "Better to wear it than to waste it. May I?" She gestured to my dress.

It had been a battle to get the dress zipped, so I nodded.

"How are you doing?" she asked kindly as she unzipped me and helped me out of the gown. It felt a little weird to be in my underwear in front of her. But since everything about this situation was strange, I tried to shrug it off.

"This is a lot," I confessed to her.

Celia placed my gown on the bed and picked up the sweater. When she went to remove the tag, I realized she was going to help me get dressed.

"Oh, you don't..." I trailed off, stopping myself from making the mistake I'd made earlier.

"Good girl," she murmured with approval. "You're learning."

She helped slip the sweater over my head. "I don't mind helping you dress." She adjusted the sweater's neckline to fall over my shoulder. "I used to be a lady's maid."

"Camila's?" I guessed.

"No." She shook her head, sadness glinting in her gaze. "Before I became a vampire. Since Julian turned me, I've worked only for him."

"Oh." Jealousy I didn't quite understand flared inside me. I did my best to shrug it off as I tugged on the buttery-soft leggings she'd found me. "Um, I feel a little bad asking this, but when did Camila die?"

The clothing she'd brought me, while older, judging from the tags, was in remarkably good condition and not nearly as old-fashioned as I expected.

"It was recent," she admitted in a low voice. "She was taken from us in the nineteen-eighties. Far too young. I'm afraid the family is still grieving. Especially Julian."

I was wearing the clothes of a woman who had died before I was born. I expected to feel freaked out, but instead, there was only sadness.

A piece of Julian that had eluded me before suddenly clicked into place. "That's why he was asleep," I said to myself, and her mouth fell open. "Oh! It's really none of my business. I shouldn't be so nosy."

First his bank balance, and now I was prying into the details of his sister's death.

"I'm merely surprised he told you. He can be quite…secretive," she said, choosing the final word carefully. "Most vampires carefully guard their private lives."

"And Julian?" I asked, even though I felt I knew the answer.

"He's built a fortress around it," she whispered, passing me some socks. "No one gets inside."

"How did I?" I realized too late that I'd asked the question out loud.

"I hate to tell you this, but I suspect you're only at the gates." She *tsked* soothingly when my face fell. "Don't fret. It's further than he lets most people get."

I sat down and pulled on the socks. Why had he shared any of this with me? No wonder she'd looked surprised. Unlike the others, Celia had to know that this was all an arrangement. She knew he and I were practically strangers.

"Thank you," I said.

"For?"

"Being kind," I said with a sigh. "I don't think I'm going to get a very warm welcome from everyone else."

"Sebastian liked you. Or he likes not being the one in trouble for once," Celia said with a small smile. "Not everyone in this house is your enemy." She regarded me with a look I couldn't quite place. Then she bent and gathered my dress in her arms. "I'll have this cleaned for you."

I nodded. She left again, and I made my way back to my crossword, but I found myself too preoccupied to continue it. I'd been staring at it for five minutes when her words finally sank in. Not *everyone* was my enemy. That meant some were, and I was sitting alone and unprotected. I curled my knees to my chest and wrapped my arms around them.

Would the next vampire to walk through the door be a friend or an enemy?

CHAPTER TWENTY-SEVEN

Julian

I hadn't seen her move. Perhaps because I hadn't expected it. My mother hadn't been so riled up since her days as a suffragette. I blinked, straining to see the silver glinting at my neck. My eyes flickered back to her. In the dimness of morning, her dilated pupils were boundless black. Yeah, I'd pissed her off all right.

If someone walked into the room, they might mistake the scene. Sabine, though much taller than most women from antiquity thanks to her vampire genes, stood a good foot below my massive frame. If she were a human woman, I could simply overpower her and confiscate the sword. But she was a vampire, and an angry vampire mother could decimate an entire city within the blink of an eye. Physically, she was as strong as I was, and she'd seen even more battlefields than me. More than one vampire female had brought me to my knees in my lifetime, but it had been centuries since my own mother had.

A slit throat wouldn't kill me, and no doubt, she would love to put me out of commission long enough to see to Thea herself. That I couldn't allow. I opened my mouth carefully so as not to jostle the blade, which despite its years was still *quite sharp*.

Sabine hissed in warning.

"You will listen to me now. If you are past the point where reason will suffice, I will physically persuade you," she said. Despite the anger seething from her, the sword didn't move a fraction of an inch.

"Never spare the rod, my darling," an amused but familiar voice boomed from the doorway.

I didn't dare crane my neck. I hoped the unexpected entrance of my father would distract her.

But her gaze, and her weapon, remained resolutely on her wayward son. "Nothing a mother cannot handle. Welcome home, my love. I wasn't expecting you."

It could have been two weeks or two years since he'd been here. I never asked about such private matters. My parents' marriage was best described as volcanic. One always seemed to know when the other was on the verge of eruption and left until the ashes settled. As vampire marriage lasted longer than mortal unions, it was a matter of survival. Lesser unions had ended in bloodshed and beheadings. But as the sires of one of the oldest and wealthiest vampire bloodlines, they were committed to making it work. So far, they'd only gone to war with each other once, a couple hundred years ago. Most of the family had survived. A lot of humans hadn't.

"Do I smell breakfast?" Dominic Rousseaux moved into view, tossing a worn leather jacket on the settee. I had a vivid memory of him doing the same with a battle-worn cloak once when I was little, and getting blood on the upholstery. Mom's eyes narrowed as if she was sharing the same recollection.

I wasn't quite sure what year my father was born. He'd never been particularly open about his life before he became a vampire. It was an unspoken rule amongst the original vampires not to speak of their lives before they changed. Some people believed they didn't remember their human lives or how they came to be the first of our kind. I just assumed it was probably a lot to keep track of. I didn't remember half of my time and I was their child.

But Dominic looked like the statues of warriors from the ancient world. No one would ever mistake his towering, brutal figure for human. He looked as if he'd been hewn from marble—a larger-than-life statue, cut to mythic proportions.

"Hey, Dad," I said stiffly. "A little help?"

But he knew better than to take anyone's side—even his own son's—over his wife's.

"Your son brought home a woman," she told him.

"That was thoughtful," he said, looking between us. "I'm starving."

A rumble tore through my chest and free of my throat before I could stop it. The vibration from it bumped the blade, nicking my skin, but I didn't care. Something snapped inside me, and I knew. Mother or not—vampire or not—I would kill the woman holding me, and her husband, before anyone laid so much as their eyes on Thea.

"He's also in thrall," she added.

"So I see." Dominic joined us, flanking my other side as he took measure of the situation.

"I am not in thrall," I bit out, wondering if it would be easier to fight them both than continue this insane conversation. "Thea is human. She had no power to place me under her spell."

But hadn't she somehow done it anyway?

"I could hear her blood-song from the front drive," my father said softly. "Even I wouldn't be able to free myself from that *cantatio*. There's no shame in it. It happens to all of us from time to time. Some humans are more tempting than others. Perhaps your mother should see to this problem of yours."

It was as if the words had sucked all the air from my lungs and replaced it with molten rage. Instinct took hold of me. Blood pounded inside me, and I stopped hearing anything they said. Something primitive drove me: the urge to fight.

To protect.

I swung my hand up, catching the blade, and wrenched it from Sabine. I flipped it into my uninjured right hand and brandished the now rust-stained sword. The choice—the movement—was lightning fast even for me. It was though some new, deeper instinct had overtaken me.

"If you please." I took a step toward the door that led to the stairs, positioning myself between my parents and the bedroom where Thea slept. I felt better instantly. Neither of them could get past me without testing just how far I would take this. I hoped neither of them would try their luck. "I can explain."

"This should be interesting," Sabine said drily, glaring at her empty hands.

I motioned for them to sit. It didn't escape my notice that they took seats on opposite sides of the room. They had been married for thousands of years and shared the unspoken language of lovers, so I had to tread carefully.

The sky outside began to lighten ominously. A crack of neon orange spilled daylight on the horizon. Thea would wake soon, and I needed them to be on their best behavior. Or it was time to get her the fuck out of here. Either way, it would be a lot easier to see her home safely if my parents didn't take up arms.

"Just listen." I didn't hide the exhaustion I felt. The throbbing of my wounded hand now mirrored that of my head, making it even more difficult to ignore the urge I felt to return to where I'd left Thea. "I'm not in thrall. It is so much worse."

Before I could continue, Sebastian walked into the room, scratching his head and blinking blearily. "What the hell is going on? You scared off my friends."

"The party ended hours ago," Sabine snapped. Clearly, she was out of patience with all her children this morning already, and it was only dawn.

"Sorry!" He held his hands up in surrender as he dropped into a chair by the fire. He nodded to our father. "Continue with the family meeting."

"This isn't a meeting." I was getting more irritated by the minute. I hadn't expected to leave Thea alone this long. I'd kept her up late enough she was probably still sleeping, but each second that passed increased the uneasy feeling in my chest.

"Your brother is about to explain why he's ignoring The Rites and bedding a mortal instead." Sabine's smile could kill a man.

Sebastian looked from her to our dad and then to me. "Well, don't let me interrupt."

I shot him a look. So much for taking my side.

"It's bloodlust," I explained. I recounted what had happened with Bellamy during the party. "I nearly lost control. I can't even remember the last time I had bloodlust that badly."

"You have been asleep for a while..." Sebastian chuckled as if the idea of his older brother failing to control his sexual appetite amused him. Considering he slept with half the warm bodies he met, I imagined it was a foreign concept to him.

"I thought she was your girlfriend," Sabine said wanly.

"She is," I confirmed. That was the arrangement. "We hadn't gone to bed yet."

"And now that is taken care of," she said, "so it's time for you to think about marriage."

I'd expected her to say that. "I am thinking about marriage."

Sabine got within an inch of me—a new sword produced out of seemingly nowhere—before my father caught her around the waist and held her back.

"You are a full-blooded Rousseaux—the heir to this family!" She continued to brandish her sword. "If you think that you can marry some random human just because she's pretty—"

"Darling," Dominic interrupted her in a soothing voice. "Perhaps we should discuss this when we're all calmer."

"I am calm!" she shrieked, kicking him in the shin.

"You're holding a sword," Sebastian offered in a helpful tone.

She glared at him and turned the sword in his direction. "It's your turn next."

"Fine." He shrugged. "It hardly matters. And then it will be Lysander's and on down the line," he said, referring to our brothers.

There was a resignation in his voice that I'd never heard before, but now wasn't the time to discuss it.

"You didn't come all the way home to pass judgment on a female," I said to my father.

His head tilted, blue eyes growing wary. "Someone infiltrated the house last night."

"It can't be the first time someone crashed a party, Mom." Sebastian laughed.

But neither of my parents joined him. "This is a serious matter. That vampire wasn't acting alone."

My frustrations over Thea faded a little. "What? There were more?"

"Not last night." Sabine's mouth flattened into a grim line. "But that mask—that mark—there have been other incidents, always started by a vampire sporting that red slash."

"Who are they?" Sebastian asked, suddenly serious.

"We don't know," our father admitted. "There's some evidence that it's a radical group of turned vampires."

"Radical?"

"They don't want to play by the Vampire Council's rules," Sabine added.

There were plenty of vampires who would agree with them, myself included. But if my father had come all the way home, it had to be more serious than they were letting on. I thought of Thea sleeping upstairs. I'd left her unguarded. "Are they a threat?"

"It remains to be seen," she said coolly. "But we will be stepping up our security. I plan to speak with the Council and encourage them to do the same. I'm sure whoever these brutes are, they'd love to ruin our social season."

She wasn't answering my questions. It was clear she knew more than she was admitting. But my parents had always kept secrets. From us. From each other. Vampires were naturally secretive in nature. Usually. Maybe that's why I'd found Thea so intoxicating. For some reason, I felt I could open up to her.

"Why don't you check in on your girlfriend?" my father suggested. "Sebastian, make sure there are no lingering guests." We'd been given our marching orders. He dismissed us with a wave, turning to Sabine and beginning to murmur to her in low tones.

No one could calm Sabine down better than our father. It was a skill he'd perfected over the centuries, after usually being the one to piss her off. He kept his hold on her until we were out the door.

"Do you know anything about this?" I asked Sebastian as we left.

"Not really. There are rumors, but if they just crash parties, they seem harmless to me."

I hoped he was right.

"You aren't seriously thinking about marriage," Sebastian remarked as we made our way down the corridor. "You can't have known her more than a few days."

"Two," I told him. "And no, I'm not thinking about marrying her. I just don't want to spend the next year parading around like a peacock to secure some new family alliance. I haven't been married in nine hundred years. Why would I agree to take a wife to please the Council?"

"Maybe it's time," Sebastian said, to my surprise. "I mean, nine hundred years is a long time to be a bachelor."

"I'll remind you of that on your birthday in seventy-five years," I said drily.

"I've been married. That one time in Vegas."

"I don't think a twenty-four-hour fling with a stranger counts."

"The Council has admittedly higher expectations," he said with a grin, but it quickly fell from his face. "Not that it matters."

It was the second time he'd said it. It wasn't like my brother to be gloomy, especially after an orgy. "Not looking forward to your turn?"

"I don't care." He shrugged his broad shoulders. "Honestly. It's just as easy for me to find someone with similar sensibilities—"

"Meaning someone who also wants to screw other people?" I guessed.

He nodded. "It's just a political arrangement. Why do you care?"

There were things he didn't know about Camila and her arranged marriage. Things I'd promised never to tell him. Even now, decades after her death, my blood-vow prevented me from telling him the truth. "I like Thea."

"That I understand. She smells sweet, but how does she taste?" he asked.

I went rigid, and darkness crept along the edges of my vision. Sebastian stepped away quickly. "Forget I asked, brother. It was curiosity. I didn't realize..."

"It's just bloodlust," I said through gritted teeth, forcing myself to push it down. My plan to take Thea home immediately had just gotten delayed by half an hour because of his careless remark. Now I needed to satisfy myself again.

It would be easier if Thea wasn't a virgin. As it was, it seemed my bloodlust would continue until I figured out how to disentangle myself from her.

Sebastian laughed, already heading down the corridor. "Keep telling yourself that, brother."

CHAPTER TWENTY-EIGHT

Thea

I lingered in Julian's room, feeling increasingly silly as the seconds ticked by. I didn't particularly like feeling trapped like a hotel guest; however, not wandering around a house of horny vampires felt like a pretty solid strategy. But the longer Julian stayed away, the harder it was to ignore a new awareness. I woke up feeling like a sex goddess, even if things hadn't gone that far. Now I couldn't help but feel hurt by his absence.

Had I been ghosted? By a vampire?

Surely he would have told Celia to have me leave.

After another twenty minutes, hurt transformed into indignation. Maybe he had all the time in the world—he was immortal and could afford decades-long naps, after all—but I didn't. If he had gotten what he wanted from me, he could be man enough to say it to my face.

I opened the door and walked straight into him.

"Where are you going?" he asked harshly.

"I was looking for you." I crossed my arms over my chest and raised my chin to show just how unimpressed I was with being left to wake up alone. Considering he was practically twice my size, I doubted he noticed.

"You found me. Come on." He strode into his room without so much as a second glance. He called over his shoulder. "Are you coming?"

Julian Rousseaux wasn't just a grouch in the morning; he was a total asshole.

Fine. I would go back into his room, but only so I could tell him off. I walked inside and slammed the door behind me.

Julian pivoted, one eyebrow raised. "Something bothering you, pet?"

"You!" I exploded. "First, I wake up alone, which is no big deal. I don't even know if vampires sleep. Or maybe you needed to find a coffin or something. But then, you just leave me up here forever with no clothes or explanation. And after all that, you come up here and practically order me back into your room. If you think this is how our arrangement is going to work, then allow me to clear a few things up."

Julian's eyebrow smoothed back into its usual position, but he said nothing.

"Well," I prompted, "aren't you going to say anything?"

"I was waiting for you to clear things up," he said, shrugging his shoulders. It was only then that I noticed his eyes were darker than usual. Crap on a cracker. Had I just pissed off a vampire in a blood rage? Even in my feverish state last night I'd seen enough to know that any mistake might be the last I ever made.

He continued to wait, his eyes growing darker with each second of silence that passed between us. That left me with two problems. Something was definitely wrong with Julian, and I didn't actually know how to clear things up. I knew what I was mad about. That part was pretty damn clear. I just wasn't sure that making demands of him was the best idea, especially right now.

I decided to switch tactics. "Where were you?"

"I assume Celia told you I was speaking with my parents." He didn't move. At all. It was like a statue had spoken and then returned to its solid form.

"Yes, I mean, she said you were talking to your mother."

"My father arrived this morning."

Now I was beginning to feel a little silly, but that didn't change certain facts.

"What are you really upset about?" he guessed when I remained silent.

"It's just..." I screwed up my courage and decided to let it all out. We were keeping enough secrets with our arrangement. We didn't need to keep them from each other. "I didn't expect to wake up alone."

There was a pause. Julian remained eerily still. He'd never looked more like a vampire to me than now, and I'd seen him attack more than one vampire. Then, he'd looked like a warrior. Now? He wasn't breathing. There was no sign of movement, but somehow, a brutal energy radiated from him. He finally blinked, but the darkness in his eyes remained. "I apologize. It was thoughtless. I hadn't expected to be away so long."

I swallowed his apology and finally nodded. "Is everything okay? With your family?"

"I think it's best if you steer clear of my mother," he said with a laugh that sounded less than amused.

I thought of what Celia had said earlier about not everyone in the house being my enemy. Maybe it was time to start making a list of whom I *should* avoid. "And your father?"

"I won't know until he meets you."

My heart dropped into my stomach, but I forced a quiet, "Okay."

"But he's not meeting you today," he said to my relief. "I need to get you home." He stopped and studied me for a minute. "Where did you get those clothes?"

"Celia," I said nervously.

"Of course." He managed a tight smile. "She's better at being considerate than I am."

"She's nice," I agreed, earning a chuckle I didn't quite understand. "I can be ready to go in a minute." I looked around the room, trying to remember what I'd done with the small purse I'd been carrying yesterday. By now, my cell phone had to be dead. Panic began to set in when I realized I'd failed to text Olivia. She was probably freaking out, and if she was freaking out, she might have called my mother and—

"Wait," he interrupted the runaway train of thoughts in my head. "I'd like to give you a proper good morning."

"A proper what?" I asked in confusion. He gave me a meaningful look that turned my core into molten lava. Suddenly my arousal and my anxiety were dancing around each other. I had no idea which would win. "Oh. I mean, that's not...I..."

"That's not what, pet?"

"You don't have to. I'm not mad anymore," I said quickly.

His jaw clenched, and he turned away from me. When he finally looked back, his eyes were the color of midnight.

"Oh!" I took a step away.

"I'm going to have to insist." His teeth remained clenched together as he spoke, and I couldn't help noticing that his fangs had lengthened.

It was what had happened last night, but this time I had no idea what had set it off. That's why he'd been so annoyed when he came into the room. Was he going to do this every time I saw him? That would get old fast unless he followed it up the way he had last night.

I bit my lip, torn between needing to check in with my friend and wanting him to erase all thoughts of anyone but him from my mind.

"It's very hard to resist you when you do that," he seethed.

"Huh?" I asked, and he relaxed a bit as I released my lip. *Oh, that.* He took a step closer, but I held up a hand to stop him. "Is this...normal? The bloodlust, I mean?"

He shook his head.

Somehow I already knew that. "Is there something I can do to help?" It was hard to even ask, because part of me selfishly wanted to keep him in this primal state, where he cared only about pleasuring me. But underneath the predator, I sensed pain. It wasn't just something he couldn't control. Staying in this state was hurting him.

"Only three things can sate bloodlust," he said in a strained voice.

I'd been thoroughly introduced to the first method last night, but I wouldn't mind a refresher. "Do whatever you need." I cleared my throat, trying to sound less emotional about the idea of offering myself to him completely. "I'm yours."

"That's a dangerous invitation to give a vampire," he growled.

"What will it take?" I asked, edging closer to him. "To make you feel better?"

He shook his head, but as soon as I was within reach, his hand shot out and grabbed my sweater. Drawing me closer, he pulled me roughly against him. With one swift motion, Julian lifted me from my feet and carried me to a chair. I felt a flash of disappointment he didn't take me back to his bed, but he quickly distracted me. Sinking into the seat, I found myself straddling him. If there was any doubt this was bloodlust, the rock-hard erection pressing into me erased it. A strong hand wrapped around my neck and guided my lips to his.

The kiss was full of a hunger so achingly deep it made my soul hurt. I couldn't kiss him hard enough or deep enough to satisfy the need I felt. Was this what he was fighting? Did he want me this badly? Could humans experience bloodlust, too?

He continued to explore my mouth even as his hands crept under the cashmere covering my breasts and found my nipples. I moaned into his mouth as he began to massage them. He did it gently at first. Then his touch became rougher until I was gasping with pleasure. He twisted and played with the sensitive buds, earning me jolts of pleasure that suggested there was so much more to come.

Julian pulled away and yanked the sweater over my head. Tossing it to the ground, he bent and took my left breast in his mouth. His tongue flickered possessively over the hardened tip, and I felt myself spiraling inward. When he dragged a fang across my tortured skin, I found myself bucking against the hard bulge in his pants.

"That's right," he coaxed as I ground against him. "Show me

how beautiful you are when you come, pet."

A strangled cry escaped my lips, but I didn't stop. I couldn't. He returned to worshipping my breasts, and I felt my release build. If it was like this with most of our clothes still on, how much better would it be if he were *inside* me? I knew he'd refuse to sleep with me, but I couldn't deny how much I wanted it—how much I wanted him.

"Don't stop," I urged him as he moved to pleasure the other one. He clamped his mouth over its peak and sucked so hard that I felt his fangs needling my skin.

"Come for me, pet," he ordered, grabbing hold of my hair and jerking my head back to extend my neck. His lips moved up and hovered over the exposed flesh.

Without thinking, I asked for the only thing that could make this moment better. The only thing I wanted more than this. "Julian, bite me."

CHAPTER TWENTY-NINE

Julian

"*Julian, bite me.*"

I didn't think twice. I plunged my fangs into her neck, ready to savor blood that had called to me since the moment I saw Thea. It spilled hot and fast over my tongue, but I tasted nothing. The promise of her *cantatio*—her blood-song—remained unfulfilled. I drank harder, desperate to sate the gnawing hunger inside me. And then she went limp in my arms.

No!

I snapped myself out of the fantasy just as my fangs extended, nearly nicking the delicate skin of her throat. It took every last ounce of my self-control to stop myself from fulfilling her request and dooming us both. Instead, I stood up, dumping Thea onto the floor in the process.

"What the—" She stared up at me, reaching to rub her backside.

I wanted to kneel down to check on her, but I resisted the urge.

"I warned you never to offer a vampire your blood," I said through gritted teeth.

"I didn't think that after last night..." She trailed off. There were tears in her voice, and I couldn't resist looking down to see how badly I'd hurt her feelings.

I didn't find rejection on Thea's face. I found defiance. She glared at me, lifting her chin as though to prove that she was offended, not hurt. But I'd heard the pain in her voice. I knew the truth. She was hurt, and she refused to show it. I found myself impressed with my little pet. Still, I couldn't reward her for putting her neck on the line. Literally.

"I won't drink your blood," I said firmly.

She opened her mouth and shut it again quickly. Finally, she spoke. "But it would help, wouldn't it? You said there were other ways to sate your bloodlust."

I ignored her and walked across the room to find the stupid, tiny phone Sebastian had given me. It was on the nightstand.

"Wouldn't it?" she repeated, refusing to be so easily dismissed. She got to her feet and moved to the other side of the bed.

It took me a moment to remember how to send a text message. I sent one to Celia before turning my attention back to her. "What would you like me to tell you?"

"The truth, for starters." She crossed her arms, looking so adorably put out that I felt myself beginning to calm down. "*Would it help?*"

I closed my eyes, searching for the correct lie, but I couldn't bring myself to be dishonest with her. Was this another one of her weird tricks? First, I couldn't compel her, and now I struggled to answer her questions? "Yes," I muttered when I failed to come up with an excuse. "It would help."

"And I'm willing," she said, her voice thick. She cleared her throat and recommitted to her offer. "You can feed on me. I want you to."

One honest answer would stop this, but it would have consequences. It was the only answer I could find that would keep her safe. However, I seemed to be out of choices. "Has it occurred to you," I seethed, "that I don't want to feed on you?"

Thea's shoulders slumped, but she fought to hold her ground. "You *won't* feed on me!"

"I don't...want...to!" I roared.

She cringed away, beginning to shake. This time she couldn't hold back her tears. She reached up and wiped them away. "You don't mean that."

But she no longer sounded sure of herself.

Mission accomplished, but the victory was hollow. I'd made her doubt how much I wanted to feed from her. I couldn't risk explaining more to her without revealing that I didn't want to feed on her because I knew I would never be able to stop. One taste would never be enough. I heard her blood singing, and I'd lived too long to pretend I'd be able to control myself once I started. It would end just as my fantasy had. And I would never forgive myself if I killed her.

"I've been here for over ten of your human lifetimes," I continued coldly. "Do you think one night with a mortal woman is enough to make her irresistible to me?"

It was the question I was asking myself. It didn't make sense. But bloodlust rarely made sense. That was why I couldn't give in to it. I wouldn't be a slave to the vampire inside me. Not now. Not after all this time.

Her lower lip trembled, but Thea was strong. She would move past this, and if she didn't, it might be better for both of us in the end. My mother had made it clear I would not get out of finding and marrying a wife this year. So how could I use Thea like that? Keeping her wouldn't just be selfish. It would be foolish. How many more times would she offer her veins to me? Perhaps it was best if I ended this now.

Thea did it first. "Fuck you, Julian."

I didn't go after her as she walked out my bedroom door. It slammed shut behind her, and I stayed by the nightstand, holding my phone. It buzzed with some type of bloody alert, but I didn't dare look down at the screen. I wanted to go after her. I couldn't risk even the slightest movement. Not until she was gone.

Minutes ticked by, and finally, Celia found me still standing next to the bed.

"Julian," she said my name carefully. "I got your text."

I didn't dare blink, but I allowed myself to ask her, "Is Thea gone?"

"I put her in a car as you requested," she said. "The driver will see her home."

"Is the driver a vampire?" I asked through a clenched jaw.

"He's human. In thrall to one of Sebastian's men," she said. "She'll be completely safe."

I relaxed, feeling the weight of self-control slip off my shoulders. But while there was physical relief, the desire remained.

"Can I get you anything?" Celia asked. We'd been together long enough for her to know when something was wrong. It had to be obvious now.

"Blood," I gritted out, "from the vein."

She lifted one silver eyebrow but made no comment. "Give me a few moments."

Celia disappeared to call one of the family's *cortège*. Like most of the older lines of vampires, we kept a collection of humans who volunteered to serve as walking blood donors. They received help or protection, and we always had fresh blood. Willing humans could always be found. I wasn't a fan of the practice, but sometimes circumstances called for unwanted solutions.

A half hour later, she ushered a petite brunette into the room. The woman was young and stood only a few inches taller than Thea. Her features were delicate and pale, as well. She was pretty, even, but not as beautiful as Thea. My eyes flashed angrily to Celia. I knew what my assistant was up to.

"I thought perhaps you might need the other kind of satisfaction." Her face remained composed, as if to point out that—unlike me—she was in control. "She's willing to see to *all* of your needs."

The woman watched me with wide eyes from across the room. They skirted over my frame as if trying to decide if she'd made a mistake. But then her tongue darted over her lower lip. She dropped into a curtsy. "I am at your service, Lord Rousseaux."

I groaned and rolled my eyes, shooting another barbed look at Celia. "Did you tell her to say that?"

"That is how Lord Sebastian likes to be addressed when we..." She flushed, her cheeks turning a promising shade of red.

"I am not Lord Rousseaux," I corrected her. I beckoned her to straighten up.

She did, blinking at me in confusion. "But you are the eldest son, which means you are next in line to be head of the family."

All of these things were true. I just wasn't sure why a member of our *cortège* knew so much about the inner workings of vampire politics. And right now, I didn't care. "You can go," I said to Celia. I would speak with her later about her suggestion.

She tilted her head, saying nothing as she left.

I circled the brunette. She swallowed and reached for the buttons of her shirt.

"What are you doing?" I asked her.

She paused. "Getting undressed."

"That's unnecessary," I said drily. Even without feeding, my bloodlust had ebbed away. Only hunger lingered. I wagged a finger at her. Slipping off one of my gloves, I held my other hand out. She placed her own in my palm, wrist up. At least she was well-trained.

"You may use your fangs," she said as I brushed my index finger over her wrist. "Anywhere you would like."

At another time the offer might have tempted me, but she was only a means to an end.

"I am not as perverse as my brother," I said in a low voice. "This will suffice." I drew my finger over her vein, and it sliced cleanly open. Lifting it to my mouth, I drank for a moment. Her blood tasted like ash on my tongue, and I resisted the urge to spit it out. I swallowed, but only so I didn't hurt her feelings. I wouldn't wreck two women's days in one morning. Biting my bare finger, I drew a drop of my own blood and wiped it across her wound. The bleeding stopped instantly, and she sighed with pleasure as the venom-tinged blood found its way into her system.

But the venom had other effects. She moved closer to me, batting her lashes. "I will go to bed with you."

"No, thanks."

Her mouth fell open. She shut it quickly and regained her composure. "I know what to expect, and I want—"

"No," I said with deadly finality. "Thank you. You're dismissed."

She huffed out of the room, still cradling her healed wrist. I hardly cared what she thought of me. There was a reason why I never called upon the *cortège*. They had a tendency to get excessively generous with the wealthier patrons. But I wasn't interested in anything she had. Even her blood had failed to please me. But her blood had cleared my head enough for me to see what I had done.

I hadn't wanted to feed. I'd wanted to feed *from Thea*. Nothing else would satisfy me. Some part of me had known, had lashed out before I could make that mistake. Because if last night had taught me anything, it was that one taste of Thea would never be enough. And while I might not have had her blood or her body, I'd tasted enough of her to be ruined for anyone else.

No, not ruined. That was the unsated bloodlust talking.

Would I ever be satisfied without having her? Could I even stay away with her lingering in my thoughts?

Without thinking, I found my keys and phone and rushed toward the garage. One of my old cars had to be down there still. I'd swipe one of my brother's if I had to. Nothing would stop me from what had to be done now. It was my only option. Something I hadn't done in my entire nine hundred years on this planet.

I had to beg Thea to forgive me.

CHAPTER THIRTY

Thea

The Rousseaux family driver delivered me to my apartment with a few polite words but little conversation. Considering I didn't trust myself *not* to burst into tears if he asked how I was doing, I was grateful.

I climbed the stairs up to my flat and paused at the door. I couldn't stomach the thought of facing my roommates. Yesterday, Olivia had polished and painted me into a goddess for my first official date with Julian. Since I hadn't come home from that date, she was likely waiting inside to ambush and demand details.

Only an hour ago, I would have giddily told her all about the night, leaving out the vampires, of course. Which meant leaving out *a lot*, come to think of it. But now? Now I didn't want to think about it ever again.

I didn't want to think about *him* ever again.

And the worst part was that I was probably just another broken heart in a string of broken hearts dating back nearly a millennium. All the things Julian had seen, the history he had lived, the women he'd gone to bed with, I was little more than a blip on his timeline. He'd probably already forgotten about me and was busy getting ready for tonight's debaucheries.

It felt like an invisible hand was squeezing my chest, and any minute now, I would break. I took my house key out and slipped it into the lock. If I was going to break down, I wouldn't do it in the hallway. I had a scrap of pride left.

I held my breath as I opened the door, but it was quiet and dark. Olivia was already gone to the studio or classes, and Tanner must be asleep or out. The universe had granted me this one small mercy. I didn't have to surrender the last bit of dignity that I had explaining how spectacularly stupid I'd been.

Of course he didn't want me.

We barely knew each other, and it wasn't like I had a lot to offer, no matter how much he liked how I played the cello.

Cello. The word struck me like a thorn, puncturing through my rationalizations. He'd given me a half-million-dollar cello. How did I explain it to people?

Far more worryingly, what was I supposed to *do* with it?

I stomped into the living room and found it waiting in its case. He'd been the one to reject me, which meant I was pretty sure it was mine to keep. But I wouldn't: I'd sell the damn thing, use a little money from the sale to buy a decent cello to replace mine, and send the rest of it back to his filthy rich family in a huge envelope. An envelope filled with glitter.

The best revenge.

I smiled, thinking of what Sabine would think about getting glitter-bombed. Maybe it wasn't the most mature plan—and I'd probably chicken out—but for now, it was enough to relieve the raw ache in my throat.

Picking up the case and wondering exactly how to go about selling an item of this kind of value, I couldn't resist the urge. Yesterday I had only been able to look at the magnificent instrument in reverent silence; now I took out the cello, along with the bow, and settled onto a kitchen stool I used for practicing.

The instrument was exquisite. Knowing that my time with it was short, I let myself run my hands up and down the surface, appreciating its craftsmanship. It was the sexiest thing I'd ever had between my thighs, except maybe—

"Don't think about him," I ordered myself, wiping a renegade tear from my cheek with the back of my hand. "Just play."

Music was my escape. It was there when I was little, and Mom was barely keeping food on the table. It was there when I didn't fit in during my high school years. It was there when Mom was so sick the doctors had told me to prepare myself.

Nothing could touch me while I played. I could play the notes of a seventeenth-century genius in my twenty-first-century apartment. Music was timeless. It was boundless. When the cello was at my fingertips, I was free.

I found myself playing the Schubert from the cocktail party the other night. I'd played this a million times before, but now the piece had a whole new meaning. Without the other instruments to support my part, it felt hollow, as though it was searching for its soul. The lonely notes I played chilled me to the core, but I couldn't stop. I doubted Schubert had written it about a vampire. Then again, maybe he had. The music felt like it belonged to me. I was the maiden, and now I knew the darkness of death. I tried to run from it. But darkness had played with me, coaxed me into trusting it. I had let it touch me.

I wasn't sure I would ever be the same. I wasn't certain I wanted to be.

I didn't realize I was crying until I reached the final notes. It seemed I had finally found something music couldn't help me escape.

Him.

I lingered with the Grancino. Some selfish part of me wanted to keep it. It was all I had to prove I hadn't imagined his dark touch. It was all I had to prove that—for a moment—I had belonged to Julian Rousseaux.

It was a depressing enough thought to snap me out of the melancholy the music inspired. I stood up and put the cello resolutely back in its fancy purple case. I could say I'd played it. That was enough.

Determined to gather up the broken pieces of my last two days and put it all back together, I found my charger and plugged in my phone. It flashed a battery warning symbol, and I left it to charge while I went to shower. Our bathroom was cramped and perpetually cluttered with Olivia's tights and Tanner's hair crap, but it had one spectacular feature. Good water pressure.

I stripped off Camila's clothes, wondering if I should just throw them away. In the end, I left them in a ball in the corner. Olivia would never forgive me for tossing vintage cashmere. She could have it. Stepping into the shower, I turned the heat up until the water practically singed me. I stood under it, willing it to wash away all the insane choices I had made since I'd stumbled across Julian. When that didn't work, I found a bar of soap and a loofah and tried to scrub him away. In the end, my skin was pink and tender. But he wasn't quite gone. I turned off the water and reached for a towel.

Someone was knocking on the door. No, *banging*.

It sounded like the door was going to be knocked off its hinges. There were only two explanations for it. The first was that someone was breaking down the door with a battering ram. The other...

"Crap on a cracker," I muttered to myself.

I wrapped the towel tightly around me and cracked open the bathroom door at the same time Tanner poked his head out of his room. He rubbed his eyes, blinking at me through the steam escaping around me.

"What the hell is that?" he mumbled.

"My boyfriend," I muttered.

"Am I still asleep?" Tanner asked, blinking rapidly. "Did you say *boyfriend*?"

Now was not the time to try to explain my insane relationship with Julian. I grabbed Tanner's doorknob. "Go back to bed. I've got this."

"You sure?" He looked toward the door, his face growing concerned. "He sounds a little intense. Is this that guy who sent you the cello? Do you need me to make him go away?"

"He's just excitable," I promised. I loved Tanner for caring enough to step in, which was why it made it so hard for me to lie to him now. But it wasn't exactly like I could tell him the truth. We got into a fight when Julian wouldn't drink my blood and broke up after knowing each other, like, five minutes. This was clearly a case where telling a white lie was for the best. "My phone was charging. He probably tried to call. He's worried the building isn't safe."

"That's right." Tanner yawned. "He's rich. I bet he thinks this is a slum."

I forced a smile and shut the bedroom door before he could keep asking questions.

As I padded into the living room, I realized the door hinges were actually rattling. I started to unlock the door, and the pounding stopped.

"Thea?" Julian's panic-stricken voice boomed from the other side.

Like all smart city dwellers, we had multiple locks. I finished turning them but kept the chain in place.

Julian exhaled heavily when I peeked at him through the crack. His blue eyes blazed with an intensity that sent my stomach into somersaults. "You scared the shit out of me," he said. "You didn't answer your phone, and no one came to the door."

"I was in the shower," I said, doing my best to sound cold and angry. That was pretty hard as my body realized there was only a door and a towel between me and an overbearing vampire. Thank God I'd decided to keep the chain in place.

"Let me come in and explain."

"I think that's a bad idea." No, it wasn't a bad idea. It was a terrible idea.

"Thea, it's not what you think."

"Are you sure? Because I think you want me to be your girlfriend, but you seem to think you can make up arbitrary rules about how that will work," I hissed in a low whisper. "And I think your family hates me, but you expect me to take your arm and pretend that this is a real relationship to get you out of some stupid arranged marriage."

"Maybe it *is* what you think," he admitted with a groan.

"Good. I'm not done. You think I'm fine for a blow job but *not* to feed from!"

His eyes closed as he took a deep breath. "Keep the door chained."

"Thanks, I will."

"Until I get this out," he continued in a sharp tone. He paused for a moment and locked eyes with mine. "I *want* to feed on you."

"But—"

"I *refuse* to feed on you, Thea," he cut me off. "That's not the relationship I want to have with you."

"But I saw what vampire relationships looked like last night. It's pretty normal to feed off the mortal half."

"During The Rites, it is common to feed off familiars," he said in a strained voice. "But I don't want any part of The Rites."

I didn't have a comeback. He'd made himself clear in that regard from the beginning.

"So you don't need blood?" I eventually asked.

"I *do* need blood."

"Where do you get it?"

"From voluntary donors who serve our family. Blood banks we established in the city. Sometimes I hunt."

I swallowed as I processed the word. "Hunt what? Deer?"

"You've been reading too many books, pet. I hunt humans, but I promise I only drink from ones who deserve it," he added.

I didn't know how to feel about that. Rational, thoughtful Thea knew it was barbaric. But this strange, new Thea had agreed to his arrangements. The part of me that had found pleasure—in his arms, on his mouth and tongue—thrilled to know he was every bit as dangerous as I fantasized.

I couldn't give in to that part of me. No matter how much I wanted to. "Okay, just give me one good reason you won't feed off me."

"Because I respect you," he answered without hesitation.

Damn. That was a really good answer. Not what I'd been expecting. Not even a little bit. And it didn't mean we were done having this conversation, but at least I understood. Kinda.

I shut the door in his face for the second time since we'd met, but only so I could unfasten the chain. I opened it to find him standing in the doorway. His strong hands—hands I knew were capable of violence and pleasure in equal measures—braced each side of the frame. He lifted his head. "Does this mean I'm forgiven?"

"I haven't decided," I said softly.

His eyes raked down my body, and I remembered I was standing in nothing more than a towel.

"I should change—" I only got halfway through my plan when he scooped me off my feet and slung me over his shoulder.

"What are you doing?" I demanded as he carried me inside, slamming the front door behind us.

"Helping you decide, pet." Then he carried me into my room and threw me onto the bed.

CHAPTER THIRTY-ONE

Julian

There was barely room to move in her bedroom. But I only needed the bed. I dropped her onto it, and her towel fell open in the process, treating me to a glimpse of the body that had occupied my every waking thought since the moment we'd met. A primal instinct rose, seeping out in a low growl.

Thea's eyes widened, and she tugged the towel back around her to cover up.

"Don't," I said as I reached to unbutton my shirt. "I want to see you, pet."

Her hands continued to clutch the towel, but she nibbled on her lower lip. "I haven't forgiven you yet, remember?"

"Then let me apologize." I shrugged out of my shirt and let it fall to the floor. Her gaze swept down me appreciatively, causing another surge of feral desire to swell within me, barreling straight down to my dick. Thea's eyes paused on the fly of my trousers. The longer she looked at my erection, the harder I got. Which was precisely why my pants had to stay on.

She seemed to know what I was thinking. "Why am I the only one expected to get naked?"

"Because," I said, sinking to my knees at the edge of her bed,

"I'm here to apologize to you."

"You don't need me naked for that." She wasn't going to make this easy.

I placed a hand on each of her knees, feeling the warmth of her skin through my calfskin driving gloves. "I'm sorry," I said in a low voice, earning a shiver from her. "I never intended to make you feel unwanted."

Thea remained quiet for a moment before she nodded. Her eyes were bright, shining with unshed tears, and I knew just how spectacularly I'd fucked up before. We needed to talk. I needed to re-establish some important boundaries, even if it meant revealing vampire secrets I was sworn never to discuss. I wouldn't hurt her again—especially not to protect old laws.

"I'm sorry I asked you to bite me," she whispered.

My eyes flashed, and I sat back on my heels to put some physical distance between us.

"You warned me not to offer a vampire my blood," she continued.

"And you did anyway." I barely contained a smile. I shouldn't like her defiance, not if it put her in danger. But there was something about it that gripped me. Maybe it was because she was so fragile, but I would never have expected to find such fire in this tiny human female.

"I just..." She took a deep breath. "I suppose I thought it might be different if we were already...intimate."

"Let me be clear on something. Refusing to drink your blood is because I respect you, and it is also to protect you," I admitted. "A vampire in the throes of bloodlust can't always stop themselves. You have a precious talent. I won't take that from the world."

Her mouth formed a tiny *O*, but her eyes were unreadable. Finally, she managed a grin. "I'll try to help you keep your fangs off me."

I was relieved to hear her make a joke, but I needed to be clear on how dangerous her request had been. "It is difficult enough for me to resist you. Tempting me is forbidden. Are we clear?"

"What if I forget when…you know…?" Her whole body flushed, and the air around me filled with the inviting scent of violets mixed with sugar and almonds. And there was a new aroma, as well: honey drizzled on juicy, sun-ripened melons. I'd learned from experience that I might not have drank her blood, but I couldn't get enough of her taste.

"If you forget, I will remind you," I said meaningfully.

"How?" She sounded suspicious. Good, that meant she was paying attention.

"What happens to disobedient pets?" I pressed a kiss to her soft thigh, and she shuddered.

"I don't understand," she said, sounding slightly strained. "You don't mean…"

"I will teach you a lesson," I continued.

"I thought you already had." Her words sounded thick and crowded on her tongue. More notes of ripe melon filled the air. I was losing her attention to her growing desire—and running out of room in my pants.

"That was a lesson in pleasure, meant as a reward," I explained. I pushed onto my knees to see her whole face as I delivered the critical bit of this lecture. "If you test the boundaries I've placed for your protection, I'll be forced to give you a different lesson—a punishment."

Her eyes, which had been half closed in greedy anticipation, flew open. "You wouldn't!"

"I promise you I will do whatever it takes to ensure your safety," I said firmly. "Don't look alarmed. I suspect you will enjoy our lesson as much as the others I've given you."

"What does that mean? That you'll ground me?"

"No, Thea." Now I understood her reaction. She was envisioning some modern form of punishment dreamed up by enlightened mortals. "It means I'll spank you."

Her breath hitched, and the honeyed-melon scent overpowered the violets entirely. Thea squirmed under my gaze. She licked her lower lip. "I'm not sure how to feel about that."

Her body told another story. I wasn't entirely sure punishment would make my limits stick. "Is that because the thought of punishment arouses you?"

"I...what...no..." Her response was as flustered as her need was growing. "Why would you think that?"

"I smelled it," I explained to her. "Your scent changed when I mentioned spanking. Would you like that, pet? Would you like me to bend you over my knee and turn your ass the same lovely shade as your cheeks are now?"

She struggled for a moment before she finally murmured, "I don't know."

But I knew. It made sense. Thea had been as drawn to me as I was to her. She craved the darkness inside me. That's why she had asked me to drink her blood. I'd shown her pleasure the night before. I'd opened her eyes to a new world filled with both beauty and shadow. Now she wanted to taste both.

I rose to my feet and took a seat at the edge of her bed. Then I pointed at my lap.

She sat up and looked at me for a moment, obviously nervous, but her arousal continued to fill the room. It hung so heavily I was finding it hard to keep myself in check.

"I came to apologize, pet, but it seems you require more lessons from me. I will stop if you ask," I promised her, "and I will do nothing that leaves a mark."

Her head fell down, and I lifted it with my index finger. Her cheeks were now so red I could hear blood throbbing under the delicate skin.

"Why are you embarrassed?" I asked her gently. "There is no shame in taking what gives one pleasure."

"You said I had to stay on my best behavior," she admitted shyly, "and I wanted to see how far I could push you until you punished me."

"Why is that?" I already knew the answer, but I wanted her to understand. Understanding was key to acceptance, and I needed

Thea to know nothing was wrong with her.

"Because I want you to spank me." She swallowed, and I remembered her mouth on my cock. "I don't even know why. I've never…"

"There are many things you've never tried," I reminded her. "And it's hardly unusual to desire a little pain mixed with pleasure."

"Will it hurt?" she asked.

"If you want it to."

She squirmed a little on the bed. "And you'll stop if…"

"Yes. Always."

"I'm not sure you understand punishments," she said, narrowing her eyes a bit.

I burst out laughing. "The punishment was about teaching you boundaries, pet." I clicked my tongue against the roof of my mouth. She was about to feel silly. "What better way to teach you to appreciate mine than to show respect for yours?"

Her mouth fell open as she realized what I meant.

"There are lines we cannot cross," I told her quietly. "Lines I will not cross. You are only beginning to find your own limits."

"And you're going to help me with that?" she asked in a wry tone.

"Someone has to," I said, sighing heavily before smirking at her.

She stuck her tongue out at me.

"Careful, pet," I warned her. "Being disrespectful will find you over my knee."

She gulped before raising her chin and simpering, "Promise?"

I pointed to my lap. There was a moment of hesitation, but then Thea crawled over and laid her belly across my knees.

"You are so lovely when you come," I told her. "So alive." I placed a gloved hand on her butt and rubbed small circles over her bare flesh. Thea moaned. The sound sent a jolt to my dick. This was why she pushed my buttons. "I can only imagine how perfect your backside will be with my handprints on it."

"Julian," she said cautiously, "will you take off your gloves?"

The request wrapped itself around my chest and squeezed.

Perhaps, one day, I would feel safe fulfilling it, but today wasn't that day. "I can't, pet. I'll explain later, but first..."

I widened the rotating motion of my palm, continuing to warm her skin.

"Fine," she said, sounding a bit annoyed and breathless at the same time.

"You seem to be having difficulty respecting my limits," I murmured as I used my free hand to brush her hair behind her ear. She turned her face to the side, resting it against the mattress, to search my eyes.

"Sounds like I need to be taught a lesson." She wiggled her lower half as though I might be more inclined to deliver said lesson if she was better on display.

"We can always stop," I said, looking into her eyes. She gave me a small nod.

I lifted my hand and delivered one light but firm smack. Thea gasped, and I paused my hand midair to give her time to stop me. But her breathing morphed to hungry panting instead. I brought my hand down again and waited before delivering one more.

"Do you like being spanked?" I asked as her ass took on a rosy glow.

Her eyes closed briefly, her face wracked with desire. "Yes," she whispered, and my cock twitched along with my palm. "A few more times."

I spanked her until the rosy hue deepened into a deep, throbbing red. Then I flipped her onto her back. Thea blinked at me, barely moving as I reached between her legs and urged them open.

"Did you enjoy your lesson, pet?" I asked as I knelt between her spread thighs.

She nodded, biting her lip. "But now..."

I lifted an eyebrow and waited for her to finish. That was proving as hard as I was because I could think of nothing more than showing her how different pleasure felt on the edge of pain.

"I feel like I'm going to explode," she admitted softly. "I need you."

"Shhh," I soothed her. "I'm right here." Dipping down, I placed my mouth over her swollen mound and savored the wet heat I found there. Pulling back for a moment, I stared up at her, darkness coloring my vision. "I will never need your blood as long as you give me this."

Thea grabbed hold of my hair, her hips bucking up as they tried to relocate my now absent mouth. "Show me."

She didn't have to ask me again. But that didn't stop me from devouring her until she came twice: the apology I'd meant to deliver and another just because I wanted more of her. She collapsed against the mattress, and I gathered her in my arms. Despite her languid limbs, she reached for the buckle of my belt.

"No, pet." I stopped her. "I was apologizing, remember?"

"I thought you were teaching," she teased. "What if I want to return to the lesson?"

"Later," I said meaningfully. "Rest. I kept you up half the night last night—"

"I'm not complaining," she interjected.

I ignored her. "And I plan to keep you up longer tonight. If that is permissible?"

"It *is* permissible." She burrowed against me, sighing happily.

I smiled, recalling how insatiable I'd been after my first lover. Some things didn't change, no matter how many centuries passed.

After a minute, Thea began to softly snore, and I reached into my pocket for my phone. There were a few missed calls from my family and a text from Celia. My family could wait. I had no plans to do anything but enjoy the exquisite creature next to me this evening. But as soon as I read Celia's message, I regretted letting the outside world intrude. My plans would have to wait. I let Thea sleep a little while longer before I kissed her forehead and coaxed her to open her eyes.

"Pet, I'm afraid we have somewhere to be, and there are things we'll both need to attend to before we leave," I told her gently, unsure how she would take this news. Not that I had any choice but to deliver it.

"What? Where?" she mumbled sleepily, trying to bury her face in my chest.

I suspected my answer would wake her up. "Paris."

CHAPTER THIRTY-TWO

Thea

"You aren't really going to go," Olivia said, taking a seat on my bed and folding her legs gracefully under her. I was a little jealous of how smoothly her dancer's body made her every movement.

She looked out of place amongst my shabby bargain-store possessions. Her own room, while not much larger, was decorated in shades of pale pink. There were even framed pictures on her walls and curtains on the window. I'd never really bothered with my own space. My bedroom had no windows. It was just four boring walls. No pictures. No matching pink bedding set. It was just a place to keep my things. With the hours I usually kept, I'd insisted the others take the rooms with views of the outside world. But now, my room felt much smaller than it had before. It felt like a cage I'd been trapped in, and I was on the verge of breaking free.

"Of course I am." I continued riffling through my drawers, looking for anything that felt even remotely sophisticated enough for a trip to Paris. I wasn't having much luck.

"What about your mom? School? Auditioning for the fellowship?" Olivia demanded. "I can't believe *I'm* the one saying this to *you*, but you can't just skip out on your whole life for some guy."

What she meant was that this was usually my job. I was the one talking Olivia down from following some random producer to Los Angeles or making Tanner actually leave the apartment during daylight hours. I went to class. I rehearsed constantly. I'd never missed one of my mom's chemo appointments. Until earlier today, I'd even had a job on top of all of that.

"Thea, what's going on?" Olivia pressed, and I realized I'd been caught up in my own thoughts. "He can't be that good in bed. Maybe it's just because he's your first..."

I whirled around, a bunch of panties in my hands, and gawked at her. "You think I *slept* with him?"

"I don't know!" She threw her hands in the air. "You're running off with a guy you just met, and you didn't come home the other night."

Both were good points. "Do you really think I would finally sleep with someone and not tell you?"

"I don't know what's going on with you," she said softly.

I stopped stuffing clothes into my old suitcase and sighed. But before I could figure out what to tell Olivia, my phone began to ring. I checked the screen and put it back down. I could only deal with one disappointed person in my life right now.

"What do you want to know?" I asked, abandoning my crappy packing job and joining her on the other end of the bed.

"You haven't slept with him, but..." She trailed off with a wicked grin.

"We've kissed." I didn't really have words to describe the other things we'd done. At least, none I could imagine saying aloud.

"Kissed?" she repeated with downturned lips. "Tell me that you aren't blowing up your whole life for some rich guy you've only kissed."

"And some other stuff," I said.

"Thea!" Olivia grabbed a pillow and whacked me with it. "Stop being so shy. Has he gone down on you?"

"Yes," I said, starting to flush. That inevitably reminded me of the last time my cheeks had been this hot, and I blushed even harder.

"Ohhhh! And he must have been good at it since you're following him all the way to Paris for more," she teased. She waited a moment before her next question. "And what about you? Have you given him a—"

"Yes," I cut her off.

"Impressive." She nodded her head like she was an expert on the subject. "You must be really good at it if he's taking you to Paris."

"It's not just about sex," I told her. I took a deep breath and admitted the truth I'd been keeping secret—even from myself. "I really like him."

"I hope so." She rolled her eyes. "That's a long flight to take with someone you don't like."

"Olivia," I said her name forcefully enough that she fell silent, "I *really* like him. I might..." But even though the right word was there on the tip of my tongue, I couldn't actually say it.

"You are *not* in love with him!" She jumped off the bed. "Red flag! Reality check! You've known him a couple days. You've only been on one real date."

"I know. I barely know him, but I can't explain it," I muttered and got up to finish packing.

But Olivia swiped my bag and held it over her head like a hostage. "You can't go. I won't let you. You have worked way too hard to just drop everything for some guy, no matter the quality of the orgasms he delivers."

"That's not what this is about," I said hotly. The phone rang again.

"Is that your mom?" She pointed to it. "Does she know what the hell is going on?"

"I'm talking to her lat—"

Olivia dropped my bag and grabbed the phone.

"Don't answer that," I hissed, but it was too late.

"Hello?" she answered. After a second, she nodded. "No, she's right here." Olivia stretched the phone out to me with a haughty frown. "It's for you."

I narrowed my eyes at her and grabbed the phone. "Hello?"

"Thea?" a worried voice responded. "It's Professor MacLeod. I just received a notice that you are dropping your coursework for the semester. Is everything okay? Is your mother...?"

"Everything's fine," I said, closing my eyes. I should have known it wouldn't be as easy as walking into the registrar and telling them I needed to take leave for the rest of the year. "I had an opportunity I couldn't pass up. I'll be back next fall."

Olivia's mouth dropped open. I hadn't gotten around to telling her this bit yet. I might as well do it now. That way, if she killed me, Professor MacLeod would be able to testify in her murder trial.

"A year? But Thea, I have to tell you—you were the department's best candidate for the Reeds Fellowship."

Tears formed a lump in my throat, and I turned away so Olivia wouldn't see. I hadn't expected him to say that. MacLeod was a hard-ass on a good day. He'd always been tough but fair. The idea of him tipping his hand was hard to process. "I was offered a job," I told him quietly. "It's going to allow me to pay off my mother's medical debt."

Silence stretched across the line and in my bedroom. Neither MacLeod nor Olivia seemed to know what to say. After a moment, he cleared his throat. "Are you certain that's what your mother would want? I don't think she would want you to give up your music, even for that."

He was right. That's exactly why I hadn't found the courage to tell her yet.

"It doesn't matter what she wants," I said resolutely. "It's what I want. I understand if this means I can't return to the program."

"Of course you can return," he said gruffly. "I just hate to see you waste time."

"Thank you for your concern," I said. "I have to go, though."

"If anything changes..."

I hung up, somehow feeling better and worse at the same time.

I knew I was right. This was my life, and only I could choose how to spend my time. But that didn't mean MacLeod's shock and disappointment didn't sting. It was only going to be worse when I finally told my mom.

Turning, I found Olivia had sat back down on the edge of the bed. There was no indignation or amusement on her face now. Instead, she looked lost in her own thoughts.

"What?" I demanded. "Go on. I know you have something to say about this."

She took a deep breath and turned worried eyes on me. "Thea, are you becoming an escort?"

"What?" I burst out laughing before she could repeat herself. "Why would you think that?"

"You just said you're leaving for a job that's going to pay off your mom's bills—and I know how much those bills are," she reminded me.

Olivia had held me through many long nights when things didn't look good for Mom. She had seen the bills. She knew why I was working at the restaurant and playing with the quartet when I was already burned out. I refused to take out more student loans in addition to what we already owed.

"I'm not an escort. Promise." I drew a cross over my chest with an index finger.

"Then which is it? Are you running away with your boyfriend, or are you being paid to go with him and, you know..."

"Julian is my boyfriend." I swallowed at the funny taste the word left on my tongue. I hadn't really called him that much. "But when he asked me to travel with him on business, I told him I couldn't because I needed to finish school and get a better job to pay the bills. He offered to pay the bills so I could take a year off."

"You're going to let some guy you've known less than a week pay off hundreds of thousands in medical debts?" she shouted.

"He's rich," I reminded her. "That kind of money is nothing to him, but it's everything to me. I won't have to wait tables or take another job when I graduate. I can just focus on finding a chair with a symphony and doing what I love."

Olivia clamped her mouth closed, and I braced myself for another eruption. Instead, to my surprise, she shrugged. "You're right."

"What?" I hadn't heard her correctly.

"You're right. He's a billionaire. He could probably pay our rent with his pocket change." She stopped and leveled a serious look at me. "But have you done a background check? Are you sure he's legit? I don't want to get a call that I have to go all Liam Neeson on some pervert's ass because you're kidnapped."

I tried to stop myself from giggling at the idea of Olivia rescuing me from a shadowy cartel, but I couldn't.

"I'm not joking." She stuck her lower lip out in a pout. "What if you're wrong about him?"

There were so many things I wished I could tell her about Julian. If she only knew how strict his boundaries were, she would be packing my bags herself. But I couldn't drag her into this world.

I hadn't asked to learn about vampires or the magical world. I hadn't chosen to be dragged into that world. I wouldn't let the same thing happen to my friend, and if I told her, I would be doing just that. There was only one thing I could do. Sitting down next to her, I put one hand on top of hers.

"I'm not wrong," I murmured. "I wish I could explain it. I just know."

"That he's not going to dump you in Paris?" she asked flatly. "That he's not going to hurt you?"

A chill ran up my spine like an icy fingertip, but I forced a smile. "You've got to trust me. I know what I'm doing." I bumped my shoulder against hers. "I'm still the same Thea who thinks everything through before she does it. I'm just a little more..."

"Slutty?" she offered, unable to hide her grin.

My own mouth twisted in bemusement. "I was going to say *worldly*."

"Fine." She stood up and pointed to my phone. "Now call your mom."

"I will."

She peeked into the bag on the floor. "You aren't going to Paris with a billionaire and wearing this stuff, right?"

I leaned down and zipped it closed. "Thanks for the tip."

"Of course, you'll probably be naked the whole time." She clutched her chest dramatically. "Who needs clothes?"

I wished that was true. Then again, after getting a taste of how vampires socialized, she might be right. I made a mental note to ask Julian exactly what I needed to pack again.

"What time do you leave?"

"He's picking me up in the morning," I told her.

"Okay, let me get a hug now." She threw her arms around me with the passion of someone saying goodbye for much longer than a week or two. "Don't get kidnapped or murdered. And whatever you do, don't get pregnant!"

"I won't!" I said, laughing.

She shot me a look as she pulled away. "I'm serious. No glove, no love."

"Promise," I said. If Olivia only knew the truth...

Maybe agreeing to drop everything and get on a plane to Paris was a bad idea. But at least I didn't have to worry about getting pregnant.

CHAPTER THIRTY-THREE

Julian

It had been forty-eight hours since I last saw Thea. Not that I was counting, precisely. I hadn't lived over nine hundred years to suddenly count the passing of hours. Yet, here I was—so what the hell was wrong with me? And, what was worse, I soon wouldn't have her to myself. I would have to share her with all of Paris.

French vampires were notorious snobs, and I was no exception. Unlike most of the older French lines, our family had staked outposts throughout Europe, then more in America and Asia. To some of the other French vampire families this was enough to erase any notion of our shared French blood. But Paris doors were always open to the name Rousseaux, and that access also entailed social obligations. A Rousseaux was expected to accept any formal invitation.

That was the problem with having old blood. We adhered to tradition at all costs.

The same couldn't be said for most Parisian covens.

A few who never bothered to attend social events in America did so only because they refused to leave Europe. Despite the arrogance, the season always came to them. Everyone found Paris romantic, even vampires.

Maybe that's why they put on such a good show. This season's scheduled events sounded even more excessive than usual, something I needed to prepare Thea for on the flight over.

I was only a few blocks from her apartment when my phone rang over the BMW's speaker.

"Fan-fucking-tastic," I grumbled when my father's name flashed on the dashboard's screen. Since he wasn't my mother, I decided to answer.

"Yes?"

"I'm supposed to ask if you're coming to Paris," he said, sounding irritated to be playing the role of messenger.

"Do I have a choice?"

"And if you're bringing the human," he added, ignoring my question.

"Why doesn't she ask me herself?" So far, my mother had gone through Celia, my father, and even Sebastian to relay details about the events in Paris over the next two weeks. "And why are there so many fucking parties?"

"San Francisco was unofficial," he confessed in a lowered voice. I suspected he didn't want my mother to overhear him saying that. "These are the first events of the season. As the eligible Rousseaux, you are ex—"

"I know," I cut him off. I'd heard this lecture before, and I'd watched Camila sit through it when it was her turn. "Is that the reason you called? To relay her messages?"

"I guess we could confide in each other," he said harshly, "or you could tell me about your day?"

"I'll take it that is it." I reached to end the call.

"There's one more thing," he said, stopping me. There was a long pause, which meant he was about to deliver bad news. "There is an event Thea will need to attend. It's private—"

"Put her on the phone," I interrupted him.

He paused as if considering my request before finally caving. "Give me a moment."

I heard my mother's voice pitch up to an octave that allowed it to be heard with perfect clarity, even from across a large, echoing room. "I'm very busy seeing to the packing. Can it wait?"

"Put her on," I told my father again.

I heard him pass it to her along with a whisper to behave herself. Was he trying to make things worse?

"So you're speaking to me again?" she said.

"Which event will Thea need to attend without me?" I demanded, slamming my palm on the steering wheel. "She's not a familiar."

"But you *are* thinking about marrying her," she responded smoothly. "Or have you reconsidered?"

I saw what she was doing. She would keep pulling threads until she found the one that would unravel my well-woven plans. I couldn't let it happen. "No, but those events are for familiars," I countered.

"They are for all possible consorts," she corrected.

"And that now includes humans?"

"If you're concerned, then maybe you should leave her at home."

"I don't see why she needs to attend a private event. Nothing is decided," I said through gritted teeth. "And I won't have Thea at a party for witches."

"Your French side is coming out," she said with a sniff. "You're acting like a snob."

I rolled my eyes. If anything, I was acting like her.

"Besides, I've already registered her for the *Salon du Rouge*."

I stopped the car in front of Thea's building, wondering why I bothered trying to speak. Sabine never heard a word I said.

A few questionable characters shuffled down the sidewalk outside. At least taking Thea to Paris meant getting her away from this far-from-ideal living situation.

"Does she have appropriate clothing?" Sabine asked.

"She'll be dressed," I snapped.

"That is not what I asked. I will not have you parading a mortal around in clothes from a thrift shop."

"I have to go." I ended the call before she could add to her growing list of demands.

I climbed out of the car to find Thea waiting on the sidewalk. She was dressed in a pair of torn jeans that rose high on the waist, showing off the curves of her hips, an oversize cardigan, and a cropped black T-shirt that had two words printed over her pert breasts: *Bite me.*

I raised an eyebrow. "I'm not certain your shirt respects my boundaries, pet."

"I've had this for years," she said with a barely contained giggle. She hoisted her small hand luggage higher on her shoulder. "I thought it was funny. Given the circumstances."

Given the circumstances, she was going to wind up with my fangs deep in her neck if she kept pushing my buttons. I had more restraint than human males, but even I had my limits. I lifted the bag from her shoulder and looked around. "Where are the rest of your bags?"

"Just my purse." She patted the small bag hanging near her hip. "Everything's in there."

"We're going to be gone for two weeks, at least." Maybe she'd misheard me.

But Thea shrugged her slight shoulders, looking unfazed. "I can always find somewhere to do laundry."

"Do laundry?" I repeated.

"Yes," she said slowly. "You put clothes in the washing machine, add soap, and it cleans them."

"I know what laundry is," I growled. "But why not just pack more clothes?"

"These are my clothes. And when Celia texted me the information, she promised she would send the green dress." The matter-of-fact innocence of her response was adorable.

It made me want to pat her on the head—or maybe swat her on the ass. Either way, something would have to be done. Preferably before my mother found out she'd been right to ask about her wardrobe.

"Ready?" I asked, knowing there was nothing I could do at this moment.

"*Oui,*" she said brightly and followed me to the car.

But her demeanor suggested otherwise as we headed toward the private airfield where my family kept our jets. She was a bundle of nerves. Her scent was sweeter than usual, and it filled the cabin, likely her hormones pumping glucose as a response to some stress. She fidgeted in the seat next to me, tapping her fingers on the center console or readjusting her seat belt.

Finally, I reached over and took one of her hands. I wrapped my gloved fingers around her pale, bare ones. It was strange to touch a woman's hands so intimately, even if no magic sparked under her skin.

"Are you okay?" I kept her hand in mine.

"Oh." She bit her lip until it was slightly puffy. "Promise you won't laugh."

"That's an odd answer."

"Just promise," she said more forcefully.

"I won't laugh," I said firmly.

She took a deep breath and blurted out, "I've never been on a plane before."

"You've never... Why do you have a passport?"

"My mom and I borrowed her boss's condo in Mexico a few years ago," she explained. "We drove past the border and stayed a few days."

I stole a few looks at her, trying to understand what her life was like. She'd never been on a plane. She'd never been with a man. What exactly had she done? No wonder she was so great at music. Or was this typical for this stage in a mortal's life span? There were so many places she'd yet to experience, foods she hadn't tried. Her whole life was ahead of her, and I had already done it all.

"You're quiet," she said after a minute, squeezing my hand. "Nervous about flying?"

She grinned up at me like she was letting me in on the joke.

"I was just thinking about all the places I'm going to take you," I murmured.

"In Paris?"

I raised our joined hands and kissed her knuckles absently as I exited the highway. "All over the world."

I glanced over at her again and found her blushing.

"Are you sure I'm the best person to take with you?" she asked to my surprise. "I'm hardly some familiar trained to attend these parties. I'm going to embarrass you."

I nearly drove off the road, but I managed to straighten the wheel. Obviously, this wasn't just anxiety about flying. I didn't answer her until we'd reached my private hangar. Turning my head, I locked my eyes on hers. "You are exactly the person I want by my side. You deserve the world. Let me give it to you."

Thea's throat slid as she nodded.

"Now that we've settled that." I gently released my hold on her hand. "Shall we?"

But Thea turned her attention to the scene outside her window and stared. "Where are we? Where's the airport?"

"We're traveling by other means," I told her. I didn't want to risk using the words private plane while she was already struggling with imposter syndrome.

"Please don't say coffins," she whispered.

I couldn't contain my laughter. The fact that she was so serious made it even funnier. "That's definitely a myth."

"Good," she said with a resolute nod.

"Now that you know I'm not dragging you across the ocean in a coffin, are you ready?"

She bobbed her head, still chewing nervously on her lower lip.

I climbed out of the car, went around to her side, and helped her out. As soon as she was on her feet, she grabbed a fistful of my shirt and kissed me. It was hot and quick, and when we broke apart, she wore an unsure smile.

"What was that for?" I asked her.

"For luck." She took a deep breath. "Let's get this over with."

I took her hand and continued to the other side of the hangar. As we rounded the corner, Thea gasped.

"What is that?" She pointed at the private jet waiting on the tarmac like she'd spotted a cockroach.

"Our ride."

Thea stayed locked in place, staring at the massive executive liner. I stopped and swiveled toward her. "Come, pet, let me show you the world."

CHAPTER THIRTY-FOUR

Thea

Paris was alive. The city teemed with life. I stared out the car window, watching the crowds of tourists on the sidewalk. I'd fallen asleep on the flight, lulled into an easy slumber by the insanely comfortable seats on Julian's private jet. I was still tired, but excitement and sheer force of will kept my eyes plastered open. A car zipped dangerously close to ours, and I shrank back out of instinct. Next to me, Julian laughed, not bothering to look up from his phone.

"That car almost hit us," I told him, pointing out the tinted window.

"I forget this is your first time in Paris," he said, still absorbed in his phone. "Don't worry, Phillipe has everything under control, pet."

I glanced at the uniformed driver who had retrieved us from the private airfield outside Versailles.

"I will keep you safe, mademoiselle," he said with a heavy accent. He smiled at me in the rearview mirror.

A low growl vibrated from Julian, and I shot him a look. "Behave yourself."

My boyfriend had gone from perfectly friendly to ice cold toward Phillipe after the driver took my hand to help me into the back of the Bentley. I made a mental note to grill Celia about Julian's beastlier tendencies the next time we were alone. Were all vampires so possessive? Or had I just lucked into a particularly domineering one?

"I will try," Julian promised, taking my hand and lifting it to his lips. He paused with it a breath away from his mouth. His nostrils flared before he finally kissed it softly. He lifted his eyes, searching mine for a response.

"Okay." I did my best to sound like a hard-ass but failed miserably. It was impossible to hold him accountable with his electric-blue eyes piercing me. I managed to tear my gaze away, sucking in a deep, steadying breath. I had a year of this ahead of me, and I was going to enjoy every moment of it. But for now, we were in mixed company. I peered over at his phone screen. "What are you doing?"

"I have recently discovered I can read all my newspapers on this infernal thing."

I pressed my lips together to keep from laughing. That made him sound every bit as old as his years. I kept the thought to myself. Of course he wouldn't be doing anything as silly as games. I'd seen the stack of newspapers his assistant had brought to his room the morning after our first night together. "It's a bit more convenient."

"Indeed." He dropped the phone into a cup holder and turned toward me. "We have a day or two until the first event. There seems to be some question about the official schedule."

"Oh." I blinked as I processed this. "I thought we had to be here by tomorrow."

"Time operates differently in Paris. No one rushes around like in America. Anyway, this will give you a moment to acclimate to the jet lag," he said, "and perhaps shop."

"Shop?" I raised an eyebrow. "I wouldn't even know where to begin." Never in my wildest dreams had I imagined shopping in Paris. Mostly because even going to Paris had seemed so out of reach. "I'd rather be with you."

Julian leaned closer, angling his head to plant a kiss on my neck.

"It's too tempting when you wear your hair up," he warned me. Then he sighed. "We have all night, and I suspect you will need to add some items to your closet before the events begin."

"Is there something wrong with my clothes?"

"No, you are perfect." Another dizzying kiss. "But you will need more than one dress."

"Oh." That made sense. "Sorry, I'm not used to anyone noticing me, never mind remembering what I wear. I'm usually stuck in a corner with my cello."

"I suspect you've been blissfully ignorant to the attention you receive," he said.

"I doubt that." It was laughable. I'd never had anyone so much as offer to buy me a drink at an event.

"I do not." His eyes raked over me, slowly erasing any doubt he meant what he said.

But I was preoccupied with something else he'd said. "Oh no."

"Is something wrong?" He went rigid, already on guard to deal with whatever troubled me.

"I should have brought the cello!" Why hadn't I thought of it? I'd been too preoccupied with my underwear and toiletries. It was just more proof that I was an amateur traveler. "We're here for two weeks. How will I practice?"

"We can find one in Paris." Julian dismissed it like the oversight meant nothing. "I'll have someone see to it."

"Promise me it won't cost half a million dollars," I said firmly. I didn't care how much money Julian had, and by all indications he had a lot. I didn't need to run around collecting priceless instruments.

"If you wish."

I narrowed my eyes. That had been too easy. "Or more than half a million."

This earned me a low chuckle. The sound buried itself in my stomach and grew warm tendrils inside me. "Ahhh." Julian tipped my chin up with his index finger and kissed me. "Now you're learning, pet."

Before I could make further stipulations regarding his generosity, the Bentley pulled to the curb in front of a limestone building that rose four stories up. In a city like San Francisco, it might look short, but in Paris, it stood proudly amongst its neighbors. The street itself was quiet, compared to the city we'd driven through so far, and it was comprised of a dozen similar buildings. Each with its own beautiful doors and wrought-iron balconies.

"Allow me to get the door," Julian murmured before vanishing with superhuman speed out his side of the car. I waited dutifully, eager to avoid any more growling if I could. Phillipe seemed nice, and I didn't want him to lose his head by upsetting the overprotective vampire. My door opened, and Julian extended his hand. I took it, noticing as I rose from the car that Phillipe had stayed far away from my side. Apparently, he didn't want to lose his head, either.

"It's beautiful," I said softly. The building's arched door boasted a swirling Art Deco design that looked so Parisian I could scream. Above it, a pair of balconies distinguished each individual floor. Bright pink flowers grew in planter boxes hanging from each railing. In the twilight, the whole thing took on a rosy glow that made me feel strangely content. I'd been here all of an hour, and I already felt at home.

"Shall we?" Julian guided me toward the entrance.

Before we reached it, an older gentleman opened the door and stepped to the side gracefully. "Welcome home, sir." He paused, tipping his head to greet me. "It is a pleasure to have you with us, Mademoiselle Melbourne."

"Thank you," I said brightly, reaching to shake his hand.

He blinked rapidly as he took it, and I realized I'd made my first American mistake.

"Am I supposed to kiss his cheeks?" I whispered to Julian.

His laughter bellowed through the massive, two-story entry and bounced off the marble floors back at us.

"I'm sure that Hughes would prefer you did not."

"The master is correct," Hughes added, shifting uncomfortably.

"I am just a butler."

I managed a smile, wondering if I could look up proper French greetings online.

"Would you like the tour?" Hughes said.

I opened my mouth to respond, but Julian beat me to it. "Please."

The butler led us farther into the foyer, where a grand piano sat untouched next to a pair of double doors. Heavy drapes hung around it, pulled to the side with thick braided cords. But it was what I glimpsed just beyond the glass that stunned me.

"Is that..."

"The reason I bought the place," Julian said, taking my hand and leading me over to the doors. He opened them to a stone terrace. Unlike the iron ones facing the street, this one looked out over a long green space, and just past it, the Eiffel Tower rose in the evening sky. Julian urged me onto the balcony so I could get a better look.

I had expected to find the tourist landmark cheesy. How could it not be? But just as we stood there, it flashed into a thousand points of light, the beginning of a spectacular light display.

"I'm told the locals hate it," Julian whispered as he moved behind me. His strong arms wrapped around me and drew me close to him. "It's for the tourists."

"I can see why," I admitted, feeling breathless. Paris definitely lived up to the hype.

"It turned out well," he continued, nuzzling my neck. I had a feeling it wasn't a coincidence that it was becoming his favorite spot.

"What? The tower?" I was still mesmerized by the light show.

"The apartment. It wasn't finished when I purchased it in the eighties."

If it hadn't been finished, then... I twisted in his arms. "Are you saying you've never been here?"

"Not in its current state. I asked a friend to oversee the completion of the project. Let's see how she did."

She? I hoped he meant Celia.

Before I could ask, he tugged me back inside, and we continued our tour. Hughes showed us the kitchen, which looked like something out of a postcard with its black enamel oven and gold hardware, then to a sitting room off the main entrance, which had been decorated with extravagant paper murals of exotic plants and animals. Green velvet couches sat opposite each other by a large, unlit fireplace. Across from it, another sitting room decorated with gilded plasterwork was a slightly softer room in terms of design, but I could only imagine how much the furniture cost.

"Perhaps we should explore the upper floors ourselves," Julian suggested in a low voice only I could hear.

I licked my lower lip and nodded. So far, Paris had lived up to every romantic notion I had. All that was left was to be seduced.

"I will see to the luggage." Hughes tipped his head with an understanding smile.

"Take your time," Julian said. He knitted his fingers through mine and led me up the grand staircase off the foyer. We paused on the second floor. "To be honest, I don't remember what I had done to these rooms."

"I hope they aren't hiding your coffin behind one of these doors," I said seriously.

"Yes, let's hope." He rolled his eyes. He reached for the closest knob and opened it to reveal a room of mirrors. "Ah, the studio."

"It looks like a ballet studio," I said, crinkling my nose. "Is there something you aren't telling me?"

"It was original to the property. I decided to keep it." There was more to this story. I could sense it, but Julian didn't seem to want to share it.

"Next," I said, not wanting to ruin the mood. Behind another door, we found a library with shelves that reached to the top of its ten-foot ceilings. A brass rail ran along the center shelving, allowing for the use of a rolling ladder. A number of oversize chairs upholstered in thick linen filled the space, each with a different antique table beside it. A quick perusal of the shelves resulted in spotting books in dozens of languages, most of which

I couldn't identify.

"One more," he said, "and then we can continue to the upper floors."

Something about the way he'd said upper floors made my skin tingle. We opened the final door to reveal a large screening room. For the last room on the floor, it was a disappointment after the others.

"These are all guest rooms and a few rooms for the staff," he explained, continuing past the third floor. "The room I wanted to show you is this way."

He led me to the fourth floor, where only one door waited. I held my breath as he opened it to reveal the main bedroom. It was drenched with luxurious silk draperies, gorgeous antiques, and a large terrace that extended out over the green space below and offered a spectacular view of the Eiffel Tower.

But I barely processed any of it, because waiting on Julian's bed was the most beautiful woman I'd ever seen.

And she was completely naked.

CHAPTER THIRTY-FIVE

Julian

"Jules, you brought a snack."

Thea swiveled to face me and raised an eyebrow. So far, she was taking finding a naked woman in my bed well. Too well. Maybe she was spending too much time around vampires. Still, this was going to be hard to explain.

"Actually, I brought my girlfriend," I said in a tight voice. "Jacqueline, this is Thea. Thea…"

But Thea had gone from curious to some mixture of amused and flabbergasted. Maybe the casual introduction had been too much.

Jacqueline slid from the bed and sauntered toward us, acting blissfully unaware of her own nudity. I knew her better than to believe she'd just forgotten she was naked. It was a power play, intended to size up the newcomer in the room. She planted one hand on her hip and offered Thea the other. "*Enchanté.*"

"The same," Thea murmured, her eyes darting around as if looking for a safe place to land that wasn't Jacqueline's breasts.

"I'm sorry for the intrusion. I didn't expect to see Julian with a human."

Thea blinked, obviously startled by her bluntness.

"Well, we certainly didn't expect to be seeing so much of you,"

I said through gritted teeth. "Perhaps some clothing?"

"Oh, of course." She waved a delicate hand as if it was all a silly mistake and then sashayed toward the en suite bathroom. She left the door slightly ajar, dressing within plain sight. "I wish I'd known you were bringing someone. I would have stayed dressed." She poked her head out and slid her gaze down Thea once again. "Then again, I could stay naked, and we could all—"

"Get dressed," I cut her off. Next to me, Thea was turning red. "And maybe call ahead in the future?"

"You gave me the key." Jacqueline came out of the bathroom, tying the belt of a khaki coat dress.

"A mistake I won't repeat." I reached for Thea's hand, but she seemed oblivious to me. I couldn't blame her; Jacqueline could dazzle any creature. No one—vampire, familiar, or mortal—could resist her.

Jacqueline tossed her luxurious blond tresses over her shoulder with a careless ease that made Thea's eyes widen. I could almost see my girlfriend calculating where she stood next to this mysterious vampire. But before I could correct the misunderstanding, Jacqueline continued. "You asked me to decorate. I decorated. And this is how you greet me."

"Jacque, you were naked in my bed." I glared at her.

"Come on, it was funny!" She looked to Thea for confirmation but got none.

Instead, Thea finally found her voice and blurted out, "Um, who are you?"

"Jacqueline DuBois. Julian's oldest *and only* friend."

"Oldest is true," I muttered. "We grew up together."

"Oh," Thea responded in a small voice, her eyes finding the floor.

"Wait, does she think…?" Jacqueline reached out and smacked me in the chest so hard that I nearly flew back and hit the wall. "You haven't *told* her about me?"

"No, he hasn't." Thea held up her head, doing her best to hold her ground, even as her lower lip began to quiver.

"You dick. Now you made her cry." Jacqueline wrapped an arm around Thea's shoulders before I could stop her. Thea seemed too surprised to say anything. I couldn't blame her for that. The whole situation gave off a distinctly scandalous impression.

"*You* made her cry," I pointed out.

But Jacqueline was ignoring me. She lowered her voice—as if I couldn't hear her. "He didn't say anything about me? Jacqueline? Sometimes he calls me Jacque? Or Jackie?"

"No." Thea shook her head.

"It's your fault if you didn't prepare her," Jacqueline argued.

I opened my mouth to protest, but Thea beat me to it.

"Are you his real girlfriend?"

Jacqueline looked at me, her eyes brightening merrily, and then we both burst out laughing. "Oh, honey, no!"

"You have a key," Thea pointed out, "and you were naked..."

"That was an inside joke," I explained quickly, before turning on Jacqueline. "I can't believe you actually did it."

"I promised you the most beautiful house in Paris and the prettiest female I could find waiting for you in bed," Jacqueline reminded me, still hugging Thea close to her. "I was trying to give him some incentive to give up his stupid plan to take an eternal nap."

"Eternal?" Thea echoed the word, glancing over at me. She knew about my time-out from the world, but I hadn't filled her in much on the reasons why I'd gone to sleep. Thanks to my best friend, I was now going to have even more explaining to do.

"I see your ego is still intact," I said, turning the conversation back to Jacqueline's transgression. "Or is there a shortage of pretty women in Paris these days?"

"I said the *prettiest*." She looked Thea over again. "Although I might have competition."

"She's my girlfriend, not yours."

"I can look," she said defensively.

"But no touching." It was best to remind Jacqueline of this rule, especially where Thea was concerned.

"Wait, are you flirting with me?" Thea asked suddenly.

Jacqueline loosed a bell-like laugh. "A little."

Thea turned on me. "And you aren't going to rip her head off or anything?"

"Has he been ripping people's heads off a lot?" Jacqueline asked slowly, but she didn't release Thea.

"Only once," I said before Thea could tattle.

"Only once?" Jacqueline shot an impressed look at Thea. "He must really like you."

"So...she's not a threat to you?" Thea pressed.

"Her? No," I said with a chuckle. "She's practically my sister."

"And you two have never..." She trailed off with a look as pointed as my fangs.

"No," Jacqueline said, but once again, I found I couldn't lie to Thea.

"When we were kids," I admitted, earning me a frustrated look from Jacqueline and a frown from Thea. "You have to understand that teenage vampires are..."

"Horny," my old friend finished for me. "And it was the fourteenth century. There wasn't much else to do. I slept with everyone just to keep from staking myself out of boredom." The corners of Thea's mouth danced up slightly, and Jacqueline took this as a sign of forgiveness. "And, honestly, you are much more my type than Jules. He doesn't know how to have fun."

"Stop hitting on my girlfriend." I pinched the bridge of my nose. "Remind me to have the locks changed."

"That is unfair. I did an exquisite job on this place." Jacqueline spun Thea to face her. "Don't you think?"

"It's beautiful," she said sincerely, looking a bit dizzy at the change in conversation.

"You have to see the bathroom. It's fit for a queen." She grabbed Thea's hand, shot a triumphant look at me, and dragged her into the en suite bath.

This was my fault. I should have guessed that Jacqueline would have heard I was returning to Paris and surprise me. It wasn't that I was avoiding her. I'd simply expected to have some time to prepare Thea to meet her and to speak privately with Jacqueline about what was going on. But the trouble with best friends, especially ones you'd known forever, was that they might pop up anywhere at any time. Even naked in your bed.

I was really going to have to explain that better to Thea later.

I wandered onto the terrace, taking in the view of *La dame de fer* and wondering exactly what to do next. I hadn't seen Jacqueline in decades, and the fact she was here meant she expected to catch up. I wouldn't risk overwhelming Thea, not on the cusp of the Parisian social calendar. That was bad enough. But Jacqueline had something no one else in my life offered—what I needed most.

Perspective.

My parents were too caught up in the politics of The Rites to be trusted. Sebastian was too busy fucking everything that moved. And Celia had an annoying habit of dropping cryptic remarks and then refusing to elucidate what she was getting at. Jacqueline was as blunt as a sword's hilt and as sharp as its blade. It was one of the reasons we got along. There was no time wasted on tiptoeing around the facts. She called me on my bullshit. I called her on hers. It worked for us. Most of the time.

The last time I'd seen her had not been one of those times.

"Your lovely companion is tired," Jacqueline's musical voice called as she escorted Thea back into the bedroom. "She needs a nap."

"I'm fine." But even as Thea said it, her hand snapped up to cover a wide yawn.

"I can see that," I said drily. "I should see you to bed."

"It's two meters away." Jacqueline rolled her eyes. "She can see herself. She needs rest, not an overbearing vampire keeping her up."

Thea's mouth clamped shut as if she was holding back laughter.

"I left the two of you alone for five minutes, and you're in cahoots," I grumbled.

"Cahoots?" Thea repeated, giggles spilling out. "Okay, *old man*."

I glared at Jacqueline, who held up her hands with wide eyes. "Why are you looking at me like that?"

"Because she spent a moment alone with you, and she's calling me old man again."

"You are old," Jacqueline said with a shrug of her slight shoulders, earning more laughter from Thea. She nudged Thea toward the bed. "Rest. I need to catch up with Jules, but tomorrow..."

Thea nodded to some unspoken plan. If she had any lingering concerns about my friendship with Jacqueline, they weren't enough to keep her from climbing into the bed and collapsing against a mountain of silk pillows. I moved to Thea's side, past an increasingly amused Jacqueline, and leaned over her. "I'll wake you at midnight. It's the best time to see Paris. Now rest, pet."

I brushed a kiss across her forehead, earning a soft sigh that only reminded me I hadn't brought her up here to rest. A spark of darkness flickered inside me, and I moved quickly away before my bloodlust took over and stole Thea's chance to sleep.

By the time I reached the door, she was already snoring softly. Jacqueline joined me, lapsing into silence as we made our way to the fifth floor, which wasn't a floor at all.

"I think you have the best view in the city," Jacqueline said as we stepped onto the roof. Before, this had been nothing more than a flat opening, devoid of any personality. Now it was filled with silk cushions in the colors of precious gems amid small tables meant for conversation. As usual, it seemed my best friend wanted me to make more friends. The whole space was clearly intended for entertaining.

"It's why I bought the place," I reminded her. "The market value will only increase."

She groaned, even though she knew me too well to be surprised. "And it will be a lovely place to raise a family. Plenty of room for little vampires."

"Not you, too." The last thing I'd expected from her was pressure to marry. Whatever end of the spectrum my mother was on, Jacqueline usually took up residence at the other end of it. But it seemed the season was messing with even the most libertine among us. The next thing I knew, Sebastian would be planning my wedding. "Is everyone around me obsessed with the bloody Rites?"

"The Rites?" Jacqueline turned on me, crossing her arms, and glaring. "You think this is about those stupid rituals?"

"What else would it be about?"

She stared at me for a moment, studying my face as if looking for some clue. Just as I grew tired of being watched like a lab rat, she threw her head back and laughed. The sound of it filled the rose-colored sky.

"You really don't know," she said, her eyes gleaming wickedly as she finally contained herself.

"What now?" I muttered. "If they've found some new archaic bullshit to—"

"Julian," she interrupted, grabbing my shoulders and looking me directly in the eye, "you're mating."

CHAPTER THIRTY-SIX

Thea

A cool breeze drifted across my body, and I rolled over...into a sleeping vampire. I blinked dreamily as my eyes adjusted to the dark bedroom. My brain woke up in the process and filled in all the short-term memory bits still hazy from sleep. I was in Paris—in Julian's bed. Warmth spread through me as I remembered, stopping when I reached the part where I found Jacqueline in his bed. I lifted my head and looked around the room, relieved to find we were alone.

Julian's self-appointed best friend—as she had called herself in the bathroom—had been a bit of a shock, but she seemed nice. At least, nicer than most vampires I'd met so far.

But more than anything, I wanted to be alone with Julian. I'd only been here for a few hours, but already I understood why they said Paris was a city for lovers.

I watched him sleep just long enough it wouldn't be creepy. His face was relaxed and peaceful, not caught in the lines of grumpiness or bloodlust that usually plagued him in equal measures. Like this, his beauty was mesmerizing. The primal masculinity that radiated from him was still there but entirely under his control. The sharp lines of his face softened with sleep, drawing attention to the perfect bow of his lips. Every ounce of me wanted to lean over and kiss him.

But I was pretty sure I should brush my teeth first. Besides, I doubted it was a good idea to wake a sleeping vampire.

I slipped out of my bed, then freshened up in the bathroom. I'd have to thank Jacqueline later for keeping it well-stocked. She might not have expected him to bring someone home, but she'd prepared it in case he had. There was extra toothpaste and mouthwash. Hanging on the back of the door were two fluffy black robes. She'd pointed them out to me earlier, eager to show me every treasure I had at my disposal. Maybe I was being naive or too trusting, but other than finding her naked, I liked Jacqueline.

Quietly, I discarded my traveling clothes, which I'd been wearing far too long to feel comfortable in. I didn't want to risk looking for my luggage, so I wrapped myself in a cozy robe and then tiptoed past the bed, holding my breath, and out onto the terrace.

It was quieter than when we'd arrived. The traffic sounds had faded into the background as most of the city slept. But another magic had descended in the absence of day. Glittering lights punctuated the midnight sky, and the Eiffel Tower glowed in front of me. There was something about being here that felt like coming home. That was silly, considering I'd never been here before. Even so, a beautiful ache cracked open my chest, and I found myself longing for my cello. I didn't know how else to express my growing feelings.

"Beautiful." Julian's quiet voice broke the spell and placed me under a new one. Whatever magic ran in his veins only required one word to cast itself over me.

"Yes." I sighed as he moved behind me and circled my waist with his strong arms. Melting against him, I admitted, "It's the most beautiful city I've ever seen."

"I was talking about you, pet." He nosed my hair away from my neck so he could kiss it.

I melted against him. We'd been on our best behavior for far too long. I couldn't stand another minute of resisting him. Craning my neck to get a better look at him, I bit my lower lip.

"Is that an invitation?" he asked darkly.

"Um-hmm." I nodded. Still, I couldn't stop myself from baiting him now that we were alone and rested. "I feel terrible to have ruined your surprise."

"Surprise?" he repeated, sounding confused. But what I meant caught up with him before he'd finished speaking. He groaned. "I'm sorry for that debacle. Jacqueline is, well, Jacqueline."

"How illuminating." I laughed. "She seems nice. She wants us to go shopping."

Julian's eyes widened for a second, but then he relaxed. "That seems like a good idea. She'll be better at that than I would be—I'd only be trying to undress you the whole time."

"Then I should go?" I was still a bit confused by their dynamic.

"Jacqueline is important to me," he said, swiftly adding, "not romantically. She is my oldest friend, and she has put up with my shit better than anyone I've ever known. I would like her to get to know you."

"Why?" The question slipped out before I could stop it.

But he showed no sign of annoyance that I questioned him. "Because you are also important to me."

His words—or rather, the way he said them—caught me off guard.

"And you'll need things to wear. You didn't pack enough clothes," he added.

I was pretty sure he meant I hadn't packed the *right* clothes.

"Then I'll go."

"This afternoon," he said firmly. "There's an event you need to attend in the evening."

"With you?" I asked slowly.

"No, this event is only for females," he said casually. "The *Salon du Rouge*. You'll be expected to attend. I'm sure Jacqueline will go with you if you ask."

"Okay." I had about a million more questions about this female-only event. I was here to pass as Julian's girlfriend, stay at his side, and basically act as an amulet to ward off overeager familiars. It seemed silly to attend events by myself, unless…

Unless Julian was beginning to see me as part of his world. A thrill shot through me, but I tamped it down before it could spread its vicious deceit all the way to my heart. That wasn't how this worked. We had an understanding. We had boundaries. I'd come to Paris knowing that, and I couldn't waste the moments I had with him hoping for an unpromised future.

My stomach growled, shattering the blissful moment.

"You're hungry," Julian said, starting to pull away, but I caught his hand.

"No, I'm not." I was ravenous. My body was clearly confused as to what time it was or when I was supposed to eat. But I wasn't ready for this moment to be over. It was too perfect.

"Liar," he accused in an amused murmur. He planted kisses along my shoulder, nudging the robe to give him more access to my skin. "It's my job to care for you. Let me."

My breath hitched as he spoke. He had been attentive since the moment we'd met, even when that attention was coupled with annoyance or frustration. But now it had a new partner. There was a tenderness I hadn't heard before when he spoke, and something else that didn't match the Julian Rousseaux I had known before:

Tentativeness.

But why? What on earth did a nine-hundred-year-old vampire have to be uncertain about?

Regardless, I had not flown all the way to Paris to lose an opportunity like this. I twisted in his arms, hooking an arm around his neck, and dragged his lips to mine. Julian groaned but didn't resist. Instead, he slid his hands past my robe and grabbed the fleshy part of my hips. His fingernails dug into my skin, nipping at it with their sharpness, and my eyes flew open.

I pulled away, waiting for him to realize his mistake, but he didn't. "Julian, your gloves…"

"Yes?" His eyebrow curved into a question mark. "Would you like me to put them back on?"

"N-n-no," I stammered. My brain scrambled for any clue—any moment to latch on to—that would explain this sudden change of heart. "I just thought..."

I didn't know what I thought, because this was all happening so fast.

"I wanted to feel your skin on mine," he explained softly. "I told you before that we wear gloves to protect others. Our nails are quite sharp."

"I know," I teased him softly. His grip on my hips loosened a little.

"Did I hurt you?" he asked, his eyes shadowed with concern. "If you would like me to stop—"

"What's a little pain mixed with pleasure?" I reached down and covered his hand with mine through my robe. "Don't stop."

"There's another reason we cover our hands, pet," he explained softly. "Our magic rests there, or what's left of it."

"Magic?" I repeated. "I thought witches..."

"Vampires, especially old vampires, carry magic, too."

"You have magic?" I asked, and he nodded. It was a little hard to concentrate with his bare skin on mine. He was warmer than I'd expected him to be. I wondered how it would feel if his hands slipped farther down between my legs.

I was so preoccupied I didn't realize Julian had fallen silent.

"I'm sorry," I said quickly. "It's a lot to process."

"You should eat. You're beginning to smell like pure sugarcane," he said softly. He tried to withdraw his hands, but I held one firmly in place.

"Why do you cover up your magic?" I asked, realizing that he might never be open to this topic again.

"So we don't use it," he said, surprising me. "Sometimes when we touch someone else..."

My eyes widened as I began to understand. "Is it dangerous?"

"No and yes."

"That's very helpful," I said drily.

"It can be used to hurt someone, but only in those of us born long ago. Most modern vampires couldn't light a candle with their magic. But more importantly, it carries life. Why do you think vampires feed on human blood? It sustains our immortality."

I shook my head. I suspected that everything I'd read or seen in movies was wrong. So far it all had been, anyway. He didn't sleep in a coffin. I'd seen him in a mirror. And Jacqueline had worn a St. Michael's charm.

"There's a little magic in all creatures, even humans who have long forgotten or shunned it. It sustains our own lives. But the truth is that we cover our hands because vampires believe sharing our touch is one of the most intimate acts we can experience."

My mouth went suddenly dry at the implication of his words. He had chosen to share it with me. I swallowed. "What are the other acts?"

He tilted his head, looking confused.

"The other acts?" I pressed. "You said it was one of the most intimate acts. What are the others?"

He nodded. Bending lower, he brought his lips to brush over mine before sweeping them across my jaw to my neck. "To feed, obviously. It's one of the reasons we usually drink from a cup."

"Usually?" I asked.

"No one is perfect," he said lightly. "Sex," he answered next, and I felt myself flush with heat. "Naturally. Although sometimes sex is just fucking."

I nodded, even though I really couldn't claim to know anything about it.

"And the other?"

"You'll laugh," he said, but I shook my head. Still, he answered with a bemused smile, "The most intimate act is to hold bare hands."

A nervous giggle escaped me, but then I realized he was serious. "Holding hands? Really?"

"It's hard to explain."

But I wanted him to explain because I wanted to know...if

someday he might hold *my* hand. My eyes found the floor, too embarrassed to ask.

"So, if you're touching me now..." I trailed off, gathering up my courage to ask what I really wanted to know. "Does that mean you'll take me to bed?"

CHAPTER THIRTY-SEVEN

Thea

After several hours spent creatively christening his Parisian flat, I no longer doubted Julian wanted me as much as I wanted him. But despite him showing me all the interesting things he could do with his newly liberated fingers, I was still a virgin. What I couldn't quite figure out was why the hell he kept resisting something we both wanted. Every time we got close to crossing the line, he managed to pull us back to safety. Even now, pressed next to Julian in the backseat of his Bentley, I couldn't keep my thoughts from straying to all the close calls we'd had the night before. He looked almost as good in his cashmere coat and gray suit as he did naked. Almost.

"Are you certain you don't want me to come with you, pet?" Julian asked for the fiftieth time since we'd finally gotten up for the day.

I shook my head and pasted a smile on my face. "I'll be fine—as long as Jacqueline doesn't bite."

"She'll have me to answer to if she does," he promised darkly. The car pulled over, idling at the curb. He leaned over and stole a kiss. "If you change your mind…"

"I will call," I said. "Make sure you actually have your ringer turned on, old man."

"Don't worry. I think I have the hang of this damned thing." He held up his phone. His gloves were back on, but I couldn't resist reaching over to brush a sliver of his bare wrist. His eyes widened slightly. "Careful, or I'll take you right back to bed."

"Promise?" I licked my lower lip, earning a frustrated groan from him. "Then what would I wear to all the events? I'd have to go naked."

"Stop putting ideas in my head, pet," he groused. His hand flashed inside his coat's breast pocket, and then he held up a thin, black card. "Speaking of, you'll need this."

I hesitated, staring at the credit card. It was weird to take his money. We'd only known each other a week, but he seemed utterly nonchalant about giving me access to his bank account. "I have a little saved up. I can use that—"

"I promise you that 'a little savings' and 'shopping with Jacqueline' are incompatible concepts," he said drily. "You'll need this, trust me."

"But..." The look he gave me ended the argument. I sighed and took it from him. "Thank you. What's my budget?"

"Budget?" he repeated.

I resisted the urge to roll my eyes. "How much should I spend? I don't want to max it out."

Julian's lips pressed into a thin line, and it took me a second to realize he was trying not to laugh.

"Don't worry about that," he said. "It won't run out."

"Julian, I don't know..."

"I've spent nearly a millennium padding my bank accounts," he said firmly. "Besides, the card is in your name."

"What?" I nearly dropped it. Turning it over, I found my name listed above his. "Wait. How did you get this so quickly?" We'd only discussed shopping yesterday.

"Banks tend to respond quickly to my requests." He pressed his index finger to my chin and tipped my face up. "Stop worrying about money."

"That's easy for you to say," I muttered.

"Just give it to Jacqueline and tell her I said to use it wisely," he said, sounding annoyed.

"Wisely?" I narrowed my eyes, staring into his sparkling blue ones. Why was it so hard to think when he looked at me like that? "So there is a budget!"

"Jacqueline's interpretations of 'wisely' will be more in line with mine, pet," he said with a slight chuckle. He kissed the tip of my nose. "Trust her. I do. You can tell her anything, and she will look after you. Now go before you wind up attending all the events naked."

"Why do I have a feeling that *wouldn't* be frowned upon?" I unfastened my seat belt.

"I would frown on it." His voice was raspy as if the thought had thickened the words on his tongue. "I don't think I would be able to control myself."

"Oh." He had a point. Maybe I should try it and really rattle him. "I'll find something to wear." My door opened, Phillipe on the other side. But I couldn't resist the urge to lean back in. I smiled wickedly. "I'm sure they have a sale rack."

"If they do, Jacqueline won't let you near it."

As if summoned, Jacqueline appeared at my side, turning heads all around us in her ivory sheath dress and scarlet overcoat. Her blond hair fell in thick waves around her shoulders, and her face was completely bare, except for her lips, which were painted the same vivid hue as her jacket. She poked her head inside the Bentley. "She's safe with me, Jules."

"Just keep your hands to yourself," he told his old friend, shaking his head, "and don't let her see any price tags."

"Done!" She straightened, offering me a blinding smile. "Shall we?"

I followed her inside the large department store, feeling more out of place than ever. I blinked at the armed guards inside the entrance, even as other shoppers pushed past. Brands I recognized only from movies and magazines had little shops all along the perimeter. As soon as we were through the doors, a security guard moved toward us. I nervously slipped the credit card Julian had given me into my old thrift store purse as the man approached us.

Was it that obvious I didn't belong here? I'd chosen the most sophisticated outfit I'd packed—a pair of cropped black leggings and a wispy white blouse I'd borrowed from Olivia. I didn't think I looked that out of place, and there appeared to be several tourists wearing jeans shopping nearby. The guard bypassed me entirely and went straight to Jacqueline, who greeted him with a kiss on each cheek.

"Jean-Pierre, you're looking very handsome." She dusted something off his shoulder, and the older man turned candy-apple red. "I've brought a new friend. I believe Sophie is expecting us."

"Oui," he said, glancing over me. Confusion flashed across his face, but to his credit he recovered quickly. He gestured for us to follow. The crowd parted for us. I wasn't sure if that was because we had an armed escort or if Jacqueline simply had that effect.

Everywhere I looked, I found some new beautiful object waiting: silk scarves in every color and pattern I could imagine, delicate bottles of perfume displayed like pieces of art, and shoes, and purses. It was a bit overwhelming. As we passed, I swiped a look at the tag hanging from one of the scarves and nearly fainted. This was not your average department store.

"I arranged to have my private stylist work with us," Jacqueline explained when we reached a door marked *privée*. "But if you prefer to shop the floors, we can."

I quickly shook my head. I wouldn't know what to look for.

"I gave Sophie your measurements, so we should have somewhere to start." Jacqueline's mouth twisted as she studied my bag. "But I think you will need some handbags as well."

"No." I shook my head. "I don't need a new one."

"Don't confuse need with want while shopping," she said with a soft laugh. "It takes all the fun out of it."

"I...I don't really shop," I admitted to her as we were shown into another room.

"Because you don't need to?" she guessed as her eyebrow rose. But her voice was warm as she spoke. There was none of the judgment I'd felt in the presence of Sabine or, to some extent, even Celia. It seemed impossible, but I was beginning to believe Jacqueline was not only friendly but kind. "Julian mentioned you are a student. I imagine that doesn't allow for many luxuries."

"Unless food is a luxury, then no, it doesn't."

"Then allow Julian to spoil you a little," she advised, mirroring Celia's words. "Besides, Julian's consort will be expected to dress well."

I thought of the green velvet gown I'd worn a few nights ago. It had felt ridiculously over the top when I'd put it on in my apartment, but in the company of vampires and familiars, I'd blended right in. I nodded, but there was one thing I found a bit odd. "Consort?"

"Girlfriend," she corrected herself. "Lover." She waved dismissively. "I can be a bit old-fashioned."

Lover. If she only knew. I thought of what Julian had told me—that I could trust Jacqueline. I wondered if that extended to *really* personal matters like my vampire boyfriend not having sex with me. There was no one else I could talk to about it.

An older woman approached us before I could summon the courage to bring it up. Her hair was knotted at the back of her neck into a perfect chignon, and she wore a stern expression. She greeted Jacqueline and began speaking rapidly in French. A few minutes later, they were both laughing.

"Come. Sophie has curated some choices for you." Jacqueline guided me toward the many racks of clothing waiting in the room. "It will take you a while to try this all on."

"Wait." I stared at the racks, which had to contain a hundred different pieces, at least. "All of this is for me?"

"It's a start," she said, pursing her lips. She riffled through the hangers and then plucked a striking black dress from one. "Try this."

Looking around, I realized there was no dressing room.

Apparently, vampires thought nothing of being naked in front of strangers. I shimmied out of my clothes. Jacqueline's eyes pinched a little, and she said softly to Sophie, "Pull some lingerie as well."

"Oh, I don't—"

"Nonsense," she cut me off, already knowing that I was going to object. "You will need appropriate pieces to wear under these clothes. It's a need." She smiled. "But we will find some scandalous pieces to tease Julian with, too."

"I'm not sure how he'll feel about that."

But Jacqueline only laughed harder.

Sophie reappeared with a small treasure chest's worth of filmy chiffon and lacy nothings. They patiently showed me how to use a garter with stockings, and I couldn't help but admit that I'd never felt so sexy.

I lost track of the hours they spent zipping and tying me into gowns and dresses. Eventually, they segued into everyday clothing after what seemed like an impossibly high number of Jacqueline's asserted must-haves. I could have cried when Sophie presented me with a pair of jeans. Then I caught sight of the price tag.

I shook my head. "I have jeans," I told Jacqueline.

"And you have a purse," she said with a shrug of her shoulders. "If you won't spend Julian's money, I will. And before you argue with me, I'm under strict orders to get you everything you might need for the rest of the year."

I doubted I could ever need this many clothes, but arguing with Jacqueline was proving as pointless as arguing with Julian. Maybe it was a vampire thing. I nodded, grateful that I'd have something casual—if I could just forget the price tag—to wear. But the movement made my head spin, and I stumbled on my feet. Thankfully, I wasn't wearing any of the stilettos that had been added to my ever-growing pile of purchases. I pressed a hand to my forehead as a wave of dizziness hit.

"*Merde*," Jacqueline swore under her breath, keeping her voice low. "You're hungry. I forget humans eat so much."

"Or anything," I said faintly. Julian and I had been too preoccupied to eat a proper breakfast this morning. Checking my phone, I realized it was already nearly two.

"Let's get you something to eat," Jacqueline suggested, "and then we will choose what you're going to wear tonight."

"The *Salon*," I said, feeling my appetite vanish. "Are you going?"

"It's not meant for me," she said. Her gaze narrowed. "You look nervous. Has Julian told you what to expect?"

"No," I said with a grimace, "and the last party he took me to was an orgy." Unfortunately, Sophie returned just as the last part of the sentence left my lips. Her mouth fell open, but she quickly rearranged herself back into a composed professional.

Jacqueline's eyes danced with laughter at my *faux pas* as she hooked her arm through mine. "Come. There is a little tea room. Let's have a bite and talk."

She said something in French to Sophie, who nodded.

"I feel bad," I admitted as we left. "She's been waiting for me to choose things all day, and now she has to wait longer."

"The bill will make it worth her while," Jacqueline said with a wry smile. "And she isn't waiting for us. I already saw to the purchases. We just need to pick tonight's ensemble."

"But I have Julian's card." Or my card.

"I've waited for nearly eight hundred years for Julian to find someone for me to shop with. This is my treat," she said, waving off my objection. "Now, let's get lunch."

The tea shop was tucked into a private nook away from the mass of shoppers.

Jacqueline ordered for me, and before I could blink, a tray of mouthwatering pastries was in front of me, along with a steaming pot of tea. I poured myself a cup and took a grateful sip before turning my attention to the sweets.

"Let me guess," she said, watching me. "He forgets to feed you."

"Only sometimes," I corrected her, closing my eyes in rapture as I lifted a buttery pastry to my lips. I paused. "Sometimes I forget to feed myself."

"Well, that will change," she said mysteriously. "He's learning. I doubt he expected to find himself attached to a human."

"I didn't really expect to be attached to a vampire," I admitted. I picked up a beautiful chocolate tart next and took a bite, groaning with pleasure. "Sorry. I didn't realize how hungry I was."

"Don't apologize for your nature." Jacqueline poured herself a cup of tea and took a few sips. "So, about tonight. You must have questions."

I swallowed my food and reached for a napkin as my heart began to race. This was my chance. "I have a lot of questions...not just about tonight."

"About vampires?" she asked. "Or Julian?"

"About everything," I confessed.

"And Julian isn't answering them?"

"Some." I took a deep breath and plunged forward. "But there are questions I'm not sure if I can ask. I can't decide if he's protecting me from his world or keeping his world from me."

"I see," she said thoughtfully. She traced the rim of her teacup, and I wondered if I'd crossed a line.

"I'm sorry," I blurted out. "I shouldn't ask you to talk behind his back."

But Jacqueline only giggled. "I was only deciding where to begin," she told me. "But I'll leave that to you. Thea, what do you want to know?"

What did I want to know? What *didn't* I want to know?

"How not to stick out?" I admitted, flushing a little as she tilted her head, confused. "I'm a *human*. If I was a vampire or a familiar, I would be prepared for tonight."

"Even they aren't fully prepared. That's what this evening is about. The *Salon du Rouge* is a chance for familiars to learn more about what will be expected of them if they marry a vampire. But it's also a chance for vampire mothers and sisters to decide if a familiar would be up to the task of being a vampire's wife."

"That's what's going on this evening?" I snatched another piece of cake up and stress ate it. But it didn't help. "Wives? There were male familiars in San Francisco. Is this some warped version of a vampire ladies' night?"

Her mouth twitched. "I'm afraid so."

"Is Sabine going to be there? Why would Julian make me go to that? He knows she'll never approve of me, and it's not like…"

Part of me wanted to spill all the details of my temporary relationship with Julian, but it felt like breaking a promise.

"I'm afraid you might be right," she said gently. "Sabine is very traditional."

"She wants Julian to get married so he can make another little vampire." A sour taste filled my mouth. "But he doesn't want babies."

"You two have talked about babies?"

She seemed to have missed the important part of that information. "He just mentioned his mom wants him to get married and have a baby. He didn't seem particularly enthused."

"He has good reasons, even if he might need to rethink them," she said cryptically. "I think you might be helping him rethink them, actually."

"Me?" I nearly spilled my tea. "I doubt it. I can't have his babies, anyway."

"Regardless of what the Council or Sabine or anyone else thinks, a family can be made, Thea. Maybe you won't have babies, but you two could make a lovely family."

Her words sent my heart into my throat, but I tamped down the thrill. There was no way that was happening, and even if it did…

"From people he's turned?" I was trying to imagine Celia as my stepdaughter. I wasn't really sure how to feel about it.

"Or ones you choose together. The families we find are the families we keep."

"I don't think Julian plans to keep me." My chest squeezed as I said it. He'd told me I could trust Jacqueline, and I needed someone to talk to.

She tilted her head and studied me quietly for a moment. "Why do you think that?"

"Because we have an arrangement," I confessed. She listened as I filled her in on the story of how we'd met and the arrangement we'd made and the fact that he refused to sleep with me. By the time I finished, my cheeks were burning, but she only looked amused.

"Interesting," she said, a smile playing at her lips. "Julian has always had a soft spot for virgins, but there are rules."

"Rules?"

"He must have forgotten to mention them." She rolled her eyes and muttered, "Males. Yes, there are rules. Have you heard of thrall?"

"I'm not sure."

"It's basically when a mortal is under the influence of a vampire. Many mortals choose to be enthralled and serve our kind."

"Why would they do that?" That had to be the equivalent of choosing to be a walking blood bag. I didn't understand.

"Money and power. We try not to get involved much in human affairs, but sometimes they seek us out for help. And then there are some who have a taste of our venom and become addicted."

Having experienced venom, I understood.

"So you enslave them?" I asked.

"Think of it as a magically enforced nondisclosure agreement. The humans are always given the terms of the arrangement," she explained.

"If they refuse?"

"We compel them to forget they ever met a vampire or that we exist at all. We aren't interested in enslaving anyone."

"But you use them for blood?"

"Only if that's part of the agreement," she said. "Some humans only serve as lawyers or guards or accountants."

I couldn't wrap my head around the idea of a vampire's accountant. It was just too mundane. "Wait, am I in thrall?"

"I think he's more in thrall to you," she said with an unladylike snort. "Which brings us to vampires having sex with virgins. There can be a problem."

My eyes narrowed. Julian had very conveniently left this part out. "What kind of problem?"

"If a vampire has sex with a virgin, the effect on the virgin is like being under thrall but turned up to eleven. The virgin is tethered to the vampire."

"Until the vampire releases them?" I guessed.

"No. Death is the only release."

My stomach flipped as I processed her words. This was why Julian wouldn't take my virginity. "But wouldn't you all be tethered to whoever you first..."

"Vampires are careful in regard to their first time." She flashed me a sheepish smile that lacked her usual confidence. "Most families match their children, and when they come of age, they're expected to..."

I thought I might be sick. "And you?"

She nodded, taking a deep breath. "It wasn't so terrible, except that my parents wanted me to marry the match. Thankfully, he wasn't interested in marriage, either."

"And Julian knew this about tethering? Why wouldn't he tell me?"

I deserved to know. I needed to know!

"To start with, tethering is expressly forbidden by vampire law, and it's one law Julian will never break."

"Why? He doesn't seem to care about dragging a human into The Rites, and that's forbidden."

For the first time, Jacqueline hesitated. She bit her lip before she shook her head. "He has his reasons—*good* reasons. Ask him."

I gulped down that bit of information and focused on the other question preoccupying me. "Why wouldn't he just tell me?"

"I think he's worried it will scare you away." Her face screwed up like she shared his concern.

"But what if we'd slipped and accidentally... I wouldn't have known what had happened until it was too late."

"That's less forgivable," she admitted. "I suspect he's relying on centuries of carefully cultivated restraint and a fair amount of self-loathing to keep that from happening."

"Why even risk it?" Was I asking her or myself? "Why didn't he just leave when he found out?"

"Sometimes, what we intend to do is different from what fate has in store. I think even Julian's restraint is no match for destiny."

"Destiny?" I shook my head with a laugh, though my heart warmed at her easy assertion that her best friend and I were fated. "I'm not sure I believe in fate."

"How long have you known Julian?" she asked. "A matter of days? A week?"

I nodded.

"A blink of an eye for a vampire and hardly any time for a human, even, correct?"

"Yes. I guess so," I said.

"Now, answer one question honestly for me." She leveled a fierce gaze at me. "Are you in love with him?"

CHAPTER THIRTY-EIGHT

Julian

Thea barely spoke on the drive home from shopping. She angled her petite body toward the window, watching Paris fly by in utter silence. Judging from the bags that made their way into the Bentley's trunk—according to Jacqueline, these were only a small portion of the purchases—the trip had been a success. But Thea remained unreachable, even though she was sitting next to me.

By the time we arrived back at the house, I was beginning to panic. I went around and opened her door. Thea didn't look at me as she climbed out. Instead, she rushed into the house, passing a confused Hughes, who shot me a questioning look.

"Thea!" I called after her, but she didn't turn around.

I shot a quick text off to my best friend.

Did you break my girlfriend?

Three dots appeared and then disappeared. I waited, but no response came. Jacqueline and I needed to have a little talk. I'd expected her to fill Thea in on some of the more delicate particulars of vampire society to keep her safe, but exactly what had she told her?

"Have you upset Mademoiselle?" Hughes asked as though reading my mind. "I could arrange to have flowers delivered."

"That won't be necessary," I said, starting up the stairs after her. I paused on the third step. "On second thought, yes. Flowers seem like a good idea."

I went to the bedroom and found it empty. She wasn't in the bathroom or out on the terrace. As I turned to look for her, some of the housemaids began carrying in the shopping bags.

"Shall we hang these in Mademoiselle's closet?" one asked.

I nodded, too distracted to care what they did. They could cut them into tiny pieces and toss them about like confetti for all I cared.

She wasn't on the rooftop, either. Finally, I made my way down to the library. I found Thea there, tucked into a window seat that looked out over a little alley below. It was the least scenic view in the house, but she stared out to something beyond the glass.

I approached her cautiously, worried she would run again. "Was it that terrible? I promise never to make you shop again."

She glanced up at me, looking startled to find me standing there, then shook her head. "Shopping was fun."

"That is the least convincing you've ever been, pet." I sat next to her, but she shrank away as if she didn't want me to touch her.

"The shopping was fine." She turned toward me. Her green eyes were hard, glittering emeralds. "And the conversation was *illuminating.*"

"I see." I clenched my jaw, wondering if I'd made a mistake. I'd known Thea would ask Jacqueline the questions she didn't dare ask me. I'd thought I could guess what those questions might be. Maybe I had been wrong. Whatever she'd learned from my best friend hadn't just upset her.

Thea was pissed.

It radiated off her. Ginger and cinnamon mixed with her floral aroma, spicy and sharp notes of warning. I'd messed up. But how badly?

"Thea, I don't know what she told you," I started, earning another fierce glare. "But whatever she said, it's the truth. Jacqueline wouldn't lie to you."

"But you did," she accused.

"I've never lied to you." I couldn't. I had tried. No wonder I was fucking things up.

"You told me that you wouldn't sleep with me because my virginity was a precious gift or some other bullshit," she seethed.

I could hardly resist the urge to smile. Whenever Thea cursed, it reminded me of a kitten trying to act tough.

"I meant that," I said softly. "Whatever other reasons I had, I meant that first and foremost."

"But you let me push you, knowing that if you lost control, I would be tethered to you. That is screwed up!"

"I know." I nodded, feeling a heaviness settle on my chest. "I won't lose control."

"Really?" She lifted her chin, blowing a renegade strand of hair out of her eyes, before pressing on, "So the bloodlust and the blood rage are you being *completely* in control?"

"Yes," I hissed. "I would never endanger you, and I will *never* break that law."

"Liar," she said softly. "Just being here puts me in danger, and if I can't trust that you're telling me everything I need to know..."

She glanced away, her throat sliding as she swallowed whatever words finished her thought. If she couldn't trust me, what? Where did that leave us?

"I wish I'd brought my cello," she said suddenly. "I feel like I don't know who I am anymore."

Her words felt like a knife through my heart. "I would never change you."

"You made that clear," she said in a flat voice.

"Can you understand the boundaries now?"

"Yes," she admitted, but she took a deep breath. "But I'm not sure why I'm here anymore. Jacqueline said... It doesn't matter."

"What did she say?" I asked, but Thea remained quiet. I slipped my glove off and reached for Thea's face. Cupping her chin in my hand, I stroked my thumb across her cheekbone. "Pet, what did she say?"

Thea nuzzled against my bare skin. "Nothing."

"What?" I asked again.

"I need time to think," she said, standing abruptly and knocking my hand away. "And I have to prepare for this evening's event."

"You don't have to go to that," I said quickly. The last thing she needed was to deal with my mother and a bunch of snobby vampires and familiars after what she'd discovered today.

"Why? Because I might find out all the secret expectations for vampire wives?" she asked, crossing her arms over her chest. "Too late. I know that you're trying to avoid having kids, so you're shacking up with me—a mere mortal who can't give you any."

"I don't think of you that way, and I don't want you to go anywhere you're uncomfortable."

She rolled her eyes. The defiance sent a jolt to my groin. I wanted Thea every waking moment. How was it possible that I wanted her even more when she challenged me?

"I'm going," she said in a clear, strong voice. "I'm not afraid of your mother or the others. Not anymore. Not since I know that I can never be what they want."

"It doesn't matter what they want."

"Will the Council agree? You've bought yourself some time, but eventually you're going to have to marry a familiar and make vampire babies."

"Like hell I do," I roared, knocking over a reading stand and sending an antique volume of Shakespeare flying.

"What other options are there?"

I gave her the first one that came to mind. "Pack your bags. We'll go to Venice or Hong Kong. You name the place."

"I'm going." I heard the resolution in her voice, and I knew she wasn't talking about some new city. She would attend the *Salon du Rouge*, and I couldn't stop her.

"Why?" I asked.

"Because I want to see your mother's face when I tell her I'm not going anywhere," she said with a wicked shrug.

"You aren't?"

"Honestly? I don't know," she said, dampening the relief I'd felt at her words. "I have to think about things, but since I basically blew up my life to come here with you, at the moment I don't have a choice. You're stuck with me for the next year. I'm not going to spend the whole time avoiding your mother."

It was hardly reassuring, but it was better than thinking she might leave now.

"So that's what Jacqueline told you—about how vampire babies are made?"

"That's some of it." But she didn't offer to share any more of what she'd learned. "I should get dressed."

"Would you like help?" I asked, dashing off a wicked grin.

But she wasn't having it. "I'm still mad at you, so no."

"Are you certain? I can be very persuasive." I hooked a finger in the waistband of her pants.

"I'm afraid that area is off-limits until I decide."

"Decide what?"

Thea looked me dead in the eye. "If you're worth the trouble."

• • •

I spent the next hour pacing the lower level. It was bad enough she knew the truth, but how much worse could it be after tonight? Why had I surrendered and allowed her to go? She wasn't a familiar. As a pureblood heir, marrying her would cause a scandal. Our family had never fully recovered from the last one.

Fabric rustled near the stairs, and I turned to find Thea standing at the second-floor landing. She'd chosen tonight's gown to go with the theme: the *Salon du Rouge*. The candy-apple-red silk twisted at the bodice, revealing the slight swell of her creamy breasts. A halter strap circled around her neck like a choker, and a silk rose was pinned to the side, over her delicately pulsing jugular. She might as well have worn her "Bite me" shirt.

As she started down the stairs, her bare legs slipped through slits in the gown's skirt. She was walking temptation.

I moved to the end of the stairs and waited. When she reached the final one, I extended my hand. "I think you're the most beautiful thing I've ever seen."

Her eyes landed on the glove I wore, and she swept past me. "Don't wait up."

"Pet," I said softly. "It's not too late to change your mind."

She whirled around to face me. Her sharp eyes swept down me, an unreadable expression on her face. "Just wish me luck."

I caught her hand and spun her toward me. "You don't need luck."

"I don't?"

"No one will doubt why you're there."

"Why?" She challenged me with wary eyes. "I'm not a vampire. I'm not a familiar. I have no place in your world."

I brushed a kiss over her bright crimson lips. "No, you aren't those things," I murmured. "You're a *queen*, and a queen directs her own empire."

Her mouth twisted a little, but she pulled away and tucked her velvet clutch under her arm. Her hips swayed as she walked to where Phillipe was waiting with the car. He opened it for her, his eyes widening, but quickly looked away.

At least he was learning.

Thea paused and threw a look over her shoulder. "I'm a queen?"

I nodded, my mind already thinking of all the ways I would apologize to her later, starting with stripping her out of that dangerous dress she was wearing.

"I'll be home by morning."

"Pet," I growled. "I would prefer—"

But she was already in the car. The queen had made her move.

CHAPTER THIRTY-NINE

Thea

I wasn't used to being angry. Not this type of angry, anyway. I'd been pissed when Mom's cancer came back. I got mad whenever Olivia finished the milk and put the empty container back in the fridge. And more than once, I'd cursed Tanner's name for not changing the toilet paper roll. Those were all *Past Thea* problems. *Past Thea* scraped together rent, held down two jobs, and went to school. In every way, *Past Thea* had it worse than me.

Except one.

Past Thea didn't know about vampires. She never worried about bloodlust or ceremonial rites or how to walk in five-inch heels. And she definitely wasn't in love with her temporary vampire boyfriend.

I kept hearing Jacqueline's musical voice, a trace of a French accent wrapping around her words, as she asked me that question.

Are you in love with him?

Never mind that I hadn't answered her. Never mind that it was apparently just to provoke a reaction. Never mind that I told myself I didn't know yet.

Because it didn't matter.

We couldn't be together. I knew that now. There was no way I was enslaving myself to him for the rest of my life—even if mine would feel short in comparison. It was the only one I had. And there was no way I was staying a virgin and settling for only part of Julian.

Not that it was up to me anyway.

He needed to marry and produce baby vampires with some beautiful familiar. He might not want to, but sooner or later, he'd meet someone who held his attention. He'd find a woman to make his wife.

Would it be next week? Next month? Could he resist the Council for a whole year like he planned? And what the hell was I supposed to do? Staying meant falling harder for him. Part of me—the deluded part—hoped maybe I could catch myself before I tumbled head over heels. But going back now was impossible. I'd taken a leave of absence from school. My mother would barely speak to me. I'd lost any chance at the Reeds Fellowship. Carmen had even texted that the quartet had found a new cellist. Julian was the one who'd asked me to leave my life behind, but I was the one who lit it on fire in my hurry to join him.

That should have been a red flag.

I dabbed the corners of my eyes, trying to stop my tears before they fell. There was no way I was going to face Sabine Rousseaux with mascara running down my cheeks. I might have made a mistake coming here, but I didn't for one second believe what she thought about me. I slipped my velvet opera gloves back on. Not being a vampire or a familiar, I didn't need to wear them, but tonight I wanted to make something clear.

I belonged.

Julian had chosen me, and I wouldn't cower to Sabine or any other vampire.

"Mademoiselle," Phillipe said from the front seat. "We've arrived."

Peering out the window, I tried to get my bearings, but it was difficult because night had fallen. A limestone wall with a large iron gate blocked me from seeing much. I didn't honestly know what to expect. Jacqueline had given me more details about this evening while we picked my gown, but I hadn't really absorbed a word she'd said. I'd been too preoccupied with the question she'd asked me over tea.

Phillipe opened my door and hovered nearby. Clearly, he didn't want to risk Julian's blood rage by giving me his hand. I passed my Chanel clutch to him so I wouldn't lose my balance as I stood. The shoes Jacqueline had advised me to wear were dangerous. On the plus side, I could probably use one of the stilettos to stake a vampire if I needed to.

He passed my evening bag back to me when I was on my feet. "I will be nearby waiting."

"You don't have to do that," I said with a frown. "I have no idea how long I'll be."

"Orders," he explained.

Of course my overbearing boyfriend would demand he wait.

"I insist," I said. I hated the idea of him waiting around when he could be enjoying the city. "At least go get a coffee or something."

"Monsieur Rousseaux made things quite clear," he said meaningfully.

He'd compelled him. Why didn't that surprise me?

Another car arrived, and a few women spilled out from the backseat, dressed in red. Jacqueline told me we were expected to wear red this evening. I tried to convince her to let me pick another color, just to annoy Sabine, but she was firm on the matter.

The group made their way toward the iron gate, and I followed at a close distance. In the end, I'd asked Jacqueline not to come along. I wanted to do this on my own. But I realized now that it had been a mistake not to pay enough attention to her instructions. I had no idea where I was going, and queen or not, a few directions would have been helpful. I listened as one of the women spoke to an attendant waiting past the gate.

Unfortunately, she spoke in French.

Tonight was already off to a great start. I hurried behind them when the gate opened, but before I made it past, the attendant stopped me.

He asked me something in French, and I shook my head.

"Sorry," I said apologetically.

He narrowed his eyes. "Family name?" he said in a thick accent.

I swallowed. "Melbourne."

He studied his list. "I don't have a Melbourne."

"I'm a guest of Julian Rousseaux."

His eyes flashed up. "I will need to check."

"Sabine invited me," I added.

"I see." He flipped through his pages and paused to read something scrolled across the bottom in flawless calligraphy. "There you are."

Something about the way he said it told me whatever was written on that paper was far from pleasant.

"Please enjoy your evening," he continued, his eyes scouring me like he was taking notes. "They will announce you at the entrance. You may wish to give the Rousseaux name."

Because I was a nobody—by their standards.

I strolled through the brick courtyard. Part of me didn't want to go in. The rest of me was learning how freaking hard it was to walk in heels on uneven ground. By the time I reached the front door, I knew what I had to do.

Another attendant dressed in a simple black gown greeted me. She was friendlier than the man at the gate, but probably only because I'd made it past the gate in the first place. "Name?"

I took a deep breath. "Thea Melbourne."

I might be Julian's guest, but I was my own person—whether Sabine liked it or not.

"And you are a familiar?" she asked gently. "Is that your family name?"

"Yes, it is my family name, but no. I'm not a familiar. I'm a guest."

She waited as if expecting me to say who my hostess was, but I simply smiled. She turned and called to the attendees visiting in the lounge, "Mademoiselle Thea Melbourne."

Heads turned in my direction, but I kept my own high, looking over the tops of them. I didn't need to know if they were gossiping or leering. Julian thought I was a queen? Acting like one couldn't hurt. Not amongst this crowd.

"Thanks," I said quietly, taking a step inside.

"Good luck," she whispered.

By the time I made it past the entrance, nearly everyone had returned to their own conversations. Half of the women present wore red, and the other half wore white. Closer inspection led me to suspect the females in white were vampires, which meant the red attire must be for familiars. No wonder they'd thought I was a familiar at the door. But unlike that night in San Francisco, there were no males present.

The massive hall opened on either side into larger rooms. As my heels clicked against the black marble floor, I realized there were dozens of people present—if not hundreds. Crimson peonies were artfully arranged in silver vases and urns everywhere I looked. Their petals spilled open in lush, exotic blossoms that filled the air with their sweet fragrance.

"Thea!" a friendly voice called, and I turned, almost tripping over my own feet, to find Quinn Porter, the kind familiar from the night of the blood orgy, waving a gloved hand at me. Like me, she was dressed in red, but she'd opted for a fitted pantsuit. Its jacket was buttoned at her waist. She wore nothing underneath. The effect was breathtaking.

"Quinn! You look gorgeous," I said as she greeted me with a hug.

"You do, too. I love your dress." She grabbed my hands and smiled. "And gloves, I see."

"I'm trying to blend in," I muttered.

We looped our arms together, and she steered me toward an empty corner. "You are the talk of the night."

"What? Me?" My stomach flipped over. I could only imagine what Sabine had been telling people.

"Someone let it slip that the eldest Rousseaux was off the market.

There are a lot of broken hearts here tonight. I'd watch your back," she advised.

"He's hardly off the market," I said with a frown. Not that I wanted to advertise that, either.

"But you're here," she said.

"Yes, I am. So?"

"Humans aren't invited to the *Salon du Rouge*," she whispered, looking around as if she was worried she'd been caught sharing secrets with me.

"You're a human," I pointed out.

"I'm a witch. Trust me, to them it's not the same thing." She shook her head. "The only time a human attended the *Salon*—"

But before she could finish, a gong rang out. Conversation instantly died, removing our cover, and everyone turned toward the sound.

Naturally, Sabine was the one standing there, a mallet in her hands. She placed it on a silver tray, which was immediately whisked out of sight along with the antique brass gong. Did they have a gong for everything? Her black hair was swept into a tight bun at the top of her head. Black liner curved into dangerous points at the corner of her eyes. But it was the white silk gown she wore that demanded attention. It left nothing to the imagination.

"Vampires must have good genetics," I muttered. Quinn giggled next to me.

"Most of them. Why do you think so many of us want to be turned?" she said softly.

I remembered what Jacqueline had said about marriages between vampires and familiars. It seemed Quinn hoped to be made into a vampire if she took a husband of her own.

Before I could ask her about it, Sabine began to speak.

"Welcome to the *Salon du Rouge*," she said. Excitement rippled through the room at her announcement.

"Tonight, you will learn exactly what is required of each of you to serve as a proper vampire wife."

"This ought to be good." A few women nearby glared at me, and I fell silent. But there were a few others giggling in the crowd. She made it sound like we were joining a sorority.

Sabine raised her perfect brows with a cutting smile. "Don't worry. Your male counterparts will also receive instructions tonight on how to be a proper and, most importantly, *obedient* husband."

That explained where all the men were. I held back a snort at the archaic idea. But then it hit me, Julian was at home. He wasn't attending some lesson on the duties of a vampire marriage.

"The *Salon* is one of our most ancient traditions, and attending it is a privilege. For most of you this is your first *Salon*, so you must understand that what happens here is not spoken of outside these walls. The secrets you learn here must never be divulged. To that end, you will all be compelled to never speak of what you experience this evening."

Butterfly wings fluttered in my stomach as she spoke. I glanced around and discovered I wasn't the only one who looked nervous. Several familiars, in their red outfits, were eyeing the door.

"Tonight, we share freely with each other so that each of you— vampire or familiar—will be prepared to take the remaining Rites."

People began to whisper around me. I turned to Quinn, whose eyes had widened. "Remaining?"

"Tonight, you will be tested," Sabine said over the murmurs of the crowd. Turning back, I found her eyes watching me as she announced, "Welcome to The First Rite."

CHAPTER FORTY

Julian

Somewhere in Paris, my mother and my girlfriend were in the same room. I hoped they were both still alive. I paced the length of the sitting room, one eye on the clock over the mantel and another on my phone. I'd lost my damned mind. This was all because Jacqueline had put ideas in my head.

Thea wasn't my mate.

She couldn't be. In my nine hundred years, I'd jumped between enough relationships and beds to know that mating was a pretty story vampire mothers told their children at bedtime. It was a fairy tale. Nothing more. No one I'd known had ever actually mated with anyone.

I sent another message to Jacqueline, who was definitely avoiding me after today's shopping trip with Thea. I wanted to know how much she'd told her and what exactly would happen tonight at the *Salon du Rouge*, though my mother had promised it would be harmless. If there was some possibility of a relationship with Thea, the sooner I got my family on board, the better.

Hughes entered the room and watched me for a second. I could only imagine what he thought of my agitation. "Sir, you have guests."

That was the problem with being in Paris. Acquaintances were bound to turn up. I thought I'd have a few more days before I had to welcome any. I sighed. "Show them in."

I wandered over to the antique bar cart in the corner, then poured myself a Scotch and braced myself for small talk. Maybe it would distract me from the wild panic that had enveloped me in Thea's absence.

"Nice digs, governor," a cheerful voice called, and I turned to find my brother Benedict standing with an unopened bottle of Scotch. Sebastian was next to him. "I brought a housewarming present."

I crossed the room in two strides and greeted him with a hug.

"You never hug *me* when I come to visit," Sebastian complained. But he was already prowling around the room, and when he reached the velvet sofa he dropped into it, kicking his feet up.

"You had Celia wake me up," I reminded him.

"That was Mother," he pointed out. "And I brought you an entire blonde."

Benedict chuckled. "Some things never change."

"Some people, you mean." I took the bottle from him and read the label. It was fifty years old and from a small town outside Edinburgh that was known for only two things. "This ought to be good."

"Say what you want, but werewolves know their whisky," Benedict said. "Shall we finish off what you started?"

I stared at him for a moment, wondering if he'd been sent here to deliver some family edict on my recent choices. Benedict's brown eyes—which had a warm, deep glow that reminded me of logs on a fire—studied me back. He looked good, dressed in a cashmere suit that was tailored to fit his massive vampiric frame. His tie hung loosely around his neck as if to signal he was ready to relax.

Benedict was the diplomat of the family. The man we sent to handle everything from strained relations between rival bloodlines to Council issues to our increasingly tenuous relationships with other species. If he were human, he'd be a prime minister or a president. But vampire law dictated that we never hold official positions in human governments.

"Let's open this one." He gestured to the bottle he'd brought.

Of course, Benedict was talking about Scotch, not Thea.

"I'm sorry. I'm distracted. Let me get you a drink," I said. The sooner I could convince my brain—and my dick—that Thea wasn't the center of the universe, the better. I was certainly acting enthralled...

I poured a drink into two crystal glasses and brought one to each of them.

"To family," Benedict said, raising his.

Sebastian rolled his eyes, his own glass already at his lips. "It's just us. You don't have to be the golden child."

"Believe it or not, I actually meant it," Benedict muttered, shooting him a weary look. "Even if you're here."

"I'm touched, brother." Sebastian pressed a hand to his heart. Then he downed his entire drink in one gulp. He looked around the room, then back at me. "Where's your sweet little human?"

My spine stiffened as I felt the increasingly familiar rage begin to take hold. All I could manage was to spit a single word in his direction. "Out."

Sebastian tossed a cocky grin at Benedict and then laughed. "I told you."

"Shit," Benedict murmured, taking a sip of his Scotch.

"And you didn't believe me." Sebastian leaped onto his feet and headed for the bottle of booze. I stepped into his path before he could reach it.

"Told him what?" I demanded. The room darkened around us. I rounded on Benedict next. "What? What didn't you believe?"

"Calm down." Sebastian brushed past me. He picked up the bottle and took a swig from it.

"Help yourself," I grumbled. I took a deep breath and pushed back the turmoil stirring inside me. "Now, will one of you tell me what the hell you're talking about?"

"According to Sebastian, you have a girlfriend—a human girlfriend," Benedict said.

"Is that why you're here?" I edged closer. "Have you been sent to talk sense into me?"

His mouth twisted into a bemused line. "Are you hoping I will?"

"Thea is a means to an end. Nothing more," I informed him.

"Really?" Benedict sounded unconvinced. "Look, I've spent enough time around politicians to know spin when I see it."

"I'm not spinning anything." I cracked open the bottle he'd brought and poured myself a drink.

"A means to an end?" he said, repeating my words. "What end?"

"I don't have to tell you that they enacted The Rites." I sank into a leather chair by the window. "She's a distraction. If I'm seeing someone, I can't be expected to prance about looking for a wife, can I?"

"Interesting." Benedict took another drink, but I spotted the smile he tried to hide.

"You should both be thanking me." I pointed my index finger at each in turn. "The longer I drag this out, the longer you have until it's your necks on the line."

"And how long do you think you can keep our mother at bay?" he asked, voicing the question I'd been asking myself since I'd found out The Rites would continue indefinitely.

"I don't know," I admitted, dropping my head in my hand. "Maybe one of you should just stake me."

"That seems like a dramatic solution," Benedict said.

"But points for style," Sebastian added. He sat down again—this time on the Persian rug—and continued nursing his bottle. "Why not just get married?"

"Seriously?" Rage boiled inside me, but I tamped it down. "Why don't *you* get married?"

"I will—when it's my turn." He smirked.

Without meaning to, I hurled my glass at his head. He ducked just in time, and it shattered against the wall behind him.

"I don't see what the big deal is," he continued, completely unfazed by the outburst. "It doesn't change anything. Look at Mum and Dad. They do whatever—and *whomever*—they please."

"Yes, what a shining example of marital bliss for all of us," Benedict said drily. "But—and I hate to say it—he makes a decent point. It's not like you need to give up your human. Plenty of vampires keep pets after they're married."

It was a casual remark. He had no way of knowing about his slip of the tongue. Pet. That's what I called Thea. I meant it affectionately. Or had a part of me meant to keep her all along?

"Just find a familiar that pleases our parents, knock her up, and move on with your life," Sebastian added. "You need the blood anyway. Even your wife will understand that. She can't argue with your need to feed, and from what I hear about marriage, she'll be happy to let you keep fucking your pretty human if it keeps the peace."

Something snapped inside me. One minute, I was listening, disgust snowballing inside me. The next, I had Sebastian by the throat, his feet dangling a foot from the ground. Sebastian opened his mouth, but the only sound he made was a gurgle.

"Stop calling her my pretty human," I roared. "Stop talking about fucking her or keeping her on the side." My hand crushed into his larynx. Blood beaded from where my fingernails had broken his skin.

A firm hand clapped onto my shoulder. "Julian," Benedict said my name gently. "Put our brother down before you pop off his head by accident."

"It wouldn't be an accident," I seethed.

"Believe me, you have my empathy, but you don't really want to behead your brother."

I wasn't entirely certain that was true. Slowly, I forced my fingers to relax until he fell on the floor. Sebastian touched his neck gingerly. When he pulled back bloody fingers, he chuckled. "I told you it was bad."

"You're doing that infuriating thing where you act like I'm not here," I warned them. Another surge of adrenaline hit me, but I managed to stumble back to my chair. Benedict picked up the bottle and poured us all another drink.

"It seems like things are a little more complicated with your human than you're admitting." Benedict held up a hand in surrender. "No judgment. We're here to help. Sebastian told me something was up."

I glared at Sebastian, who didn't even have the decency to pretend he hadn't been gossiping behind my back.

"Now, where is your girlfriend?" Benedict asked, choosing each word carefully, so he wouldn't set me off.

"She went to a party." I downed my Scotch with one swallow and beckoned for another. As a vampire, it was hard to get drunk—but not impossible. I aimed to try.

Benedict sank into the chair opposite of mine. His drink remained untouched in his hand. "I've never seen you like this before. I mean, I understand the urge to rip Sebastian's head off—"

"Hey!" Sebastian interjected. "This is what I get for trying to help."

Benedict continued, ignoring him, "—but it's not like you to be so..."

"Grouchy?" I offered.

"No, you're usually grouchy," Sebastian said. Clearly, he wasn't worried I would finish what I'd started with his neck.

"Violent. Possessive." Benedict settled against his chair. He swirled the amber liquid in his cup. "I've heard stories about recent blood rage and bloodlust outbursts."

"Mother is exaggerating," I said.

"Is Bellamy?" he asked seriously. "No wonder the rumor is that you're off the marriage market."

"I was never on the market," I said bitterly. This was turning into the worst family reunion ever.

"You never will be at this rate." Sebastian dipped his finger into the bottle's neck and then flipped it over. He pulled his finger free and wiped away the blood on his neck from our disagreement. The wounds were already healed. No permanent damage had been done, and he didn't seem angry with me.

I just couldn't understand why.

"What's going on?" Benedict asked. "What's so special about this girl?"

I shifted forward and leveled a searing gaze at them. "If I tell you, you can't tell anyone. Not Mom or Dad. Not even Lysander or Thoren." The last thing I needed was more of my brothers involved in this mess.

"Your secret is—"

"I need you to promise." I dragged a nail across the palm of my hand. Blood welled onto the spot, and I stuck my hand out.

"Seriously? A blood vow?" Sebastian laughed, but he shut up when I turned a furious look to him. "Fine! Keep your gloves on."

He slipped his own gloves free and repeated suit, then reached over and shook my hand. "I swear to never tell anyone that you are batshit crazy because you're my brother, and I love you—even though you tried to kill me."

"I'm holding you to that," I said gruffly. "And I'm sorry I tried to kill you."

Sebastian shrugged. "It happens."

Benedict watched the exchange in silence. I looked at him and waited. Sebastian might complain about being asked to make a blood vow, but he'd always say yes. Benedict was more careful with the secrets he agreed to keep. Committing to a blood-vow was a somber choice for him. He had to be wondering what secret I was keeping that required such an extreme measure.

Finally, he stood and removed his calfskin gloves. A moment later, he made the vow. "I'll take your secret to the grave."

I sighed with relief. They waited expectantly.

"Thea is a virgin," I said before I lost my courage.

"I was not expecting you to say that," Sebastian admitted,

sounding on the verge of laughter.

Benedict wasn't nearly so amused. "What the hell are you thinking? Is this why you're practically ripping people's heads off for mentioning her? Virgins and bloodlust don't mix, dickhead."

"Thank you," I said drily. "I hadn't noticed."

"Seriously, Julian. You need to let her go before it's too late for you both."

"I can't. She knows about our world, and she already drew some attention. It wouldn't be safe." It was as reasonable an excuse as any for keeping her with me.

"Compel her, buy her a small fortress in the middle of nowhere, and move on. You don't want to tether a human."

"I have to agree," Sebastian interjected. "It's never pretty."

"Does she even know what would happen if you gave in and slept with her?"

"She knows, and she's pissed. She went shopping with Jacqueline earlier."

They both stared at me.

"She's shopping with Jacqueline? No wonder half the vampires in Paris think you're one walk away from the altar." Benedict stood and began pacing around the room. "How did she react when she found out?"

"Not well." It tasted sour to admit. "It's not like I *want* to tether her."

"At least she doesn't want to be tethered," Sebastian said helpfully. "Only the weird ones go for that."

"There's something else," I said slowly. My brothers stopped and stared.

"At least we know she isn't pregnant," Sebastian muttered.

Benedict continued, ignoring him. "What could be worse than getting involved with a virgin?"

"It's something Jacqueline said." I hesitated, but I couldn't ignore what I'd already pieced together. "There's something different about Thea."

"That's the bloodlust talking," Benedict said, but I shook my head.

"No, I mean it. I can't lie to her. I can't compel her."

"Impossible," Sebastian said softly. "Maybe you were just having an off day."

"I tried more than once," I said bitterly. "I've known her a week, and if one of you tried to step between us, I'd rip your head off."

Benedict swore under his breath. "You can't really think..."

"She's my mate," I murmured. A weight lifted off my shoulders. I'd spent the last twenty-four hours telling myself the exact opposite. I might not be able to lie to Thea, but I could lie to myself. I knew that now. Just as surely as I knew Jacqueline was right.

Thea was my mate.

For a split second, joy welled inside me—warm and promising and hopeful. But just as quickly, dread replaced it.

"No," Sebastian said. "Mating is a myth. I've never known anyone who actually mated."

"She can't be your mate," Benedict said quietly. "Not yet. Not if you haven't..."

"I know." My voice sounded hollow, as if it was coming from someplace far away instead of my own throat. There was a catch. We all knew the fairytale stories of mating, and we all knew how the bond was sealed.

"Fuck," Sebastian groaned. "We should have brought more Scotch."

"Where is she tonight?" Benedict asked. I knew what he was thinking. He wanted to see us interact with his own eyes. He'd never been Jacqueline's biggest fan. He probably thought she was putting ideas in my head.

"The *Salon du Rouge*," I said, feeling the beginnings of a headache. Between constantly suppressing my bloodlust and my recent outburst of blood rage, I needed something stronger than Scotch.

"What?" Sebastian spun around, bottle in hand. "Where is she?"

I repeated myself. Sebastian shook his head, worry contorting his face. It looked so out of place that it might have been comical if we weren't talking about Thea.

"Julian, do you know what goes on there?" he asked.

"No one knows," Benedict snorted. "That's the point. It's for the females only."

"*I* know what's happening there tonight." Sebastian glared. "I heard it from one of Mom's friends."

"Get to the point," I said. Whatever it was couldn't be worse than knowing Thea was my mate and I could never have her. Not unless she let another man have her first. I couldn't care less about some stupid party in the face of knowing that.

It turned out I was wrong.

"Julian," Sebastian said my name like it was fragile. "She's at The First Rite."

CHAPTER FORTY-ONE

Thea

This was not what I'd had in mind for the evening. After Sabine's dramatic announcement, the familiars and I had been ushered down an ancient stone staircase into an underground room. Its stone walls and floor lent a damp mustiness to the cold air. Ornate torches burned around the perimeter, but their flames did little to light the subterranean cavern.

"I don't like this," Quinn muttered next to me.

I shivered, wishing Jacqueline had given me a wrap to wear with this dress. Maybe she hadn't known about this part. Perhaps I hadn't been paying enough attention when she'd warned me.

Quinn wrapped an arm around my shoulders, and we huddled together. Several others around us followed suit. No one spoke above a whisper.

"Did you know this was The First Rite?" I asked Quinn.

She shook her head. "Everyone failed to mention that, and believe me, I asked about tonight. They must have meant it when they said we aren't allowed to talk about it."

"Probably because they make sure we can't."

"You think they're going to compel us?"

I looked around. This place was only a step up from being a

catacomb or a dungeon. Whatever was about to happen was going to be memorable. There was no way every familiar who attended the *Salon* would keep this secret.

Before I could tell Quinn this, Sabine descended the stairs. In her hands she carried a basket shaped like a cornucopia. Next to her, an older woman wearing a red gown stood with her hands clasped, bound together by a dark rope. Behind them in two lines, beautiful women dressed in white followed their lead. Each carried a small basket of her own.

We all fell into silence as Sabine stopped.

"Tonight, we pay homage to the Bona Dea," she said in a clear, strong voice that echoed off the stone walls. "Damia—mother of us all. From you, our life springs eternal."

"Damia—mother of us all," the woman in red next to her repeated. "From you, our magic bears fruit."

"What in the ever-loving shit?" Quinn whispered.

My thoughts exactly. I felt like we'd wandered into the initiation ceremony for some cult. I spotted more than a few other women glancing around. We weren't the only ones wondering what we'd gotten ourselves into.

"We welcome your spirit among us," Sabine continued.

"We walk in your presence," the woman in red added. She bent, unwrapping the cord that bound her wrists, and dropped it to the ground. But it wasn't a cord at all. It hit the stone with a hiss that made my stomach fall along with it.

"Oh, hell no," I said as the snake began to slither across the floor.

The familiars parted, lifting skirts and looking around, panicked.

But there was nowhere to go. Vampires were blocking the stairs, and there were no windows. Sabine called out in a calming voice, "Men have made the serpent your enemy with their lies. You have been taught to fear it, but it only seeks to give pleasure. All of you here know the exquisite pleasure of the flesh. Damia teaches us to embrace that pleasure. Pleasure is power. Pleasure is feminine. Pleasure is the seed that will bear beautiful fruit. The snake is her servant, and it will not harm you. It seeks only to deliver its offering."

"We walk with it to remember that we are the power in this world," the woman in red continued. "Our bloodlines endure. Our fruit prospers. Damia embraces us and blesses us. She ripens our wombs and prepares them to receive our protector's seed."

Quinn giggled breathlessly, and I elbowed her in the side. I couldn't exactly blame her. It was a bit over the top.

"And tonight, we will offer Damia our blood in appreciation for her gifts. A single drop from each of you, that we might continue to receive her blessings."

Despite Sabine's reassurances about the snake, several women continued to move out of its path as she spoke.

"Fear has no place in pleasure," she cried out to them. "The serpent is a friend to all that know its embrace. Show your courage, and be found worthy. A familiar must never fear the fangs. Tonight, it will not touch the daughters of Damia. You have prepared yourself for your place at her side."

"So the snake is a vampire? Am I getting the symbolism right?" Quinn asked.

My heart began to pound so hard that it sent blood roaring through my veins. All I could see was the snake moving through the crowd. I didn't care what it symbolized. I cared what it was looking for.

"Thea," Quinn said quietly, "you look terrified. You heard what she said. The snake won't touch any of us."

"Unless—"

Before I could finish the thought, the women behind Sabine cried out in unison: "We welcome your spirit among us. We walk in your presence."

Raising their baskets, they emptied them, spilling more snakes onto the stairs. Sabine smiled as she lowered her cornucopia, and serpents began to spill from it. They uncoiled like black ropes, crisscrossing each other as they spread across the dank rooms.

"Damia." Sabine lifted her head and bellowed, "We embrace

you. We offer our faith without fear. Bless us in The First Rite."

"This just got so much worse," Quinn said, sounding completely freaked out. But she didn't move. None of the familiars moved. This was the test.

One I wasn't going to pass.

"Damia calls you forth." Sabine removed her gloves and handed them to a woman behind her. Another passed her a silver chalice. "You are found worthy. Come to—"

Gasps from the crowd cut her off, and she fell silent as the snakes all began to move together, forming a thick line of writhing darkness. Serpents slithered around the feet of familiars, moving to join the others in a black parade. A few women looked like they might pass out, but it soon became clear the snakes were banding together, as if herded by some invisible force.

"Oh, fuck," I muttered as they slithered closer and closer. The first serpent, the one the woman in red had released, reached my feet. It took every ounce of restraint I possessed not to move as it began to climb my skirt. The rest joined it, forcing Quinn to move away as the snakes encircled me like a wreath. A moment later, the first one slithered up my stomach past my breasts and slowly made its way to my neck. Its scales scraped across my bare skin, and I felt acid rise into my throat. It coiled around my neck and rested its head against my throat.

I didn't dare move. Sabine had said the snakes wouldn't touch the daughters of Damia. I hoped she was just talking about witches, but the sinking feeling inside me knew it was so much worse than that.

Everyone had fallen silent, but now whispers began again. If I wasn't the talk of the party before, I would be now. Sabine, who had stayed utterly still, snapped back into action. Depositing the chalice into her companion's hands, she swept down the steps and marched toward me. The snakes that circled me parted for her. She stepped closer and plucked the snake from my throat. It unwrapped itself into her hands, and she tossed it to the ground.

"Well, well." Her blue eyes flashed like lightning in the dark. "It seems one of us doesn't belong here."

We glared at each other.

"I think you already knew that," I said.

"Quiet, vestal." Her voice was a deadly whisper meant only for my ears. She lifted her voice and addressed the group. "The Rite will continue. Sister Agnes will accept your offerings to Damia, and then we will proceed to the upper rooms for entertainment and conversation."

The woman in red, who must be Agnes, moved to the side of the stairs. Familiars formed neat lines, each eager to offer their drop of blood and get away from this horror show.

I, on the other hand, was surrounded by magical snakes and one angry vampire mother. Sabine grabbed my wrist, flinching slightly when her bare skin met mine. But she didn't drop her hold. She yanked me toward the stairs and away from the rest of the guests.

Quinn shot me a worried look as I passed her, and I did my best to force a smile. I doubted she bought it.

Sabine's nails pierced my skin, and I yelped. But when I tried to pull away, they dug in deeper. "Stop fighting me," she murmured. "Or you might not make it out of here alive."

She dragged me upstairs to the now empty corridor and finally released me. Blood welled from the puncture marks she'd put into my wrist. Sabine's nostrils flared, and her eyes darkened. I wrapped my hand around the wounds quickly.

She laughed, tossing her head to the side. "I am not my son. Your blood does not tempt me."

"Could have fooled me," I shot back.

She rounded on me, backing me toward a small corner off the foyer. "Is this your plan?" she demanded. "Is that what has my son so ensnared? Has he been feeding off you?"

"W-w-what?" I sputtered. "No!"

"I knew I smelled something in your blood," she continued without acknowledging my response. "A virgin! What the hell is

Julian thinking, or is this some petty revenge against his family?"

"This might shock you," a calm voice interjected, "but this has nothing to do with you, Sabine."

She spun around, stepping out of the way so that I could see my savior.

Jacqueline.

My shoulders sagged in relief to find Julian's best friend standing there dressed in neither the vampires' chosen white nor the red of the familiars. Instead, she wore a black leather dress that hugged her willowy body and stopped a few inches above her knees. Her blond hair was gathered in a loose braid that hung over her shoulder. But it was the unimpressed look on her face that stood out the most.

"Jacqueline," Sabine said, her voice dripping poison, "you've deigned to join us. Although I see you still don't respect our traditions."

"Really?" she said to Sabine. "I thought you would have learned your lesson when Cam—"

"Do not say that name to me," Sabine cut her off. "And this is different. Julian is the heir to the Rousseaux bloodline. I will not have him tethered to some mortal."

"That is not for you to decide," Jacqueline said firmly. She pushed past Sabine and took a place at my side.

"Vestals are not admitted to The First Rite. The last time a virgin breached the *Salon du Rouge*, she was sacrificed to Damia to show our penitence." Sabine glared at me. "I saved your life, girl. You owe me."

My mouth fell open. She could not mean any of that.

"Well, thank God it's not the eighteenth century," Jacqueline deadpanned. "No one is going to sacrifice a virgin in the twenty-first century."

"I wouldn't expect you to understand." Sabine sniffed with obvious disdain, redirecting her disgust at my friend. "You never have. If you had agreed to the arranged marriage, this wouldn't be happening at all."

"Not this again." Jacqueline exhaled heavily. "Julian didn't want to marry me any more than I wanted to marry him."

I turned surprised eyes on her, but she shook her head. Now wasn't the time or place for her to tell that story.

"Sometimes marriage is about duty," Sabine continued.

"Maybe it shouldn't be," Jacqueline said. "And it's not up to you who Julian picks. If he chooses Thea—"

"He will not choose her!" Sabine shrieked. "He will not fall victim to some gold-digging virgin."

Her words cleared the final shock clouding my brain, and I realized I wasn't going to let anyone—even Julian's mother—speak about me like that. "Why would I *want* to sleep with him?"

"Of course you would deny it," Sabine said dismissively.

"I'm not about to be your son's slave—and it doesn't matter because what we do and don't do is none of your business!" I stomped my foot, forgetting I was wearing dangerously tall heels, and nearly broke my ankle.

"No woman would pass up the chance to permanently bind a vampire to her."

"But I'd be the one getting bound, so I guess it's up to me." At that moment, I didn't care what I'd said before. No, I wouldn't allow myself to be tethered. But that was *my* decision, and there was no way I would allow Sabine to have any input in it.

Sabine's eyes narrowed as a wicked smile curved across her face. "I see my son was smart enough to keep that from you. I'm surprised Jacqueline didn't spill that little fact."

"Sabine, enough," Jacqueline said in a low voice.

But I turned a sharp look on her. "What are you talking about? I know what tethering is."

"No, it appears you do not," Sabine said in a haughty tone. "Because if you did, you would know that it binds *both* parties. The female is subject to the male's orders and whims, but in return, she receives lifelong protection from him. He must guard and care for her. The tether can't be broken."

Something in my chest split into two. Now I understood why Julian had kept this from me. He'd meant it when he said he would never lose control. But only because he knew what would happen to him if he did.

He would be forced to keep me.

My stomach lurched, and I nearly vomited. Managing to keep control, I grabbed my skirt and started toward the door.

"Thea, wait!" Jacqueline called after me.

"Don't you dare," Sabine said. "Let her go. The sooner this charade ends, the better. She will have no place in this family. I will not have my son indebted to this human."

That was it. I spun around a few steps from the front entrance. "I don't want your family or your money or even your son."

"Good." She lifted her head, triumph written across her striking face. "I pray Julian comes to his senses as well."

Tears smarted my eyes as I turned toward the door, but Jacqueline was standing in front of it.

"Move," I demanded.

"No, I won't let you leave thinking he's afraid to be tethered to you."

"Of course he is," Sabine added as she moved closer. "Let her go and put an end to this."

"I'm afraid that's impossible," Jacqueline snapped. "There is no end to this."

"I wish you had just told me—spared me," I said softly, not caring if either heard me. "If I had known he didn't want me, either, I wouldn't have come."

"Either?" Sabine repeated. "You can't expect us to believe *you* would let him go. Not when you're so close to claiming your prize."

"He wasn't a prize to me." I choked on a sob.

"Please, Thea," Jacqueline pleaded. "If you just talk to him..."

I shook my head. I hadn't known what I'd do when I came here tonight. "I can't trust him."

"It's not what you think," Jacqueline said. "He never even

worried about being tethered to you, himself."

"Lies!" Sabine called. "No vampire wants to be bound to a woman with no means of escape."

I knew she was right. Even my own father had left my mother while she was pregnant. I'd seen it happen.

True love. Destiny. Soul mates. Those things only happened in books.

"Julian didn't care," Jacqueline continued loudly, "because he's already bound to her."

"Impossible. She's still a virgin!"

Jacqueline looked to the floor and took a deep breath. When she lifted her face, she glanced between us nervously. "That doesn't matter." She cast another worried look at me before facing Sabine. "Thea is Julian's mate."

CHAPTER FORTY-TWO

Julian

I swallowed the last of my drink and, reaching to refill it, discovered the third bottle of Scotch already empty. My brothers seemed at a loss to offer me any input on my situation. Instead, we drank in silence—until we heard the front door slam.

"Uh-oh," Sebastian said with a grin. "I think the little woman is home."

"I dare you to say that again and see what happens," I warned him.

He rolled his eyes. "I hope she has a better sense of humor than you do."

"She's scarier than I am."

Before Benedict could add anything to the conversation, Thea swept into the room with Jacqueline by her side. Neither looked pleased to discover me in the company of my brothers and empty bottles. I lurched to my feet and started toward Thea.

She crossed her arms as I approached. Fury radiated from her, and I slowed my approach. She was much taller than usual in her heels, but I doubted that's what made her appear so formidable.

"Pet," I murmured as I stepped closer.

She raised an eyebrow, looking around the room. "Having fun?"

"Just having a drink with my brothers," I said with a shrug.

"A drink or an entire bar?" She wrinkled her nose. "You smell like a distillery."

"We were catching up. Benedict is in town." I gestured over my shoulder to where he was slumped on the couch. He'd lost his suit coat along with his tie. His shirtsleeves were rolled up, and he was still nursing his last drink.

"Hello." Benedict waved. An hour ago, I wouldn't have expected him to be so friendly. The bottle of whisky he'd polished off between now and then must have helped.

I checked my watch. "You're home early."

"Sorry to interrupt," she said in a calm voice.

"No, I'm glad you're back." I reached for her, but she shrank away.

"Uh-oh," Sebastian called from the sofa.

"Are you all drunk?" Jacqueline asked with a sigh. "Tell me that you saved me some."

"Vampires can get drunk?" Thea thawed momentarily, and I glimpsed the curiosity I'd first fallen for underneath the icy attitude.

"No, not really." I shook my head and winced. Pinching the bridge of my nose, I peeked over at her. "Maybe a little, but it wears off quickly."

"Lucky for you." She wouldn't look at me. In fact, she seemed to be inventorying the room in an attempt to avoid making eye contact. Was she still mad about earlier? Or had the *Salon du Rouge* been worse than I imagined?

"Want a drink?" Jacqueline called to Thea as she opened a bottle of gin.

"No," Thea said quietly. "I want to lie down." She turned to me, her gaze fixed on a point just over my shoulder. "What room would you like me to stay in?"

I shook my head, trying to process her question, and was rewarded with another piercing throb in my head. "Our room."

"You mean *your* room?" she corrected me.

Shit.

"Maybe we should—"

But Thea turned and swept away. I stood there, watching in silent shock, as she made her way up the stairs. Jacqueline moved to my side, sipping her drink without comment.

"So that's Thea?" Benedict said. "She's pretty."

We all swiveled around to stare at him.

Benedict lifted his hands, shrugging his broad shoulders. "What? I'm trying to be supportive."

"At least the whisky seems to have checked Julian's blood rage. I think an hour ago that observation might have resulted in loss of limb," Sebastian said. Then he turned his attention to me. "By the way, brother, I think she's mad at you."

"Tell me something new." I swore under my breath.

"Tonight didn't go so well," Jacqueline said.

"Do I want to know?"

"Probably not," she admitted.

"Are you going to tell me?"

"I'm through being in the middle of this." She shook her head. "But you should probably go talk to her."

"I'm in trouble, aren't I?"

"Were you in trouble before?" she asked.

Fuck, what did that mean? I nodded.

"Well, you're in deeper shit now. Can I give you some advice?"

I groaned but remained silent.

Jacqueline cocked her head, her blond braid falling over her shoulder. "If that's going to be your attitude..."

"Please," I said penitently.

"Fine," she agreed and lowered her voice. "Take her on a date. A proper one. You might want to romance her a bit."

"Is that a good idea?" I muttered.

"That depends," she said casually before finishing her gin. "Do you want to lose her?"

I didn't say anything. I didn't have to. She already knew the answer. I wasn't sure I had a choice. Even now, it felt like my body was being tugged up the stairs.

"I better…"

"That's a good idea." She smiled and turned to my brothers. "Care to see what trouble we can find at this hour?"

"I guess." Benedict didn't sound very enthused.

Sebastian was already on his feet. "The night is young."

I left the three of them bickering about what *arrondissement* they wanted to head toward. Taking the steps two at a time, I prayed I would find Thea in the bedroom we'd shared since our arrival, not in one of the guest suites.

Relief washed over me when I found her in our bedroom, but it was short-lived when I saw her arms full of her belongings.

"I just need to grab a few things," she said, looking past me again. But the crack in her voice told me she wasn't just angry. She was hurt.

I covered the distance between us in a split second, stepping into her path to stop her from leaving. "Pet, what's wrong?"

"I need to think," she murmured after a strained moment of silence.

"About?"

She shook her head. Tears gathered in her eyes, but she didn't blink. I suspected she refused to let them fall.

"God, you're gorgeous when you're stubborn."

"I'm not being stubborn." Her voice shook as she lifted her chin, glaring at me. I raised my eyebrows, and she sighed. "Okay, maybe I am being a little stubborn."

"You need to think," I said, struggling to respect her wishes. Right now, my whole being wanted nothing more than to carry her to bed and make her mine. The hesitation I'd felt about bedding her when I first learned she was a virgin eroded more with each moment that passed. "I can respect that."

She gave me a doubtful look.

"But this is your room as much as mine." I prowled closer.

"Not remotely." She shifted, nearly dropping a pair of jeans in the process.

There was no way I would let her hole up in another room. She belonged here. She belonged in my bed. "You take the bed."

"And where will you sleep?" she challenged me.

"Elsewhere."

"You want me to take *your* bed?"

"Pet, I might go crazy if you try to sleep in anyone else's bed," I said in a strained voice.

"Even my own?" she asked. Her lips tugged up at the corners. She thought she had me.

I dared to trace a finger down her cheek. She shuddered when our bare skin made contact. "Especially your own."

Because being in her own bed meant she would be back in San Francisco. My own plans wouldn't take me back there this year, if not longer. Just the thought of her being that far away sucked the air from my lungs. Was this ever going to get easier?

She studied me for a moment, her face full of her own questions. After a minute, she turned and dumped the clothes in a nearby chair. "Fine. I'm going to get undressed—*alone*."

I remained silent as she made her way to the bathroom. It was a victory, if only a small one. She shut the door, and I picked up her clothes and carried them to the closet. I wanted no reminders that she'd almost left. I'd just finished rehanging everything when she emerged from the bathroom. Her face was freshly washed, and she was wrapped in a cashmere robe. She continued past me with a look of pure determination. When she reached the bed, she slipped the robe off quickly, granting me a flash of ivory satin, before she climbed under the covers.

"I think I've got it from here," she announced.

Every instinct in my body screamed to join her. I had never wanted anything more—not sex or power or blood. Instead, I nodded and took the chair I'd just cleared.

"What are you doing?" she asked.

"Going to bed."

"Julian." She stretched my name into five syllables. "You have plenty of beds in this house."

"I don't mind the chair."

"You said you would sleep—"

"Elsewhere," I pointed out. "The chair is elsewhere."

"I thought you meant another room." She tugged the sheets up to her chin.

"Then I hope you learned something about agreeing to an arrangement."

Her eyes narrowed, but she burrowed into the bed. "Nothing's going to happen to me."

"I know that." Nothing would happen to her because I wouldn't let it happen.

"I'm not going to be able to fall asleep if you're just sitting in that chair staring at me."

"Maybe I can help." I rose from my seat, but she held out a hand to stop me.

"I don't think that's a good idea."

"Relax, pet. I'll behave," I promised her. She clung to the sheets like they were a shield. I sighed and sat down at the end of the bed. Lifting the bedding, I drew her feet one at a time into my lap. "Believe it or not, I can put you to sleep without an orgasm."

Was it my imagination, or did her face fall a little at that?

It didn't matter. Taking one of her feet in my hands, I began to massage gently. It took effort to control my own strength to not injure her unintentionally.

"That feels amazing," she said breathily as her limbs visibly softened and she relaxed into the pillows.

"I figured it might after wearing those shoes."

She sighed. "So this is the perk of having a vampire boyfriend?"

God, that term felt so grossly inaccurate. I shoved the urge to say so back inside me. "One of them."

"There are others?" She grinned at me. It was tentative and a little cruel, and I loved her for it.

"I'd be happy to show you."

Her throat slid. "Don't tempt me. Tonight anything from my ankles up is off-limits."

"Noted, but pet, forbidden fruit tastes the sweetest."

"If you want fruit, try the kitchen," she said in a dry tone. "There's no fruit here tonight."

"About this evening..." She closed her eyes, moaning softly every now and then as I worked, which was pure torture. After some time, I switched to the other foot, feeling smug to see the effect this was having on her. It wasn't nearly as much fun as watching her climax until she couldn't stay awake, but it was something.

"Ummm-hmmm," she murmured dreamily.

"What happened?"

"Nothing," she said, sounding even more tired than before.

"Sebastian said it was The First Rite."

That got her attention. Her eyes snapped open. "You knew?"

"Not until after you were gone," I said quickly, realizing my mistake. The last thing I needed was for her to think I'd sent her off to a vampire ritual unprepared. "Can you tell me about it?"

"Actually, I can. I left before anyone could compel me to never speak of it." But she didn't continue.

Maybe I'd asked the wrong question. "Do you want to talk about it?"

"Not really," she said. "I mean, there were snakes and chanting and blood offerings."

"Blood offerings?" I repeated. Darkness gripped me, threatening to take over.

"I didn't get that far, either," she said, sounding mildly annoyed but not angry. "I wish they would have compelled me to forget everything that happened."

"Was it that bad?"

"*There were snakes,*" she said forcefully. "*Lots of snakes. On me.*"

I would have to ask Jacqueline to tell me precisely what The First Rite entailed.

"I take it you don't like snakes?" I guessed.

"Not anymore."

I chuckled as I tucked her feet back under the covers. Thea turned on her side, wrapping her slender arms around a down pillow.

"Why didn't you go to The First Rite? The one meant for the males?" she clarified, her voice barely a whisper.

I stilled, barely containing the surge of rage I felt. "It seems they forgot to invite me."

Thea shifted, peeking up from the pillow. "You didn't know." She forced a brittle smile. "It was to learn how to be a proper vampire husband, anyway. Not something you care about."

I shook my head, hearing it for the lie it was. Couldn't she see that? No wonder she was so upset.

"I would have gone, Thea," I told her softly.

Our eyes locked as we both digested what that meant—what dangerous ground we were both treading.

I stood up, but before I could return to my chair, she blurted out, "Don't. Sleep in the bed with me."

I took a few steps closer and leaned over to kiss her cheek. "You need time to think."

She shook her head and reached for me.

"I will be right here." I resumed my place in the chair. "And when you wake up tomorrow, I would like to take you on a date."

"A date?" she repeated. "The last time you said…"

"A proper date."

"What about all the parties we came to Paris to attend?" she asked. Did I detect a hint of hope in her voice?

"We have the theater tomorrow evening, but we're free until then."

"The theater? That sounds positively normal," she said.

"It won't be," I promised. Nothing vampires did *ever* fell under that category.

Thea was quiet long enough I thought she'd fallen asleep, until she whispered, "There's something you should know."

"What?" I didn't like the way she said it. Who knew what else had gone wrong this evening?

"Don't be mad."

I gripped the arms of my chair and waited.

She took a deep breath, then dropped a bombshell. "Your mother knows I'm a virgin."

CHAPTER FORTY-THREE

Thea

I woke in the morning to find Julian asleep in the chair. He was still dressed, and it looked like he hadn't moved an inch during the night. I stared at him for a moment, trying to process everything that had happened in the last twelve hours. I'd been covered in snakes, his mother knew the status of my virginity...I'd been covered in snakes.

And apparently, I was Julian's mate.

Now that I was calmer, my brain zeroed in on those last words Jacqueline had said before we'd left the Salon. *Thea is Julian's mate.* I'd been too upset by everything to question her on the way back to Julian's house, but now my mind raced. What the hell did that mean? Was he *my* mate?

I needed to know more about this whole mating thing, but how could I ask him? Jacqueline said he seemed to be fighting it. Why? It felt like my head might explode from the sheer number of questions that wanted to come out. But as I watched the sharp lines of his face, softened by sleep, a deep ache swelled in my chest.

Yesterday, I wasn't sure if I could stay.

Today, I wasn't sure if I could leave.

I slipped quietly from the bed and tiptoed into the en suite bath.

Closing the door as quietly as possible, I went about my morning routine. Between getting dressed up last night and knowing I would be expected to again this evening, I decided to skip makeup altogether. I splashed a little cold water on my face and reached for the towel.

Julian handed it to me.

"Oh my God!" I clutched my chest as my heart tried to escape through my throat. Taking a few deep breaths to calm myself, I glared at him in the mirror. "Make some noise!"

"I could demand the same," he said drily, but his face remained contorted with anxiety. "You weren't in bed when I woke up."

"I didn't go far. You were still asleep." I patted my face dry before applying some sunscreen.

"Still…" His hands found my hips as he leaned to nuzzle my shoulder. He lingered there, his eyes closing for a moment as he inhaled. "I'm sorry."

I should have pushed him away, but I didn't want to. After everything he'd kept from me, I should have been angry. I should have been demanding answers. Instead, I only wanted to stay like this, with him. It felt so simple in these moments that I almost forgot how complicated our relationship was becoming.

"Sorry for what?"

"Do you want a list?" His eyes met mine in the mirror. "To start, I should have told you about tethering."

"You think?"

"I'm not sure why I didn't," he admitted, planting a kiss on my shoulder that made me shudder with pleasure. "I'll tell you whatever you want to know about weird vampire shit."

"Really?" I arched an eyebrow, debating if that was a sign that I should ask him about what Jacqueline had said. For some reason, despite the offer, I wasn't ready to ask about it. The truth was that I just didn't believe her. Julian barely knew me. He couldn't possibly want to be stuck with me for the rest of my life. I might not understand what vampire mating entailed, precisely, but I'd seen enough nature documentaries to understand the basic concept.

"But first," he said, and I caught my breath, waiting for his condition, "I want to take you on that date."

"Now?"

"Yes." He paused, his eyes darkening slightly. "Sooner rather than later."

"Because we have the theater tonight." I sighed. Attending a theater in Paris sounded like a dream. Unfortunately, knowing I would be attending with an audience of vampires sent that dream into nightmare territory.

He kissed my shoulder again and shook his head. The five o'clock shadow dusting his chin scratched my skin in a tantalizing way. "Because if you don't put some clothes on soon," he said with a thick rasp, "I'm going to carry you back to bed and spend the whole day with my face buried between your legs."

Warmth pooled in my core, and my knees nearly buckled. I gripped the marble counter to keep upright. "That's tempting. I'm not sure I want to get dressed."

His low chuckle made my stomach flutter. "I'm afraid that if we don't make an effort, we will spend every moment we have in Paris in bed or at a bloody event."

"We could just spend all our time in bed and skip the bloody events," I suggested. Cautiously, I brushed my index finger across the top of his hand. His eyes hooded, and a low rumble vibrated in his chest.

"Careful, pet," he warned me. "I'd rather not spend the day in a fit of bloodlust."

I wanted to point out that there was a way to cure him of that, but I needed to decide if I was willing to pay the price it would exact on both of us. I lifted my hand and reached for my hairbrush. Swallowing, I forced myself to think of something normal to say. "What should I wear?"

"Whatever you like. Although I prefer when you wear nothing."

"I think the weather is a bit cold for that." A smile tugged at my lips. Despite everything, there was something deeply satisfying about being wanted as much as I wanted him.

"I'm going to take a shower, and then we'll explore."

On cue, my stomach growled, and he smirked.

"We'll start with breakfast."

"Me and my stupid human stomach," I muttered. Now that a day in Paris was on the table, stopping for breakfast sounded so mundane. "I bet you wish I didn't have to eat all the time."

"I wouldn't change a thing about you, even your stupid human stomach." He moved to the shower, turned toward it, and began unbuttoning his shirt. "It's my pleasure to care for you."

A new hunger developed as he spoke. My eyes followed the progress of his nimble fingers as he unfastened the final button. He slipped the shirt off and hung it on a nearby hook. By the time he reached to unbuckle his pants, I was starving.

"If you keep looking at me like that, neither of us will make it farther than the next room," he said, nearly growling.

"Sorry!" I heard the shower turn on as I reached the bathroom door. I couldn't help but steal one peek.

Julian stood under the showerhead, letting it wash over him. He turned and shook the water from his hair. "You have about three seconds to get your pretty little ass out of here before I put you over my knee. Boundaries, pet."

My eyes swept lower, pleased to see that he was at least as aroused as I was. I blew him a kiss and shut the door behind me. Now I had another problem. What did I wear on a date in Paris with a vampire?

"You've got champagne problems, Thea," I said to myself, unable to hold back a grin, as I headed toward the closet to figure it out.

• • •

I couldn't stop checking out Julian's ass. I'd opted for the designer jeans purchased during yesterday's shopping trip, paired with a blush-pink sweater and oversize cashmere jacket. Julian had taken one look at me, walked into the closet, and returned wearing a ribbed black sweater that clung to his muscular body, a loosely knotted tartan scarf, and a pair of jeans that looked like they'd been gifted to him by the gods.

"It's like you've never seen a man wearing jeans before," he said, catching me in the act again.

"I've never seen *you* wearing jeans before," I corrected him. Lifting my face up, I grinned. "Why do you wear anything else?"

"Jeans still feel a little modern for my tastes." He hooked an arm around my shoulder as we turned off the house's quiet, tree-lined street.

"Modern?" I snorted.

"Sometimes you forget I'm an old man." He leaned over and kissed my forehead.

I grabbed the hand dangling over my shoulder, frowning to feel his calfskin gloves. They were buttery soft, and in the fall air, they hardly looked out of place, especially paired with the leather jacket he'd grabbed on our way out the door. It was simply that the gloves reminded me of every obstacle that stood between us.

"Here." He guided us into a small bakery. "Best breakfast in Paris."

I listened as he ordered in flawless French—as if he needed to get any hotter—and a few minutes later, we each had a steaming hot café and a fresh croissant. I took my first bite as we stepped out the door and stopped in my tracks. A dozen layers of flaky, buttery heaven melted across my tongue. I groaned in approval.

"You're making me jealous of a pastry, pet," he murmured as he coaxed me gently back onto the sidewalk so other customers could enter.

I swallowed and licked my lips. "You should be. I think I just lost my virginity to it."

"You're hilarious," he said darkly as he steered me down the street.

"This isn't like the croissants back home," I admitted as I took another bite.

"You approve?"

"I'm thinking about marrying it," I said with a sigh. "Where are we going?"

"To one of my favorite spots in Paris," he said.

"When was the last time you were here?" I asked, sipping my coffee. "What if it's not there?"

"That is one of the things I love about Paris," he told me as we crossed the street and continued past a row of beautiful limestone buildings. "It doesn't erase its past like some cities. The new grows around it."

"Nothing ever changes?"

"No, things change, but the important things do not." A horn honked as we cut across another street, and Julian shouted at the driver. "Unfortunately, some things do. I miss the days when it was all carriages—except for the smell."

We continued down the street. Julian pointed out architecture and told stories about every spot we passed.

"You've spent a lot of time here," I said as we waited for our chance to cross a larger intersection.

"I've spent a lot of time everywhere," he said with a shrug.

Eternity allowed for that, I supposed. The crossing light turned, and Julian slipped his hand into mine as we stepped onto the street.

This wasn't a date. It was a scene from a movie. Each second that passed was even more impossibly perfect than the last. I never wanted it to end.

The streets grew more crowded as we continued. Everywhere I looked, tourists snapped photos. Boutiques gave way to shops selling tiny Eiffel Towers and cheap sunglasses. This was Julian's favorite spot in Paris? I guessed things had changed a little, but I gasped as we rounded the corner, and I spotted part of Notre Dame.

I'd seen pictures of it before the fire, but even now, surrounded by scaffolding, it was amazing. Julian stopped beside me.

"What the hell happened here?"

I blinked, momentarily confused. "The fire…"

"Nobody mentioned a fire," he told me, and I remembered that he'd been asleep when the landmark burned. "I suppose Celia had to leave a few things out of the dossier. I'll have to remember to tell her in the future that I care more about things like this than the advent of social media."

My stomach clenched at his use of "next time." Did he plan to go back to sleep when the season ended? I didn't have the heart to ask. Instead, I forced a smile.

"Come on." He tugged me toward a stone bridge that sat over the Seine. We crossed quietly, hand in hand, and entered another world. The chaos that enveloped the city faded with each step we took.

"Where are we?" I looked around at the old stone buildings.

"Île Saint-Louis," he said as we passed some quiet bistros. "I spent most of the eighteenth century getting into trouble here."

"Trouble, huh?" It seemed impossible to imagine trouble could be found in the quaint neighborhood. He guided me down a side street and paused in front of a nondescript gate.

"And this is Paris's best-kept secret. At least, I hope it still is." His crooked grin made my heart skip a beat. He pulled off a glove and then placed his palm on the iron gate. It swung open, revealing a courtyard that seemed impossibly big given the street it sat off.

"How?" I peered inside.

Julian put his glove back on, smiling at my amazed expression. "Welcome to *Île Cachée*."

CHAPTER FORTY-FOUR

Thea

I stared at the world waiting beyond the gate, but I couldn't process it. Turning, I looked back at the street. Graffiti blighted a building, flyers cluttered a nearby streetlight, and traffic hummed in the background, punctuated by honking horns. Behind me was Paris. In front of me was an entirely different world.

"*Ill what*? Remind me to learn French," I grumbled.

"*Île Cachée*. It means the Secret Island."

I narrowed my eyes as I followed him past the courtyard and down the cobbled street that couldn't possibly be there—except I was walking on it. "But how does it fit?"

"The island the rest of the world knows is under a glamour," he explained. I stared at him again. "An illusion. The world only sees half of it. It appears to those without magic as half its size."

"And this is the other half?" I asked, catching on.

"Yes, pet. This place is known only to vampires and familiars."

"And now me."

He nodded, but I was already looking around, trying to take everything in.

There were no souvenir shops or tourists with cameras. People on the street were dressed in an amusing array of clothing, from petticoats and styled wigs to a man with a sword strapped to his side.

"Not all of us transition well to the changing times," he whispered.

"So I see."

It felt like stepping back in time. Chestnut trees towered along the quiet path, sending gold-dappled light dancing around us. Their rust and goldenrod leaves fluttered despite the lack of breeze. I watched as a single leaf fell from the tip of a branch. It danced to the stones below, landed gracefully, and vanished. I blinked a couple of times. When I looked up, the leaf was back on the branch. As I watched, it performed its lovely dive again.

"It's enchanted," I said, feeling stupid. Of course it was. Everything here was. Julian chuckled and pressed closer to my side.

"Magic is strong here. It's protected," he told me as I watched more leaves fall, vanish, and reappear. "Visitors are limited so that no one draws too much from its source."

"There is a magical reservoir in Paris?" I didn't know why that surprised me. There was something magical about Paris, from its dreamy avenues to its rose-tinged light. It seemed fitting to find magic at its heart.

Julian leaned over and kissed my forehead. "That's one way of looking at it."

"Does that mean witches can use magic here?"

"No, it's forbidden. Spellcraft, potions, anything that comes out of your standard grimoire, but not true magic."

"Standard grimoire?" I repeated, my mouth twisting. "You make it sound like something I can pick up in a corner store."

He pointed to a blue-lacquered shop across the street where stacks of books perched in the windows. "There's probably a few in there."

"I'll keep that in mind," I said, feeling slightly dazed. We continued, passing impossibly tall shops filled with strange objects, squat bistros crowded with tables, and windows crammed with spectacles that widened my eyes and flushed my cheeks. In one shadowy storefront, ropes and chains hung next to what I feared was an actual iron maiden.

"Is that...?" I nudged Julian.

"Vampires like to mix pain and pleasure. It's natural to us," he said with a shrug.

"Wait." I stopped in my tracks and peered into the dark window. "I thought it was a torture shop."

He snorted and moved behind me. Julian lowered his mouth to my ear and whispered, "Look closer."

Straining my eyes past the show-stopping front window, I caught sight of a woman, bound in red rope and little else, dangling from a golden hook. A group lounged on chairs beneath her, discussing something.

"Why is she hanging there?" I murmured.

"*Look*," he commanded in a dusky tone that stole my breath.

I peered through the glass and caught sight of dark liquid dripping from her bound arms. As I did, one man below lifted a glass, catching the dripping liquid deftly, and brought it to his lips.

I gasped and tried to back away. Julian tugged me back to the cobbled path.

"Is she...okay?" I asked when my shock wore off.

"Yes." His dark laugh raised goose bumps over my skin. "She's enjoying herself. Some mortals choose to serve vampire masters."

"Their blood?" I blurted out.

"Amongst other things," he said.

"She was a human." I glanced back toward the black shop.

"Yes." He didn't say more.

The bakery next door seemed positively *tame* compared to that. But the aromas drifting from it made my head swim. I took a step closer, but Julian drew me away.

"That's not a good idea." He tipped his head toward a sign hanging over the door with the words *Enchanté: Sorts d'amour* stenciled in gold letters.

I raised my eyebrow.

"Love spells," he said, sounding a little strained. "It's hard to even walk past without getting ideas."

I bit back a grin. "Maybe I *would* like to go in there."

"You don't need any help," he promised.

The enticing aroma gave way to soap-scented smoke billowing from the shop next to it through large open windows. Pillows and tables dotted its interiors, artistically scattered to make the space inviting. Resting on cushions, a few patrons passed a pipe back and forth.

"Opium," Julian confirmed, moving us along.

We passed a woman sitting at a bistro table, sipping an electric green liquid. She smiled as a man joined her with more of the strange drink. On and on it went. Shops filled with silk gowns and expensive suits, bookstores cluttered with leather tomes, darkly thrilling bars and restaurants serving items that were forbidden or illegal in the human world.

At the end of the street, a large open market buzzed with activity. A banner hung over it, seeming to float in midair, which read *L'apothicaire* in thick, block lettering. Crates sat on tables, spilling their strange wares, some of which were moving. I didn't look too closely at those items. There were bottles and herbs and wild, unearthly plants.

"Mostly for potion making," Julian said.

It was beautiful and overwhelming. "I could explore here for hours."

"There are spots like this in every major city in the world—places where the magic runs so deep it's like an oasis," he explained. "I want to take you to them all."

My heart stuttered at the thought of more days like this. Days with him full of magic and wonder and beauty—and the nights... My skin heated as I considered what they would be like.

I took a deep, steadying breath and noticed a man watching us from across the cobbled street. He waved at me. "I think someone recognizes you."

Julian glanced up, and the ghost of a frown flitted across his face. A moment later, a man not much taller than me joined us. Cold, dark eyes studied me as he greeted Julian. "Rousseaux! I'd hoped to run into you."

"Boucher." Julian shook his hand. The man wore velvet gloves, and I wondered if he was a vampire. I wouldn't have guessed it based on his appearance. He looked ordinary compared to the others I'd met of the species. "May I introduce Thea?"

Boucher moved to greet me with a kiss, but Julian growled.

Actually *growled*.

We both stared at him.

"I see you've made a match," Boucher snorted. He continued to search my face. "If you'll pardon me, I feel I know you from somewhere."

"Thea was at the cocktail party in San Francisco."

"Ah yes, and what is your family name?"

I stiffened. "Melbourne."

"Thea was one of the musicians," Julian explained to him.

"Interesting." If Boucher had opinions about our relationship, he kept it to himself. "I'm sure your mother is delighted to have a musician in the family."

"Perhaps, if she can see past Thea's humanity." Bitterness coated Julian's words.

Inside, I thrilled that he said nothing about Boucher's assumption regarding our future. But I tamped down my excitement. It was nothing more than part of our arrangement. Julian needed to appear seriously attached to me.

"What do you play?" Boucher asked.

"The cello." Even thinking it was painful. "When I'm home."

"You must take her to see Berlioz. He's working on something new," Boucher said to Julian.

"God help us," Julian muttered.

"Hector Berlioz?" I asked, my eyes widening. "But he's been dead for centuries!"

"Don't tell him that. I believe he convinced someone to turn him so he could finish an opera," Julian said. "It's still a work in progress."

"You're familiar with his work?" Boucher sounded impressed. "Now you must take her. But be forewarned. He's been especially moody of late."

"I was already on my way there. I'm hoping he has a cello."

"Of course he does." Boucher waved his hand but then leaned in. "The question is—will he sell it to you?"

"Some things never change." Julian smiled like Boucher had issued a challenge. "Will I see you tonight?"

"Yes, I am *officially* allowed to return to the Garnier." He narrowed his eyes. "As if they could keep me out!"

"Perhaps we'll see you."

We said goodbye, and I rounded on Julian. "I want to meet Berlioz."

He laughed and pointed down a quiet side street. "This way."

A music shop waited at the end of the cobblestone alley. But not just any music shop. In the windows, instruments played themselves.

Julian paused. "Listen."

I closed my eyes and did as instructed. A familiar melody found its way to me, and I smiled.

"What do you hear?" he asked.

I opened my eyes and studied him. "Schubert? Don't you recognize it?"

"They play a different song for everyone," he murmured. "The song we want to hear."

I swallowed that tidbit of information, not sure how to digest it. I started to ask him what he heard when the door to the shop flew open. A short man regarded us from the doorway with wild eyes. He shook his head, sending his mass of graying curls in every direction.

"Human," he said, staring at me.

"Oh, um, yes." I wasn't sure if he was waiting for a confirmation.

"I'm not interested," he said to Julian and made to shut the door.

Julian caught it with the toe of his boot. "I'm not selling snacks,

Berlioz," he said. "She's a cellist."

I forced myself to stay calm and not overreact that I was meeting a composer believed to be dead for over a hundred years. Berlioz studied me for a second and then snapped, "We'll see about that."

He moved inside the shop without another word. The door remained open, and Julian started toward it.

"He doesn't believe I'm a cellist," I said under my breath to Julian.

"He suffers from lack of company." Julian shrugged. "Some think it's bad for him—that it's driving him mad."

"Do you?"

"I think he was already a little eccentric before someone made him a vampire, pet."

"That's reassuring." But my concerns died as I stepped inside the store and took in the piles of priceless instruments and rolled-up scrolls shoved all around in every nook and cranny.

Julian whispered, "Touch nothing, unless—"

He fell silent as Berlioz approached and shoved a cello into my hands.

"Play," he demanded.

I took it with trembling fingers and nodded. But as soon as it was in my hands, I relaxed. "What would you like me to play?"

"What you wish," he said vaguely, cocking his head.

It was a test. I smiled at him, knowing this was a test I would pass.

• • •

An hour later, we emerged, and the shopkeeper himself was arranging the delivery of a cello to Julian's house. I'd won over Berlioz, who usually refused to sell his wares, when I'd played Part Four of his *Symphonie Fantastique* from memory.

We wandered through the streets, peering into shop windows

past trailing ivy. Julian kept buying me pastries as if he wasn't sure how much food a human needed to consume. I didn't complain. Eventually, the sun began to fade, coloring the light rose.

"It's perfect," I said as I drank in *Île Cachée* at twilight.

"Indeed," Julian murmured. I looked up to find him watching me. He smiled sadly and looked at his watch. "Unfortunately, we should head back to the house."

"Can we come here again?" I asked.

"If you like." But the same sadness that tainted his smile coated his words.

If there was time. We only had a few weeks in Paris, and tonight the social season would kick into full swing for both of us. Julian paused under a stone arch and drew me to him.

"Did I do okay?" he asked, brushing a gloved finger across my lower lip. "I'm a bit rusty when it comes to courtship."

I nodded, my mouth parting instinctively at his touch. "Your courtship skills are intact."

"Are you mocking me, pet?"

"A little," I admitted, grinning up at him. He lowered his face over mine, bringing his lips a breath away.

"May I kiss you?" he asked softly.

I blinked, surprised by his request.

"It's a proper date," he reminded me when he saw my reaction. "I'm courting you, remember?"

"Court away," I said breathlessly.

He brought his lips to mine slowly with a deliberate reverence that unraveled me. A raw ache filled me as the kiss deepened. He took his time, moving his mouth slowly as if savoring my taste. The rosy afternoon twilight had faded into evening when he finally pulled away. Julian took my hand without a word and guided me away from the magical spot. As we stepped out of *Île Cachée* and the glamour faded, the sounds of a busy city flooded the air around us.

I sighed. "I could stay there forever."

"If only we had that long." He said nothing else until we reached the house.

"I should get ready," I said with a groan as soon as we were inside. "If only I were a vampire, it wouldn't take so long to get pretty."

He went rigid and turned from me. I froze, realizing how stupid I'd been to make the glib comment. After a moment, he turned back. The edges of his eyes were black, but it was clear he was regaining control. I waited for a rebuke for my careless remark, but none came. Instead, he swept a ravenous look over my body. He moved closer and reached between my legs. I inhaled sharply as he pressed his palm against the growing ache there.

"Will you leave this bare under your dress tonight for me?"

I nodded, my mouth going dry at the implication of his request.

"I promise you'll be rewarded, pet." He stepped away without a second glance, leaving me to wonder what he planned to do.

CHAPTER FORTY-FIVE

Julian

*T*he *Palais Garnier*, known more infamously as the Paris Opera, loomed ahead, rising above the crowded streets and traffic like a beacon. To most people visiting the City of Lights, the Eiffel Tower was the center of the whole metropolis. To vampires, it was the Opera. Tonight, however, none of it mattered because I couldn't take my eyes off the woman at my side.

Thea remained quiet throughout the ride. Her hand, clad in a velvet, elbow-length glove, rested under mine as we waited in the line of cars. I suspected she was occupied with the same thought haunting me.

If only I were a vampire, she'd said.

For the past few days, I'd been obsessed with the possibility she was my mate. Or, rather, the impossibility. Now, I wondered if the reason I fought the idea so hard had less to do with her being a human and more to do with what being a human meant: a mortal lifespan. I clasped her hand more tightly, as if she might slip away any moment.

Thea glanced over and smiled, but her eyes betrayed that her thoughts were somewhere else. Whatever was on her mind haunted her, too.

"What are you thinking, pet?" I asked her before she could ask me.

She turned nervous eyes on me and lowered her voice so Phillipe couldn't hear. "That everyone is going to be staring at the virgin."

More than ever, I wished I could joyfully relieve her from that burden. "You said that they planned to compel the familiars not to speak of it."

"That doesn't mean they won't remember," she pointed out.

"Yes, but only half the people will be staring."

Her lips pursed, unimpressed with my logic. It was a tad slim. "Another crappy vampire pep talk."

"Another?" I lifted an eyebrow.

"I called Jacqueline while I was getting ready."

"What did she say?" I asked curiously.

"That they would be staring at me because I was hot," she said in a matter-of-fact tone.

"She's not wrong."

I swept my eyes down her, allowing my bloodlust to darken my eyes just enough for her to know I meant it. Her velvet gown was strapless, showcasing her bare shoulders and the arms made shapely from years of playing cello. She'd pinned her hair to the side with a delicate gold comb, showcasing her slender neck. Between the way the dress clung to every curve and hollow of her body and the veins pulsing in her throat, I couldn't stop thinking about claiming her with my body—or my fangs.

"Every male in there will want to fuck you, and every woman will want to be you."

"Because I'm with you?" A smile tugged at her lips to show I'd succeeded in my attempts to distract her.

"Because they know you're mine."

She laughed. "You're pretty cocky for an old man."

"They won't stare because of *whom* you belong to," I whispered into her ear. "But because of *how* you belong to me."

"How is that?" she asked softly.

"Completely." I kissed the spot below her ear, earning a shiver. "Absolutely. Unequivocally."

Her tongue swiped over her lower lip as she leaned closer. "Then why am I—"

"We've arrived," Phillipe interrupted.

I used the interruption as a diversion and got out of the car. I knew what she was going to ask. Now wasn't the time to discuss our shifting relationship or remind her of the necessity of limiting our physical intimacy. I wasn't sure how much longer we could avoid the reality of our situation.

Circling the car, I helped Thea from her seat and offered her my arm. She took it, adding, "We're not through discussing this."

But as we stepped inside the Palais Garnier, she fell silent. Thea looked around with wide eyes as she tried to take it all in at once. For a moment, I saw this place I'd been a thousand times through her eyes. I marveled at the sweeping stone staircase, at the murals painted overhead, at the mirrors that seemed to make the guests milling about the grand foyer part of its extravagant scene. Unfortunately, the moment ended abruptly as we were swarmed. The vampires who refused to return to the States all wanted to say hello or have a word.

But mostly, they wanted to get a look at Thea.

Maybe Sabine hadn't compelled everyone at The First Rite, after all. Thea shot me a panicked look as more and more people accosted us. She had to be thinking the same thing.

"You've arrived with your little girlfriend," an imperious voice sliced through the crowd.

The guests surrounding us parted ways to allow Sabine to walk through. She'd gone for black—an unusual choice for her. Dark lace rose high on her throat and down to her wrists. All around her, vampires whispered their admiration, but I got the distinct impression the dress was a message. She was in mourning.

"Mother," I said coldly. The vampires who'd greeted us before slowly vanished, as if they sensed a storm brewing. But I noticed more than a few curious onlookers eavesdropping.

Boucher appeared at my mother's side. "Julian," he said, "and the lovely Thea."

"Don't tell me you're encouraging this," Sabine hissed, glaring at him.

"I was simply saying hello." Boucher sighed. "And I came to speak to you. There's been a last-minute change. One of the sopranos has vanished."

"Of course," she said heavily. "Have we checked all the boxes to make sure someone didn't take the liberty of stealing her as a snack?"

"We're in the process of that," he assured her, "but Berlioz must be talked down. He's convinced that the debut will be ruined."

"Berlioz is debuting a new opera?" Thea asked excitedly.

Sabine turned cold, glittering sapphire eyes on her and glared. "You've heard of him?"

"Thea is a cellist," I reminded her, trying to salvage this situation.

Thea gave her a pretty smile and added, "We met him this afternoon, and he didn't mention it."

"You...met...Berlioz?" Sabine sounded pained. She glared at me. "What was she doing on *Île Cachée*?"

"I took her on a date," I said, intervening before one of them throttled the other.

"I see." A muscle ticked in her jaw. She swiveled her face slowly to Thea. "Berlioz is premiering a new opera he's written for the evening. *The Symphony for the Dead*. I hope you both enjoy it."

Something about the way she said it made me suspect we wouldn't.

"Excuse me," Sabine added.

"Go where you're needed," I said meaningfully. Sabine swept away in a huff, leaving an apologetic Boucher with us.

"I didn't think she could hate me more," Thea said.

"Sabine doesn't like anyone," Boucher reassured her.

"She likes you."

"My dear," he said, his beady eyes glinting, "she tolerates me. There is a difference. I do sincerely hope you enjoy yourself this evening, in any case. I should go mediate between those two."

"We will," I muttered. Boucher took his leave, and I immediately spotted Benedict in the corner. Thea noticed him at the same time.

"Your brother is here," Thea said. "Or one of them. Should we say hello?"

I shot her a questioning look. Wasn't one family confrontation enough for the evening?

"I'm trying to be polite," she explained as I steered her toward the sweeping staircase. Peonies, roses, and lilies encircled its stone railings, making the already lavish interior more decadent.

"Polite and vampires don't mix well, pet."

"Will we be sitting with your family this evening?" she asked carefully as we reached the first floor.

"We have a private box," I said through gritted teeth. It was a small mercy, and I owed Boucher for allowing me to keep my usual seat in the house.

"Is this a favor or..."

"I've kept a box for years, but tonight we're using the box next to it." That was all she needed to know.

"Is there something wrong with yours?" she asked.

"Box three is more private than mine. I didn't want to share." I tossed her a suggestive grin. That much was true. My box had a curved half wall between it and the seventh. After sharing Thea for half an hour with vampire society, I wanted her to myself.

I guided Thea through the crowd, ignoring the curious eyes that followed us. When we reached box three, I was relieved to find it open and waiting.

"Are you usually in box one?" she asked.

"No, five," I said absently as I peered in to find the box had been arranged per my requests. Instead of the typical eight chairs, only two waited. The chairs were positioned farther than normal for the best view but back far enough to ward off most, if not quite all, of the prying eyes.

I began toward it, but Thea didn't move. She was mesmerized by a plaque on the box next to ours.

"*Loge du Fantôme de l'Opera*," she sounded out the French, and her eyes widened. "Wait, which box did you say you keep?"

"Box five," I admitted, already knowing why she'd asked.

She grabbed my arm, her velvet fingers clutching me tightly. Even through the layers of cloth, I felt a prickle of something inexplicable, but Thea didn't seem to notice. "Are you telling me that you're the—"

I groaned, knowing that she was going to enjoy teasing me about it for the rest of the night. "I owed Leroux money—or so he believed."

"And you didn't pay him back?"

"There was some debate as to the validity of his claim. He believed he'd won a round of piquet. I believed he was a cheater."

A soft laugh fell like music on my ears. I'd earned another smile. Even after the disastrous confrontation in the lobby. "Was he a cheater?"

"Most certainly. All writers are." I extended my arm toward the box. "So he wrote the bloody book and told everyone he'd based it on me."

"You don't seem to mind using the phantom's box," she pointed out as she swept past me. I followed, shutting the door softly to outsiders.

"Perhaps I will sweep you into the bowels of this place, to my secret lake, and give you a private lesson. Would you like that, pet?"

"Do I need another lesson?" she murmured. She stood, half in shadows with her evening wrap draped off her shoulders. Even in the dimly lit box, I saw the pulse at her neck.

The space darkened as bloodlust thundered inside me. Thea glanced at me and stumbled back a step, her body making contact with the red satin lining the wall. The reflection off the fabric cast a red hue over her pallid skin. I'd been wary of bringing her here, especially after the idea she'd planted in my head. These were close quarters for a human and a vampire. At least at home I could touch her.

I did my best to keep distance between us as we took our seats. Still, despite my instinct to protect her, an invisible hand seemed to hook around my heart, pulling me gently but insistently back to her.

"Come," I said with a thick voice, "and I'll tell you where Leroux got his ideas."

"From you?" she guessed as she took my hand.

I nodded, and she laughed.

"A cheat *and* a thief?"

"Don't forget a liar when it suited him," I said with a wry smile.

"And he was your friend?" she asked.

I moved next to a chair and waited for her to take a seat. "*Acquaintance* would be a better term. He couldn't win at any game he played."

"But you played him anyway?" Her eyes narrowed with disapproval, but she was still smiling.

"Someone had to take his money," I said as I sat next to her. "Why not me?"

"Because you have more money than God," she said with a snort.

"Yes, and I use it more wisely," I told her. On the evening that Leroux had lost a considerable share of his newspaper earnings for the week, I'd purchased a woman's freedom on the walk home. A young virgin being sold on the streets. Leroux would have drunk the money away. I'd done something useful. I'd given the virgin to a convent.

Apparently, my ethics had slipped in the last century because I was finding it hard to think about anything else but Thea and her problematic virginity. "Everything was for sale in Paris those days, and a man like Leroux wanted everything."

"And how did you become the Phantom?" She tugged her wrap higher, covering some of the exposed flesh I couldn't stop staring at.

"He had a talent for taking the truth and making it sensational," I told her. "The reservoir below us became a hidden lake, and the passages were made for a ghost to walk about the theater. But the reality is the reservoir is there because this used to be swampland."

"And the passages?"

"Vampires love the opera. It can inflame us, though," I said with a shrug. "In its early years, it was necessary to occasionally remove our human guests when a vampire lost control."

"Remove because..." Thea swallowed, shaking her head. "Never mind. I don't want to know. Do you think there will be problems tonight?"

"There are very few humans here this evening," I reassured her. "And there are rules about these things now. It's frowned upon to take a date to the opera and drain them."

"Well, when you put it like that," she said drily. "So, Leroux knew you were a vampire?"

"No." I laughed at the thought of telling a man like that about my world. "But I did admit the passageways were there to remove incapacitated guests. He just thought I meant drunk people."

She giggled, but before the conversation continued, the lights in the auditorium dimmed slowly and then brightened several times. Thea turned from me toward the stage, her entire face lighting up. "I can't believe I'm sitting at the Paris Opera with the Phantom himself."

"I never should have told you that story," I muttered.

"Don't worry." She patted my hand. "I've figured out what we're going to be for next Halloween."

I rolled my eyes as the lights went down the last time. Thea's attention was now entirely devoted to the stage as the orchestra began to play. Her eyes closed as the music swelled through the air. She was next to me, but she'd been transported somewhere else. When a soprano took the stage and began the first aria, Thea opened her eyes and craned her head to watch the action.

"I wish I understood French," she admitted.

"She's singing about her love that has been taken from her," I whispered. "He has gone off to war and died."

The soprano was talented, as Boucher had said. Pain rose in stabbing notes as she told her story. It was a misconception that vampires were without feelings. Simply, we'd learned to divorce ourselves from the mortal world long ago—so we wouldn't suffer further grief or loss.

Until we went to the opera, where we couldn't ignore emotion any longer.

The story continued, and a tenor entered. The young man had returned from the war, but he was no longer a human. He'd been turned into a vampire, and he didn't recognize his love. Thea gasped when he attacked the woman, and her hand tightened on mine. Of course Sabine had approved of this new production.

Thea watched with unwavering interest, and I watched her. Each gasp and sigh she made lodged itself inside me, amplifying the emotional intensity I felt during each scene. Tears filled her eyes as the woman hid from her lost lover. She stole a glance in my direction, palpable fear on her face. Her biochemical reactions to the opera sent her blood singing in her veins until I couldn't resist her any longer.

I gazed out across the audience and found all eyes were trained on the stage. The debut seemed to be a hit, which made it easier for me to lower to my knees.

"What…?" Thea said softly when I released her hand. I answered her by moving to kneel before her.

"I'm right here," I whispered as I drew off my gloves. I slid my bare palms up her calves and urged her to scoot toward the edge of her seat. "That's a good pet. Keep your eyes on the stage and try not to let anyone know what I'm doing down here."

"Wouldn't want a Rousseaux to be caught on his knees?" she teased in a whisper.

"I wouldn't want to make every male here jealous. You smell delicious. May I put my mouth on you?"

Thea sucked in a sharp breath, hesitating a moment before finally nodding. I lifted her skirt, allowing it to drape over her thighs, and discovered she'd done as I'd asked. She was completely bare under her skirt, and I inhaled her scent as I pressed a kiss to her inner thigh. A duet began on stage, its longing mirroring the hunger I felt now. I tugged her ass to the edge of the seat, hooking my arms around her thighs to balance her, and lowered my lips to her delicate flesh. A moan slipped free from her as my tongue parted her folds.

I lifted my eyes and found her straining to remain composed. Her fingers gripped the armrests as I slowly circled the tip of my tongue over her swollen clit. Another gasp, drowned by the duet to all but my ears. Her tiny sounds of pleasure blended with the opera, and I found myself devouring her, desperate to taste her climax. Thea's legs began to tremble, and she cried out as the duet peaked, flooding my tongue with her essence.

I couldn't stop. The song shifted into a fierce clash between the soprano and tenor, and I sucked and licked. Thea grabbed hold of my hair, her whole body trembling as I stole more pleasure. Finally, her thighs clamped around my head, a signal that she couldn't take anymore. But I couldn't stop. Her scent drove me, fueled by the music, and I shifted my lips to the soft inner thigh clenched around me. Thea relaxed with a sigh, her thighs blossoming open to present a new temptation.

The duet shifted to an *aria parlante*, and the tenor, now singing alone, grew increasingly agitated. I felt his frustration burning through me, and without thinking, I lowered my mouth to the crease of her inner thigh and did the unforgivable.

CHAPTER FORTY-SIX

Thea

It might have been a kiss. His lips were soft on my skin. My eyes shuttered at the contact, and I drew a ragged breath, waiting for the pain. It came with a stinging swiftness that sent my hands clawing for the armrests I'd just released. I gripped them tightly as the sting melted into something else. A prickle of fire and ice—my nerves fired so rapidly that I couldn't process what I felt until it began to spread.

The clash of heat and cold built between my thighs and spread to my core. I felt it all—the pressure of Julian's mouth on my flesh, the blood spilling against his teeth, the venom filtering through my bloodstream.

Somewhere my brain protested this development. Julian had bitten me.

Not just bitten me. He was feeding.

I should stop it, but I didn't want it to end.

I wanted him to take more. I wanted him to take all of me.

A new sensation blossomed in my chest. It felt both familiar and different. My heart swelled, as though it would crack open and spill out, like my blood on Julian's tongue. This new feeling commingled with pleasure, building a crescendo inside me.

The aria hit its final, dramatic climax, the audience burst into applause, and I shattered.

They were calling for an encore by the time I dared to open my eyes. When I did, the world was different. *New.*

It wasn't the first time Julian had pleasured me with venom in my system. But then he had used his hands and mouth to coax out my climax.

All he had done was bite me this time.

Later there would be consequences. But as he lifted his head, I found his eyes black as obsidian and his lips stained red. A second passed as we stared at each other. We'd crossed a line, and I knew now there was no way either of us could go back.

And then Julian casually got up, wiping his mouth with his thumb, and took his seat. I waited for a moment, trying to figure out what had just happened. As the applause died down, the opera resumed, and I dared a glance at him. His eyes remained black, and his hands gripped the wooden armrests as mine had moments ago.

"Julian," I whispered, reaching for his hand as my heart began to race. This time from panic.

"Leave," he snapped.

"What?" The theater was still relatively quiet as the next scene began, and a few heads turned our direction at the outburst.

"You need to clean that up," he said in a low voice. "Go to the bathroom until the bleeding stops."

I stared at him. The love I'd felt a moment before seeped away as I stared at the stranger next to me. "Are you—"

"*Get out of this box before I kill you,*" he said in a furious whisper, his eyes never leaving the stage.

I stumbled to my feet and fled from the box. The restroom was nearby, and I dashed inside it. After checking to ensure I was alone, I locked the main door and collapsed against it. Tears came as hard and fast as the final orgasm Julian had delivered only moments ago. No matter how hard I tried, I kept seeing his face and the look of unfiltered hatred on it. It was how he'd looked at me the first time

I saw him in San Francisco.

I realized he wanted to kill me then, too. Not in a murderous, psychopathic way. It was more complicated than that. Julian wanted to drain me because of what he was.

He'd warned me never to offer him my blood. Now I understood why.

An hour ago, I would have trusted him with my life. Did I still? And what had I expected?

I wiped away my tears, staining my gloves with mascara. I couldn't sit in here crying all night. I stood and moved to a long mirror meant for ladies to check their gowns or stockings. Instead, I lifted my skirt. Clutching it to my chest, I examined myself and found I was still bleeding from the wound. I cursed under my breath and went to the sinks. Wetting a hand towel, I cleaned the spot, discovering two perfectly round puncture wounds. I held the towel over them, waiting for the bleeding to stop. After a few minutes, I checked to find it had. Carefully, I made sure there wasn't a drop of blood anywhere before dropping the towel in the trash. If Julian couldn't control himself, could others?

I couldn't stay in here forever, though, and by now, Julian would have control of himself. I unlocked the door and stepped out, determined to march back to box three and demand we leave. We needed to talk before he succumbed to his self-loathing. Because, despite the roller coaster of emotions he'd just put me through, I finally had my answer.

He was my mate.

I still didn't really know what that meant. It was just a feeling. It was something in my gut that told me this was it. *He* was it.

Honestly, I wasn't entirely happy about it. Mainly because being bound to a stubborn, grumpy vampire wasn't something I'd planned on. Not that I could have planned it if I had wanted to. I made my way slowly into the corridor leading back to my seat, trying to decide which questions to ask him first. I only made it halfway before doors began to open along the corridor. Guests spilled out around me, moving to the restrooms or to the bar for a drink during intermission.

I fought my way through the crowd, trying not to accidentally touch anyone. I realized I'd left my stained gloves behind in the bathroom trash. Maneuvering around a group, I walked straight into Sabine.

She cast a disapproving look at me as a massive male vampire joined her.

"Thea, what are you doing here without a chaperone?" she demanded.

"I don't need a chaperone," I said, rolling my eyes. I didn't have the patience to deal with her. Not now.

"This is her?" Her companion looked me over. "She's shorter than I imagined."

"Now is not the time, darling," she hissed at him.

But he smiled broadly at me. "You must be Julian's girlfriend."

Sabine actually winced at the word.

"I'm Dominic Rousseaux, Julian's father," he explained, ignoring his wife.

"Oh. It's nice to meet you," I said, mustering up the politeness Julian had warned me against. Why did this have to happen now?

"Where is my son?" he asked.

"Hopefully, he's not out picking up more strays." Sabine sniffed. Then she went still. Her nostrils flared, and she turned on me. Her gloved fingers caught my wrist, clenching it so tightly I thought she might break bones. "What have you done?"

"What?" I tried to pull away, aware that more than a few people were watching. Right now, I would give anything for a distraction. She couldn't know that he'd bitten me, and, even if she did, why would it matter?

"I smell—"

A scream cut her off, followed by several more shouts. I turned and found myself face-to-face with a scene that looked like a horror film. Figures dressed in black filled every staircase and began grabbing vampires. I spotted a red slash across the breast of one of the attackers just as he grabbed a vampire woman and shoved a stake through her heart.

It wasn't like in the movies. Vampires *bled*. A lot.

I let out an involuntary gasp as the female vampire's blood gushed over her evening gown, her skin turning ashen as she bled out. After a moment, she went totally still. The attacker threw her on the ground and lunged for another vampire.

And then all hell broke loose.

I didn't know if I screamed, because those around me drowned my cries. Within seconds there were more attackers clashing with vampires.

"Get her away from here," Dominic ordered, shoving me toward Sabine. He moved toward the chaos. Sabine gripped my arm and dragged me away.

"We have to help them," I shouted at her.

"You don't stand a chance against them," she yelled at me as I fought her. "Those are vampires."

"But the men in black…"

"*Are vampires*," she repeated, yanking me along. "I can't believe this day has finally come. This is why you shouldn't be here. The bloodlines need to be strengthened, so we can fight these monsters. Instead, I'm babysitting you."

I wrenched free of her hold. "I don't need a babysitter."

We regarded each other for a minute, and then I tipped my head adding an unspoken request. *Go.*

She could fight. I couldn't. She was needed there. I wasn't.

"Run," she snarled, then launched herself toward the fray.

I looked around for a weapon but found nothing. I doubted I could even pick up one of the antique candelabras.

But Sabine hadn't delivered me to safety. She'd herded me away from the pack. A vampire in black saw me and started toward me. His hand tightened on the stake he held. It probably didn't matter if I was a vampire or not. A stake through the heart would kill me.

I ran toward our box, praying Julian was inside, but it was empty. Shoving at the door, I tried to hold it against the attack, but I wasn't strong enough. Just as Sabine had said. The vampire pushed open the door, knocking me to the ground in the process.

"*Carpe Noctem!*" he called as he lifted the stake.

"I'm human!" It was the only card I had. But it wasn't enough to save me. It only changed the game.

"A human?" he crowed, standing over me. "Someone brought a snack. Let's remind them what humans are meant for."

I cried out as he grabbed me and lifted me to my feet.

"You don't belong here, but you knew that." His eyes were entirely black, and I knew nothing could save me now. "You belong on a dinner plate."

He dropped his face to my neck, and I braced myself for pain. None came.

Instead, I crumbled to the floor. Looking up, I saw my attacker's body sway and then topple toward me. Headless.

Before he fell on me, strong arms lifted me from the ground and rushed me away. I buried myself against Julian's chest, soaking up the safety I felt in his embrace. Yes, I still trusted him. No matter what he'd done. No matter how he felt about it. I knew he'd never be able to hurt me. I had just faced a monster with no man inside. Julian wasn't a monster. No matter what he thought.

But when we reached an emergency exit, he stopped.

"Take her to my house and make sure no one gets in," he ordered someone.

I clung to him as he tried to pass me off.

"It's okay," he coaxed me. "Sebastian is going to get you out of here."

"I'm not leaving without you." I protested while he placed me on my feet. "If you're going back in there, I am, too."

"You are so brave, pet. It is the first thing that I loved about you." He grabbed me and yanked me hard against his body. His lips crushed against mine, and a sweet taste flooded my mouth.

Venom.

This time it wasn't an accident. Venom flowed through me, and a fuzzy lightness overtook my brain. Julian released me into his brother's waiting arms.

"She is going to be pissed at you." Sebastian sounded a million miles away.

"I don't care as long as she's alive," Julian barked. I tried to move toward the sound of his voice, but Sebastian kept hold of me.

"Don't do anything stupid," Sebastian told him, "like get killed." *Killed.*

In my foggy brain, I remembered a hard lesson. Vampires could die. I'd just watched one die in front of me. Julian turned to go back to the attack.

"No!" I yelled. "Please! I love you."

It was enough to make him pause. His head turned just enough for me to see his eyes were completely black. He smiled and vanished into the chaos.

CHAPTER FORTY-SEVEN

Julian

There was death everywhere, and Thea loved me. The taste of her blood still lingered on my tongue as I threw myself into the violence. I locked the thought of her inside me. I couldn't afford to be distracted, but knowing she was waiting for me at the other end of this drove me.

A vampire in black started toward me, stake raised. I waited until he was close enough to lift his hand to strike. Dropping low, I spun and swept his feet out from behind. His body flew backward, but I was already up. I hooked an arm around his neck and wrenched his head from his body. A few feet away, another vampire rushed toward a group of guests clustered together. I lifted the head in my hands and launched it at him, hard. It hit the vampire square in the shoulder blades. The impact caught him off guard, buying time for the group to run back into the theater.

I grabbed the stake from my attacker's limp hand. "Thanks."

Now I had a weapon, at least. If reports were true, these vampires were mostly young and recently turned. We had centuries more experience in battle than our attackers, but we were outnumbered. I spotted my mother and father working together to take down a small, coordinated group of terrorists. At least my own parents knew how to fight. There were plenty of vampires here who were unprepared. Bodies lay everywhere.

My eyes fell on a familiar writhing on the ground with a stake in her chest.

"P-p-p..." she said. Her hand reached out limply as blood sputtered from her lips. I knelt to inspect her wound. The stake had driven clear through her breastbone, splintering the bones in its path. A few shards stuck out from where her flesh had torn to reveal her heart. There was too much damage. Not even magic could save her.

Drawing her mangled body into my arms, I took her hand and held it. Her magic pulsed against mine, growing fainter with each slowing beat of her heart. Her head lolled back, and she forced out a few final words. "Take. It."

Electricity sparked like lightning against my palm as she passed her magic into my body. With one final crack of energy, her body went limp.

Her magic roared through me as I laid her gently on the blood-soaked tile. I was about to stand when a vampire flew over my head and smashed into the wall. She went limp, crumpling into a heap of black clothes, blood covering her. I whirled around to thank my unexpected ally, but she was already dashing toward the stairs. She was dressed in black. It wasn't one of us who had saved me. It was one of them.

What the fuck? I vaulted over a body, my eyes tracking my savior.

Her dark hair swung around her face, obscuring it from view as she escaped. Without thinking, I followed, leaping over the railing and, barely, landing neatly on the lower staircase. Her head turned slightly toward the sound of my landing. It was only a glimpse, but it was enough to stop me in my tracks.

It wasn't possible.

Snapping out of my haze, I started after her. I made it a step before a body fell from the first floor, hitting the steps in front of me with a sickening thud, almost taking me out. My eyes lifted to find Bellamy standing at the railing. "Sorry, Jules!"

I nodded and continued after the terrorist who'd saved my life. But she was gone. Bodies cluttered the floor of the lobby. I wondered how many had died and how many had escaped. As I walked among the fallen, I spotted faces I knew as well as strangers among the dead. Footsteps fell behind me, and I whipped around to face another attack.

But it was my father and Benedict. They closed the distance between us in two long strides. My father caught me in a hug.

"Thank the gods." He drew away, his face grim and lined with grief. "We can't find Sebastian."

"He got Thea out of here," I told them.

"He left?" Dominic bellowed.

"I'm the better fighter, so I stayed. He saw to his family."

"That mortal of yours is—"

"Is my mate," I cut him off with a snarl.

Benedict stepped between us. "We know where he is now," he said to our father. He shot me a warning look. "Let's make sure they're all gone."

"Fine," I muttered.

"Whatever."

"Mom?" I asked Benedict as we fell into step together.

"She's offering mercy to those that need it."

I swallowed, remembering the first time I saw my mother following a battle. Unlike the males, who'd joked and boasted after the fight, she'd walked back onto the field and offered death to any who sought it. That was how I learned she was known as *angelus mortis*.

The angel of death.

We stuck close to each other as we swept the building looking for survivors, but there were none. A couple dozen had fallen. Given the brutality of the attack, I was surprised it wasn't more. Its swift execution and the equally fast retreat told me this was a rallying cry, not a full-blown attack. More would follow.

"Why do this?" Benedict asked as he studied the body of one of the attackers. "They could have done it while we were watching the opera—locked us inside and burned us alive."

Benedict, always the politician, had never had the heart of a warrior. He'd seen plenty of battlefields, but the art of war eluded him.

"They didn't want to kill us," Dominic said quietly.

"What is this?" My brother pointed to the death around us.

"A message," I answered.

"From whom?"

"I don't know." I thought of the woman who'd saved me and fled, dressed like the others. She was one of them, whoever they were. I remembered the look of their clothing: black, with a single slash of red across the breast. "I think there was a male at Mother's orgy wearing a mask almost exactly like the uniform these attackers wore. Mother had security escort them out. Who was that?"

"Now isn't the time nor place," my father said darkly, adding quietly, "Only the blood can be trusted."

Benedict nodded, accepting what he was saying: only our family could be trusted. But after what I'd experienced tonight, I was no longer sure. Like him, though, I understood this needed to wait.

Dominic didn't speak again as we finished our sweep of the floors. We found our mother administering a swift death to a familiar on the third floor. Nearby, a few black-clad vampires lay dying with mortal wounds.

"Mercy for them, I presume?" Benedict asked, starting toward them.

"No!" she ordered, rising to her feet. Her black gown caught the light, revealing sticky, wet spots on the fabric I knew was blood.

"You never discriminated before," he pointed out.

"Only warriors deserve honor," she said coldly. She walked to one of the dying males and spit on him. "These are cowards."

Not one of us argued with her.

"Has anyone been called?" Dominic wrapped an arm around her, drawing her to him. Death always brought out each's affectionate side.

"There was no need. Everyone was here," she said flatly. "Boucher is dealing with the humans who were present. And the Council is convening to discuss next steps."

Dominic looked around and sighed. "This is a mess."

She smiled wearily at him and pulled away. Moving to Benedict, she examined him for a moment before giving him a tight hug. She hesitated when she reached me, but the bitterness I'd felt earlier this evening was gone. It had been stolen from me.

"Mother," I said softly.

"Son."

I wrapped my arms around her, knowing that our differences would never come between what we were to each other: family.

Sabine pulled away and glanced around, her expression turning to panic.

"Sebastian?"

"He's fine," my father said, shooting me a glare. "He saw to the safety of our son's *mate*."

Sabine's eyes narrowed, but she didn't say anything.

"You don't seem surprised, my love. I found this revelation shocking." He glanced at my brother. "Does anyone tell me anything?"

"Later," she said tersely as a group of well-dressed vampires approached us.

"Sabine, Dominic," the tallest female greeted them in a somber tone. "The Council is gathering, but we will be speaking with every pureblood sire this evening. Tonight's attacks change certain priorities. You will join us."

"Of course," Sabine said, bristling a little at the command from her fellow Council member. Her eyes strayed to the female's pristine clothing, and her nostrils flared with distaste. There wasn't a speck of blood on them or a hair out of place among the lot. Most of the Vampire Council let others fight their battles. Not my mother.

"Your sons are not needed," she continued, "*for the moment*."

I didn't like the sound of that, but I was more than happy to get the hell back to Thea.

"I'll drive you home," Benedict offered. "I assume Sebastian took your car."

"Probably." I just hoped he'd let Phillipe drive.

My brother had parked his Mercedes in the car park beneath the theater, in our family's reserved section. I paused when I saw the tan interior and grimaced, inspecting my own blood-soiled clothing. "I'm afraid I'm going to stain your seats."

"So will I," he said with a shrug.

"You've been in France too long," I muttered as I slid into the passenger seat. I buckled my seat belt and reached into my breast pocket for my gloves. Drawing them over my bloody hands, I felt the fresh magic from the familiar dampen.

"You had your gloves off," Benedict noted lightly.

"It worked out," I told him. "A familiar passed me her family magic before she died. It's been a while since..." It was unusual for a familiar to pass their magic in its entirety to a vampire. The woman who'd died in my arms tonight must have felt she'd had no other choice.

"If you took a wife—a familiar wife—you would have access to her magic." He kept his eyes on the road. "It could make all the difference."

"For what?" I asked. Even now, after everything that had happened, my family wanted to marry me off to an old familiar family.

"For whatever happened tonight." He cleared his throat. "You said there was one at Mother's party. Now this. I knew that tensions were high, but I never expected violence."

"Tensions?"

"There's talk we've become too docile. Everyone has an opinion. Whoever this group is, it seems they are siding with the more extreme voices. The ones who want us to take back the night."

"*Carpe Noctem*," I muttered.

Benedict lifted an eyebrow.

"That's what the vampire who crashed Mom's party yelled."

"This attack," he said, taking a deep breath before saying what I already knew. "It was planned. They must have people inside our circles."

I hesitated, torn between telling him who I'd seen on those stairs and keeping it to myself. Before I could make a decision, he continued, "What if there's another attack?"

"We fight again." We'd all seen enough war to know that.

Benedict pulled the car in front of the house. I looked up and found a light on in the studio window. I couldn't see Thea, but I knew she was there.

"Should I come in?" he asked.

I shook my head. Clapping a hand on his shoulder, I forced a smile. "Can you drive Sebastian home? I'd like to be alone with Thea. She's never seen anything like that."

"Yes," he said hesitantly, "but, Julian, be careful."

"I am," I said tightly.

"This mate thing..." He glanced nervously at me. "You can't expect the family to accept it. You know they won't, especially if the bond isn't..."

"Thank you for your concern," I stopped him and opened my car door. A couple passing me stared at my blood-stained clothes. I needed to get inside to clean up before I went to her. The last thing Thea needed was to see reminders of tonight or proof of the violence I'd encountered once we'd parted.

"Julian," Benedict called my name, and I leaned down to the window, "is she really worth it?"

I looked back at the warm glow of the window and caught the faint notes of a cello in the air. I shut the door with a definitive "yes."

CHAPTER FORTY-EIGHT

Thea

Even the cello couldn't calm my mind. I sat in the ballet studio. Something about it reminded me of practicing with the orchestra or peeking in on Olivia during rehearsals. It was a place that felt more like home than Paris did at the moment. As soon as Sebastian had brought me here, I'd traded my evening gown for a silk robe, dragged a footstool into the room, and began to play. Berlioz had seen that the instrument arrived in pristine condition, already perfectly tuned, and I was grateful for his attention to detail.

I hoped he had survived the attack.

The bow felt good in my hands as I began playing every piece I had ever memorized. My bare feet felt like ice on the cold wooden floor, but I didn't care. Julian's venom still burned inside me, but even it wasn't enough to distract me. I was determined to escape the prison of waiting. There was a time when music would have been enough to transport me to another place and time. Tonight, my mind and heart kept straying to Julian—wherever he was. Sebastian's reassurances that he could handle himself only reminded me that the man I loved was fighting people who wanted him dead. What if they took him from me?

What if they took my mate?

Without meaning to, I began to play Schubert—the piece I'd been playing the night I'd met Julian. *Death and the Maiden*. It was almost enough to make me laugh now. I closed my eyes and let the panicked notes of the music reflect the turmoil churning inside me. It shifted between sad longing and fear and something that felt like a chase. I followed suit, my heart rising and crashing along with the score. The *andante con moto* began, and tears burned my eyes. I refused to open them. I refused to cry until…

Julian gently placed a hand on my shoulder and murmured, "Don't stop."

I'd been so lost in my thoughts and the music that I hadn't heard the door open. I did as he asked. I continued to play as he knelt behind me and rested his forehead against my shoulder. I peeked in the mirror through my wet lashes. He'd stripped himself of his tuxedo, his hair wet, as if he'd just showered. And then it hit me—why he'd want to immediately bathe. My bow slipped for a moment, splintering the air with a missed note. Julian didn't budge. I continued on. He looked as if he was praying. Was he?

Later, I would ask him about what he'd lost tonight. Or rather, what we'd lost, because any grief he carried was mine now, too.

I paused as I reached the end of the *andante*, and he pressed a kiss to my back. "Keep playing, pet."

The heat of his mouth lingered on my skin, the silk no match for his kiss. I continued. Now that he was here—now that I could feel him, each moment I played, I slipped further into a state of peace. After a few minutes, an arm wrapped around my waist. I barely noticed until his hands slipped my floral robe off my shoulders. My eyes shut as cool air nipped at my bare skin. I wore nothing underneath the robe, and Julian let out a slight hiss of approval.

"Keep going," he instructed me. His mouth traveled along my spine. I sighed, trying not to tremble as he kissed my bare skin. He took his time, worshipping my flesh, and slowly returned to my neck. I felt a fang drag across my shoulder, and I sucked in a steadying breath. I doubted I could keep playing if he bit me. My core throbbed at the thought of him feeding on me as I played for him, and a soft moan spilled out. He paused, allowing the sharp points to press against my skin before he planted a kiss over the spot.

No bite.

He moved his mouth to my ear and spoke just loud enough for me to hear over the music. "I have imagined this since the first time I saw you play. Open your eyes while we play together."

I sucked in a deep breath and allowed my eyes to flutter open. Julian rested his forehead against my shoulder as he moved his hand down. His fingers spread me open, and I nearly missed a note.

"Should I stop?" he asked.

I shook my head, determined to continue and let this be our reality instead of whatever we'd left behind tonight. He lifted his head, his eyes meeting mine in the reflection, and then he began to play. His fingers danced over my swollen flesh, igniting the venom in my bloodstream. I couldn't see them as the cello blocked all but my shoulders up from view in the mirror. But I felt each longing note. Music built inside me, rising and bringing with it a staccato series of throbs. Each beat of pleasure was violent and promising. I thought of the opera—of his fangs inside me—and I lost control. The bow clattered to the floor. I reached behind me and wrapped my arm around his neck, leaving him to orchestrate the final bars of our duet.

Cries spilled from my lips as he brought me to a crescendo and held me as I fell into his music.

When all that remained was the lingering rhythm of my pulse, he steadied me and took the cello from my hand. I saw myself in the mirror. Floral silk puddled under my spread legs, my skin glistening with the wet heat of climax, and every inch of my body on display. I stared at the stranger I saw there.

She walked with death.

She knew desire.

She craved the forbidden.

Julian returned and stood behind me, his hands on my shoulders and his eyes sweeping across the body on display. I allowed myself the same pleasure. There was no mistaking him for a human. He had the body of an ancient god, not that of a man. His muscled chest was so well-defined, so perfectly chiseled, that it looked as if he had been sculpted from marble. He was simply perfection.

No words passed between us. But something else grew inside me. Not the constant hunger I felt for his touch. That was always present. This sensation planted itself in my chest as we watched each other in silence. It blossomed and stretched until I was sure I would crack open. I was changing. I couldn't deny it. I wouldn't.

I knew what I wanted.

I lifted my hand and placed my palm carefully over the hand resting on my shoulder. His nostrils flared at the audacious touch, but he didn't pull away. It was the most intimate message I could send him.

My hands contained no magic. I had none to offer. I only had one thing to give him: myself.

Every bit of me. My heart, my soul, my body, and with it, my future.

"Take me to bed," I murmured.

Julian remained still. A muscle clenched in his jaw, but he didn't hide the battle in his eyes. He released me and stepped away. My heart splintered, until he moved around the stool and scooped me into his strong arms, urging my legs around his waist as his mouth found mine. I coiled my arms around his neck, pressing myself against his skin. He didn't falter or pause as he carried me out of the studio and to the bedroom.

He laid me carefully across the bed and hesitated.

I stretched my body, rolling onto my stomach, and reached for the drawstring of his silk pajamas. He didn't speak as I unknotted it and pushed the pants off his narrow hips. His erection sprang free, and I shifted onto my hands and knees. Taking his length in my hand, I stroked as I lowered my mouth over him. Every muscle in his body went rigid as I pleasured him. A hand fisted my hair, trying to slow me, but I didn't stop. I couldn't. All I wanted was to erase his memories of tonight, even if only for a stolen moment.

His fingers tightened, but I continued until a growl ripped through the air. A moment later, I was in the air as he tossed me onto my back. He pounced, his strong arms caging my body as he hovered over me. My legs fell open in welcome. Julian's head lifted, and he drew in a deep breath, drinking in the air. When he looked down at me, his eyes were black.

I had no idea what I was doing. I only went on instinct. I lifted my hips to brush against him, and his mouth opened. Fangs descended, and I steeled myself.

I knew what I wanted: to be his in every way he wanted me.

I turned my head to the side, offering him my neck. Out of the corner of my eye, I saw agony flash across his face. He reached out with one hand and gripped my chin. I closed my eyes, ready for his bite. Instead, he turned my face back.

"No, pet," he said stiffly. "Not like this."

I opened my eyes and stared into the black pools of his eyes. "I'm *your mate*, Julian. I am *yours*. All of me. My *body*. My *blood*. You can have both. You can have *everything*."

His mouth crashed against mine. A fang nipped my lip, and an iron tang filled my mouth as the kiss deepened. I didn't know if he'd meant to spill my blood or if it was an accident, but I didn't care. Julian shifted, his weight pressing against me, and then I felt his hand between my legs. I moaned into the kiss as his thumb brushed briefly over my clit. Then it disappeared. Before I could cry out, something softer and broader swept over it. I was so lost in his kiss that it took me a moment to realize what it was. It nudged against my entrance, and I gasped. Julian reared back and watched me as he dragged the tip of his cock along my seam.

His breathing was ragged, and his eyes remained black as I writhed under him.

"You don't know what you're asking," he said hoarsely. "You don't know what you're giving up."

I swallowed. I'd thought of nothing else since I'd learned the truth. I understood. "I choose this," I whispered. "I choose you. I choose to be tethered."

His eyes closed, and then very slowly, he pressed against me. My body protested, a circle of flames erupting where he'd yet to breach me. I clawed at the sheets, grabbing fistfuls of fabric to squeeze as I waited for him to take the last of my innocence.

Julian brought his lips to mine and kissed me until I was breathless. The fire cooled as he began to stroke himself along me again. "I will never deserve you."

"You've got me anyway," I said fiercely. There was so much for me to learn about him. I'd only glimpsed some of the shadows of his past, but with every second that passed, I was more certain that my life was inextricably linked to his. Julian's forehead pressed against mine as he started to slowly push inside me. I caught my breath, waiting for the pain, but nothing happened.

I opened my eyes to see his blue eyes gazing down on me. Sorrow burned in them. "I can't," he said, cutting me off when I opened my mouth and adding, "I won't, Thea."

Sharp pain sliced through me, and a moment later, fat tears rolled down my cheeks at his rejection. He turned away, and I felt a stab of embarrassment for being so pathetic.

I tried to squirm out from under him, but he held me firmly.

"I won't," he repeated, breaking my heart again, "because I love you."

And then he reached over and pressed his palm to mine.

CHAPTER FORTY-NINE

Julian

'd never held a lover's hand before. As my whole body waged war over whether to take her, there was something about this simple touch that changed everything. Tears rolled down Thea's cheeks. Her head turned to the side, and she stared at where our hands were clasped. Leaning down, I kissed the tears from her face. After a moment, I rolled onto my side and gathered her into my arms. I tucked her against my massive form and took both her hands this time. Twining my fingers with hers, I held her there until her uneven breathing calmed.

"I know it's not sex," I murmured into her hair, "but for a vampire, it's much more intimate."

She made a soft, noncommittal noise and tightened her fingers. "Explain why again?"

"Maybe it's just a legend. There are stories—older than me," I added.

"That's hard to believe," she teased, but her words sounded hollow. "Stories about what?"

"The first magic," I whispered. "When I was a child, *eons ago*, my mother would tell me about a time when magic pounded in human blood. Back then, magic was life itself." I lifted our clasped right hands and released hers. Pointing to the lines, I continued, "You could see magic in the lines of your palm."

"Like palm reading?" she asked skeptically.

"I believe palm reading is its bastard child, so yes, in a way. The lines of the palm corresponded to various powers—elemental, earth, sexual—"

"Sexual powers?" she interrupted, laughter in her voice.

I relaxed a little to hear it. "Yes, attraction was once the provenance of witches, sirens, and other creatures. When magic disappeared, it was still present in the veins of thousands of witch bloodlines, but most couldn't access it."

"So the familiars really can't use their magic at all?"

"Not true magic. Only the spells and potions that have been passed down from generation to generation."

"But what does that have to do with vampires? I heard you two are always fighting with each other about which of your kind came first."

"That is true to an extent," I allowed. "However, I've always believed witches were here first."

She twisted slightly to look at me. "Really?"

"It makes the most sense to me." I lifted her hand to my lips and kissed it. "But regardless, it's only stories. There are probably plenty of scientific reasons that magic dwindled."

"It's sad, though," she said softly. "To only ever feel that you're half of what you're meant to become."

I stilled. Maybe I hadn't distracted her at all. "You are everything you need to be, and you will only continue to find yourself."

"But I will never be your mate." She returned her gaze to the wall across the room. Seconds ticked by as I tried to think of something to say to her. But that proved impossible. How the fuck was I supposed to tell her she was wrong?

I couldn't, because I knew she was right.

There was only one way to make it happen. I couldn't believe I was even considering it. It was fucking insane, but we would be, too, if we didn't find a way to solve our problem. We were at a crossroads. We had to choose a path. "Thea, there is a way."

I heard her breath catch. A moment passed, and she prompted, "I'm listening."

"If you weren't a virgin," I began slowly, "then there would be no risk to—"

"Then screw me already," she blurted out. She let go of my hands and flipped over to face me.

"*I* can't," I repeated my words from earlier. Pain ghosted through her eyes.

"I don't understand how I'm supposed to lose my virginity if you don't take it," she said defiantly.

She really belonged to me. Pride swelled in my chest as I looked at this unexpected mate of mine. But now wasn't the time to go all gooey. Not when I was going to have to spell it out in painful detail. "I would not be the one to take it, pet."

Her face went blank. She blinked a few times and continued to stare. "I don't understand."

"I think you do," I said carefully. I braced myself for a wave of blood rage and plastered a limp smile on my face. "I'm certain there will be any number of men ready to help you with the issue."

Her jaw dropped, and then she sputtered, "You want me to *find some guy to fuck*?"

I felt none of the amusement I usually experienced when she cursed. I couldn't. Even hearing her say it had me on the edge of violence.

"I *want* to take you as my mate," I said in a strained tone.

"That I can agree to." Thea pushed herself up on the bed and crossed her legs, treating me to a glimpse of the subject in question. I groaned as I grabbed a pillow and tossed it into her lap.

"I can't think when I'm looking at that."

"In that case." She picked up the pillow and threw it on the floor. "Are you really okay with sharing my body with another man, even once?"

I was across the room before she blinked. My fist drove through the plaster wall as my brain imagined what I would do to the man who laid a finger on her.

"That's one way to answer," she said from behind me. "Julian, I'm not going to sleep with another man. I won't do that to you."

I withdrew my hand from the hole, plaster crumbling to the floor, and shook off some of the dust. I squared my shoulders and turned to face her, doing my best to appear composed. "I give you my blessing."

"Fuck your blessing," she yelled. "I've waited my whole life *for you*. I knew that when we met. There has to be another way."

"Chastity is an option," I said drily.

"I doubt it," she shot back. Thea scrambled off the bed and moved toward me. "Someday, you will slip. I know because you slipped earlier tonight. Did you plan to feed on me?"

I swallowed, my thoughts growing dark. "No."

"Exactly." She crossed her arms over her small breasts. "It's only a matter of time."

"That sounds like a challenge, pet."

"No. It's common sense." She sucked in a choppy breath. "You nearly took me tonight."

"I know," I said bitterly.

"Don't sound so happy about it," she muttered.

"I'm not." I paced across the floor, throwing glances at her as I made my rounds. "It's unfair to you."

"It's unfair to both of us," she corrected me. "I know what tethering demands of you."

I snorted. "I don't care about that. The moment I saw you, I knew I would either protect you until you left this world or..."

"Or?" she prompted.

I pivoted so I could look her directly in the eyes. "Or I knew I would be the one to take you from it. Tethering is dangerous... You have no idea the risks, even with the best of intentions. The tether acts of its own accord. If it deems there is a threat, it will respond with lethal force or force you into action. It's not a romantic thing."

She didn't so much as flinch. "I'm not romanticizing it. I already told you, I am yours completely. If that—"

"Fuck," I interrupted her. Had things already gone too far? She couldn't really mean what she implied. "You already sound tethered. Can you imagine how much worse it could get?"

"I have, and I'm willing to take that risk."

"You are so maddeningly stubborn," I said through gritted teeth.

She shrugged one of her shoulders. "Maybe, or maybe I just have more faith in us."

I lost hold of the last shreds of patience keeping me together. One moment she was defying me across the room, and the next, I was only a few inches from her. "I will never tether you," I snarled. Her eyes widened, and I knew I was scaring her. Good, maybe she'd finally hear me. "I will never watch someone else I love be bound like that."

Her lower lip trembled as she processed this, and then she asked the obvious question. "What do you mean by 'someone else'?"

I saw the woman running down the steps at the opera in my mind. I closed my eyes. "My sister," I said softly. "Camila was tethered to her husband. It ended...poorly."

Thea stayed quiet this time. Revealing this seemed to snuff out her argument. She closed her eyes and took a deep breath. "I think maybe I need a minute alone."

"I understand," I said stiffly. I strode into the bathroom and grabbed a robe. "I'll be elsewhere."

Thea didn't look at me as I slipped it on and started toward the door. I only made it a few steps before I returned back to her. Propping her chin on my index finger, I studied her for a moment. "We will find a way."

"I really want to believe you." She tried to smile, but it came out tortured.

I brushed my thumb over her lower lip. "I'll find some wine. Maybe something to eat."

She nodded but refused to look at me.

To leave her there was more painful than any of the wounds I'd endured on battlefields over the centuries—and I'd taken more than a few that would have killed a human. Everything was changing. I'd felt it in bed. The mating bond had tried to snap into place. It tried even as I held her hands. But I'd resisted. My reward was feeling like I'd been ripped in two.

I closed the door to the bedroom and then worked my way toward the stairs. The farther I got from her, the easier it became to rationalize my decision. When I reached the final step, I was sure I'd done the right thing. But before I could continue to the kitchen, the doorbell rang.

Hughes appeared as if summoned. He stopped when he spotted me in my silk dressing robe.

"Perhaps I should get the door?" he suggested.

"I agree."

He nodded and proceeded to the front door as the bell rang again. Whoever it was needed a healthy dose of patience shot up their...

When Hughes opened the door and greeted my guests, I stopped on the spot.

My mother, still wearing her bloodstained ball gown, stood there, surrounded by the other members of the Vampire Council. She caught sight of me in the entry, and her eyes narrowed at my state of undress.

I wished more than ever that I had some of Benedict's people skills. As it was, I frowned. Tying my robe tighter, I padded toward them with bare feet.

"Shall I show them in, sir?" Hughes asked me quietly as I reached him.

"I'll handle this," I told him. "Why don't you find us a bottle of wine? Actually, find us a couple." I waited until Hughes was gone before I gestured for them to enter. "Come in. I assume you're here to speak with me."

"Indeed," one of the ancient vampires said solemnly. He looked me up and down. "That is, if you aren't currently occupied."

"I'm not." I'd been sent away...by my mate. My mate who refused to see reason. My mate who felt rejected.

I started toward the attached sitting room, but my mother cleared her throat. "Perhaps somewhere more private?"

I led them to the formal sitting room and closed the doors behind us. Gesturing for them to sit, I remained standing. The last thing I wanted was for any of them to get comfortable here. "Is this about what happened this evening?"

"Yes and no," one of the Council members said cryptically.

"Thanks for clearing that up." I sauntered to the bar cart and poured myself some of the Scotch my brothers had left.

"This is about The Rites," my mother said carefully.

Of course. I took a lingering sip of my drink before turning to her. "Already? You've only had one so far."

Her eyes flashed murderously as I revealed that I knew what had happened the night of the *Salon du Rouge*.

"As you know, The Rites are enacted for the betterment of our species and the strengthening of our alliances with the magical community," an old vampire with a nose like a pointed stake said.

"Yes, I know what they are," I said impatiently. "Are you planning to go to every eligible vampire's house tonight and give them a lecture?"

I looked to my mother to see if I was on track, but she had turned away, veiling her face in shadows. A moment later, I understood why. She'd known why they were here.

"That won't be necessary," the Council member said. "You are the only one acting in defiance of the law."

"Law?" I nearly choked on my Scotch. "When did The Rites become law?"

"An hour ago," she said coldly.

My fingers tightened around my glass. I barely processed it when it shattered in my hand.

"And we are here to deliver your final warning."

CHAPTER FIFTY

Thea

It took me a few moments to collect myself before I realized I wouldn't get anywhere by pushing him away. Yes, his plan was stupid. No, I would not sleep with someone else just to clear the way for us to be together. I had no idea where that left us, but we wouldn't get anywhere unless we faced our problems together.

I went to the closet and got dressed in case the bell I'd heard earlier meant guests had arrived. The last thing I needed was to walk into a roomful of vampires half naked. I pulled on a pair of the designer jeans Jacqueline had picked out and then found a soft, cashmere sweater. Slipping on a pair of velvet flats, I made it nearly out of the bedroom when I heard the alert on my phone.

I'd placed it on the charger when I got back from the opera, determined to call my mother when the time was right in California. After what I'd experienced tonight, I regretted not calling her sooner. She might still be mad at me for taking the semester off, but I didn't care. Life was short. I'd had a front-row seat to that lesson tonight.

I unplugged it and saw a half-dozen missed calls from her. Before I could hit redial, the phone started to ring again.

"Mom?" I answered swiftly. "I'm so sorry. I was going to call you in a bit."

"Am I speaking to Thea Melbourne?" a stranger's voice asked me.

I froze, my heart leaping into my throat. I nodded.

"Um, hello?" the stranger said.

"Oh!" I startled. "Yes, this is Thea." I checked my screen and saw that the call was definitely coming from my mother's phone. The heart in my throat plummeted to the floor.

"This is St. John's Hospital. A patient was brought into the emergency room earlier, and we found this number listed as her emergency contact. Do you know the owner of this phone?"

"It's my mom," I whispered, clutching the phone like it could anchor me.

"Would it be possible for you to come to the hospital?"

"I'm in Paris." A raw ache crept into my words. I fought to control my panic. "Is something wrong?"

"Normally, a doctor would want to speak with you in person, but I guess it might take you a while to get here." I heard fingers typing on a keyboard. How could anyone multitask at a time like this?

"Is my mother dead?" I blurted out.

"Oh, sugar, no!" she said gently. "But she's not awake. The doctors are trying to figure out what happened. Should I have them call you when they know more?"

"Yes," I said so quietly I wasn't sure she'd hear me.

"And is it okay for them to call when they have a minute?"

"As soon as they know anything," I said, snapping into action. I was already out the bedroom door and racing toward the stairs. I froze when I caught a glimpse of several people leaving. As Hughes saw them out, I recognized the dark, perfectly coiffed hair of the one lingering at the rear. "And I'm on my way."

Sabine swiveled toward my voice, her eyes pinning me to the spot. The look on her face sent a chill racing through me. But she didn't say anything. She simply murmured something to Hughes and stepped out behind the other guests.

"I'll let them know," the nurse on the other end said.

"Thanks." I hung up with her and dashed down the stairs.

"Where is he?" I asked Hughes.

"In the drawing room." But I was already racing down the hall. "Can I be of service, mademoiselle?"

I shook my head, my heart pounding as I rounded the corner and found Julian staring out the window into the sparkling night.

"My mom," I said, gasping. I was barely holding back tears. "I'm sorry. I need to get home right away. The hospital called."

Julian didn't turn toward me. He continued to look out the window. His palm rested on its sill, and I found myself calling out again, "My mom! Look, I know we're fighting, but—"

"We aren't fighting," he said quietly. "Is that what you think?"

I paused, unsure how to answer that question. "It's not important. My mom is in the hospital. I need to be with her."

"I understand." Julian didn't look at me as he spoke. He walked past me and deposited a handful of glass on the bar. Had he just been holding it the whole time? I gawked at his bloody palm, trying to figure out how he'd injured himself and why he was acting so weird.

"It looks like you should be in the hospital, too." I went to him, but he continued to stare past me. "Julian?"

"It will heal," he said dismissively. "So. You need to go home."

"Yes, can we leave soon?" I asked.

There was a pause before he answered, "I'm afraid I need to stay here."

I nodded. I wanted to understand his position. He was expected to stay here. But it hurt that he wouldn't come with me. "Can you come soon?"

"Oh, pet." Something about the way he said it made my stomach clench. "I'm afraid that's not possible."

"I don't understand," I said slowly. I searched his face for clues to his sudden distance. We'd just been holding hands in bed. Was he that upset I didn't want to sleep with another man? But I might as well have been analyzing a mask. His face betrayed nothing.

"I believe this is our swan song," he said in a hollow tone.

Tiny fissures cracked my heart. "A swan song is an ending..."

"Exactly." He glanced at me for just a moment. His blue eyes burned through me, but he quickly looked away. "This was always inevitable. I guess it's better to end it now before anyone gets hurt."

"Hurt?" I stared at him. What was he saying? What was going on? "Does this have something to do with your mother—"

"No. I've been fooling myself. I see that now."

A sob broke free from me. I stepped in front of him, trying to force him to look at me. He couldn't mean any of this, not after what he'd said. He loved me. I loved him. But Julian's eyes looked past me. "Why are you doing this? We love each other."

"Sometimes you are so human," he said in a brittle voice. "I suppose it's easy to believe love is enough when your life is a blink of an eye."

"Love will be enough." I believed that. Why couldn't he? "We'll find a way."

"You weren't meant for my world."

"I'm meant for *you*," I said in a soft voice. He was my mate. Maybe it wasn't official, but that didn't change anything for me. Not the way I felt about him. Not what I was willing to do to be with him. But staring at him now, I knew something had changed for him.

And then he delivered one final blow. "I can't marry a human. I can't marry *you*."

"Because they told you that you couldn't?" Was that why Sabine had been here?

"Because I won't. You were just a pet. I always knew that." His words sliced through my heart. I couldn't breathe. I shook my head, unwilling to believe him. He couldn't mean that.

I reached for his hand and clasped it. Julian didn't pull away. His eyes shuttered, his body stilling under my touch. He understood what I was saying.

If it was true—if he didn't want me, he wouldn't let me touch him like this. He'd told me it was the most intimate act for a vampire.

I meant more to him. I wasn't just a pet. He was lying about his feelings. I just didn't understand why. I opened my mouth to demand an answer.

Instead, Julian stepped away and yanked his hand from mine, his rejection strong but not violent. My reaction was the opposite. I crumpled into a chair, sobs racking through me. He loved me. I was sure of it. Knowing that only made the pain more acute. He couldn't love me as much as I loved him. If so, he wouldn't be able to endure this now. He wouldn't be staring at me with a placid, unyielding gaze. He wouldn't be walking away.

"I'll arrange your travel." And then Julian left me there to pick up the pieces of my broken heart.

I sat there for a few minutes or perhaps hours. I lost track of time until Jacqueline peered into the room. I looked up at her, my face saying what I couldn't. She rushed over, dropped to the ground next to where I sat, and wrapped her arms around my shoulders. I wasn't crying anymore. I didn't think I could find another tear inside me. Not for him.

"Poor darling," she murmured. "I will never understand males."

Behind her, someone entered, and for a moment, my heart soared with hope. It crashed when I spotted Sebastian hanging back. He watched us silently. He didn't look surprised or concerned, only somewhat wary. If he had an opinion on his brother's actions, he kept it to himself.

I'd been stupid to think I could fit into Julian's world. Not when his entire family refused to give me a place in it. Why was Sebastian even here?

"The plane is seen to," he said, answering my unspoken question. "We can leave when you're ready."

He'd been summoned to take me away. The last of my hope died. Julian wouldn't even personally take me to the airport. It was too much to process. But I knew one thing. My eyes drifted toward the ceiling to where my belongings waited upstairs. "We can go now."

"You're already packed?" Jacqueline asked, her eyes narrowing with suspicion.

"I don't want any of it," I said softly. I couldn't stomach the idea of being reminded of the future I'd lost—the future Julian had ripped away from us.

"Nonsense." Jacqueline got up and brushed off the knees of her leather pants. "You're taking all of it and some of his shit, too. I'll pack it myself."

I didn't try to argue with her. She was probably right. I should take it all. I didn't know what had happened to my mom, but I did know there would be more medical bills now. I could sell the designer clothes to help pay for them. It would only cost me a bit of my soul each time.

Jacqueline disappeared up the stairs, and I waited. I wasn't even certain what I was waiting for. Sebastian stayed uncharacteristically silent. He didn't crack a joke or smirk.

He knew something. I was sure of it.

But I couldn't care anymore. The real world tugged at me, dragging me back to the life I was meant to live. Maybe this had all been a dream. My mother needed me. I wouldn't waste more time on the man who'd broken my heart.

When Jacqueline reappeared, hauling an overstuffed suitcase, I was already on my feet. I walked toward the door. I'd just reached it when the sound of shattering glass stopped all of us. My body tried to turn toward the noise and the man who I knew had made it. I closed my eyes and refused to allow myself to look. Still, I let myself linger a moment as though he might appear on the stairs.

But Julian didn't come after me.

He didn't say goodbye.

Neither would I.

ACKNOWLEDGMENTS

Some books bang around in you for a while before they come out, so to everyone who listened to me ramble about my vampire book idea for years: thank you!

I never expected to get a call that a publisher wanted Filthy Rich Vampire. I've had the pleasure of watching Entangled become an empire, and it is an absolute privilege to be published by them. I'm eternally grateful to Liz Pelletier for her guidance, friendship, and vision. Liz, this is the beginning of something beautiful!

Thank you to the entire Entangled Team for working to take this story to the next level. Special thanks to Elana Cohen, Lydia Sharp, Rae Swain, Jessica Turner, Curtis Svehlak, Bree Archer for all their help, insight, and notes.

I owe huge thanks to my powerhouse agent Louise Fury, who has always been team sexy vampires, and to the amazing co-agents at The Fury Agency and The Bent Agency for all you do! A special thanks to my foreign rights agents for bringing my words to readers all over the world. You rock!

I couldn't do this without my on-the-ground team. Big thanks to Michelle and Shelby for keeping me focused and on track—which is a monumental task. My endless gratitude to Graceley and Paper Myths Media for all their hard work on this book.

It takes a village to keep writing. A huge thanks to my writer friends who have been there through this crazy process, including

Audrey, Cora, Amy, and many, many more. And big hugs and thanks to my reader group, Geneva Lee's Loves, for being my happy place.

Thank you to Josh for for all the developmental dopamine. Thank you to Rosa and Shelby for the eagle-eyed proofreading. Someday I will figure out lay vs lie.

And to my family for giving me both a reason to write down these crazy stories and the support and love to do so. Thank you to my older kids, James and Sydney, for brainstorming sessions about magic, and to my little one, Sophie, for being an endless source of it. And thank you to Josh for being my mate, my tether, and my #1 fan.

Filthy Rich Vampire is a steamy romance full of extravagance and an ending that will leave you on the edge of your seat. However, the story includes elements that might not be suitable for all readers. Violence, familial estrangement, blood rituals, beheadings, mind-altering substance use, and death are shown on the page, with sibling death and discussions of cancer in the backstory. Readers who may be sensitive to these elements, please take note.

I thought a weekend away would be the perfect escape. Until I woke up married and trapped... by the king of the Dark Fae.

the
dark
king

GINA L.
NEW YORK TIMES BESTSELLING AUTHOR
MAXWELL

For Bryn Meara, a free trip to the exclusive and ultra-luxe Nightfall hotel and casino in Vegas should've been the perfect way to escape the debris of her crumbling career. But waking up from a martini-and-lust-fueled night to find herself married to Caiden Verran, the reclusive billionaire who owns the hotel and most of the city, isn't the jackpot one would think. It seems her dark and sexy new husband is actual royalty—the fae king of the Night Court—and there's an entire world beneath the veil of Vegas.

Whether light or shadow, the fae are a far cry from fairy tales, and now they've made Bryn a pawn in their dark games for power. And Caiden is the most dangerous of all—an intoxicating cocktail of sin and raw, insatiable hunger. She should run. But every night of passion pulls Bryn deeper into his strange and sinister world, until she's no longer certain she wants to leave...even if she could.

*The lone wolf answers to no alpha or pack.
He is both judge and executioner
for rogue werewolves.*

TAMING THE WHITE WOLF

USA TODAY & NYT BESTSELLING AUTHOR

N.J. WALTERS

White wolf Devlin Moore has spent nearly the last century following his destiny: hunting rogue werewolves. His fate is to be the only one of his kind—hardened, feared, and brutally ruthless. Only now, Devlin's not alone. *There are two others*. And if that wasn't unsettling enough, Devlin is drawn to New York City for what appears to be a human...

As far as Devlin can tell, vibrant artist Zoe Galvani is no threat. But there's something about her— from her unusual eyes that look similar to the same shocking hue as his own, to his growing need to mark her as *his* that suggests magical forces may be at play.

Now there's no escaping each other, or the attraction that grows stronger by the second. But no one, especially a human woman, should have this effect on a lone wolf. And just when he's sure that having her could be his undoing...the truth steps out of the shadows.

an imprint of Entangled Publishing LLC